Incorporation

Incorporation

WILL WILLIMON

CASCADE *Books* · Eugene, Oregon

INCORPORATION

Cascade Books
An Imprint of Wipf and Stock Publishers
199 W. 8th Ave., Suite 3
Eugene, OR 97401

www.wipfandstock.com

ISBN 13: 978-1-61097-470-7

Cataloging-in-Publication data:

Will Willimon.

Incorporation / Will Willimon.

x + 256 p.; 23 cm

ISBN 13: 978-1-61097-470-7

1. Clergy—Fiction. I. Title.

PS3623.I80 I47 2012

Manufactured in the USA.

Hope Church, though a capacious congregation, could not possibly accommodate all of the events and characters in this novel. Everything herein is a figment of my imagination.

Now you are the body of Christ and individually members of it.

—1 CORINTHIANS 12:27

Contents

Prelude

As he jogged the familiar though risky route from the church office— cheerfully dodging the ever demanding faithful—down the hall to the sanctuary, hymnal in hand, not five minutes before the beginning of the service (he could already hear hints of the portentous prelude), Stephen instinctively gave his cincture a final, reassuring jerk and tugged the button on the neck of his alb. Behind him flapped the ends of his purple stole. Having vested so often for sacred service, he could make such adjustments even while moving hastily, having no need of a mirror.

He smiled as parishioners passed.

"Stephen, please, *please* don't forget to remind them about the Youth Car Wash for Haiti," an aqua-pantsuited parishioner said. "Remember, you forgot last Sunday. Next Saturday. It's important. OK?"

"Sure," he said, suppressing his resentment with a subtlety gained through years of practice.

"Pastor Steve," a high-pitched, tiny voice peeped from his back. He stopped and turned to find a little girl just behind him. "Can I ask a question?" she said, her plain face brightening into a smile.

"Sure you can." He mused at the inopportuneness of questions, even when asked by "the least of these," to someone in his line of work at this hour, in this place. He knelt down next to her.

"When did you choose to be a preacher?" she asked. "Like in the ministry."

Her innocence in asking so huge a question momentarily transfixed him.

He looked into her little face and knew that she knew not what she had asked. Memories rose to his mind that would take a long time to tell and, in any case, could not be told to her, despite Jesus' "for to such belongs the kingdom of God."

Prelude

"Sometime let's talk," he said as he gently patted her back, then rose. "I didn't choose it; it chose me."

Seeing she was puzzled, he explained, "It's kinda complicated."

Good Friday

Spring sun, and all apple green, budding, fresh and clean, nothing to testify to this day's theological significance—apogee of the bloodiest week of the Christian year. Good Friday sepulchritude was jarring on such a bright spring day, the church once again out of step with the natural world.

Simon wheeled into oak-lined Hope Boulevard. Fifty yards before the church, the branches overhead parted and he relished the unobstructed view. The sight of the tower rising before him, its gray stone glistening in the incongruous, midday Good Friday sunshine, made him smile. Some kid in the church had quipped, "That bell tower looks like a giant." This was true—a Gothic Goliath surveying his ecclesiastical domain, overseeing an asphalt parking lot. Though Simon Lupino did not fancy himself as naturally spiritual, to his credit, his delight in this vista had continued undiminished. Twenty years of cantankerous parishioners, a stolid board, and commonplace fellow clergy—all playing their middling parts against a backdrop of antiquated toilets, overloaded circuitry, and cracked plaster—had not squelched Simon's reverence for this panorama or his delight that it was his. The burden of the building was light compared with the privilege of serving a church so fine as Hope.

Simon's sunny situation was fortuitous—midcareer, Midwest, midlife, midyear, midday—master of an ecclesiastical kingdom that would evoke pulpit envy in any ambitious pastor. Hope was in the top ten percent, maybe the top five of American churches. When he arrived, Hope contributed a measly one grand to benevolence and mission; this year's money for good work was over a million. The majority of clergy are sentenced to obscure, pointless parishes, where they languish unappreciated and barely make ends meet. Simon savored the serenity of knowing that he had twenty of his twenty-eight years under orders living every pastor's dream.

Incorporation

Though his sense of self-satisfaction was hard-earned, Simon was gracious enough to know that he was here—this morning, in this high mood, at this church, with this life—as a recipient of undeserved good fortune. Modestly he attributed his position to "good luck" rather than divine providence.

As a young cleric spiraling upward, all that Simon had asked for was the opportunity to have a church that appreciated his talent and, through his exercise of his personal gifts, to make someone's sad life happier and the world a bit better. In the day's cheerful spring sunlight, his ecclesiastical accomplishments arrayed before him, Simon could say with the psalmist, "my lines have fallen in pleasant places." He was at a golden age, attained by few ecclesiastics, when he could take pleasure in what he had produced. A visionary transformer more than mere manager, an energetic enabler more than cautious caregiver, content and satisfied, his cup overflowed.

Simon's car was sleek, dark blue, clean, German. (He had leased the car in expectation of a long sought car allowance. Though the perquisite had been slow to materialize, he wouldn't allow the board's sluggishness to detract from his enjoyment of the perfect car.) The church lawn fit Simon's spirit—grand, green, and manicured. He had an Easter sermon in the oven for presentation the day after tomorrow. The new four and a half million mission/education/fellowship/inspiration wing caused him particular pride. True, he had hoped to chip away more progressively on the building's debt, but with less than two million to go, the church's indebtedness could not diminish his triumph. What a morning.

The German sedan showed Simon's adoration—to the point of preoccupation—for efficiency, whether in cars, coffeemakers, or churches. When interviewed recently by the drab denominational monthly and asked, "What is the key thing you have done to put Hope Church where it is?" Simon responded, "Excellence. I have stressed excellence in all that we do. Too often churches content themselves with second best, average. I'm not much interested in what is traditionally called 'sin,' but 'sin' in my book is mediocrity. 'Excellence' is our management mantra."

A solitary Unitarian/Universalist-like Saab greeted Simon in the lot, probably someone fussing with Easter flowers. His spirit rose; the Saab was solid evidence of an ever so slight leftward lean of the congregation in recent years, the fruit of his prophetic preaching.

How many pastors of his rank would report for work on a holiday Friday, he wondered, even by noon? Not many, particularly after his leadership of the previous weeks' exhausting Lenten ecclesiastical lollapaloozas.

He congratulated himself on decisively terminating Good Friday worship rather than allowing the sparsely attended liturgical relic to die a slow death. Now on the verge of Hope's grand Easter crescendo, the depressing forty days of Lent almost at an end, he was spirit-pumped.

As Simon sped up the walk, he was annoyed to see a hunched over old man shuffling toward the office door. No doubt this mendicant hoped for charity amid the Holy Week zeal that was bubbling up from the faithful. What self-respecting church could deny a urine-saturated indigent on Good Friday? Simon begrudgingly admired the determination required by someone in his condition to crawl all the way to Hope, even for an affluent, suburban handout.

"May I help you?" Simon called out politely.

"No," muttered the man, undeterred in his shuffling, forward movement, barely looking over his shoulder.

"Hello? Seeking assistance?"

"Only Jesus can help."

"Unfortunately, this is not the door for such inquiries," said Simon, positioning himself defensively between the inerloper and the church's entrance. Gesturing with his free hand that held his keys, he directed, "Please go right back down this sidewalk. Then take a right, straight to the end, then left. Sign by the door says Hopeful Hands and Hearts. Got that? I'm sure that a volunteer can help you there."

"Jesus?"

The old man's mention of Jesus reminded Simon that because it was Good Friday, every do-gooder at Hopeful Hands and Hearts was on holiday. Still, the man would be off his hands (to say nothing of his heart), wandering in more distant parts of the Hope campus where, providentially, all the doors would be locked.

"Good day," said Simon, approaching the outside door to his suite. "Straight to the end, then left."

Having done his bit for charity, Simon entered a dark, oak-paneled, tomb-like side entrance hall into the administrative suite. Eight portraits greeted him—Hope's dead pastors preserved, some in clericals, others in business suits. Simon acknowledged them with a snort; he had passed by this Sanhedrin-like welcome committee nearly every day for twenty years. Each past pastor posed smugly, looking pious before bookshelves. One held a Bible. All await Simon one day to join them.

The portraits' function—immortality for clergy—had been thwarted by sloppy labeling. Last year one was revealed to be the Reverend Arnold

Incorporation

Toppson, imposter, no more than an assistant (for a scant four years), falsely designated as the Reverend Doctor Eugene Jackson. Only five—the last three and the first two—could be positively identified. The rest hung in obscurity, requiring resurrection by a persevering archivist.

Simon bustled under the bold Gothic letters chiseled above the portraits: "Our Pastors, Always Beloved."

∾

Unseen and unknown by Simon or anybody on this Friday of Trisagion, eight miles from Hope Church, where the river makes a wide, rainbow arc, a body bobbed aimlessly down the East Fork. The *corpus delicti*, now partially naked except for stripped undershorts and shirt, was that of a male between fifty and sixty years of age. The corpse had been a regular communicant at Hope, no less than a trustee. This would be his first Easter absence, now dunked into the Communion of Saints.

Every now and then the body would snag on a stump or branch in the Styx, then bob for a time until the river, unusually high and swift from ample spring rains, freed it to continue its digression. After more than eight hours in the muddy water, with the sun high and the heat rising, the corpse was swollen.

At one point the body rolled over and floated for a time on its back, stomach distended, arms outstretched, the balding, bloated corpus resembling a gray, dead fish, or a clown on a crucifix, or perhaps a dead pig.

1

Easter

He opened groggy eyes, squinting, blinded by bright Sunday morning sunlight flooding the bedroom. Bleary and dizzy, unsure of where he was, he rolled over, looked at his clock, and bolted upright.

"Nearly ten? Damn!" He gave Thea, still sleeping, a shove. "Sugar babe, arise! We overslept! Move it! Get up!"

Stephen staggered toward the bathroom, scratching himself, heavy-headed and dull, wobbling his way past unpacked boxes like a corpse coming to life. Thea tossed the sheets, kicked her left leg over the side of the bed, and rolled, groaning, "I told you that two bottles would be too much. I think I died."

Then began a wordless, frantic dash—bumping about, jumping around with one leg in and one leg out, the pulling on of clothing, brushing of hair, rapid slurping of juice—in which they were dressed and on their way in less than twenty minutes.

"Happy Easter, Babe," Stephen finally spoke as they entered Main Street. "My First Sunday as the new and improved version of the Reverend Doctor Martin Luther Damn King." He smiled, flashing the winning grin that enabled him to charm his way into or out of almost anything.

"Whatever," Thea sighed, patting him on the shoulder, offering her first smile of the morning. "Your big day. Hope that Hope meets your expectations, I hope, I hope, I hope."

Ten minutes later, they joined a procession of cars moving down Hope Boulevard accompanied by clanging bells, the intimidating Gothic bell tower ascending before them. Thea helped herself out of Stephen's car. Stephen bounded from the driver's side, thoughtlessly slamming the door so quickly that he caught the bottom of his sport coat. Fortunately, he halted in time not to rip the coat—his only quasi-formal clothing.

"Let go of me," Stephen cursed, fumbling for his keys, suppressing what he would have liked to say to the clutching door since he now stood in the middle of a church parking lot on his first day of ministry. As he took hold of Thea's hand and led her into the walkway, he realized that for the rest of his life he would be getting out of a car, entering the church on Easter, once again to discuss Jesus raised from the dead, leading the faithful in their biggest day of the year, forever doomed to wear the requisite coat and tie.

He felt a mild pang of regret.

"Charlotte," said a man nearby who was struggling to extricate a black-cased trombone from the backseat of his Toyota, "you have made us late for my most important engagement of the year. I hope you are happy."

She sat impassively in the front seat, looking unhappy. This was his sole annual gig, the amateur trombonist having long since been dropped from any gathering of musicians other than the Hope Brass. He scurried alone toward the bowels of the looming building, thrusting in front of him his black case, trombone at the ready.

The pealing bells were deafening. In the parking lot near the tower, early arrivers exiting their cars were forced to shout in order to be heard above the clanging and banging. Whenever the big bass boomed, the world trembled. The bells had been pealing in strident sequence since dawn, much to the chagrin of godless, would-be dead-to-the-world-sleepers-in a mile around.

The lawn, enriched by last week's rain, was verdant, lush, an Edenic green. The sky was bright, filled by ample April sun—nature now in synch with the church's liturgical year.

Just beside the trombonist's Toyota, a couple emerged from a nondescript Dodge van with their three tastefully smocked and frocked children in Easter outfits. In this neighborhood it was a moral achievement not to overdress one's children.

The Smiths (Ida and Bob), the Franklins, the Gunters, and the Rendles, all of them regulars, assumed their usual berths. A pert twentysomething eased her small blue bubble into the space between two large sedans. Though unacknowledged by anyone, she smiled anyway. A gaggle of three or more persons of indefinite identities followed, one in a Jaguar, all equally unacknowledged. Interlopers were normal on Easter; the regulars considered it bad taste to make much of their presence in the procession that moved from bright spring sunlight into the darkened interior of Hope.

∞

Twelve minutes' drive from the gradually gathering Easter throng, in a not nearly so nice part of town, a half-dozen sleepy-looking children slouched around a table at the community center, about to be breakfasted by Mary Lupino.

"Eggs! Eggs makes me sick," said the little girl as Mary scooped a spoonful of scrambled eggs and plopped them on a light green plastic plate. "I threw up eggs last time I tried 'em."

"Alright dear," answered Mary cheerfully. "You may enjoy the potatoes and toast. Eggs are an ancient Christian symbol for the resurrection. And these eggs are free range! Let us pray."

Mary bowed her head and put her hands together. None of the children took her cue.

"Thank you God for this Easter day and for the gift of this food. Remind us of the farmers who labored to produce this, as well as all seasonal workers, particularly the ones who are undercompensated. Help us remember those who are not so fortunate as ourselves, especially those who are hungry on this day . . ."

"Get your filthy fingers out of my plate!" growled one urchin to another.

"Equip us, we pray, to change the world for the better," Mary continued, undeterred by the childrens' poor manners. "Motivate us to do something about the needs of other people, to use our gifts responsibly in your service in the making of a more just world. Use us as your hands reaching out to respond to the pain of others. Amen."

"Where's the bacon?" demanded a feral boy who appeared to be about six or seven. "Can't have no breakfast without no bacon."

Mary chirped sunnily, "We don't have bacon, dear. I'm a vegetarian. I think you'll find that you'll be just fine without bacon. We must be ecologically responsible."

"I thought you was a Christian," said the boy glumly.

"That too. Having better luck with the veganism than the Christianity this morning," she muttered to herself. "Now, everyone eat up. We must leave for church in about fifteen minutes."

"There ain't no cereal? I like Fruit Loops. Never heard of not having no cereal," said another as he kicked the child seated next to him.

"Ow! That hurt!"

Ignoring the exchange, Mary said, "We are going to church for the most special day of the year. Easter!"

"Are we gonna see the Easter Bunny?" asked the littlest of the bunch.

"No, this isn't about the Easter Bunny, dear," chirped Mary.

"Ain't no Easter Bunny no way," one child declared.

"We are going to church to pray, and to praise God," Mary instructed.

"Ain't no Easter Bunny, ain't no God, no Santa Clause neither," he continued to lecture the others.

"Shut up!" yelled the oldest girl, an obese child with stringy, blonde hair. "Don't you blaspheme! There is too an Easter Bunny! Brings people toys and eggs. Brung me a big chocolate bunny last year with yellow eyes. Some blue shoes, too. So there!"

"I hates eggs. Eggs makes me sick," droned the other little girl.

"Now children, eat up," said Mary as she bustled about in the kitchen, stashing the pots and pans. "The eggs are organic. Aren't they wonderful?"

For a moment Mary considered her situation—stuck in a dingy, linoleumed room that reeked of disinfectant, standing at a sink, her hands submerged in greasy dishwater, confined with cast-off kids while everyone else donned their Easter finery—and she was filled with satisfaction.

"The van will be leaving in five minutes! You will hear some wonderful music. Our church is so large and beautiful. If you are all good, nice Mr. Judd will take you to McDonald's after service. Won't that be fun?"

"Mister Bud? That's his name?" shouted one of the children. Everyone giggled hysterically. "Mister Buuuud!"

Mary felt, for just a second, a tad bit of resentment toward Jesus for saying, "let the little children come to me, for such is the kingdom of Heaven," then recovered her senses.

"I seen an Easter Bunny at the mall wonst," testified the eldest girl. "Lady, do you think the Easter Bunny's real?"

"Get in the van," Mary explained.

∞

Meanwhile, in the church parking lot, the stage was set for the entrance of Sybil Warrenton Smith Vestal. Though Sybil was usually tastefully late, aware of the crush of the Easter crowd, she was present and accounted for a full half hour before the prelude, jauntily displaying herself (even though the morning was still cool) in her vintage, topless ebony Mercedes. She was adorned in large sunglasses and a lime-green scarf draped over a green dress that was rather low-cut for ecclesiastical wear, though on more lackluster Sundays Sybil had been even more suggestively attired. She waved eagerly to anyone who glanced her way.

Sybil had married a series of well-heeled men, tripping multiple times across the oceans and, when she tired of them, tossing them aside, jettisoning them like empty champagne bottles. Having acquired a fortune through strategic matrimony and even more skillful divorce, Sybil had, Jabez-like, expanded her holdings. She was a favorite of nearly everyone in the congregation (save a few envious women), managing to unmarry periodically without incurring ill will even among her ex-husbands, her serial failures in marriage offset by her success in divorce.

Next an older couple arrived. As he helped her from their dark blue, unadorned Ford, she straightened her skirt and patted her bluish-gray hair. As Gerald Glumweltner waddled round them, bustling into the building, a large vessel under full sail, the man asked genially, "Just arriving, Gerald?"

"Surely you jest!" (He hated the laity's "Gerald," preferring to be called "Dr. Glumweltner" since winning his D. Mus.) "Been here since dawn. Do you think the choir pulls off what we do by miraculous divine intervention? I'm retrieving a piece of music I had worked on at home for the last two weeks!" he said, panting as he pushed his girth past their slow sidewalk procession.

In his bustle back to the building, huffing and puffing, Glumweltner nearly tripped over a child who had broken free of the grip of her mother, Gwen Stone, and was making a run for the front lawn. Glumweltner recalled Gwen's departure from the altos in humiliation when her husband (chemical salesman, basketball All-American) went out for a gallon of milk one evening—and never returned. That was two years ago. The twenty-yard trek from the parking lot left him winded and also wondering if Gwen might be open to an overture for a date.

A now unbroken line of people was welcomed at the left tower door—formally and perfunctorily—by the Reverend Johnson Quail, Minister of Administration and CFO of Hope Church. Quail had been to seminary, switching careers after a mercifully short stint as manager of an engineering firm in town. He was "Mr. Quail" to some, "Dr. Quail" to those who first met him, just "Quail" to the Senior Pastor when he was annoyed with him, "Johnson" when he wasn't, and "Pastor" to none.

"Happy Easter, Mr. Quail," said one of the women upon entering the narthex. "Hasn't the Lord just blessed us with a beautiful day?"

Incorporation

"Good Morning," said Quail in return, standing guard on efficiency, crowd flow, and corporate tone, annoyed that Henry Niculous had failed to meet him as they had agreed last Sunday. Lay disrespect for clergy time was widespread, but Quail was troubled that Niculous—one widely respected for his mingling of piety and punctuality—would stand him up like this.

"Meeting someone, Mr. Quail?" asked a random worshipper.

"No, I am not."

At the end of the line was a well-dressed couple, followed closely by their sullen, scowling teenager, made to appear at church under duress; their uncertainty betrayed them as members of the "Christmas and Easter" class of casual attendees. Three morose youths, dressed defiantly in denim, shuffled in, the Thomases and their stooped, doleful son James. Then a garrulous group brimming with glee over their good fortune at the day's weather. The sun! The trees!

Two Asian women, holding huge, black, floppy Bibles, incongruously appeared.

Quail rushed to intercept them. "Excuse me. Excuse me. The Korean service is at two this afternoon, not now," he said in a highly articulated way, as if talking to a couple of kindergartners holding crayons.

The women smiled, bowed cordially.

"Your church meets at two this afternoon. At two. In the Great Hall. Great Hall. Were you not told?" he asked.

"This our church," one of the women responded.

"No, this not your church. Your church not here. It around back. In Great Hall, and not now. Were you not told? It at two."

They smiled, bowed, and forged on, impervious to Quail's pig Latin attempts to deflect them.

Then the Senior Managing Pastor's wife, Mary Lupino, herding—genially but with difficulty—a band of multicolored, breakfasted children out of a green van (emblazoned with the words "HOPE CARES"). Even the Christmas/Easter irregulars did not need to be told that the children had been gleaned from the community center or that Mary was a clerical wife.

Next came a handsome nineteen- or twenty-year-old, in good spirits, holding a large paperback Bible in his left hand and escorting a young woman in a green blouse. "He is raised!" he was overheard to say to one elderly couple.

"Yes, these days I'm often amazed," replied the man.

Unremembered by Quail, the youth was Jack Hodges, on a swimming scholarship at the state college. He and his girlfriend, Alexis, had returned home having had a religious experience (so it was rumored) during a Campus Crusade retreat in February. Though both shared a youthful prejudice against mainline Christianity, when you want Easter done right, they had reasoned, go to Hope.

Then Dr. and Mrs. Sydney Kline and their well-groomed and deferential teenagers. A prominent internist, Kline had been quite a rover as a young man but now lived rumor free; he was reputed to have "got religion," though no one seemed sure of where.

Jane Whetsell and her sister Maryanne. Their long-deceased father, John Whetsell, gave one of the largest gifts to build the first educational wing of the church back in the thirties.

"You must be our new Youth Pastor," Jane robustly greeted a young African American man just stepping onto the sidewalk with a young woman.

"Why, yes, I am," Stephen replied, fighting back the devilish temptation to ask the woman, "How did you know?"

"Well, I'm Jane Whetsell," she said, thrusting at him a menacingly strong hand. "And this is Maryanne, my sister." Her sister smiled but said nothing.

"I'm Stephen," he said as Jane vigorously shook his hand. "And this is my girlfriend, Thea." Thea smiled as Whetsell Number One wordlessly grabbed and jiggled her hand and arm. The sisters Whetsell looked to Thea like characters in some PBS miniseries—hearty, officious, solid, English, Miss Marple sorts in sensible shoes. Jane Whetsell wore tweed, even on Easter, as if it were her standard battle fatigues. Thea simply smiled, noting that these people sure seemed to enjoy grabbing other people's hands.

"My very first Sunday," gushed Stephen, attempting to present himself favorably to the older women. "It's just unbelievable that a place like Hope should be my very first church. What a privilege to work with Dr. Lupino. I heard about him in seminary. A great model. I'm pumped, excited. Unbelievable."

"Have you yet met our famous pastor?" asked Jane.

"No. He wasn't involved in my selection process, which may have been good since I might not have gotten hired if he had seen my resume," said Stephen with a beguiling, toothy grin.

"I presumed that you had not yet had the privilege. Well, you are destined to be a great addition to the life of our congregation. I was on the Education Committee that recommended augmentation of our youth ministry. You have the honor of being *primus,* our first Associate Pastor for Youth. I examined your resume and thereby learned of your stellar academic record," said Jane. "*Summa cum laude.* Young man of letters. Do you read Greek?"

Thea at first thought Jane had asked, "Do you reek geek?"

"I'll count on you to show me the ropes," said Stephen.

"I try to stay abreast of all things Hope," said Jane, swelling with pride. Thea, noting Ms. Whetsell's ample bosom, corseted in stretched tweed, smiled at how funny "abreast" sounded in some contexts.

"And so, Thea, will you also be moving here with our newest cleric, Stephen?" asked Maryanne, simply being nice. Thea explained nervously that no, she was in grad school in cross-cultural anthropology, that she hoped to visit on weekends, that it was only a three-hour drive, that this semester she had a late Friday seminar every week, and that though "the ministry thing" was all his and not hers, she was so glad that Stephen was being given an opportunity like Hope.

"Well, you are more than welcome at our rambling Victorian abode when you need to overnight, should you be visiting Stephen," chirped Maryanne. "In our father's house on Elm Street there are many rooms," she said with a grin. The matriarch's biblical allusion sailed past the two uncomfortable young people.

Though Stephen was relieved when he and Thea finally joined the press of people entering the narthex, there bidding farewell to the bustling sisters and merging anonymously into the Easter multitude, he also delighted that someone had recognized him.

Now a steady stream of cars quickly filled the lot. Any experienced observer could predict that the service would be especially packed, even for a celebration of the resurrection. Perhaps this attendance spike was economically determined. What the downturned economy taketh in offering receipts, the economy giveth in worried, depressed people packing the pews, at least on Easter, thought Quail as he surveyed the scene and did a quick estimate of the size of the house. He alerted the Chief Usher to be prepared to retrieve extra chairs from the Great Hall. Today's offering was sure to be more fulsome than an average take.

As the hour approached eleven, the bells pealed more exuberantly. A few choir members in white surplices and red cassocks began clustering in corners of the narthex. A reluctant acolyte—managed officiously by the Tsar of the Altar Guild, nemesis of generations of prepubescent males whose manipulative mothers had forced the miscreants into acolyte service—was shoved toward the door leading into the sanctuary, pouting at being thrust into duty.

"And put on those gloves," she ordered. "I don't give a rip whether you want to or not. Didn't I tell you, 'No chewing gum'?"

The Senior Managing Pastor entered the narthex, smiling broadly to the milling choir. A gaggle of sopranos made way for his eminence. He planted a kiss on the cheek of an aging alto and then gave a pat to a soprano.

"Hey, happy Easter to you!" snorted an older man in the narthex. Attired in an incongruous bright green vest, he spoke at a volume usually reserved for taverns.

"Shhhh!" the Tsar scolded, asserting her authority beyond prepubescent acolytes.

The organ gave way to the Hope Brass. Crucifer, clergy, and choir formed a line for the processional hymn. Preservice chaos bowed to liturgical order. Dear old Herbert Cohellen, retired pastor who had settled at Hope, had been invited to march in the procession and to make the announcements, his chief liturgical sinecure. The pimple-faced crucifer continued to lean upon his cross—stolid, bored, as if to say to all, "I'm not really here." (His expression was not unlike a few in the choir.) The Hope Brass smothered all polite conversation in the narthex once the ushers opened the doors to the sanctuary.

"Tenors! Tenors!" shouted Gerald. "For God's sake put yourselves in line. I need all of you if we're going to pull this off! Charles, all you basses look at me on that stanza when the anthem picks up steam! Look at me! Scott! That's you!"

"Has anyone seen my Harold?" asked a confused older woman in lavender. "I wonder if he has already taken a seat? Harold?"

After politely smiling, everyone turned away.

"Let's do this thing, good people," said the pastor jovially to the choir. "You all look wonderful."

"Joe, give the high sign to Grimballs," ordered Gerald after confirming the presence of the Senior Managing Pastor. (The choirmaster referred to the organist as "Grimballs" behind his back.) A bass turned around and flipped a small switch. Organist cued, Easter ensued. "Show time," Gerald said, adding "break a leg"—in a near pitch-perfect imitation of the late Orson Welles—as encouragement to the first wave of sopranos flowing into the aisle in the wake of the crucifer. To the last in line, he said, "Move it, honey," patting her rear with his chubby, perspiring hand.

Through doors held open by ushers, the procession began moving to the strains of "Christ the Lord Is Risen Today." Other ushers stood by with folding metal chairs, ready to sweep in behind the choir with additional seating. The congregation, which on many Sundays was half-hearted in its singing, now with pews packed, bordered on enthusiastic.

Christ the Lord has risen toda-ay, A-a-a-alleluia!
All rejoice and angels sa-ay, A-a-a-alleluia!

"Dum de dum, de dum dee dee," Gerald stood at the door hammering out the tempo in the air for each successive wave of choristers. "Tenors, it's all up to you," his bass threateningly boomed as they moved passed. "Scott!"

With morning light streaming through the windows in a strong blue cast, the soaring arches, the well-ordered choir and noble organ, the brass interludes between the second and fourth stanzas, and an eager, full house, Hope today approached the thrilling. The energy remained high as the service progressed—prayers well formed, elevated language fit for the occasion, a fresh new anthem, "Life! Life! Joy! Joy!" with tympani.

There was a collect, thanking God for life and the sun, the grass, and democracy. Then a selection from *Messiah*, keyed to the day. A Scripture reading. Another hymn—a new one—that seemed to annoy some in the congregation with its unfamiliarity. A prayer of intercession by Herb in which God was informed of assorted health needs within the congregation and lectured on key current events. An acolyte nearly fumbled an offering plate when it was handed to him by the ushers, but otherwise the production was flawless.

Herb wrestled with the announcements, strategically placed to validate Hope as an on-the-go congregation. Someone really should get the announcements printed in large type if Herb was to be the announcer. *Women Aflame Bible Study Fellowship will not meet this week, due to Easter. But the Moving Men . . . will meet this Wednesday to hear a presentation on "Ten Proofs of the . . . Resurrection." This gathering will be held in the Walter Rauschenbusch lounge. Mick McConnell's famous sausage biscuits will be served . . . The winners of the Hope Happy Hearts Easter Bonnet contest are Agnes Youlonts and Mary Summers . . . Or perhaps that's Mary Connors. Our "Send a Kid to Camp" drive begins next Sunday . . . Goal: one hundred indigent kids . . . at camp, that is. And for those of you doing your spring cleaning, the clothes closet is in need of clean, warm winter coats in all children's sizes . . .*

From here the service regained its lost momentum and cantered toward the crescendo: the sermon by the Managing Pastor. From the moment he rose to speak, ascending the pulpit's steps, delight played upon the faces of the congregation, pride at the preacher in their employ, light falling upon Simon Lupino's salt-and-pepper gray hair, his resonant baritone voice like that of a radio announcer, his masterful timing, his gestures from the torso. The preacher's bodily presence was the perfect complement to the building and the day.

The beginning of his sermon was (by skillful design) mildly disconcerting; the preacher began with a few dismal citations from the recent news about the decline of the economy, an earthquake in Asia, a mass shooting at a mall in Texas, and the failure of a hundred-year-old tire company in Akron, fare that few expected to be served during an Easter sermon. These unpleasantries were a rhetorical ploy, however, poising the congregation for a good-hearted shove into the core of his message. Simon paused for effect—a few seconds of silence, then:

Yet my friends, these stories of death, despair, and mayhem are not the only ones to be told. There is yet another word to be said. It is the word that has convened us this glorious Easter day—Life!

Easter stories are charming and beloved—the women coming to a place of death, only to be surprised by life. The stupid disciples dumbfounded by glory. The announcing angel. I plead with you not to trouble yourselves with intellectual concerns about the mere facticity of these ancient texts, not to long for raw historical data.

Andante.

I want to reframe all that to reassure you that the word that these Bible stories are trying in their own ancient ways to speak is a word more important than any of our misgivings about these primitive witnesses.

Basso profundo.

As a great biblical scholar, recently retired from an endowed chair at a university in Oregon, instructs us . . .

The preacher had forgotten the man's name.

. . . these stories of the empty tomb are metaphor, a primitive way of expressing deeper, useful spiritual truth.

That message is as near to your souls as the word that our choir has sung so well—Life! It is a word you are literally dying to hear. In the vale of the shadow of death—Life! Immortal, unquenchable life!

His voice now rose to a high-pitched, earnest fortissimo.

Believe not those who tell you that you are a frail creature of constricted vistas and constrained future! Believe not the naysayers and negativists. Believe in Life!

Easter is not about one Near Eastern man's unjust death and grim entombment. Injustice happens, particularly in that benighted part of the world. Easter is more. It is grand, cosmic, eternal, and indeed it is universal, most of all, it is relevant. It is the eternal message we hear whispered in our greatest poetry, set forth in our grandest music, and articulated in our wisest films—Life!

Now a crescendo.

I do not stand before you to argue this but rather to assert this—Life!

This glorious day with the sun shining down and the air fresh and clear is an eloquent natural testimonial to our supernatural theme—Life!

Here is the word you cannot fully tell yourself. Even as ex-President Jimmy Carter, man of malaise, has written, we live in a "culture of death." The Easter word is a defiant protest against that morbid world. And so I boldly speak it to you in the face of all your deadly, paltry "facts"—Life!

Having risked a prophetic reference to Jimmy Carter at the end of the first movement, the preacher modulated his voice into a more restrained conversational tone as he told a story about a woman who had feared that the successful, multimillion-dollar personal care products business she had founded in the basement of her home would fail under pressure from her creditors. A kind, charitable banker (who was Jewish!) had found a way around restrictive government regulations and had saved her with a bridge loan.

Life! Life! he resumed, shouting at the top of his voice in grand, closing molto crescendo. *Liiife!*

Exeunt.

By prearrangement with the musicians, these last words of the sermon were immediately followed by a building roll of tympani, the jarring clash of cymbals, and the choir's near shouting of a verse from the old favorite, "He Lives!"

He lives! He lives! You ask me how I know he lives? He lives within my heart!

A thrill ran through the congregation, their collective response to this skilled theatrical coordination between preacher and musicians. More brass, another clash of cymbals, and the organ took up the first verse of "Up From the Grave He Arose" as crucifer and clergy smoothly glided into position and the recessional began. Some in the choir, both women and men, had tears on their cheeks as they walked and sang. Some shouted more than they sang. Despite the full service, the benediction was pronounced by the Senior Managing Pastor, followed by the Sevenfold Amen, at a mere five minutes past noon, a testimony to careful liturgical execution. Choirmaster and pastor, looking at their watches, beamed, and nodded congratulations to one another on the punctual conclusion.

"Thanks for another grand service," more than one congregant was heard to say as the clergy glad-handed nearly everyone who exited, hugging some.

"What an Easter!" one portly, red-faced man in a plaid sport coat exclaimed.

"You got that right!" said an unidentified voice from the dispersing crowd. No one seemed unnerved by the backdrop of a man who was tortured to death and then brought back from the dead.

"Dr. Lupino, you really spoke to me today," said one woman. "As you know, I lost Mother just a couple of months ago. Your sermon was such a comfort. Bless you for blessing me."

Jack and Alexis emerged, smiling brightly. Jack lasted the entire service without cracking open his overly large study Bible. Later, they would have a brief evaluation while on their way to lunch with Jack's parents at the club, agreeing on the demerits of the sermon.

The person who queried, "Did you mean to criticize or to praise Jimmy Carter? I never was much on Carter," was smilingly shoved on ahead and out the door.

Pastor's wife, Mary Lupino—without much acknowledgment by her husband standing at the door—handed off her indigent wards to her assistant, Hank Judd, local attorney, public defender, and agitator on behalf of and in servant ministry to the less fortunate. The children flew out the door like birds released from a cage, at last on the way to collect their just desserts at McDonald's.

"Didn't we have more lilies last Easter? Seemed to me like we had more lilies. Did we have more lilies?" was randomly overheard in the post-service crush.

"The thing I love about this church is that you really minister to our doubts and concerns," said one with eyes slightly moistened. "I wish I could have heard your take on Easter when I was full of questions, back in college. I guess it's never too late to believe."

Pastor Lupino smiled paternally and, with one arm, embraced the grateful parishioner, then handed her onward.

After tousling the hair of a towheaded young Kline, the pastor leaned his bronzed face close to that of Dr. Kline and said earnestly, "Sydney, I really need to consult with you if you have a moment."

"Now? Sure, what's up Simon?" asked Dr. Kline.

"Well, it's rather personal. Could we step back inside?"

"Sure," said Kline.

The two stepped just inside the narthex. Simon guided his parishioner to a darkened corner—in such a large church, one could easily find a dark corner when necessary—where he whispered, "Sydney, this morning there was blood in my stool. Not a great amount, mind you, but enough to throw me. It's all I can think about. I started to call you to see if it was safe for me to preach."

"Was it good red blood—not black but red?" Kline asked.

"Why yes. Blood. At first I thought it might have been something red that I ate, strawberries or something, but no, it's blood," Simon responded. "Blood."

"Has your rectum been sore? Tender?"

"Well, yes, matter of fact I have experienced some discomfort, itching there. I was particularly aware of it during the pastoral prayer."

"Congratulations, Preacher. You have hemorrhoids! Not to worry. Typical in a guy your age. Go get some of those over-the-counter suppositories, stuff one or two up your butt, and after a couple of days of greasy suppositories, you'll probably be fine."

"Are you sure? I thought it could be cancer. I'm terrified by the thought. You know I have it in my family. My mother . . ."

"Nonsense. This is what you get for the Lord not making you a jumping, running Pentecostal. We mainliners are way too sedentary! You have probably been sitting on your butt too much—or straining during your golf swing," said the doctor, smacking him on the arm.

"I don't play golf," replied Simon.

"Say, our Bible study on Wednesdays has been going great guns," said Kline. "Half the hospital staff is there. Simon, you ought to come. It's really just about the best experience I've had with God's word in a long time. From six to seven every Wednesday morning."

Guiding Kline back toward his waiting family, Simon said through a smile, "No thanks. And happy Easter to you."

2

Low Sunday

Even the massive Easter throng is overshadowed by the Easter Tuesday descent upon Hope of a couple of thousand preachers for the national Signs of Hope conference, all of the attendees hoping to duplicate back home the wonders worked at Hope. When some of Hope's post-paschal fatigued staff questioned the wisdom of a clergy conference so soon after Easter, Simon said that was the point—hope. He cited a national study: in the aftermath of Easter, clergy tend to be suicidal.

Under Simon's leadership, Hope felt responsibility not only to be a quality church that stressed "excellence in worship, witness, and service" (Hope's Mission Statement), but also to be a teaching congregation. At the weeklong Signs of Hope, there were workshops, lectures, spectacular services of worship—traditional liturgical, multimedia, multicultural, multi-site, contemporary, ancient-future, emergent, eclectic-expressive, culture-sensitive. Hope had it all. (Hope even boasted a chef—or Manager of Hospitality—a graduate of the Culinary Institute of America.)

Signs of Hope participants were enlightened in the latest techniques for growing excellent churches—how to put together deals to buy shopping centers and retirement homes, build columbaria that paid for themselves (particularly in aging congregations), construct engaging, Web-worthy sermons, attract add-on ethnic congregations, concoct timeshare condos for the elderly, yoga classes and bridge tournaments for the stressed, pregnancy termination counseling for the young, spirituality groups for seekers, and grow state-of-the-art recording studios. They would take notes and collect packets, order CDs, and internalize the mantras of successful church leadership, all hoping to do back home what had been done at Hope.

The last morning of Signs of Hope—Thursday—Johnson Quail led a dozen clergy on an architectural tour prior to the closing plenary. The glorious building was tonic for some tired pastors, catalyst for green-eyed envy in others.

Standing in the circular drive, the great Neogothic panorama laid out before them, sunlight nimbus around his balding head, Quail expounded Hope's history:

"Built in 1926, gift of a local industrialist, Jackson, the last Neogothic project of Gilded Age guilt before the Crash. As was said in the Middle Ages, 'great sinners build great cathedrals.' The sins of Jackson must have been significant; it cost him a fortune to buy his way out of Protestant purgatory with this towering leviathan," Quail grinned.

"How much did it cost?" asked someone in the group.

"Cell phone companies squabbled over who would rent our 214-foot bell tower. Our tower rises—unexpectedly, anachronistically (and indeed phallically)—visible from the interstate." Another knowledgable grin. "Tourists are attracted like flies to a carcass after a glimpse of Hope from the highway."

"Tower bells are Taylors, the last from England before the Crash. The largest, the great bass, weighs a ton. Questions?"

Except for a stint in a miniscule church down state, Johnson Quail had never practiced sacerdotal ministry, moving into the "Ministry of Administration" at Hope Church at the invitation of the Senior Managing Pastor, who had found unbearable the pressure of administering a complex volunteer organization burdened by an aging mausoleum of a building.

Quail boasted at having resided in the "real world," a brag that he leveraged against effete clergy with little aptitude in administration. Maker of tough decisions, minder of the budget, and keeper of the architectural fabric, a strict materialist theologically, Quail enjoyed the clout of being the second highest paid staff member at Hope—a hard-working administrator devoid of both nonsense and imagination.

"How much stone was used?" asked one of the pastors.

Leading them into the building, Quail answered over his shoulder, "Cost well over a million in the twenties. Twenty times that couldn't replace it today." Quail affected a stride within the building that was counter to the gait of clergy—a business-like walk, worldly and self-assured, a clergyman camouflaged as an accountant.

Once the group was huddled inside, Quail resumed the monotone of a professional guide: "Hope reminds one of Salisbury, though Hope's Gothic is more assertive, decidedly *Neo*gothic, the sort favored by Midwestern nouveau riche in the twenties. You must admit that if Hope is fake, it's fine fake." Another unreturned grin.

"When Jackson offered money and land, he also stipulated that the church should 'update itself to the new America.' Note the central tondo and the two large Rodinesque hands, reaching upward," he said, pointing above. "Jackson was a devotee of what was then called 'muscular Christianity,' now in disrepute because of its appeal to Nazis. That devotion accounts for the pronounced pectorals of the angelic figures—'ecclesiastical homoerotic,' I call it."

Blank stares all round.

"As a proponent of what is now 'progressive religion,' our patron also felt that contemporary faith ought to be enriched with a vague aura of mystery, derived from its medieval English sources. Words from The Letter to the Hebrews were adapted for Hope's motto: *A church full of assurance of things hoped for combined with thoughtful conviction of things not seen.* You'll see it carved in the limestone above the Gothic gateway to the garth."

"Hope rose where the best people migrated and built homes to look six hundred years old, trophies of new affluence. Here Hope reigned— Gothic mirage in the middle of a park, shored up by suburban success— mercifully saved from the urban blight that has knocked out many of our rivals.

"Though our greatest asset, this old barn costs a fortune to maintain. Nearly every other once large church in our denomination is in precipitous decline, but not Hope—Hope flourishes. Packed pews are irrefutable arguments against our less visionary detractors."

"What's your percentage of attendees versus your membership?" asked the shortest of the pastors. Quail pretended not to hear the question.

"Oh. I should have noted the front, or 'East Entrance,' as it is more properly called. In the limestone tympanum Christ reigns, not on a cross, which has no place in Hope's iconography, but rather as the affirming Christ, seated, embracing a small Asian child."

Now walking down the center aisle, where a few gathered for the closing plenary, Quail shouted over the rumblings, "The true aesthetic glory of Hope are the windows, the work of the Trumbulson firm of Boston, each an irreplaceable masterpiece of the contemporary glass worker's art, twelve gigantic windows in homage to the twelve apostles, though few contain specific biblical references. Each window depicts a contemporary saint surrounded by images of his or her holiness."

Gesturing, "General William Booth and wife Catherine, John Brown, pike in hand, Abraham Lincoln as commander-in-chief of the Union Army, Booker T. Washington embracing—of course—a potted peanut, William Wilberforce and the rent manacles of slaves, Charles Darwin accompanied by a delightful dodo (subject of wisecracks), George Washington (thought by many to resemble a young Bette Davis), Thomas Jefferson (with an inset of mistress Sally Hemmings, added by a donor in 1973), Nathaniel Hawthorne with Hester Prim, and Louis Pasteur in front of brown cows. Each year Planned Parenthood gathers for a Celebration of Contraception at the Sanger window. These 'saints' are 'Hope personified,' as an early pastor put it.

"Chartres blue predominates, flooding the sanctuary with an ethereal glow," he droned over the growing din, "culminating in that massive lancet, in which you will see Christ triumphant, holding his hands out as if to embrace John Brown, Margaret Sanger, and the rest. Enough. It's time for the plenary. Unfortunately, no time for questions."

∾

Everyone at the conference knew that Hope's success was attributable, not to the church's having discovered some foolproof technique for survival, and not even to the glory of the building, but rather to its pastor, the Reverend Doctor Simon Lupino.

The main drawback of Signs of Hope was that many were doomed to leave their week of church renewal even more despondent because, though they may have learned techniques for improving their modest parishes, they also went home knowing that they were no Simon Lupino. Pastor Bob Smithson from Louisville summed it up, when interviewed by an inquiring local reporter: "You want to be a successful church? Well, start with one tall, good looking, hint-of-a-British-accent, Ivy-league educated, dark-hair-turning-silver-gray-around-the-edges pastor who in twenty years has gathered around him the richest people in the city, and backed by a six million dollar endowment, the rest is easy."

Those less afflicted with pulpit envy than Smithson agreed that Simon's achievements at Hope were remarkable. While it was true that when Simon had arrived twenty years ago—the country's brightest and most promising thirty-five-year-old cleric—he inherited a church with an already handsome endowment. It was also undeniably true that Simon had accomplished that which few of his peers had. Hope's mix of high-brow, mostly traditional worship and urbane preaching, augmented by the hundreds of small groups and study opportunities, a vigorous volunteer service program, boosted by a few strategic deaths that swelled the endowment, were savvy ecclesiastical strategy for a new millennium. By his fourth year at Hope, Simon was named "Best Performing Pastor of the Year" by the Guild for Parish Clergy.

At this, the last session, Simon stepped onto a circular stage in the center of the sanctuary. Large, glittery silver letters spelling EXCEL-LENCE had been affixed to the stage, with the letters forming EXCEL highlighted in gold trim. While the stage was sometimes used on a Sunday when Simon desired to make a particularly strong impact—such as United Nations Sunday—it was standard for the Signs of Hope conference. As the houselights dimmed, a spotlight cut dramatically through the blue air, illuminating the solitary preacher, and with two thousand expectant (if not desperate) faces trained on him, Simon began his closing keynote in a voice like an emcee's:

No one disputes that you are working hard in your congregations. I can tell by looking at your weary faces!

Muffled laughter in the audience.

The challenge before us pastors in the present hour is not hard work but smart work. Don't attempt to be the church in the twenty-first century with tools that were cobbled together in the first. Once, it was enough for a pastor to counsel the troubled and preach on Sunday. That day is as dead as John Wesley. Richard Niebuhr's vision of the "pastoral director" has finally been realized. Here at Hope, results—results—is our religion. We baptize what American business management has learned and claim these insights as God-given means of grace for the church today!

Scattered applause.

There was a time when pastors needed skills in biblical interpretation or theological rumination. Now the golden key that unlocks the future is the litany of leadership, management, and entrepreneurship. God has given us all we need.

A lethargic church awaits with eager longing the deliverance worked by those leaders who are supple and strategic. Every problem that your congregation faces can be cured by inspired, heartfelt leadership that bows at the altar of excellence!

Applause.

Thank God that the builders of Hope Church, while they genuflected to the church's medieval past, didn't erect a church using Dark Ages' building techniques. Nobody would sit under a ten-ton boss that had nothing but the engineering of medieval architecture to support it!

Again, laughter.

No, they took what had been given by the past and they adapted it for the present, fully embracing St. Paul's dictum to be "all things to all people."

Everything you have seen this week is the result of our staff praying, "God, grant us holy discontent. Stir up in us passionate desire to be excellent."

At the mention of "staff," one amid the throng took particular notice—freshly minted by Princeton Seminary, new Minister to Youth and Students at Hope, Stephen Smith, dressed uncomfortably but dutifully in his single coat and tie for his inaugural event after his first Easter at Hope, aspiring not to look stupid. As he listened, he texted Thea: "Everytg going grt. Impressive. Lupino AWESOME. Love, hugs, & kisses, etc., Stephen."

Stephen could not believe that it was his good fortune to begin his ministry at a church like Hope. Though Stephen didn't plan to be a youth pastor all of his life, and though he knew that Thea was probably right—the main reason why he was here was to add diversity to Hope's all-white staff—landing a job at Hope had made him the envy of his seminary classmates. He could structure student ministry as he saw fit, assured that an eager but underled group of teenagers awaited him. The salary was better than he had dreamed, his apartment more than adequate.

Above all he would be tutored by the best in the business. As he watched Lupino move comfortably on his circular stage, bathed in spotlight, his resonant voice booming into the vast sanctuary—using no notes—Stephen wanted to be him.

After three mostly irrelevant and rarely interesting seminary years, it was invigorating to hear someone like Dr. Lupino talking about the real world and sharing proven, workable church techniques. If Thea could hear Lupino now she would understand. Two thousand souls hung on Lupino's words.

Don't do more; do less. You must focus on "the one thing needful," the pearl of great price, the treasure in the field. Make this your sole desire, waking or sleeping, by day or by night. Make this your watchword: Excellence!

God bless you. God bless America. See you same time, same place next year!

Applause. With a wave and a broad smile, Simon exited the stage to the strains of the praise band's pulsing, reggae rendition of "Amazing

Grace" (even though Simon had spent the last thirty minutes explaining that astute church leadership was neither amazing nor due to grace.) The applause roused Quail from his slumber beneath the column next to the John Brown window. Organist Grimball looked with contempt upon the praise band's attempt to manufacture a feeling of inclusiveness with their bogus reggae—this group of suburbanite amateurs knew as much about reggae as Lawrence Welk.

As he tucked the music into his bag, a morose thought occurred to choirmaster Glumweltner: the conference had ended without lunch, forcing the insatiable chorister to forage on his own.

Stephen looked at his watch. Thea would be beginning her afternoon seminar and likely would not be able to text him back.

While Simon adored the clergy's collective adulation, he also felt pity for them, ensnared as they were in a profession that attracted the intellectually mediocre, the unsexed, the inane, and the overweight, adorned in plaid sports coats and bolo ties—all those who, if held accountable for the results of their labors, would starve.

∽

Twenty minutes after the finale, Simon strode down an adjacent hall past the Walter Rauschenbusch Lounge with Johnson Quail.

"Johnson, my man, this year's conference will prove to have been the best ever, once the evaluations are in," predicted Simon, slapping him gently on the back. "Things just clicked. Like clockwork. Can you believe that all of this began just a decade ago with nothing but a dream? Fine execution, if I do say so. I could see it in their faces. Thanks ever so much for your contribution."

"While I did not see their faces, I have seen something more revealing—the receipts. Not encouraging," said Quail, a faint note of delight in his voice as he delivered the bad news.

"What? That's impossible. Registration maxed out, and we sold twice as many Hope Packets. And the CDs! Good Lord, the CDs! CD sales alone should have put us in the black."

"Sorry, Simon. I told you we should have upped the registration fee, despite the economy. Remember the rules: when outgo is greater than income, we lose. Right? A well-wrought business plan could have been our salvation. Numbers don't lie."

"Our costs couldn't have gone up that much," protested Simon, suddenly crestfallen.

"Well, I'll explain when you have more time to focus," Quail patronized. "I'll run the numbers, do the comparisons. Don't mean to rain on your parade."

∾

Churches tend to smell like, well, churches, Stephen thought to himself as he sat in the outer office awaiting his first audience with Dr. Lupino. While sitting there, his foot nervously beating the rhythm to no particular song, he wondered—what was the source of that peculiar smell? He sniffed. Old, moldy, closed. Perhaps the musty smell was due to churches being unused most of the week. Hospitals or cafeterias smell the way they do because of what happens in them. But churches smell because of what doesn't happen there, the same way a house smells when it lies vacant.

But he was sitting in one of the most frequently used spaces at Hope—the Senior Managing Pastor's office. Mix six decades of burned candle wax, fifty-year-old vestments soaked with clerical sweat, generations of sticky Sunday school kids, potluck suppers, and overperfumed, heavily powdered old ladies noisily unwrapping mints, and you get that distinctive church bouquet, a byproduct of the faded glory of mainline Protestantism.

"Dr. Lupino can see you now. Just go right in, sweetie," said the smiling woman behind the desk who told him to call her Cloe. Stephen, roused from his olfactory reverie, stood up, straightened himself, and entered the sumptuous office.

"And be sure that you stop by afterwards, honey. I'll give you the master keys. You'll need a half dozen to get around in this old place," laughed Cloe.

Six master keys stretch the meaning of "master key," Stephen thought as he entered Dr. Lupino's office.

"You are great to meet with me after the grueling week that you've just had," said Stephen.

"No trouble at all," said Dr. Lupino, not rising when Stephen entered, peering at him over the top of his reading glasses. He gestured toward the leather Chippendale chair. Dr. Lupino's office was vast, Gothic, adorned with books, all of them perfectly set in rows on the surrounding shelves, those with leather bindings (the sort that are sold as a series of books made to look old and valuable) placeed so that they were most prominent. On one wall were pictures of Dr. Lupino hugging or being hugged by numerous local politicians of both parties. A large American flag leaned against a corner beside a pair of snow skis over which was draped a doctoral hood.

Swiveling from side to side in his chair, Simon began, "Though invigorated by Easter, I am even more pumped by the Hope Conference. Glad you were able to witness it. Annual confirmation of how much has been accomplished at Hope. Our gift to those poor souls laboring in the backwaters of Christendom."

"I really liked the upbeat nature of the conference," said Stephen, forced to sit up slightly in order to see over the desk.

"Thanks. That's by design. Be positive, even when . . ."

Simon's cell phone buzzed. He flipped it open and answered, "Yes . . . no, this is fine . . . sure. No problem. Tuesday noon will be fine. I hear your new lake house is wonderful. Yes. Good. Bye."

He closed the phone and resumed, saying, "But I wanted to orient you to life at Hope before both of us are caught up in post-Easter, pre-Pentecost stuff."

He reared back thoughtfully. "Stephen, you're smart enough to notice: Hope is not your average church. It would be a mistake to think, 'thus and so was done at Saint John's on the Expressway, so I'll continue it here as well.'"

"That's good," said Stephen, "since I've had virtually no church experience. Here I am. Blank slate."

"Relax. Inexperience is another name for 'open-minded.' Teachable. My dream was a staff that was not only dedicated but also competent. In the words of the old hymn, 'Give of your best to the Master'. Loved that hymn as a kid and prayed that one day I'd lead a church where everyone would be free to give their best. 'Give him the strength of your youth . . . join in the battle for truth.' Loved that. I tithe—as an example to our staff.

"All of our staff—or as I prefer, the Hope family—perform to the max. We aspire to the most efficient pastoral care delivery system in town, the most engaging messages (I wonder if the prosaic 'sermon' is so shopworn as to be unredeemable), and the most scintillating programs. Stephen, is that what you want?"

"Sure. Honored to be here."

"After studying your résumé and tracking down your references, I know that you will thrive. You remind me of myself at the first. Wish I'd had someone to show me around in my early days. Would have avoided lots of mistakes."

"I'm grateful because I don't feel seminary really made me . . ."

"I may push you beyond your comfort zone," Simon laughed, speaking with the sort of pontification that typifies clergy ten years Simon's senior. "But I never ask any member of the family to do anything that I myself do not do."

"I love a challenge."

"Now, tell me about your path into this work," said Simon.

"My call? When I was in college, I was summoned home. Fall, my junior year. My grandfather was dying from emphysema. He came up the hard way. My parents were caring for him in his last days. Well, I rushed to his bedside. Since he was weak, we didn't have much conversation. He said that he was tired, but before I left, he wanted to have prayer. I held his hand. He prayed that God would give him a good passage out of this life, told God that he looked forward to seeing my grandmother again, and some other things."

Simon fidgeted with his phone.

"The last thing Papa prayed was, 'And please, Lord, lead Stephen to see that he ought to be a preacher. Amen.'

"I said, 'What? What did you say?' And Papa just said, 'I've got to rest now, Stephen.' And I stumbled out. It shook me. Before the end of the following day, he slipped quietly away, leaving me holding those words, 'And please lead Stephen to see that he ought to be a preacher.'"

Simon cleared his voice. "Well, you will be immediately accountable to me, Stephen. Accountability is the source of effective ministry. I restrict the number of staff whom I supervise. No more than eight direct reports. I'm making an exception in your case, not only because I like what I see in you but also because I am convinced that there's no way that Hope can attract those in their early forties without snagging their teenagers. We get lots of people who have no interest in church but think that we can be helpful in managing the kids. Giving a credit card to one of these overindulged brats is like offering free booze to a drunk. The only control these parents offer them is free birth control!"

Stephen took Simon's hearty laugh as a cue to laugh too.

"Clueless parents. That's where we come in. Right?"

"Right," answered Stephen, making a pretense of taking notes, nodding.

"I hire good people and then trust them to do good work. No micromanager, I."

Dr. Lupino seemed to be imitating Stephen's dad handing him the keys to the family car for his first solo drive.

"Your best teachers will be other staff; I've tried to assemble the very best in the business. Have you met our chief musicians, 'G Squared'— Glumweltner and Grimball?"

"Not yet," answered Stephen. "But I've seen their work this past week."

"First rate. Like most artists, they can be a pain. Glumweltner is the more portly, Grimball the more prickly and prissy."

"I'm sure that all of us will try your patience," Stephen interjected carefully. "I guess that's the burden of being a senior . . ."

"In my vision of worship, musicians provide the musical backdrop, the stage setting, cultivating the proper emotional tone. Get the music right, you can take a congregation any where you like. Few people, even the most intelligent, make it from emotion to reason in their religion, which is why musicians are so important. I handle the head, they handle the heart. When Grimball came to us, or should I say after he was hotly recruited by us, some of his organ music was better suited for a funeral parlor than a church on the move. How he grew! Under Glumweltner, our choral music is mostly traditional, respectful of our sacred music heritage, but not stuffy, eclectic, borrowing from a variety of periods, but always with good taste.

"Then there's Eleanor in children's ministry. Every church needs an Eleanor—sweet marriage of the M. Div. and the M.S.W., adroitly handling those whom nobody else wants to bother with. Like many clergywomen, Eleanor can be a big bundle of need. In an earlier day, she would have been a nun."

Stephen strove to look thoughtful while not agreeing or disagreeing with the politically incorrect opinions being tossed at him.

"Let's see. Sam, who handles the building, Keeper of the Keys to the Kingdom. A beautiful barn we have here, but a bear to keep up. Some days I feel as if I do nothing but feed this great Moloch, with its leaking windows, deteriorating plumbing, and overflowing gutters. She's an aging dowager—not bad looking when smeared with rouge and all dolled up, but look more closely and you can see her fault lines and sags. Still, you couldn't replace her for a fortune. Hope is Mecca for ex-Bible thumping Southern Baptists who've taken up golf and are on their way up. Hope is the equivalent of becoming Episcopalian without all the lace, smells, bells, and martinis."

"It's something," said Stephen.

"Oh yes, Pastor Cohellen. You met him Easter?"

"I saw him in the service but didn't actually have the . . ."

"Herb toddles about. Wonderful help with old folks, hanging out with the Hope Happy Hearts. Periodically he is summoned to provide pastoral sedation to a matriarch who has got her feathers up. He vests and offers a patriarchal word in the service. Couldn't tell by looking at Herb now, but in his day he served some nice little churches downstate. Pouring oil on troubled waters is his ministerial specialty."

Stephen smiled. It was an honor, sort of, to be included on the inside line. Simon settled back in his chair, swung his feet up on his desk, and continued the catechesis.

"Cloe, my assistant, can get my ear. Just be sure that it's an emergency. I'm overseeing from the balcony; you work the floor. Oh, one more—Johnson Quail."

"I met him last week," said Stephen.

"Johnson is sort of pastor without pastoral portfolio. Zero people skills, God bless him. Administration is a perfect fit for his talents in finance and bean-counting oversight of the physical plant. Thank God we've got him. Flatter him with some budgetary question. He'll eat it up. I gave him his big break, and he has more than met expectations. Valuable assistant. Now, what else do you need to hit the ground running?"

"Thanks," said Stephen. "Hope is obviously well run. How do you decide on the mission, the goals?"

"Good question. Shared goals mean much in a multifaceted organization like Hope. Our overarching goal can be summed up in one word." Simon looked to Stephen for the answer.

"Uh, excellence?"

"Well done! I felt it important to keep our goal simple, memorable, flexible."

"I'm sure that setting the direction is a challenge, not only because Hope is big but also because the mission of the church is so different from that of other institutions."

"Different?" Simon asked, knitting his brow. "My discovery, in the early days of my ministry, was how similar the church is to other nonprofits."

"Well, I mean that being the Body of Christ makes the church special."

"Hmm. Can you be more specific?"

Stephen continued awkwardly, "At seminary we learned that the poor have a special place in the kingdom of God. Jesus' preferential option for the poor. And hands-on mission can be a real attraction for the under-thirty crowd."

"Of course. However, there are liability issues. The care and protection of our young people must be our highest priority. Not too sure how these hovering parents would view a field trip to the ghetto with their kiddies, you know, hobnobbing with the down and out. You would need to consult our insurance carrier."

"Sure, just talking about the future," said Stephen.

"Stephen, much that they force-fed you in seminary isn't relevant to the church as it is. Idealism is a liability for clergy. You would be wise to shed yours as soon as possible. Books on ministry can't take you as far as on-the-ground experience. My theology is Christian Realism, looking at the world squarely, without spiritualized ooze, calling things by their proper names *sans* undue supernatural reference. My model is Reinhold Niebuhr. There's quite a gap between the world of seminary books and the real world of the local congregation. Let me ask, what are *your* goals?"

"Goals? First of all, I want to survive!" said Stephen, smiling. "Having had virtually no experience preaching, I hope to look over the shoulder of a master. In fact, I would welcome your critique of my preaching, whenever I get a chance to preach."

"Well, sadly, Hope is not the place to learn how to preach," responded Simon, offhandedly tossing his cell phone onto his desk. "You are the youth pastor. While I personally would be willing to have a rookie take a swipe at the congregation from time to time," he smiled, "the board is rather insistent that I fill the pulpit the majority of Sundays. Our offering plummets on those few Sundays when I'm not in the box.

"But let me offer you a few pointers, if I may. Observation is your best teacher. The secret to preaching is delivery, presentation. That's what the laity want—*style*. I worked on my delivery so that I conveyed confidence, self-assurance, and of course, excellence. Did you do any acting while in college?"

"No, I didn't."

"Pity. Oh, another thing," said Simon, swinging his feet off the desk, sitting up in his chair, and picking up a small slip of paper. "This Jack Hodges kid has been harassing me since Sunday, dying to have some kind of a conversation about the resurrection or something. When I saw him at the front door Sunday, a buxom nymphet on his arm, I figured that he had gone off to college and had some kind of a 'religious experience.' Heard dozens over the years; no need to hear his. You are closer to his age. Hodges is an otherwise right smart young man, I hear. All-state in swimming. He'll grow out of his religious fervor by graduation, when he's looking for a job."

"Jack Hodges?" asked Stephen, taking the note from Simon and clipping it to his tablet. "I'm on it."

"Well," said Simon, looking at his watch, "got to trot across town for a meeting related to open housing. We're the sugar daddy for most of the charitable work in town. Close enough to the poor for you? You'll do just fine here, Stephen. I know it. 'To whom much is given will much be required.'"

On his way back to his cubicle, though he tried not to, Stephen remembered Thea's prediction: "Those people at that big church just want to use you. Showcase you. Your ideals will kill you."

That night Stephen slept uneasily, troubled by dreams that seemed to validate Thea's prediction. He was in a crowded, closed room with arched, Gothic windows, all shut tight. Everyone was white, watching, staring. He spoke but they just stared. Wildly shaking doorknobs, battering his fists against the doors, he was like a bird beating its wings against the bars of its cage.

He hadn't had such vivid dreams since he was a kid.

∿

That Second Sunday of Easter was anything but "Low Sunday." Simon had axed the choir director who preceded Glumweltner for attempting to slouch through the music on Low Sunday. "We've got to take advantage of the Easter attendance bump," reasoned Simon. The music was ordered to rival the triumphalism of Easter so that little of the paschal momentum would be lost.

"All fired up to laud your patron saint, Simon?" asked Gerald, waddling his way to warm up the choir.

Gerald's comment was informed by a decade of Simon's Low Sunday encomiums to Thomas and his doubts. Simon had preached at least seven variations of his "Thomas, My Friend and Fellow Cynic," praising Thomas's "probing questions." A couple of years ago, Simon had extolled Thomas's "searching intellect," ridiculing "credulous folk who accept everything at face value, lacking the intellectual chutzpah to demand evidence." Last Low Sunday, Simon had nearly overplayed his hand by gently criticizing John's Gospel for its dismissal of Thomas as "rogue disciple," saying that Our Lord himself "was made uncomfortable by Thomas's legitimate concerns."

Old Herb labored through the announcements, but haltingly:

There will be no Women Aflame Bible Study Fellowship this week due to illness. Jane Swanson is recuperating from a bad tumble last week. The "Stop Genocide Now!" meeting on Thursday has been moved from the Great Hall to the Eleanor Roosevelt Parlor. Come hear how you can stop genocide. Hope Happy Hearts is sponsoring a wine and cheese reception in the Walter Rauschenbusch Lounge after the lecture.

Finally the sermon. A brief narration of Doubting Thomas from John 20 opened this year's Thomas tirade. Simon said that in the church's wisdom, after the Easter musical hoopla, we are given this Sunday for calm, thoughtful reflection on the meaning of Easter.

I give thanks to God that Thomas was there for the soirée on Easter evening. For if my friend Thomas had not been there, I could not be here. No place for honest doubt at the Lord's Table? Don't you let the Baptists tell you that! I stand as living proof that probing doubters are close to our Lord's heart.

I have been one of those people (are you?) who never got over my childhood obsession with asking, "Why?" I kept probing, kept asking. A teacher's authoritarian "that's just the way it is" struck me, even at an early age, as irresponsibly evasive.

Grimball, lounging on the organ bench, thought to himself, *Oh dear God in heaven, not the riff on his intellectual integrity! Please God, not again.*

Right on cue, Simon boasted, *Despite the efforts of some seminary professors, my own intellectual integrity has not been stifled by those who are threatened by honest doubt.*

Glumweltner released a belch that, though mild, provoked snickering from a couple of adjacent altos.

I give thanks to God for courageous "saints" like Thomas, and his later-day brothers in the Jesus Seminar, all those who stand up to closed-mindedness and bigotry and dare to ask the sacred "Why?"

Where would we be if Pasteur had bowed to the doubts within him and had ceased his work with radium?

Here Simon made an expansive gesture toward the Louis Pasteur window, which exposed his faux pas. Pasteur was the milk man; the cows backing him in the window proved as much. Simon knew from experience to pick up his tempo slightly in order to cover his gaff. Glumweltner leaned forward in his pew, seeking to hide behind the sopranos as he fiddled with his Blackberry—positioned on his stomach—asking Bing if Pasteur was a skeptic or not; he was fairly sure that Simon had injected Pasteur into his message without checking facts.

Note how quickly the story shifts from the less well-endowed disciples, cowering like frightened rabbits behind their locked doors, to Jesus' engagement with Thomas, as if Jesus cares less for the credulous than the doubtful. Our Lord takes up Thomas's goad with gusto. When Jesus says, "Do not doubt but believe," Jesus is not rebuking Thomas's legitimate questions; he is rather praising doubt as the door to faith, affirming Thomas as a fellow searcher. Here's a man on the way to a faith worth having.

He then cited Paul Tillich, something about "new being." Though the allusion dated Simon, a German name lent gravitas even when the congregation knew nothing of Tillich's theology (or adultery). Having extensively claimed kinship with Thomas, Simon returned briefly to the metaphor of the locked door. Noting that the disciples were hunkered down on Easter night behind locked doors, Simon enumerated examples of contemporary locked doors:

"anti-abortion Nazis, the ossified and hidebound Roman Catholic curia, and then there's the Creationist lobby messing with textbooks . . ."

Johnson Quail heard none of Simon's Low Sunday homily. His absence from divine service was due to more than his having heard it all before. Quail was in his office—behind locked doors—feverishly attempting to pilot the church through the dark waters of an impending financial emergency. Sequestered, lights in the outer office extinguished, Quail pored over the books feverishly, thrilled by a true financial crisis. He was in his glory: his reading glasses perched on his flat, slight nose, his knotted brow damp with perspiration, he was a man caught in the middle of a whirlwind.

Five years ago Hope had bought, at a supposed bargain, a defunct retirement village on the west side of town. The project was a ridiculous one, and Quail had said as much, alerting everyone he could until Simon had virtually ordered him to pipe down, invoking the need for Quail to be a "team player, if you get my drift."

Quail had dutifully buried his misgivings. Simon was hell-bent on Hope's buying the village—a thoroughly faux, stucco, country French calamity. The thing was to be renamed "Hope Township"—in Quail's judgment, a euphemism for A Place Where Spoiled Rich People Go to Tell Others Who They Once Were and Then Take Their Sweet Time Dying. Quail had quite accurately prophesied that the place would be a money drain, with its shopping arcade (never more than half occupied) and its nursing center (in the red for four of its seven years). The first residents, in clenched-fist defiance of actuarial predictions as well as natural law, had lived much, much longer than they were supposed to, enjoying the benefit of having others wait on them while driving the nursing center bankrupt.

Undeterred by financial realities, Simon pushed the deal through—quite insisted on it, preached it from the pulpit, twisted the trustees' arms, and shamed all those who resisted: "It's high time that this church stood up and acted like a church, standing in solidarity with the less fortunate, reaching out in servant ministry to the community." Simon cited a predominately African American congregation in Detroit that was a major player in downtown redevelopment and a similarly entrepreneurial congregation in L.A. that owned a shoe factory. "If they can make money at ministry, don't tell me that Hope can't do better."

With these and other exhortations, Simon had rammed the deal down everyone's throat. Quail had charitably swallowed the bogus investment. Now, surveying the wreckage, Quail was literally sick to his stomach.

In the first days, Quail had feared that Simon just might be justified in his rosy predictions for Hope Township. The purchase attracted attention from the local press. Even *Money* magazine pumped the new project in a piece titled "Clergy Superstar Simon Lupino Aiming Big in Business Too." A couple of new tenants (a women's exercise center and a combo wine and cigar store) were secured for the shopping center. But a succession of CEOs had been hired and fired. At least the first two of these thieves had been skilled in running the old folk's center in a way that kept the geezers sedated; the current CEO was good at nothing, neither larceny nor sedation.

Now, with the economic downturn, three of the shopping center's tenants had gone belly up, taking thousands in back rent with them. The health department said that the sewage system needed immediate replacement (to the tune of two million dollars)—the old folks produced such a volume of waste that the settlement pond was dangerously overstressed.

The flaccid board was facing five lawsuits from disgruntled residents and their families—a broken hip per week on greasy floors, it seemed. Of course, Simon had assured everyone that Hope was immune from liability, but Quail knew that the deep pockets for this geriatric boondoggle would have to be Hope's. If Hope Township finally rolled over and died, any self-respecting, bloodsucking attorney would head straight for the church's coffers.

Incorporation

Thus Quail was engaged while Simon reveled in his yearly homage to Saint Thomas. From all that Quail had seen—his emergency salvage operation of the Hope Township books had begun on Saturday morning—the proverbial chickens were indeed coming home. His goal was to devise a plan of salvation for the project, and thus to earn Simon's gratitude for saving his hide.

Quail glanced at his watch—a quarter to noon. Simon was a stickler for ending the service at twelve sharp—prominent people are punctual people—and on most Sundays he hit his mark. Stashing the potentially damaging papers, scooping up spreadsheets and documents, he quickly slithered out of the office so that he could be in the narthex before the last gasp of the service. No one would know that he had played hooky.

As he rounded the corner, affecting his banker's gait, he discovered that he was not the only truant. Three men—Drayton, Warner, and Thomas, trustees all—were huddled in somber deliberation in the darkened well of the east stairway. Warner was an acquisitions specialist, a local Mitt Romney–type who bought and sold Berkshire Bidet five times, terminating half of the company's workforce. Drayton was the manic-depressive head of a string of trendy Asian-themed restaurants, Fu Fu Tofu. People of such consequence were not to be trifled with. In confirmation of Quail's suspicions, the conspirators were obviously embarrassed to be discovered in conclave. Quail overheard one say, "It's time to act. The bishop has got to be . . ."

Had this sneaky triumvirate beaten him to the draw on the Hope Township debacle? How could they know the numbers? He suspected them of having that low, lay, animal cunning that enabled them adeptly to sniff out clergy goof-ups. If they had wised up, it was all the more important to lay his evidence before Simon, together devise a plan of attack, and get the jump before they could make mischief with either bishop or banker.

Officiously hurrying down the hall and past the Walter Rauschenbusch Lounge without acknowledging the now scattering connivers, Quail ascended the side stairs, cracked open the door to the narthex, and jabbed his balding head inside just as Simon was winding down his doubt-filled diatribe:

And as Tennyson said, "There is more faith in honest doubt than in half your creeds."

Tennyson! Quail heard scattered, responsive applause. They ate it up, couldn't get enough of it. To give the Devil his due, old Simon was a master manipulator of the masses. As the organ exuded the first notes of the recessional, Quail sensed a sharp pain in his gut; he felt queasy, though he didn't know if it was due to his undercooked breakfast, to what he had seen of the disastrous Hope Township numbers, or to the toxic snippet of Simon's sermon.

The self-satisfied throng—blessed and sent forth to "live the questions" and "to trust your doubts more than your beliefs"—moved through the narthex and out into the warm April sunlight. Quail watched from the shadows as young Stephen tried to buttonhole a few bored youths and chat them up, to little effect. *That eager young man has a daunting task trying to get those spoiled brats worked up about anything religious*, Quail thought.

"Johnson, I know that this is a busy time of the year," said Townsend Thomas as he pulled Quail aside, "but I must see you. How's Wednesday afternoon?"

Quail smiled. They were moving fast, these rats, trying to scurry off a sinking ship. Thank God that Niculous wasn't around, pious little fake, or he would have eagerly joined their coup.

"Tough week for me, actually, Townsend," replied Quail. "Snowed under. This Wednesday I have a doctor's appointment and some unpleasant tests. Bustling time in the life of the church, too. Eastertide and all that. How about next Wednesday at 3:00?"

"Sure. Wednesday would be fine."

"That's Wednesday *week*, next Wednesday, not this Wednesday," said Quail with a smile. *If the boys want a revolution, they have come to the right place*, he thought. He had managed uppity trustees before, and he could easily do so again.

As in the gospels, so too in the church: after the resurrection, the real trouble begins.

3

The Third Sunday of Easter

A t an absurdly (for a senior cleric) early dawn hour on Monday, Simon turned into staff parking, just to the rear and to the right of the church, easing his car into the space labeled in large, eternal gold, MANAGING PASTOR. The car turned in on a dime. His determination to be an example to the rest of the staff accounted for his presence at this premature hour. "Show, don't tell" was another of his management maxims.

Simon shut his car door with a reassuring, well fit thud. As he did so, he glanced again at the wrought-iron sign designating his reserved spot. His heart missed a beat. Even by the dawn's early light he could see that some Easter vandal had scratched off the first three gilt letters so that it read, AGING PASTOR.

Though he was not a violent man—he had never once in his life struck any person (thus his clerical status)—Simon seized the sign, worked it to the right and left, and ripped it up, post and all, including a small ball of concrete and dirt at the bottom.

"Oh God," he prayed, "may that sign not have been defaced more than a day or so ago."

Body bent, sick at heart, Simon trudged gloomily up the sidewalk toward the station designated "Ministry of Administration," fumbling for his keys.

∾

Simon religiously commenced the weekly gathering at nine sharp—too many ecclesiastical agencies are wasteful in their use of time. He enjoyed

Monday staff meetings, not only as an opportunity to build community, but also as a quotidian rebuke to the church's tendency to high-flown, Sabbath-day flights of spiritual fancy. The meeting certified Monday as the most important day of the church's week, where everyone, having received their charge, surged forth to do the kingdom business, a weekly reminder that the work of the church was the world, not the church.

Stephen was already present, drinking coffee, bantering with Grimball. When Simon entered, Stephen rose and spoke an amiable, "Hi, boss." The organist glanced up, smiled a knowing grin at Simon, but tacitly. As Stephen rose, Simon remembered his satisfying introductory conversation with the novice. For a fleeting moment, Simon wistfully wished that he could have bragged to the kid that he had courageously marched with Martin Luther King Jr., that he had once met Jesse Jackson at a meeting, even that he was once on a long flight with the Reverend Al Sharpton and was impressed by his intellect. Why did he feel he was on probation with the novice, when the probation ought to be the other way around?

"Goood morning allll!" announced an uncharacteristically cheerful Gerald Glumweltner—that is, *Dr.* Glumweltner, D. Mus.—as he waddled behind Simon.

"Is it a relief to have Easter and the conference over and done with Gerald?" asked Simon, just to be nice. "Quite a load off your shoulders, I guess."

"Not at all," replied the corpulent choirmaster (who needed a lightening of the load in his gut more than his shoulders). "I've been working six weeks on our music for next Sunday. Mine is a year-round job, just like yours. As preacher, you know what I mean, since I am sure that you plan your sermons far in advance. I'm cheerful because my choir performed so well Sunday—a warm 'thank you' to all of you for your many kind, supportive words of gratitude."

Simon nodded. Pride in having Glumweltner in his stable competed with vexation at Gerald's growing impertinence, aggravated by Grimball's insubordinate mouth. Until someone discovered a cure for excessive cellulite, Glumweltner would always be out of sorts.

Cloe Strong, Simon's personal assistant, entered and took her place prim and proper at the table next to Andrea Coyne, Administrator for Print Media. Who knew what Cloe had endured over the weekend from her besotted husband? Simon frequently thanked God that Cloe kept her troubles to herself, a rare virtue among church folk. For her part, Andrea was reported to have a live-in boyfriend, a mechanic, but that was all that anyone knew about her—aside from her skill at word processing and the fineness of her supple figure—which was fine, too. Andrea not only quietly produced the weekly bulletin but also the full-color brochure for the Hope Conference. The front cover of this year's brochure featured a photoshopped image of Simon looking upward toward a church in the sky and the words, in bold green letters, "Does Your Church Have Hope for Tomorrow?"

"Dr. Lupino, will Mrs. Lupino be joining you for the Boy's Club banquet next month?" asked Cloe innocently. "I must let the folks at the club know for the head table."

"Probably not," replied Simon. "Can't count on Mary for many meals these days. Had our first breakfast together in weeks only this morning. Mary is here, there, and everywhere, showering blessed benefits as she goes. She's really quite remarkable, if I do say so."

Sam Watson appeared with notebook in one hand, coffee cup in the other. If truth be told, Sam was the only essential person on staff. Possessor of a plumbing license—more helpful at Hope than a license to preach—Sam had also committed to memory the arcane electrical system, knowledge that was indispensable in a blackout. Quail had whispered to Simon that he secretly suspected that Sam intentionally orchestrated an annual electrical outage—sometimes in the middle of a Grimball organ concert (which, though such embarrassments to Grimball delighted Quail, still suggested sloppy administration of the building), sometimes on the night of the annual church council meeting—in order to remind everyone that he alone had plumbing and wiring gnosis. Simon had dismissively told Quail that he was becoming paranoid and patted him on the back, and Sam continued, undisciplined.

Sam's gigantic ring of keys, which he plopped on the table, was testimony to his indispensability. Though everyone tastefully tried never to mention it, Sam's wife had put a bullet through her head two years ago. She was a Catholic.

And then there was Eleanor McIlvain, Coordinator of Children's Ministries, quiet, mousy, and confined to her corner. Though she had a seminary degree—earned in midlife after her husband came out and left her for an industrial architect—only one lowly housekeeper deigned to bestow the title of "Reverend" upon her; her seminary education was a distinction as superfluous as her appendix, and her "Christian Education Program" no more than a sanctified babysitting service.

Confined to the children's wing, Eleanor excelled at keeping the children from underfoot except for their annual appearance on Christmas Eve when folk drove from miles around to have a sentimental wallow. Eleanor supervised the children's seasonal production of a cardboard turkey or a sock Santa for parents. She also concocted children's theme Sundays about bunnies and talking mice who had discovered deeper meaning in their Christian discipleship, complete with in-house produced videos and hand-cut cookies in the shape of biblical personalities and Hebrew letters. In her tennis shoes and denim skirt, she dressed the part and never failed to disappoint low expectations, laboring *sans* notice, *sans* gratitude, *sans* reserved parking space.

"Sam, can you stay a moment after the meeting?" Simon asked.

"Sure. If this is about the leakage around the organ chamber, I think we are on to that," said Sam. "Roofing tar—one of God's great creations! Mr. Niculous didn't think the dribbling could be stopped for less than a thousand. Is he going to be surprised that I know more about roofing than he knows about money!" Sam shook with laughter.

"After the meeting," said Simon, smiling.

Newcomer Stephen chimed, "The music was just great Sunday, really first-rate."

"Thank you," replied Glumweltner before Grimball had the opportunity to ask whether Stephen was referring to music choral or instrumental. Too smug to receive even modest compliments, Glumweltner asked, "Have you experienced first-rate ecclesiastical choral programs in the past, or is this your first?" He sounded exactly like Orson Welles doing a wine commercial.

"Young man, that will teach you to offer unsolicited praise to a musician," muttered Quail, not looking up from the stack of papers before him. Grimball snickered and winked at Stephen: Quail 1; Glumweltner 0.

"Well, good people, the hour hath come," pronounced Simon. "All dutifully assembled. Hospital report? The little Swenson child is still at Children's Hospital. I went by last week, took one look and figured that his parent's fears were well founded. No word on the whereabouts of Niculous. Found his car, but without him."

Quail's face tensed slightly at the mention of Niculous, but no one noticed, so skilled was he at concealment.

"And of course we've got Eliot Thomas hanging on at St. Luke's. Hysterical reports that he was on his last leg were erroneous, apparently, exaggeratedly dire. Holy Saturday, Eliot was rumored to be on his way to eternity. Now, well into the Great Fifty Days of Joy, he's still among us, happily sucking oxygen and Medicare."

"Quite a heart for an octogenarian who smoked two packs a day, I'd say," said Cloe cheerfully. "God bless 'im."

"And a guy who had his share of the ladies, from what I hear," said Gerald, mouth now crammed with sweet roll, dusting his gut with crumbs and powdered sugar.

"Herb? Keep us posted on Eliot's progress or regress," said Simon genially.

Herb seemed to nod.

"Andrea, three typos, baby, in Sunday's bulletin," said Grimball as he openly slid a copy of the bulletin toward her across the table, marked up in red like a high school book report. "Read it and weep, baby."

"Clerical matters are my purview," sneered Quail, seething at Grimball's trespass.

It pained Simon to see Grimball use the meeting to take a swipe at defenseless support staff. Everybody must dominate somebody, but Grimball's prospects for having a subordinate were few. Simon was pleased to see Andrea receive the imperfect bulletin cooly, showing no intention of weeping over a few bulletin typos presented to her by an organist. "You've got quite an eye for mistakes. Let's hope that your ear is similarly sharp," she said icily.

"You go girl," stage whispered Glumweltner, adoring with silent gratitude how fine Andrea looked in her snug knitted top, but disappointed that Andrea made no response to his gracious affirmation.

Stephen ducked the sparring and poking, the jaw-jabbing and back-stabbing, though some of it looked fun. Through it all, Grimball projected an air of indifference, thumbing through sheet music as Simon checked off the agenda. Glumweltner attempted unconcern, working the email on his phone that rested on his broad belly while sucking some sort of hard candy. Cloe sat upright with pencil in hand but rarely made notations. Herb dozed, even though it was not yet midmorning, smiling contentedly. Sam doodled. Quail sorted mail, occasionally raising his eyebrows contemptuously in response to someone's statement, dismissing any comment by Grimball.

Stephen could tell that Simon enjoyed the role of president; efficient but also patient, never allowing the gathered staff to squander time with idle chitchat or to become bogged down in irrelevant details, Simon worked at having a doggedly positive demeanor. Hope was a beehive of busyness this spring. Before Stephen's arrival, the staff had agreed to Simon's target of a five percent increase in attendance over last spring's numbers. The key to a spike, according to Simon's lecture, was "all cylinders clicking," with an augmentation of small groups and other activities. He had gleaned three goals from a quick-fix management book that no church grew without: a 70 percent participation in small groups; 16 percent of the members giving 10 percent of their income; and a 40 percent proportion of young parents with children. Though Hope had far to go before it came within range of any of these lofty organizational goals, everyone had pretended to receive Simon's suspect statistics as gospel truth on boosting attendance, hoping that this was the boss's passing fancy and little would come of it.

As Simon went over all of this (as if it had not been mentioned at the last meeting), Grimball perked up and asked, "Simon, I thought that figure was 18 percent required to give 11 percent of their income. Are you sure? Then again, 10 percent giving 8 percent of their income would be a remarkable step forward around here."

Glumweltner swallowed a laugh as expertly as he had engulfed his Danish.

"Simon, I welcome the increased emphasis on accountability," said Quail, looking directly at Grimball as he spoke.

Though the staff had hoped that Simon would not remember this attendance increase dictate—he had a history of forgetting these papal pronouncements shortly after he made them—Simon had ordered Cloe to remind him to ask everyone to report. Stephen took this as a cue to eagerly announce his six-week "Power Bible Study," as well as a "Hope Floats" trip down the East Fork River. Then he made the mistake of announcing a projected youth mission excursion before summer's end.

"Er, Stephen, I thought we decided that you would go slowly on your mission trip notions. I suggest that you focus internally, organize things in house, before being distracted by external, marginal concerns," said Simon in a warm but paternal way.

"I was, uh, just saying some things that I have under consideration. I can put the rest in an email to everybody."

Eleanor then went into far too much detail about a series of special Sundays for the children, replete with puppets, a trampoline, and a movie with popcorn, including a dissertation on how surprisingly difficult it was to obtain organic popcorn in large quantities.

"Handmade puppets are a turn-on for five-year-olds whose Easter consisted of three days in the lap of luxury—with room service and Cinemax—at the Magic Kingdom?" asked Grimball.

Simon was consoled to learn that even the staff's pet peacocks, the pompous Glumweltner and Grimball, were doing their part to stimulate participation. Glumweltner descanted on the choir's dinner concert, "The Best of Stephen Sondheim," for this year's spring garden party. ("I hope to heaven that Chef will not try one of those 'Polynesian Nights' concoctions like last year," Grimball chimed in, to which Quail replied, "If Chef doesn't climb back on the wagon, the dinner will be catered."). Glumweltner was deflated by their studied disinterest in his repertoire for the evening.

Grimball contributed his lunchtime concert in May, though Simon reminded him that the goal was to boost the numbers on Sundays, not Wednesday mornings. ("Late May? I am guardedly optimistic that Chef will be either sober or dead," said Quail. "The menu is of more import than music.")

When Quail was asked to report his ideas for attendance promotion, he sighed and said, "Pass." Rearranging the deck chairs on the Titanic, as far as Quail was concerned. If they knew what he knew about Hope's burgeoning unserviced debt, they wouldn't be fretting about the number of freeloaders attracted to the Sunday show.

Simon asked Cloe to devise a wall chart on which Sunday attendance could be graphed, directing her to post the chart in the outer office, "where we can hold ourselves accountable."

No response from kindly old Pastor Herb. In fact, save his smile and occasionally blinking eyes, there was little indication that Herb was actually alive. Simon shared with most active clergy the ungenerous opinion that retired clergy were a pain to have near a working church. Yet Herb was risk free and even useful on occasion. Simon had hinted to Herb that he need not feel compelled to attend staff meetings, stressing that "we wouldn't want to intrude on your retirement or the important work you do for us with the shut-ins or Hope Happy Hearts," hoping that Herb would get the point: there is no earthly reason for you to be here. Herb appeared to be not only without guile but without much aptitude for hint taking; there he sat, consigned to the far end of the table, fading in and out of consciousness, kindly smile etched indelibly on his face, though no one knew why.

"Remember, it's not how hard we work, it's the specific, measureable results we get," Simon lectured. "Work smart, not hard. Excellence is our byword. Unless we have a goal, and keep it specific, we won't go anywhere. If you don't have a plan to go somewhere, any path takes you nowhere. Though measurability, purposefulness, excellence abide, these three, the greatest of these is excellence, to coin a phrase."

Amid this wash of high insipidities, the downer was, as was often the case, Quail's monthly financial report, which he had artfully designed for that low purpose. Easter's paltry oblation was reported and comparatively analyzed. Cash receipts were depressed, checks too. The dollars were disappointing, especially when compared with last Easter. The memorial Easter lilies seemed to have siphoned off some of the undesignated giving. Though the attendance was high, those present in the pews, if judged by what they put in the plate, were cheap.

"I hate it when they come for the show but fail to cough up the dough," rhymed Grimball, reveling in his poetical expertise. "Do they think we can shovel out this cultural feast gratis?"

Of course, it had been a grisly year for the market, so a slump was anticipated. A high percentage of Hope's hoarier members lived off their stock coupons, it was surmised. Rumors were that the ruling class was hurting more than they let on. Seasonal excursions to Florida or the islands slumped this past winter, pronounced Grimball with authority. And now the most discouraging news: the annual Hope Conference, which had left the staff with a hangover they were still nursing, was in the red for the first year since its inception.

"We've got to do a better job with our business plan on something of this magnitude," said Quail in a censorious tone. "I mean, my God, fifty thousand for technical set up? And the money we dropped on that musical group from St. Louis!"

"Fine. Next year we'll get so-and-so's nephew strumming his daddy's *gee*tar and whining gospel jingles. Excuse me. I thought this whole thing was about excellence," said Grimball with theatrical aggravation. "Guess I got it wrong."

"Johnson, not to sound pious," said Simon, "but as the denomination's most successful church, I feel we have a sacrosanct obligation to share what we've learned with those who are confined to the hinterland, to give some glimmer of hope to the hopeless—which could be our conference theme next year. Hope for the hopeless! I like it. Yes, that's a possibility."

"Let me know how many of the hopeless you attract to a conference on hopelessness," Quail scoffed.

"If you could have seen the faces of those pastors, filled with such bright optimism on the last day of the conference, then . . ."

"We're all thrilled that the rubes got high at Hope. They should have been happy," snarled Quail. "After all, they got a conference that cost almost twice as much as the freeloaders paid for it. To tell the gospel truth, they ought to be downright delirious with bliss, damn them."

"All right, all right." Simon didn't believe in circulating negative information, and he was becoming increasingly vexed with Quail's unconstructive attitude. "Cloe, make a note that we'll plan more closely for next year's event. But we will not back off on excellence. No church has higher standards. We have made remarkable progress. You all have been wonderful. I sense a new feeling of, well, *hope*." Plaudits for subordinates, even if undeserved.

"Hearing no further business, you are adjourned. Good work, good people. I am confident that we will indeed reach our goal. Let's remember our great commission: excellence. And 5 percent! Oh yes, Cloe, I seem to have mysteriously misplaced my keys. Looked everywhere. Would you see that I get a new set?"

"Can such paupers as we afford such extravagance?" muttered Glumweltner as he gathered up papers and brushed crumbs onto the carpet, eyebrows upraised, chortling. "After being warned of the preciousness of those antique keys, I always tuck mine under my pillow, first thing after my prayers each night."

"Really now, is that prudent?" said Quail, attempting to play a part in the comic opera that was the staff meeting. "Ought not you stick them up your big fat . . ."

Glumweltner scurried off to the music suite, disgusted by the whole lot of them, there to solace himself by sticking his head into a therapeutic tub of Häagen-Dazs Rocky Road.

∽

After an epigrammatic post-meeting double check with the musicians concerning next Sunday's looming service (no more pricey rented brass until Pentecost), as well as a question from Stephen about his parking space (talk to Cloe), when the room cleared, Simon reached behind the side table and presented the vandalized sign to Sam, banging it hard on the boardroom table.

"How long might the Manager of External Maintenance have left this malicious aspersion in place?"

Sam looked at the sign reading AGING PASTOR and the metal pole with the small ball of dirty concrete at the bottom. Suppressing a laugh, he offered nothing in return but a disinterested, "Humm?"

"You know, Simon, it'll cost a pretty penny to replace your master keys. Antiques," said Sam, affecting indifference to the sign.

"Sam, for God's sake, focus!" Simon chided, hoping to convey to Sam that he was as hurt as he was angry. He then wheeled around and sped down the hall toward his office after ceremoniously dropping the offending object in front of Sam.

If anyone had followed Sam out into the garth, he would have been seen hoisting the sign high into the air as if leading a procession. As he walked, he sang softly, "Lift high the cross, the love of Christ proclaim, 'til all the world sees Simon's shame . . ."

He couldn't wait to share it with the guys in the shop.

❧

Simon made it as far as the back hall, where he collapsed into a threadbare Queen Anne chair to nurse post-meeting wounds and to ponder the gap between ecclesiological life as he had intended and church as it brutally was. Monday's distance between his youthful theological expectations for the church and the midcareer sociological reality was widening into a chasm. The brilliant staff he had yesterday so laboriously assembled were today little better than junior-high Sunday-school brats punching one another, roughhousing, and making their teacher miserable. Perhaps he had been too lax in his supervision, inadequately asserting his pastoral authority? Had he overpraised their work, tempting them to think too highly of themselves?

Sinking deeper into a post-meeting mire, Simon was startled by the vibration of his cell phone. "Simon, looks like I won't be home for supper tonight," said Mary in an unintentional but almost pitch-perfect impersonation of a whining Madeline Albright. Simon fought back the desire to ask, "And what's news about that?" His Christian faith prompted him to say only, "Thank you dear. Please don't worry about me. I'll fend for myself . . . as always."

Ave Maria gratia plenita. For three decades, Mary and Simon had congenially endured. They met in "field education," as student interns at a church-run community center in the grimmest of grim Newark. Along with sufficient passion for one another, they shared a passion for ministry to the poor. Both passions—for Mary and for the poor—cooled by the end of Simon's first decade in ministry. For Simon, ministry to the dispossessed was a youthful, passing, Princetonian fling; Simon had modified his Lord's "the poor you will always have with you" to "the poor you will have with you—until you develop more sensible interests." As for Mary, the less fortunate were her enduring absorption, an endless infatuation; she had never grown out of her campus-radical-do-gooder phase.

Something better came along when Simon became head of Hope. Unlike Simon, Mary had steadfastly rebuffed the affluent, self-satisfied congregation's attempts to dampen her activist zeal. She initiated a number of commendable programs—a Spanish-speaking after-school club for kids (once featured on NPR), an expanded Feed the Homeless involving a dozen of the city's congregations, safe-sex coaching for teens, and more. It was true—Mary had single-handedly initiated Meals on Wheels during her very first year at Hope. Periodically taking pride, Simon would on occasion proclaim her benevolent endeavors from the pulpit.

"I'll tell you, the world would be a better place if we had more Marys," some well-meaning spinster would cluck. Simon would think, "The world might be better, but my life would be unendurable."

A more compliant and accommodating clergy spouse would have developed interests aligned more closely with those of the congregants at Hope. Mary had class-struggle contempt for those who sat next to her in the pew, except for the few guilt-ridden zealots like Judd whom she conscripted for her causes.

"Let's hope that Jesus keeps his promise that 'the poor you will have with you always,'" Simon thought as he watched her throw herself goofily into one righteous cause after another.

Undoubtedly Mary's barrenness was due to some biological problem, though neither of them had taken the trouble to find out. Mary's busyness—her "Hey everybody! Let's all get together and save the world this weekend!" determination—left little time for domesticity. Drunks and derelicts, pitiable old folks and wayward adolescents, victimized whales and disappearing baboons tugged at her heart more than any of her own kind.

He recalled the weekend that she presented him to her folks in Cleveland. Her childhood home was vast. Full-time maid in residence. Long, circular drive. Four-car garage. An abode better suited to condescending New England Episcopalians than flavorless Midwestern Congregationalists. Her Wellesley background rendered her irresistible. In the early days, he thought: she will lay down her sweatshirt, cast aside her braless, granola altruism, and adopt more suitable attire for folks at the club.

He thought wrong.

Simon's family of origin was modest Italian American, Waldensian. (His baptismal final *e* on Simone was dropped when he entered junior high.) If asked, he imaginatively told inquirers that his great-grandfather was a craftsman who had immigrated from northern Italy in the 1800s. The truth: his grandfather was a Sicilian who arrived just after WWI to work the mines in Pennsylvania.

How was he to know that Mary would squander her adulthood augmenting the expanse between herself and her Lawson forebears? By failing to guide Mary back to the mainstream, he had let down the Lawsons. Mary was as perseverant as a salmon in her campaign to move (and work) against the mainstream.

Simon and Mary had redeployed, without discussion or rancor, arriving at an acceptable arrangement—Simon executing his caring preacher performance, while Mary reprised her eager-beaver Jesus socialism act. Living under the same roof—except for most Friday and Saturday evenings, when Mary was ensconced with her charges in the homeless shelter downtown, thrilled (so Simon suspected) to be stuck on the shift that nobody wanted—they rarely bumped into one another at their modest (because Mary wanted it that way), concrete-colored house, seldom breaking bread, never sharing a bed. With his show and her meetings, his early morning workouts at the gym and her all-nighters bunking with the homeless, his devotion to managerial/ministerial excellence and her insatiable need to be needed, who had the oomph for marriage?

Simon strove to remember her as she had been on that first fall weekend in Cleveland, or on seminary ski trips to New England, but now all was obscured by the indelible image of Mary bustling off to some save-the-universe meeting, unsullied by makeup, adorned in sensible shoes, and wearing her no-nonsense, butch pageboy.

"Dr. Lupino, don't you fear for Mary's safety at that homeless shelter?" some parishioner would ask. He would suppress a smile, thinking, "I saw what she was wearing when she left for the shelter last night. Her safety is no cause for worry."

Simon had more than enough companionship from his cloying congregation. A person made more for ideas than relationships, he could say with the apostle, "I have learned to be content." What would Mary do with her time in eternity with all earthly wrong set right?

Incorporation

He gazed upon the lancet window in front of where he sat. He had never noticed the true grandeur of this well-carved window. The gothic tracery was elegant, beautiful, limestone fashioned so that it spiraled heavenward like a flame or hands folded in prayer. Thick, leaded glass shimmered in the late morning sunlight, showing off the elegance of the stonemason's handiwork. It was hard to imagine a time when such craftsmanship was lavished upon nothing but a window, one in an obscure side hall that few people used. Simon was transfixed by the extravagance of the workmanship, by the window's defiant uselessness—such exuberant excess offered to God. He let his mind roam in the great gap—not the one between his youthful ideals and the grubby reality of the church but rather the one between his adoration of efficiency and sensible calculation and the pointless, purposeless extravagance of the window before him, symbol of another age rebuking his modern, parsimonious adoration of efficiency. Was it possible that this creaking old building knew more than he?

Simon's reverie was interrupted by his watch. On Easter he had caught big game in his sights: an investment banker seen at the club but never before espied at church. He had invited Simon to lunch at noon. Having counted on the recent downturn to wash some well-heeled flotsam onto his beach, Simon wondered: was this banker the first of some low-hanging fruit?

∾

"I'm so glad that God has deposited you among us," said Grimball as he wheeled out of the Hope lot, one finger resting nonchalantly upon the wheel, steering as if he were picking out a new piece on his keyboard. He and Stephen were huddled in Grimball's old Volvo, sputtering their way to The Baguette on Broad. "We need an infusion of new blood from time to time—young, virile energy—a shot of testosterone will do us all a world of good. We have thrilled to the reports of your stellar seminary record and felt privileged to lure one such as you to our puny parish. And what of your very first staff meeting?" he asked. "Frightening?"

"It's all rather overwhelming," said Stephen uneasily. "This church has just got everything. I mean the building alone is unbelievable. And the opportunities."

"We need you not to waste much time being overwhelmed," interrupted the self-consciously prickly organist. "You'll find much amiss. My God, can't someone, somewhere find something to do with that sad Mr.

Quail? I mean, really? I expect a smart young thing like you won't stay overawed by us very long. To know us, really know us, is to loathe us."

Stephen looked straight ahead, careful not to glance toward Grimball.

"And how do you like our monsignor?" asked Grimball, languidly drooping his arm out the window of the Volvo, steering with his right index finger, acting as if his were an offhand question.

"Actually, I've just met him. But he seems cool. He's quite a star in our denomination. Besides, do you really think that I, lowest guy on the totem pole, barely into his third week on the job, would actually tell you if I *didn't* think Dr. Lupino was cool?" Stephen asked with a grin.

"Good point! But surely there's no harm in my attempting to trick you into veracity. As a callow youth, surely you haven't yet acquired the deceitful habits of more experienced clergy. I suppose you expect me to despise Reverend Father—as his resentful organist, chief accompanist for his weekly exhibition—but that's not the case. Simon (no need for the 'Reverend *Doctor* Lupino' pretense here) graciously summoned me from the cultural wasteland of Grand Rapids (where I was languishing in Dutch Reformed blah), upped my meager salary, and supported a complete, fabulously expensive, top-to-bottom renovation of the Great Organ, for which I shall be forever grateful. Although a restoration was what we really needed. Work in progress while I tug mightily upon the purse strings of aging dowagers. I'll lead you on an organ crawl sometime in the fall, when the weather cools."

"Sure."

As Grimball chattered on, Stephen stole a couple of fleeting glimpses at him across the grunting Volvo, noting the uncommon color he had dyed his hair, even his eyebrows: Strom Thurmond reddish-blonde. The gold chain on his left wrist matched his ring.

"Simon's achievement is quite stunning, when you think about it. Other clergy are green with envy. Though we musicians have a quite well-deserved reputation for the green-eyed monster, even the most unimaginative clergy can outdo us on begrudgement any day of the week. I told Simon that he ought to travel with a bodyguard just to be sure that some pastor doing time in Des Moines doesn't stick a stiletto through his heart."

"Like I say, I'm lucky to be here," interjected Stephen, for the first time noting Grimball's perfectly groomed fingernails, which were surprisingly long for an organist.

"Of course, he's got foibles, as any clergyman—not to disparage your profession. Sometimes he falls victim to his vanity and believes his own press releases, but he does present a sweet spirit. He's rarely more annoying than when he presides at staff meetings—unless it's when he attempts inspiration from the pulpit. Simon preaches the mawkish sermons required by belief in his sort of God—banal though benign."

Stephen fixed his gaze forward, intently looking out the windshield as if he were focusing on a far-off road sign.

"Hauling you aboard gave dear Simon another feather in his cap. 'Look at me,' he surely has said to the few clergy who don't hate his guts, 'I've landed me a finely polished, young neeegro.' Hope has been a great launching pad for more than one clergy career. You'll be no exception. Use dear Simon even as he thinks he's using you. His imprimatur on your résumé would be worth its weight in gold to an aspiring young man . . ."

Grimball swerved to avoid a young cyclist, dramatically gasped and caught his breath, yelled an obscenity into the wind, and continued without dropping tempo, "An additional word of caution that, given your intelligence, is probably unnecessary. That oily little Quail has moved in recent years from utilitarian prevarication in an attempt to save his worthless hide to more creative, recreational lying, dissembling for the hell of it. His only ministerial virtue is in making the straight crooked, valleys deeper and mountains higher. Odd to find such adept mendaciousness in one who seldom preaches."

Made uncomfortable by Grimball's corrosiveness, Stephen asked, "And what, in your experience, are Dr. Lupino's strengths?"

"Yes, unspectacular though his virtues may be, they do tend to balance his more interesting vices, don't they? How Christian of you to ask."

He smiled and patted Stephen on the arm.

"For one thing, Simon is so busy with self-promotion that he has little energy to pry into the personal lives of his parishioners—meddling is a flaw in more conscientious clergy. Simon is marvelously nonjudgmental and affirming of them in all their moral wretchedness—something about God's being gracious and just as pleased as punch that we're good enough to find an hour in our busy schedules to be with the Almighty. Simon considers himself one of God's best buddies. Can't argue with the results of his ministry. Each year, as I watch an increasing number of Mercedes edge Volvos and Saabs out of the church lot, I think to myself, 'Simon knows what he's doing.' And I think he genuinely, quite touchingly believes all those business slogans with which he saturates the staff. I say, thank God that his God has no censoriousness about our bedroom escapades. There are worse Senior Pastors, I can tell you."

Stephen wondered if this is how clergy must listen—feigning interest without assent or dissent. It seemed to Stephen unfair of Grimball to charge Dr. Lupino with having an outsized ego. It was the preacher's job to climb the pulpit every week and summon the guts to speak up for God—not a task for the insecure.

The car was close and confining, and the smell of burning motor oil wafting through the open window whenever they waited at a stoplight, mixed with Grimball's cologne, made Stephen feel faintly nauseous.

Attempting to lift the conversation out of the muck of office gossip, Stephen ventured, "How would you characterize the prevailing theology at Hope?"

"I wouldn't," responded Grimball decisively. "How wonderfully neophyte of you to suspect us of having an operative theology. At Hope we have found church ever so much easier without unnecessary allusions to the Man Upstairs," said Grimball, modulating his voice to a theatrical bass. "As I said, we are as much church as our type of God can stand."

"Well, how would you characterize your own theology?" Stephen persisted.

"Again, I wouldn't. When one works for God, I have found, it is helpful not to allow one's opinions about God to distract one from the work. Evading censure by the board is so much more important than dodging the wrath of God. Ask oneself the Jamesian, utilitarian, 'now what is the cash value of all this?' and next thing you're hanging yourself with your cincture. No, when it comes to my own religious orientation, I find church and theology don't mix. As a dealer in holy mysteries, at least in the sacred musical ones, I resonate with Al Pacino's counsel to drug dealers in *Scarface*: 'Don't get high on your own supply.'"

Stephen's seminary education had not prepared him to come up with a rejoinder.

"And what of your plans to boost the faith of the pubescents in our little parish?" asked Grimball.

"Well, I've planned a float trip down the river to build community."

"Fine. Just be sure I'm not invited. Can't imagine anything more distasteful than burrowing in the wet mud with the kiddies down by the riverside."

Stephen smiled. "I also hope to do some Bible studies throughout the summer, and a mission trip. Something in Chicago. I know a guy who runs a street ministry on the South Side. Amazing story. You know that mission work is one of the best ways to really get people's spiritual lives in gear."

"How intriguing—taking a gaggle of privileged brats to hobnob with the less fortunate! Be sure that they've got their birth control devices on board before you leave town. Strip search them for drugs, too. Oh, and keep me posted on how many takers you get for your little Huck Finn adventure."

"What books have you been reading lately?" Stephen asked for no other reason than to wrest some control of the discourse from Grimball.

"Ah, youth! Not big on books—dead ideas of dead white men mostly. Why fondle a cold book when you've got so many warm people all round? It's one of the great blessings of being in church.

"Say, have you met good, bleeding heart Virgin Mary? She is really one of the most dedicated Christians I've ever known, perhaps the only one, and the most offensive. Mary's passion for the less fortunate makes our own dear Lord look positively apathetic. Of course, it's difficult ever to catch Simon and Mary in close proximity. Simon moves in his orbit, a shining sun surrounded by a few adoring planets within the congregation. He is truly committed to that hash of platitudes that he ladles up each Sunday and bores us with at staff meetings. Sincere in his glittering banalities. I mean, since you have arrived, have you heard anything worth repeating in his pep talks? Ralph Waldo Emerson for Dummies."

Stephen hastily interjected, "I'm just a few months out of seminary. I don't know anything. But I've been pretty impressed by the few sermons I've heard."

"Come now, Stephen. Well, you are clever enough to know not to know anything in your first weeks on a new job. You'll teach me. Let's be fast friends," said Grimball, taking the steering wheel with his left hand, reaching toward Stephen's shoulder with his right.

"That would be, er, great," Stephen said awkwardly.

"I mean *friends*. No cause for alarm. You've a girlfriend and I'm twice your age, half your intelligence. But trust me; you'll need a friend now that you've entered the jungle. Watch your back."

ᖁ

Simon returned in the midafternoon, disappointed by his luncheon with the banker. The man's intention was to dither over some "faith crisis" rather than to affiliate himself with Hope. It took Simon a full two hours to terminate the bothersome banker's monologue. On his way back, he had asked himself what sort of free wisdom he would have gleaned if he had sought the banker's advice on his Pastor's Pension Plan.

"Simon, I must see you," said Quail as Simon entered the administrative suite. "It's a matter of some grave concern."

"Really? You've sounded the alarm about the budget, trashing this year's Hope Conference in the process. Must you go on?"

"It's more important even than that," said Quail sotto voce.

"Johnson, friend, are you well? You look a bit pale," said Simon, assessing him up and down.

"As a matter of fact, I am sick—sick in my stomach," said Quail, patting his tummy, "but it's not due to disease. When you see what I've got, your stomach will be churning too."

Simon sighed and invited Quail into his office. Quail disregarded Simon's well-known dislike for any real work to intrude into his "study" and plopped down a stack of folders. There, on Simon's wide oak desk, Quail pushed aside some of the artifacts and laid before Simon his summary of the situation at Hope Township. Both stooped over the charts. Though a whole weekend was consumed in the process, Quail had compiled the numbers in a straightforward way, complete with graphs, so that even Simon would see clearly the fix they were in. He had gone through the mishmash of loans that had been cobbled together for the project—all of them in arrears. Some of the operational losses were buried, requiring Quail to do some deep digging.

"And I have good reason to believe that the trustees have wised up. Three were huddled in the stairwell like rats in a dumpster just last Sunday. All of them are men of business and could easily figure out the mess we've made of Hope Township. As you see, we haven't paid a dime on the principal of the major loan in over a year, just as you directed. And now we've missed two months of interest. You have me to thank for the bank not pulling the plug on the loan. I've got a good friend at the bank—a Baptist—and I've stroked him for the past few months. It is only with the utmost difficulty that I've been able thus far to keep the facts from the nosier trustees. And God forbid if the bank president catches wind of this. The Shylocks are being lenient because we are a church. But they'll have their limits, even with a church. As you can clearly see by comparing our income versus expenses for the last three years . . ."

Simon offended Quail by glancing over the spreadsheet and then, before Quail had gotten to the worst of it, disregarding him midsentence and turning away, staring vacantly out his office window. He meant this not only as a charitable gesture, refusing to judge a friend who was embarrassing himself with his unpleasant behavior, but also as an act of pastoral care toward a brother in difficulty.

"See that bird? Been pecking like crazy at my window since last week. What do you make of that? That bird is either dumb or else knows something we don't."

"It's avian territorial protection," sneered Quail, glaring at Simon across the desk without looking toward the window.

"Do you know that for sure or are you faking? I would have thought sex had something to do with it, mating and all that."

Simon continued, "You know, this place is built, pseudo-Gothic, with these attractive but utterly dysfunctional lancet windows. No one outside sees in, which must have been their original intent. But none of us on the inside see out, being cloistered, confined. Still, if I try, the view from my office is really quite lovely this time of year. And look at those tulips! I regret that you don't enjoy the same view from your office. Yet I suspect, dear Johnson, even if you were blessed with my vista, your defeatist perspective would prohibit you from enjoying it. Reality is how you choose to look at things."

"Simon! I beg you to see the desperate situation in which we find ourselves, appeal to you for drastic, decisive action to stem the deluge that could sweep away everything for which you have worked and make you look like a damned fool—me too. You have got at least six million dollars in deferred maintenance staring you in the face right here in this crumbling wreck, commitments that you've made to a dozen social-service agencies tallying well over a million. And you talk of pecking birds at windows and tulips budding in their beds? Where in God's name do you expect to find the cash to keep up your blessed Township when it's risky to flush a toilet around here? The church is our cash cow. You have got to focus on the situation at hand," said Quail with all the earnestness he could muster.

Simon wheeled around, now looking directly at Quail. An incongruous, sinister smile played upon his face. "Be frank, Johnson. You never really backed this project, withheld from me the support for which I asked, failed to come up with adequate financial structuring, and now it appears that you have been scheming to bring about its demise. You're lacking just a bit in the loyalty department right now, Mister Johnson, if I may be frank."

"How dare you say that! I have never . . ."

"Please!" said Simon, the fake smile having vanished from his face. "If this visionary project is in difficulty, as you claim, then it is due to you, not me. I'm not the CFO! You are always trumpeting your financial genius. If I am guilty of anything, I have been too trusting. I'm the visionary, you the implementer."

Quail had never been addressed by Simon in this manner. Shaking with rage, he immediately began to realign. He surmised Simon's intent: you handle things, keep me out of it, so I can blame you when this thing blows up.

Simon regretted responding harshly to his lieutenant in his time of trial and offered, "As Emerson said, 'In battles, the eye is the first organ to be overcome.' Or was it George Bush? Anyway, the important thing is to look at this in the right way, not to cower before the challenge." His mind raced back a decade or more to the moment when Johnson Quail had come to him on bended knee, having made a mess of his little church, and Simon had rescued him from a life sentence of hard labor in an ecclesiastical gulag. Though he longed for the compassion to see him that way again, he could not, detecting in Quail a steady leak of gratitude.

Slowly, deliberately, Quail spit out, "Well, you really take the cake, Simon. You do a snow job on the whole congregation with your grandiose ideas, force me to compromise my business standards, and when it goes belly up, you blame *me*?"

"Am I to take that as criticism?" Simon asked. Then brightening, "Now, now, Johnson, let's not quarrel. We're a team. Let's not lapse into emotional talk that we might regret. I simply want to encourage you to rise to the level of your greatest excellence. You are a creative person, a veritable financial genius, I hear. I have complete confidence, at least no reason to doubt, that you will find your way out of this. You need a visionary plan, one that does not include whining and sniveling. Seize this as your kairos moment. Forswear apocalypticism. When the times are tough, the tough get . . . tougher."

"So you will not become involved?"

"I am expressing confidence in your ability," resumed Simon. "I believe in getting good people and trusting them to do good work. No one can accuse me of micromanagement. Think outside of the box. My trust for you is unshaken, even though I am disappointed by your unseemly panic. Where there is no vision, the people get confused. You'll discover light at the end of the tunnel."

Quail glared at Simon in stony silence.

Incorporation

"You know, Henry Ford was dead wrong in saying that compound interest is the eighth wonder of the world. We should thank God for the invention of the body corporate, not compound interest. The blessed concoction of the corporation removes personal responsibility from the world of business. Let not your heart be troubled, dear friend. No matter the direction this thing takes, you have wisely incorporated so that if Hope Township becomes history, we go on, you and I, unsullied. The mighty law of corporate indemnification is our bulwark. Excellence!"

Quail hated gratuitous God references. Simon only trotted out God, Quail noted, when he found himself in a pathetic position and needed to bolster his blather. Silently, Quail made for the door, clutching his papers, not awaiting the conclusion of the sermonette. He walked down the hall, ducking into the men's room because he couldn't make it as far as his office washroom. There, overcome by paroxysms of fury, brought to his knees, even as Mary had clutched the hem of Jesus' robe, Quail clutched the rim of the toilet and vomited. Depression can be an ecclesiogenic illness.

∾

Mary Lupino was party to none of these deliberations, although she had been in the building since early morning. Mary rarely ascended to the rarified climes of the administrative suite (or any other attractive area). And if anyone asked, Mary was quite willing to catalog Hope's ecclesiastical errors, the chief one being that the largest item in the budget was building maintenance. Tower of Babel. Graven image. Golden calf. She delighted in flinging, at anyone who would listen, the question, "Since when did Jesus show any interest in the acquisition or maintenance of real estate?" She never missed an opportunity to challenge congregational self-flattery or attempts to expunge guilt through a modicum of service and care to those in need.

Mary was more comfortable laboring in subterranean Christendom with fellow members of the lowly laity than she was occupying the holy of holies with the high priests. Early that morning she had parked one of the church minivans outside the entrance to the west wing. There she had descended to hard labor in the bowels of Hope, in the catacombs—a musty and windowless basement where she would be safe from the hierarchs—working with three other women to sort a mountain of old clothes that Hope's members had donated to the poor.

Because it was Hope, many of the clothes were worthlessly inappropriate for the needy. Eight evening dresses, three bridesmaid gowns, a set of souvenir lederhosen, and even a tattered blue tux had been culled from the pile of castoffs this morning alone.

"If the poor of our town ever throw an elegant eighties party, we have just the thing," said one of the women, holding up a short, heavily sequined evening dress to widespread giggles.

"Eighties?" said another. "Honey, that's got seventies all over it."

Because most of the children's clothing had been utilized for training Hope's young ones in the art of dressing for a cocktail party or employment in a stockbroker's office, it was laughably pointless.

"I'm sorely disappointed," said Mary. "We usually get our best donations from everyone's spring housecleaning. I repeatedly stressed to the congregation that what we're hurting for is good, utilitarian children's clothing. I think we'll make another appeal."

One of her fellow workers, closely examining a pink evening gown, commented to the others, "Well, look at this. Lila Thompson has enough foam padding in these cups to make her a fire hazard. And to think, all of you thought she was kin to Mae West!" Everyone laughed but Mary.

Before noon they would, with considerable effort, load six large boxes of clothing out to the van for the Urban Ministry Center. The rest would either be sold as rags or offered to a local consignment shop that specialized in eccentric and vintage garb.

"Hank is to come by during his lunch hour to help me unload all this," said Mary. "Don't know what urban ministry would do without dear Hank, a real godsend."

⟡

By the time three thirty rolled around, Quail had steeled himself for his encounter with trustee Townsend Thomas. After the awful conversation with Simon, Quail had determined that he had no future serving as the fall guy for the Hope Township fiasco. He had made a good faith effort to save Simon from himself, only to be subjected to a humiliating homily. To the lifeboats! Every man for himself.

A cover-up was futile. Thomas, who ran a string of men's clothing stores downtown and at the mall, was quite capable of figuring everything out. Any half-wit set before the spreadsheet need not be told that it was Armageddon for Hope Township. Quail busied his brain in composing a set of sermon points. His objective would be to form an alliance with the trustees, confirm their dire assessment, even praise them for their business acumen, then to assure them that he was on their side. Yet he must not show disloyalty to Simon. He had tried to be a friend to Simon, he would tell them, had repeatedly sought to induce Simon to see the facts. Now, out of love for Hope Church, he would work with the trustees as their ally in a salvage operation, heroically to lead the church through these turbulent waters.

So when Thomas arrived at the appointed time, Quail received him warmly as he went over in his mind the script that he intended to trot Thomas through.

"Reverend Quail," began Thomas—perhaps his use of this unaccustomed ecclesiastical nomenclature was Thomas's way of stressing the seriousness of the matters that lay before them—"I have enjoyed getting to know you while I was on the finance committee and now in my work with the trustees. You do so much for the Hope family."

"Thank you—you are most kind," said Quail, relieved by the warm, respectful tone that Thomas set for the conversation. "You know that I have the best interests of our beloved church ever before me. And I have much enjoyed working with you. What a joy to have a comrade, a man of business, a progressive who has successfully managed his resources. Rare in the church."

"Uh, thanks. Now I know that you don't spend all of your time in ministerial matters—though of course, administration is a true ministry—but I think that you are just the sort of person I need to talk to."

Quail found this an odd lead-in to the business at hand. Having spent so many years working for the Body of Christ, he was accustomed to people not saying what they really meant.

"I thought about talking with Dr. Lupino, but he is so busy and for some reason the Lord led me to talk with you. Wasn't his sermon great last Sunday? Anyway, this is not an easy matter for me to discuss."

"I am glad that you chose me. If the matter is what I think it is, then you were wise to come to me rather than to Simon."

"The matter you think it is?" asked Thomas.

"Oh, I try to keep my finger on the pulse of the congregation," bragged Quail. "My eyes and ears always open."

Thomas seemed unnerved. "What—what do you think I wanted to talk with you about?"

"I would rather you tell me. Don't let me interrupt. I know this is difficult."

"Well, yes, difficult," said Thomas, unsteadied by the thought that Quail had a premonition of his business. "You know that Lydia and I have been really working on our spiritual journeys. We signed up for Disciple Bible Study. And that was just great. Then we attended the Walk to Emmaus, and that really took our spiritual lives to a whole new level."

It was now Quail's turn to look confused.

"Well, anyway, we have set out to live completely sanctified lives. Believe it or not, we'd never even heard the word *sanctification* before. Guess it just sailed right passed. You know how the Lord sometimes waits to speak things until we are ready to hear. That was us: clueless about holiness of heart, hands, and mind."

Quail listened in dumb mystification.

"And Lydia and I have always had a good marriage—two great kids, lovely home. We've always been close. And affectionate. And in a way, our walk with Jesus has drawn us even closer. Except in one way. Not that sex was a huge part of our marriage before, but we certainly enjoyed—yes, enjoyed—a healthy, normal sex life. But then Lydia tells me that she just finds it difficult to integrate sex into our present walk with Christ. Not that we've ever believed that sex was dirty or anything, particularly in the covenant of marriage. It's just that, well, Lydia (this is only my theory) thinks of sex, even in marriage, as something not quite right—fine when the goal is procreation, but not when done by two people past middle age just enjoying one another. She's all spirit now and not much body. Why, we haven't been . . . intimate, really . . . in more than six months. Does that seem biblically justified to you?"

Quail had finally regained composure. "*This* is what you wanted to talk about? *This*? My hands full just trying to keep a roof on this rusting wreck, what with the plumbing and all, and you come in here with this? Why on earth did you think that I could be helpful in whatever all this is about? *This?*"

"I needed professional advice. More specifically, I've run across what Saint Paul says about marriage. Seems like Paul says that it's OK for a couple to refrain from intimacy 'for a season,' but then, well, it's almost like a duty for husbands and wives to be intimate, sexually. As you know, he says in First Corinthians 7:4 that the 'husband does not have authority over his own body.' What do you think he means by refraining 'for a season'?"

"This?" kept muttering an incredulous Quail. "How would I know—or care—what St. Paul thinks?"

"Well, you are a pastor, after all. What does it mean to have authority over your body? And I, well, I'm just your normal male." (Here Quail thought that the man was actually going to break down in tears.) "Even in church. I watch women come into the Lord's House, and I—I mean even women in the choir. Thoughts come into my head . . ."

"Look, Paul was a notorious misogynist, got hot and bothered about food offered to idols, circumcision, women speaking in church! What the hell would he know about marriage? If you only knew the truly worrisome things that are going on around here! Financial things."

"So you don't think that we need to be worried about our marriage, or what Saint Paul says on . . ."

"Look. We have people around here who have expertise in these matters, whatever in God's name these matters are. Progressive people. But I'm not one of them. There's a counseling service that rents space down in the west wing. Psychologists!" snorted Quail as he rose from his seat, slamming shut the bound spreadsheets on Hope Township.

"I enjoyed working with you on the committees and . . ."

"Good God, man, I assumed that you had come here on a matter of importance to the church. *Business* matters," said Quail as he almost pushed Thomas out of his office. He then jerked open the drawer to his desk and consumed a near lethal dose of antacids.

"Fools!" muttered Quail as he gulped down the chalky tablets. "Like being stoned to death with marshmallows! Niggling sins build trivial churches. I rescheduled negotiations with Fat Free Forever, Inc. for *this*?" (The dieting company had wanted to bargain for a large meeting space.)

As if drowning in the veniality of the laity was not enough, as he attempted an exit, he was chased down the hall by Eleanor, shouting breathlessly, "Mr. Quail! Mr. Quail!"

"What is it?" he asked, turning around with exasperation.

"I've just learned that . . . something terrible has happened," she said, her chest heaving as she labored to catch her breath.

"And what is that?"

"I'd rather tell you in your office; it's so serious," Eleanor gasped.

"I don't have time for that. What's so terrible that you must interrupt me now?"

"Well," she whispered, "it has just been reported to me that Martha Shannon has . . . has struck a child."

"And who the heck is Martha Shannon?"

"Why, Martha is the head of the Acolytes Subcommittee of the Altar Guild."

"Really? I wondered what that surly woman's name was. Never heard her called anything but Tsar," said Quail, smiling, "which seems a good deal more fitting than Martha."

"I have from a good source that she actually struck a child," said Eleanor. "I think I can verify it."

"What child?" asked Quail.

"One of the acolytes. That's all I know at this point."

"Well, did he deserve it?" asked Quail offhandedly.

"What? What do you mean 'did he deserve it'? We're talking about a young child here."

"Well, from my experiences with acolytes, I assume that he is guilty and therefore a fit subject for corporal punishment. I'm with the Tsar on this one. It would take a coldhearted, calloused person indeed not to have felt the desire to smack an acolyte at some time or another. I'm sure that Our Lord could cut us some slack on this one. I recommend forgiveness for old Martha, or Tsar, or whoever she is."

"But—but our Safe Sanctuaries policy strictly forbids that any child be . . ." gasped Eleanor.

As he turned about and hurried on, Quail said, "Sometimes you've got to do what you've got to do when you are dealing with insolence. Until more details, I'm with the Tsar on this one."

That he nearly collided with saccharine Pastor Herb toddling in from the parking lot, smiling, did little to alleviate Quail's highly aggravated disposition or his unruly stomach.

"I'm on my way to the doctor's, Herb," Quail said in passing. "Can't talk." Herb grinned incongruously, hearing not a word.

∞

That fine spring afternoon, Stephen, having registered his car and signed for license plates at the Department of Motor Vehicles, headed west on the sidewalk, wondering what he would fix himself for dinner. Macaroni and cheese again?

This would be a great afternoon for lying in Thea's arms in a patch of tall grass, thought Stephen, *rather than running errands for the Bride of Christ, trying to look busy.*

"Upon my word! Saint Stephen out and about, rubbing shoulders with the hoi polloi."

He turned and was unsurprised to confirm the voice as belonging to Miss Marple, Jane Whetsell.

"Remember me?"

Stephen smiled. In the memorable cast of characters at Hope, Jane was for Stephen among the most remarkable.

Without hesitation she seized his elbow and quickened his pace as she marched him down the sidewalk. "Allow me to buy you a drink," she said.

"A drink?" asked Stephen. "It's not even four o'clock yet."

"Relax, dear, unadulterated young Christian. There's a coffee shop up on the next corner."

"That would be great," said Stephen, relieved.

Coffee was ordered—a double espresso for Jane, a mocha latte with whipped cream for Stephen. She asked him how things were going, if he was settling in, was he happy to be at Hope? To all her questions he answered affirmatively.

"I suppose you will learn much from our senior pastor and staff?" said Jane, fishing for something.

"Sure will. I'm really lucky to be in a congregation that functions so well. It's amazing what Dr. Lupino has accomplished."

"So you feel under obligation to refer to our pastor on the basis of his honorary Doctor of Divinity degree? Fine. As for the Reverend Lupino's amazing accomplishments (*dato non concesso*), I am sure that you are bright enough eventually to ask yourself the enduring theological import of such endeavors. A young man like you has a challenge—mastering ministry and, at the same time, contributing something of value to uplift the sad state of the craft. I expect that you will need to be rather cautious in emulating many of our professional staff. *Caveat emptor!* Undoubtedly you will want to do things rather differently in your own ministry, boldly chart your own course. Take care in your *imitatio*."

"I'm not sure of your meaning," said Stephen. He was beginning to feel sympathy for Dr. Lupino. Seemed like everybody, whether staff or laity, felt free to slam the Senior Managing Pastor.

"Ah, waste not our time attempting false intellectual modesty, young Saint Stephen. Feigned self-deprecation I find tiresome."

"You seem to have quickly formed certain impressions of me that may not be accurate, since we have really just met," said Stephen.

"A hazard of my profession," said Jane.

"Which was teaching?"

"How did you know? Yes, I put in three decades as pedagogue, attempting to pump English literature into privileged prepsters until my sister and I decided to forswear the pretense of having a profession and settle down, content to live off Papa's legacy. Someone ought to enjoy the fruits of Papa's labors. Lord knows he never did. Now I'm simply a silly old woman who occasionally putters about the House of the Lord during her free time, which is really all of my time these days."

"I knew that you had been a teacher," said Stephen, "even before you told me."

"Really?"

"Of course. You haven't retired. You are teaching all the time."

"Am I? One of the challenges of teaching is not to confuse listening for learning, telling for teaching. One never knows. Even now, you're gazing at me with a sphinx-like, enigmatic stare that gives no indication of just what's happening in that good mind of yours."

"Conversation with you gets me to thinking, I can assure you. How come you know so much about theology and church matters?" Stephen asked.

"I'm flattered that you are impressed that a lowly lay person can talk your jargon. When I was young, I got in my girlish head that I ought to be a pastor, a thought so strange only God could have put it there. More than anything I wanted to study theology. So I majored in religion in college. Read everything I could get my hands on. Set out to be the Harry Emerson Fosdick of our part of the world."

"And why didn't you go to seminary?"

"Couldn't find anyone who thought a theological career was a good idea with the exception of the Lord and me! I had overlooked the *sine qua non* for a theologian!" she declared.

"Which is?"

"Male genitalia, of course."

Stephen gulped.

"OK, got to run," said Stephen, looking at the time on his cell phone. "Thanks for the drink, for the teaching, and for the anatomical, theological reflection."

"Please do not self-congratulate for your charity, for—*contra natura*—wasting a half hour humoring an old maid," Jane said as she gathered her things. "I thought you would never end our little coffee klatsch. I have been about to perish for a smoke. Until we meet again," she said, thrusting her hand toward his. She lit up before Stephen was out of sight.

As he quickly put distance between himself and Jane, it occurred to Stephen that one of the benefits of being clergy was that clergy could always plead something pressing to do since so much that clergy do is done in secret. Nobody really knows what, if anything, clergy are up to, making deceit easier to manage. Stephen's appointment, which abruptly terminated his conversation with Jane, was nothing more than a solo meeting with a box of macaroni and cheese in his monk's cell of an apartment.

∾

On Sunday, when Simon held forth from the Hope pulpit, preaching fulsomely on the assigned gospel reading, Luke 24, the supper at Emmaus, he took as his text the apostles' "But we had hoped he would be the one to redeem Israel." It seemed to Simon a fortuitous linkage with the needs of the congregation. His primary homiletical mode had been (since long ago tossing what he remembered of two anachronistic preaching courses in seminary) what he called "needs-based preaching." A one-sentence definition of Simon's homiletic modus operandi: Out of love for my congregation, I am a preacher who speaks in plain English to the felt needs of real people living in today's real world.

Simon thus strove to use the archaic biblical texts as a pretext for addressing the congregation's collective need, as a point of departure for a journey deeper inward. This Sunday, Luke 24 would be creatively utilized for a thematic sermon in which the preacher would castigate those "small-minded, small-futured people who have neither the inspiration nor the imagination to hope." Thus he congratulated the delighted congregation who were seated before him:

But we had hoped that someone, somewhere might turn the economy around.

But we had hoped that there would be world peace.

But we had hoped that I might one day have a reason to get out of bed in the morning.

Scattered laughter.

But we had hoped! But we had hoped! But we had hoped!

He was drumming his fist on the pulpit, his resonant voice raised to the level of the histrionic.

I'm tired of naysayers and Chicken Little–pessimists with their carping, negative criticism and their small-minded perspectives. Chicken Little, Henny Penny, Ducky Lucky be damned! Give me people who dream, give me visionaries who are bold enough to think new thoughts, give me a new humanity able to rise up and assume its God-given, heaven-sent opportunities! Give me Hope! Hope! Hope! Hope!

Stephen, listening, thought, "Jesus, the empty tomb, and Chicken Little?" He wondered if Dr. Lupino tended to overdo the style thing. His gestures seemed forced. True, Stephen was seated in a pew near the front, so he might not have been the best judge. Maybe this sort of preaching worked when witnessed from afar. Maybe everything in church looked better at a distance.

He could tell, from the fussing and fuming, the pounding and expounding, that the Senior Managing Pastor was worked up over something, though it was difficult to say just what. Was this sermonic "Hope! Hope! Hope!" a swipe at Quail, maybe Grimball too?

Stephen's inexperience was showing. The inspiration for Simon's sermon had been a popular clergy journal a couple of years ago.

There was a short prayer, a final hymn, then the benediction. Simon had always taken care to pronounce the benediction in front of the congregation, with his arms extended, looking them in the eye, his voice strong and reassuring, as a kind of complementary ritual conclusion to his earlier sermonic thoughts. As in preaching, in blessing a congregation, style was everything. In the early days of his ministry, he had found the act of pastoral blessing to be one of the most daunting functions of ministry. To say, "God bless you" seemed an awfully presumptuous demand to make upon God. On some Sundays, when he stood before them to bless them, and they all looked directly at him, for a moment Simon sensed the threat of a surging tidal wave of human need. Twenty years had given him intimate knowledge of their lives. He knew secrets and had witnessed some of their inarticulate pain. Most of their suffering was silent and banal, but still, Simon had found that being a witness to the quotidian agony that people hid from the gaze of others was one of the great burdens of ministry.

Although Simon had often said that one of the reasons why he was drawn into ministry was that he wanted to respond to people's need, to assuage their hurts and cares, he had underestimated the depth of their need. Sometimes, imperiled by the rising tide of their cumulative misery, he felt he might drown in their pain. For his own self-protection, he now kept his interactions with them polite and brief; one with them but not one of them, he was careful not to give them opportunity for exaggerated self-expression or embellished lament lest they elevate their aches and pains to the level of anguished despair while in his presence. He had reached his quota as a repository of their dark secrets.

He intoned in a genuine-sounding voice:

Go forth to love and to be loved by God, to be the best that you can be, confident that you are blessed. Amen.

Bustling to the back of the nave while the choir sang something about the road rising to meet you and the wind being at your back, Simon dutifully greeted people at the door. Everyone seemed satisfied with the production. As he grinned and hugged profusely, Simon struggled to hide his annoyance that the Easter crowd had dwindled so quickly in the succeeding Sundays, though it was almost reassuring to have the church sliding backwards toward normal.

"Dr. Lupino, Dr. Lupino," said a breathless acolyte, tugging at his robe as Simon was giving a farewell hug to the last dawdlers of the exiting congregation. "Dr. Lupino."

"Yes, son, what is it?"

"I think we've got a problem," said the boy.

"And what is that?"

"Somebody has died."

"What? Where?"

"In the service. Somebody dead," the boy breathlessly explained. "As we were picking up the bulletins, just like Ms. Swanson makes us, and replacing the pew pencils—even though we've told her that we're supposed to be at soccer practice at one and this will probably make us late—George noticed old man Lazar slumped down in the pew." George, standing nearby, nodded his head in confirmation, somberly adding, "We're already late for practice."

"So we looked at him, even tried to push him, and he just fell over to the side. George thinks old man Lazar might be just sleeping real hard, like in a coma like on TV, but I think he's dead."

"What in God's name?" said Simon as he rushed out of the narthex and back into the sanctuary, looking right and left.

"Over there, that pew just behind the pillar," said one of the acolytes. "See? He's dead."

"I think I've had more experience with dead people than you," said Simon to the boy. Sure enough, there was old Lazar, slumped over to the left, mouth gaping, eyes rolled back in his head. After a quick examination—sniffing his breath for alcohol and then detecting a slight movement of his chest—he determined that Lazar was neither dead, as he feared, nor passed out drunk, as he expected. Simon grabbed his shoulder and forcefully shook him.

"Lazar! Lazar! Are you alright?" he said in a booming voice that echoed throughout the empty sanctuary. "Wake up!"

"Ughh," moaned Lazar. His eyes opened. He looked up, focusing his wild eyes on Simon, who had now unhanded him and stood there, with the two acolytes, looking down upon him. Lazar then straightened himself, pulled his jacket closed, smoothed back his rumpled white hair, took another confused look at Simon, belched heavily, and, without a word, stood and walked toward the exit.

"He sure looked dead to me," said one of the boys as Simon pushed them aside and headed back toward his office.

George sighed, "Coach is going to give us almighty hell."

∽

That same Sunday afternoon, on their way back to their respective offices after a meeting of the building and grounds committee (Simon had declared that Sunday afternoons were perfect opportunities for the convening of really important church committees—no excuse for being absent), where the chief subject had been the intricacies of guttering and drainage, Quail asked, "Simon, it's ages since we've had the bishop visit Hope. I wondered if it would be smart of you to invite the old guy for Pentecost, or maybe sometime next fall?" asked Quail.

"The bishop is not one of my favorite people," pronounced Simon, not bothering even to glance toward Quail.

"Well, you'll get no argument from me about that," countered Quail, "but don't you think it might be good politics at least to have him darken our door a couple of times a decade?"

"My friend, the bishop needs us a helluvalot more than we need him. I think he avoids us because we remind him of what a lousy job he has, managing all the dead churches. No good is to be gotten by having him poke into our stuff. If he wants to prance down the aisle like a peacock, sporting his pectoral cross and crosier, let him rent his own hall. Ours is booked."

"Well, he is bishop," said Quail. "I agree to his mediocrity, which puts him in the category of every bishop I've ever known, but I wouldn't want him ever to make trouble for us."

"What trouble could he possibly make for us?" asked Simon. "As I say, he needs us more than we need him. A lot more. This is twice as big a church as that bug-eyed lemur has ever thought about serving. And he wouldn't have a camp, children's homes, warehouses for the aging, homeless shelters, nothing, without Hope. Don't worry Johnson. He wouldn't dare touch me, or you (as long as you're with me). We're footing the bill. If he wants to come over here and thank us for our generous payment of a big chunk of his salary, fine. Otherwise, I can't imagine a congregation of our sophistication tolerating His Hollow Holiness in our pulpit for five minutes."

"Just want us to obey our Lord's injunction to be 'wise as serpents,'" said Quail.

"I appreciate that in you," said Simon. "But I think it the better part of serpentine wisdom to keep that man quite at arm's length. Hope is about excellence; the bishop is the embodiment of corpulent mediocrity."

"Fine. Just asking."

"Now look here, Johnson—be frank. Your attempt to push the bishop on me doesn't have anything to do with your Chicken Little angst over Hope Township, does it?" asked Simon as he scrutinized Quail more closely, looking for signs that Quail had caught the allusion to today's sermon.

"Why, no. Doesn't seem like it would hurt either," said Quail, riled that Simon had attempted to link serious conversation with his embarrassment of a sermon.

"My friend, if you wimp out on me, just in the heat of battle, then I'm disappointed," said Simon, reaching to take Quail's arm. "Where is the old Johnson Quail? I remember when you liked nothing better than to sink your sharp teeth into a real entrepreneurial challenge. Your job is to come up with savvy solutions, not go crying to the bishop when the going gets rough. There is *nothing* that little man can do for us."

Quail found this generalissimo façade, which Simon occasionally adopted at such moments, to be distasteful in the extreme. The only reason why Quail made twenty-one thousand dollars a year less than Simon was Simon's sneaky parsimoniousness with salaries. Simon's was an unconvincing bluff that he assumed when he hadn't a clue about what to do next. "Go ahead, sink or swim, Simon," thought Quail as he turned away without further comment.

"Hey, Johnson!" Quail heard an unfamiliar voice call after him as he veered toward the administrative suite. He was surprised to see young Stephen sauntering toward him. Stephen had been wandering the building, killing time before a meeting of the youth fellowship committee in the Walter Rauschenbusch lounge. "Could I check with you about projections for the youth budget this summer? Don't want to spend money I ain't got."

After his latest run-in with Simon, Quail was not only in no mood to be trifled with, but he also found such first-name-basis informality highly distasteful, particularly when practiced by the insouciant young. He wondered if Stephen's impertinence was due to more than youthful ineptitude. Could the newest, least significant member of the "Hope family" consider an older veteran his equal? Was Stephen's use of Quail's first name, even though they had only recently been introduced, a sign that he lacked respect for the ministry of administration, or was it simply a generational quirk of the novitiate? Were Simon's demeaning actions toward him spreading even to the junior staff? He wasn't sure.

"And what was it you needed, Mr. Smith?" responded Quail in a decidedly businesslike tone.

"I need to know how much I can count on for the summer budget for youth. I'm planning on some cool stuff but wanted to be sure, what with the proration and all," said Stephen.

"Do you not possess a copy of the budget? If you take the opportunity to look, you will find that everything is there, clear as clear can be. No proration has been put into effect to my knowledge, at least not yet," said Quail.

"Good. Just wanted to double check."

"And in the future, Mr. Smith, please note that I prefer to answer inquiries about budgetary matters through email rather than in casual hallway conversations," said Quail, determined to allow neither Stephen's race nor his youth to control his professional interaction with him or his critical assessments of him. "You will find that to be a more efficient and businesslike practice."

"Sure. Thanks. I'll do just that in the future," said Stephen.

Quail noted, with pleasure, that he had induced considerable embarrassment in the young man. Without further comment, he darted into his darkening office.

"No problem," muttered Stephen under his breath as he resumed his amble down the hall, whispering, "and you can go to hell."

∾

The next afternoon Stephen lounged in his cubicle—it could hardly be called an "office"—with his feet on the desk, talking with Jack Hodges. They had chatted for a short time the previous week while riding stationary bikes at the health club, but this was to be their first time to "hang out as brothers in the Lord," as Jack put it. Trying to keep things light, Stephen opened with some banter about swimming, since Stephen had been on his school's swim team until his junior year. But Jack didn't want to talk sports; he was consumed with collegiate religious athletics.

"I had been through a time of real searching. Even purging my body in an attempt to cure myself of impure thoughts and desires. Fasting, abstinence, the whole nine yards. I was determined to make my body a temple where Jesus could reign. Put him on the throne. I read God's word like crazy, but it didn't really make any sense to me. I think I was trying to read Scripture through the flesh rather than through the spirit. Know what I mean? The letter but not the spirit. And then there it was, just as clear as day." Jack rambled on, narrating, in much detail, his experience of being saved, finally concluding with, "I knew that Christ had died for me. I just felt in my heart that Christ had something special in mind for me, work he wanted me to do. A plan. The Holy Spirit opened a door. Like Jesus switched on the light. Alexis said it showed on my face. I was born again."

"And have you gotten clearer about just what that work is that the Lord plans for you to do?" asked Stephen, the sight of Alexis passing briefly through his mind. "'Cause I have found that when God blesses you, God often gives you an assignment."

"Well, that's why I wanted to talk with you. I'm hoping that you, as a spiritual leader, can help."

"I'm not so sure that you've come to the right place, in coming to me," said Stephen, smiling. "You know I'm just a few weeks out of seminary. I'm still green. The newest pastor and all. Still, your story is interesting."

Jack adopted a more earnest, less eager tone. "Stephen, speaking of pastors, do you really think that Reverend Lupino is a true spiritual leader? Consecrated?"

"Of course. He's the senior pastor, or senior managing pastor, what-ever. He's like a star in our denomination. I don't think you could get that far in the church if you weren't a true spiritual leader."

"Do you?" asked Jack. "Do you really think that being the pastor of a big church like this is a sign that you have gone a long way in being a spiritual leader?"

"Well, I guess I mean that, all other things being equal, I can't see any reason to doubt that Dr. Lupino is a fine spiritual leader," Stephen said, uncomfortably mouthing the words he thought he ought to say.

"Really? What's your honest opinion of his sermons?"

"His sermons?"

"Yeah. I mean, I never thought that he had much substance, biblically speaking. But I've noticed, in the weeks I've been home from school, man, he doesn't ever even mention the name of Jesus! What's up with that? I don't know if his sermons have changed or if I've changed. It's like we're at a meeting of the Rotary Club or something, a coach's pep talk in the locker room before the big game. Don't get me wrong—he seems a nice enough guy, though he doesn't seem to want to talk with me. But listening to him, I can't figure out why a guy like that is even in the ministry. I mean, without Jesus, what's the point? It's like he's just in it for the show."

"I take it that in your born-again religious experience you had on that retreat, Jesus didn't say anything to you about 'judge not lest you be judged,'" said Stephen pointedly, surprised by his own candor.

Jack gulped, shaking his head. "Oh man, you nailed me on that one," shaking his head and smiling. "Point well taken. Can you cut me a little new Christian slack?" he said, grinning. "I was way out of line questioning a brother in Christ. Busted."

"Sure," said Stephen. "And if I sound a bit self-righteous myself, maybe it's because I'm struggling with some of the same questions that bother you."

"Hey, you didn't mean to say that I'm self-righteous?" asked Jack, with a toothy sort of Joe College grin.

"Look, man, this is all as new to me as it is to you. I'm just a kid trying to figure my way through the maze, just like you. Just trying to read the game and figure out the other team's playbook," said Stephen. With that, Jack got up, walked over to Stephen, and hugged him, unnerving Stephen; for a moment, Stephen was gripped by the terrifying thought that Jack might actually cry in front of him.

To Stephen's great relief, Jack released him, slapped him on the shoulder, and said, "Thanks a mil, soul mate. Gotta go. You're the best."

Stephen sat there awhile, attempting to analyze what, if anything, had happened in the foregoing conversation. His ruminations were interrupted by a light tapping at his cell door and a high-pitched "Hello?" Pastor Herb stuck in his head, gave Stephen a benevolent, elderly sort of look, and asked, "May I come in?"

"Sure. Come right in. Glad to see you," said Stephen, rising from his desk and offering Cohellen his hand.

"Settling in, are we?" the patriarch asked.

"Maybe that's too strong a word for what I'm doing just now," Stephen answered. "Just trying not to go under is maybe more like it. Treading water for dear life."

"Oh, don't exaggerate. I'm sure you will do quite well," reassured Herb. The man seemed to be typecast to play the role of the kindly old grandfather, and he played it with stereotypical ease. "Son, you remind me of my first days in the ministry, long, long ago. How vividly I recall my very first parish."

"Let me ask you," said Stephen, thinking he would humor the old guy with a church question, "what did you find to be your greatest challenge?"

Herb smiled. "Oh, I doubt that my challenges, so long ago, will be yours, but now that you ask, I think my greatest difficulty in being a pastor of a church was the church. God has forced us into a strange assignment, us pastors, to be sure. Here Jesus Christ has called us into his service, summoning us for work in the kingdom of God, his chosen spokesmen. But when he called me, Jesus failed—or at least neglected—to mention that we would be required to work with his friends, the church!" Here Herb let loose a surprisingly strong laugh.

Stephen laughed too, nodding his head in agreement.

"No," Herb continued, staring off into nowhere, a habit he affected, "I found that it is not so great a task to love Jesus; no, the great challenge is to love those whom Jesus loves!" He chortled again. "I'm sure you will have ample opportunity to rediscover the veracity of the gospel claim that 'Christ Jesus died to save sinners.' Only sinners. And guess who gets to serve the sinners whom he has recklessly saved?"

"Only sinners, only us!" Stephen responded, feeling as if he were being inducted into a fraternity, whispered a professional secret known only by those in the clergy guild.

"So, my boy, I'll leave you to your labors. Welcome aboard. Remember: God never calls a man to undertake a work that God will not also give him the gifts he needs to fulfill the task. I think that's Aquinas, maybe Augustine. If it isn't, it should be. There is so much more going on around here, among us, in you, than you will ever fully discern. Pray to God to break it to you gently."

Herb arose with some difficulty, turned, smiled, and with a wave of the hand, exited.

That night, as Stephen sat at his bare kitchen table, swigging a beer and plowing through a mound of macaroni and cheese, he thought of Jack with a kind of begrudging admiration. Who knows? Jack could be justified in his theological misgivings about Dr. Lupino. Had all of Stephen's theological study, as well as the hands laid upon his head at ordination, combined to seduce him into selling out and joining the religious establishment that he once despised? Enduring all those boring classes in theology in order to prepare himself to swallow Chicken Little sermons without choking? Was he now little more than one of the officers of a sanctified Rotary Club? He almost envied Jack's exuberant, puerile Jesusness, so eager and wide-eyed about all things spiritual. Not long ago, he was Jack. In the past few years, had he grown or had he shrunk?

Perhaps because of these contemplations, Stephen had a restless night. Once again he was tormented by dreams. The dreams that weren't sexual had him back in high school, trapped in Latin class, that hellish high-school torture chamber. He was standing, humiliated, in front of a chalkboard, while the teacher and class stared. He looked down at himself and was horrified to see that he was stark naked, with nothing to shield him from the gaze of others, nothing but a piece of chalk in his hand. He stood dumbly at the blank board—paralyzed, uncovered, trapped.

4

The Fourth Sunday of Easter

Sitting in his office on Tuesday after lunch—feet on desk, open book before him, lethargic—Simon languished, suffering from spring fever or, as it is known in the church, post-Easter blah. Cloe had been told to hold his calls. *Getting Your Church off Dead Center* lay on his desk awaiting perusal, remedy for the seasonal malady creeping over him. He had tried to read the book—the latest marketing manual by some hotshot, grinning, church-growth guru from California—but lost interest after the first few pages. Everybody told him that he ought to read books on congregational development, but the author's gee-whiz determination to indiscriminately transform the church into a used car lot was off-putting. A sentence like, "Jesus Christ wants your church to grow, to be all you can be for the kingdom," made Simon's eyes glaze over. He yawned.

Sometimes, when he felt low, Simon would recall his list of achievements. The act of cataloging them was caffeine to his soul. On this occasion, however, therapeutically meditating upon his two decades at Hope, recollecting his ministerial feats—the new educational/fellowship/etc. wing, the fairly steady growth in membership, the city's first Kwanzaa celebration, the hiring of the first African-American staff member, the Koreans (his first choice—Nigerians—had slipped through his hands), the invitation of an openly gay preacher to be his pulpit guest (not once but thrice—beginning in 1988, mind you), the Hope Township project—failed to add up to enough to buy out his blahs. His courageous 1988 invite had garnered a smattering of gay and lesbian congregants, even a transvestite tax broker. (How many churches could boast that?) But these once-prized trophies had lost their luster. Even the evangelicals on the edge of town now bragged about their rainbow cross and blustered, "Gay friendly for Jesus."

That was the challenge of the progressive, forward-thinking practice of Christianity—always some new battle to be engaged in, some new idea to be taken for a test drive, some new wave to be ridden. How oppressive it was to be under the heel of the "latest thing." Simon had always taken pride that his unique ministerial feat was his mastery of progressive, goal-oriented organizational leadership, practiced in tandem with modest, contented, low-expectation spirituality. Many clergy had one of these virtues; Simon was a practitioner of both. His genius, if it could justly be called genius, was a desire to do well in things earthly, linked with apathy for achievements heavenly. He kept his aspirations realistically institutional rather than exaggeratedly religious. Jeremiah's sober counsel to the exiled Israelites was his guiding biblical text—plant gardens, pray for the peace of the city that holds you captive, settle in, and settle down. Babylon ain't so bad, once you get used to it.

That was Simon's theology, such as it was: a theology of adjustment, practical divinity of accommodation to the facts. Others deluded themselves that they were engaged in the godly transformation of the world or on a steadily upward journey to some better place; Simon was content to work the world as it was, to be a skilled chaplain to the indomitable status quo.

Think of the misery (he had seen it in his work as pastor) that is occasioned by people who are driven by a weakness for overly wrought moral striving or cursed with a prying, snoopy inquisitiveness about things divine. Simon was burdened by neither.

Worldly wisdom fused with spiritual nonchalance perfectly fitted Simon for the demands of ministry in a modern, progressive congregation. Thank God that Providence, or good luck, had landed him at Hope. This is what people wanted—no, *needed*—in their pastor. Too many congregations, Simon discovered early on, are burdened with prissy pastors, eager beavers for God, those unnaturally obsessed with religion. These sacristy rats fled the real world for the whimsy of ministry, thinking that by working for the church, prancing in the chancel, they could turn their preternatural, adolescent God obsession into a secure—though admittedly none too lucrative—lifetime profession.

Not Simon. His feet were firmly planted on this earth; he was content with what he knew and had no need to dream of possibilities in some wished-for world. This personal realism had been graciously used by

God—or whatever one chose to call him or her—into a healing balm for those tortured, religiously obsessed souls who huddle in any congregation. If he had a noteworthy pastoral gift, it was a gift for helping others adjust to things as they are rather than waste their lives pining for that which might be. God—or whatever one chose to call him or her—graciously gives us all we need for contentment right here, right now, Simon argued. Why attempt to sing Zion's song in a strange land? Simon's credo: All we know for sure is here, now. Upon this mundane, modest plot of ground, he had erected his spiritual home, planted his garden, and prayed for the peace of Babylon.

On most pensive afternoons, this was enough.

The bishop himself had said on more than one occasion that managing a large congregation is the greatest clergy leadership challenge. For two decades, Simon had been faithful steward of that which he had been given. A church well organized—the right people on the bus, productive systems in place, all cylinders clicking, employees' strengths identified and utilized, their weaknesses ignored. Now he had time to spare. Unfortunately, he seemed to be using his free time on this afternoon to sink into the clutches of the noonday demon.

Why had he made so few real friends within the congregation? It had been months, *years* since he and Mary had been invited into one of their homes. When he lunched at the club, he lunched alone unless he invited someone on the pretense of church business. When he dutifully exercised at the club, he sweated solo. He boasted that he followed the time-honored dictum "make no friends among church members," but perhaps he was simply consoling himself—none of his congregants wanted to be friends with him.

Shortly after his arrival at Hope, he had befriended a corporate lawyer. They played tennis each Wednesday, finishing off with a drink. But their camaraderie dribbled away shortly after Simon's prophetic sermon in which he took on George and Laura Bush, daring to criticize the Bush Administration's budget as punitive toward the poor. (Simon bragged that he was one of the first to see the wiles of Laura Bush.) Congregational conservatives sang a different tune once Bush drove the economy into the ditch months after Simon's outburst. No doubt Amos, Hosea, and Jeremiah had lacked tennis chums too.

He stared vacantly at his desk. In a few hours he would be heading home to a dark house empty of Mary. That was nothing new, but this afternoon he felt it as a particularly sharp pain. A few weeks ago, his most earnest desire was a full car allowance provided by the board. Most clergy of Simon's stature had car allowances, gas, oil, depreciation. Sure, the church paid for his membership at the club (which Mary had so publicly and sanctimoniously declared off-limits for herself, even though the club boasted a dozen Jews—at least half of them lawyers—and a couple of black dermatologists). He wouldn't have bought the Porsche if he had known the board would resist this minimal perk, throwing back in his face his (in their estimate) generous salary. They had relented, finally, but only after requiring him virtually to get down on his knees, and their hesitancy had robbed him of much of his joy.

The car allowance had, in Simon's mind, become a referendum on his ministry. Twenty years of self-sacrificial labor, and what had it gotten him? A spring afternoon of gloom, a handful of dust.

He had never understood the Easter giddiness that seemed to infect some clergy at this time of the year—flowers bursting through wet ground, birds atwitter, waves of pollen sweeping over green lawns, sap rising, and Jesus come back from the dead. When you are on the other side of fifty— bearing the burden of a few professional disappointments, a wise, first-hand awareness of human limits—vernal vitality is depressing. His soul felt shrunken, desiccated. For most people, this week's tax-filing deadline was more eventful than the resurrection.

It was April in the churchyard and November in his soul—he was alone, unaccustomedly vulnerable, caught like Dante "in the middle of life's journey, where the straight way is lost." Or was it the result of insufficiently utilized testosterone?

His cell phone buzzed in his trousers. Probably Mary to let him know she was still alive but wouldn't be home for dinner, again. Against his usual inclination, he answered the phone.

"Doctor Simon Lupino," he said.

"Padre!" said a familiar but unidentified woman's voice, languid and husky. "Forgive my importunate intrusion."

Instantly he identified the deliciously raspy voice. He brightened.

"Just Sybil here. Got your personal number with a bribe. Hope I'm not barging in on anything divine or eternal."

"Sybil! What an unexpected, pleasant surprise," he said in a slightly uplifted tone that betrayed his delight.

"Hope that you are having a grand Eastertide, and some much deserved rest after the rigors of resurrection. After reading all the goings-on in the *Hope Herald*, well, I just had to pour myself a drink, put up my feet, light a cigarette, and recuperate from ecclesiastical exhaustion."

How cute. Simon rarely had personal interaction with Sybil Vestal, though she was a surprisingly regular Sunday communicant. And yet he noted in himself an odd, inexplicable excitement any time, at church or on the courts at the club, he had a "Sybil sighting." He was fascinated by her mix of urbane sophistication and devil-may-care demeanor.

"I'm pleased that you noted that I'm earning my keep," laughed Simon.

"May I help you cool down from an exhausting week, my Father Confessor?" said Sybil playfully. "An odd whim pushed me to give you a buzz and ask you to stop by. Don't know if contemporary, high-steeple clergy do house calls anymore, but you've hardly set foot in my digs, so I thought I'd try for a pastoral call into the Land of Nod, East of Eden."

Simon's heart beat faster. Like a bumbling teenager, he was unsure what to say next. Sybil was appropriately long out of her second (or maybe her third?) marriage. Her checkered marital past made her all the more interesting, certifying her as one of those enticing, the-rules-are-made-for-everybody-else-women who are the polar opposite of the dowdy, bustling, bourgeois church women, the morally serious, spiritually sensitive ones who are drawn to a pastor like flies to a carcass.

"My care for my flock knows no bounds. Always searching for a wandering soul. Would love to drop by." Then laughingly, "Our Lord said there is more joy in heaven over the retrieval of just one of the lost, than in church with the many who lack the creativity to wander."

"Wander into the wilderness and retrieve this lost one," she said teasingly. "Lost sheep here, eager to be found."

Simon's mind was racing. He was perspiring. Classy, sassy Sybil knew how to wear a dress. She moved through the halls of Hope as if on a Parisian runway. And Sybil in slacks! Few women her age retained such hips.

"Like our Lord, I'm always searching for the lost, indeed, going out and compelling them to come in," Simon answered.

Sybil's lair was her grand Tudor Revival on Elm, reputed to have been wrenched from one of her husbands in an advantageous divorce. The house was a fitting setting for such a creature. Sybil had never known life without privilege—probably couldn't remember when anyone in her family actually worked.

"To be perfectly candid, I've always thought of myself more as one of the Lord's goats at his left hand than as one of his sheep, wayward or not, on his right."

Such a tease, thought Simon, *so seductive.*

"Still, if you're in the mood for playing the Good Shepherd, any chance of a drink this afternoon on your way home, Padre?" Her tone was unmistakably flirtatious.

Simon's heart was pounding now. "Well, perhaps I could. Let me check my schedule . . ." He allowed a three-second pause before replying, "Why yes, I can. Nothing I can't rearrange for a confab with you. Pastoral care home delivery. Around fiveish, Sybil?"

"Perfect!" she responded. "Surely between now and then I can come up with some spiritual dilemma for us to ponder together."

Her daring use of *together* tingled his ears for the next two hours. He worked up this casual word into a full-blown, torrid relationship. Unprepared for her coquettish responsiveness, he was thrilled.

Sybil didn't fit the provincial confines of the Midwestern city of her birth. Summers with Daddy and Mommy up in Southampton, shipped off to a girls' school in Switzerland when she began being too attentive to the lifeguards at the club, then Swarthmore (where surely there must have been a schoolgirl crush), a master's in interior design—which she need never use—from NYU no less. Sybil was something.

Simon savored the memory of the casual, seductive way that Sybil had chatted with him before the Lenten Noonday Concert. She played the flirt with many, but that March day she had been studiedly flirtatious, wearing a purple top, which he duly noted, making a cute comment on her liturgical correctness. Sliding her hand down her finely turned hip, she had shaken her dark brown hair this way and that as she moved her finger back and forth, smiling, in mock rebuke of his impudence. It was a wonderful moment, mischievously out of character for the Lenten fast.

Perhaps even then she was testing the waters. Had he shown too much delight in her while in the narthex, coming on even in the midst of Lent? Why not? Her actions and dress seemed to shout, *the key is under the doormat.*

He joyfully meditated upon her entrance on Sundays—arriving in style in her black convertible, scarf and all, pushing her sunglasses back as she sashayed through the narthex as if to say, "The diva has arrived. If God wishes, the show may begin."

After counting the minutes all afternoon—checking his hair, sucking in his paunch—at five after five, Simon pulled into Sybil's shade-covered drive. At that hour, only a few rays of late afternoon sunlight stole through the majestic, surrounding trees.

Her secluded house had welcomed him only once, for a meeting of the Altar Guild, of all things. (Sybil was unimaginable with her long dark red fingernails, her diamond-studded bracelets, polishing the altar ware with the dowdies of the guild. He would pay good money to see Sybil tidying the crumbs and shot glasses after communion. Still, her presence at church almost every Sunday must say something.) By the time he had walked up the slate path and taken the risk of pressing his finger to her big, brass door chimes, he was in near frenzied expectation.

"Welcome!" said Sybil as she put her arm around Simon in a casual but unmistakable embrace. "You are kind to come."

Simon stepped inside, and Sybil began pouring drinks. "Can I tempt you, Padre?"

Simon stirred with anticipation of the inconceivable joy of succumbing to her temptations. As Sybil mixed and stirred, he gazed about her living room. Everything was old, probably European, and just right. All from elsewhere, the best made better by being inherited rather than bought. As pastor, Simon had been in many fine homes, but none as fine as Sybil's. He rubbed his hand along the back of the sofa.

"Well, dear rabbi, what must we discuss?" asked Sybil, settling at the other end of the sofa, kicking off her shoes, and tucking her bare feet beneath her. She cradled her drink with elegant fingers—fingers like those of Botticelli's Venus—sliding them slowly up and down the stem. "I'm as innocent as an unwashed pagan, unsullied by theological information. Let the catechesis begin."

"I would rather talk about you," said Simon.

"Me?"

"I realized this afternoon as I thought about our . . . meeting, that I know you, but not really. I see you at Hope. And at the club." (Here he indulged in a moment's meditation upon Sybil in her taut tennis whites on the courts at the club, reaching for a sideline serve, sleek and tan, graceful as a gazelle.) "But what does that tell me about you? Who *are* you?"

"Simon, you know more about me than I about you. You are unrevealing in sermons. Guarded, well secreted from public gaze. I like mystery in a man, as long as it's a mystery into which I can sneak a privileged peek, as long as the mystery turns out to be deep, dark, illicit, and naughty," she said, smiling seductively.

Simon was aroused, relishing the thought that Sybil found him enigmatic. He had always wanted to be mysterious, but until now, no one had thought he was. As a wordsmith, he figured that her "naughty," intensified by "illicit," had to be intentional. Simon, who enjoyed managing situations, working at his predetermined pace, was losing control—and he loved it. She was coming on to him.

Seizing her invitation, Simon launched into an exposition of his favorite subject:

"Me? Not much to say, really. I'm a guy who needed to be needed by others. I wanted, not just to make something of myself, which would have been easy enough, but to add value," said Simon, focusing upon Sybil's sharp brown eyes. "To transform. To build."

"A call?"

"Maybe that's the traditional name. A keen sense of my gifts. In my case, more an inclination than a call—no, a passion to use the gifts that I had been given," said Simon, "glad to be following a life that was the antithesis of my parents' solid, pragmatic path. 'Follow your bliss' was how Parker Palmer, I think, or maybe Joseph Campbell—I love them both—reframed the traditional idea of vocation. 'Follow your bliss.'"

"More alluring than a man of mystery is a man of passion," said Sybil playfully. "And God knows I'm all for bliss."

Was she gently mocking him or coming on to him? Dear God, he prayed, let it be the latter.

"Simon, can I get you another?" she asked, swaying her empty glass seductively, her glorious, long fingers fondling the stem.

"Why, that would be lovely," said Simon. Had he inexpertly gulped down his drink? Light-headed, rapidly descending an alluring path that he had presumed would take more time to negotiate, entering dark waters, slipping dreamily, dizzily downward, he found his quick descent exhilarating.

When she returned, he said, "Sybil, I love your art. As a communicator, a practitioner of the homiletical arts, I've found that few people around here care for the finer arts. You must have a fortune in Impressionists." As he reached for a cracker and a glob of softened Gruyere, Simon's left hand brushed against the white orchid on the table. He smiled; the orchids were real.

"My, my. Daddy would just turn over in his grave if he heard you call his beloved Expressionists 'Impressionists,'" laughed Sybil. Simon burned with embarrassment at this unintentional revelation of the limits of his knowledge.

"He collected them while he was in Germany doing business right after the war. Got most for a trifle. They're Fauvists, actually. He looked upon German art in the same way as he used cheap postwar German labor. As a child I detested the paintings' garish colors and dark, disturbing images. But when I did time in Switzerland, incarcerated by the nuns, I began to see the Fauvists' artistic intent. You can't find any better outside the Brücke, near Berlin, if I do say so. The Expressionists were criticized for their misogyny, but I think they've got us just right, or at least they've got me—beasts with piercing breasts and sharp teeth to tear to shreds some unsuspecting male."

"They must be worth a fortune," said Simon.

"But now, Simon, the beginning. Please. You who are so accustomed to having people narrate their stories must now tell me yours."

Resuming, he told her of the confining, featureless Pennsylvania landscape of his youth and of his growing desire—no, *passion* (instilled in him by his mother)—to escape, to follow his *bliss,* free of the place in which his parents were embedded. The movie *Jonathan Livingston Seagull* had been a revelation, had confirmed in him that he was created for grander things. Like Jonathan, he was meant to soar.

Then the second-rate church college he tried not to remember, where he was in effect trapped by the gift of a full scholarship funded by his home congregation. Still, a couple of demanding, unorthodox professors (one of whom had a German degree) introduced him to the wonders of the historical-critical method of biblical interpretation and to Tillich and Bultmann, makers of modern theology. His ebbing, inherited faith was bested by a new faith more suitable for a person now able to think for himself.

Simon also made note of a couple of girlfriends; Sybil must not think that he was an effete young intellectual. (The invitation to indulge in autobiography is a temptation to idealized self-presentation and subtle prevarication, temptations that Simon was unable this dizzy afternoon to resist.)

"And how did your sense of God play into all this?" Sybil asked.

Simon told Sybil that even before he ventured forth intellectually, he had an inarticulate sense of the divine. People responded to him, so ministry felt like a natural fit.

"And yet in the past few years, my youthful intellectual attraction to the faith has cooled," Simon confessed, lowering his voice, sounding earnest. "Sometimes, Sybil, sometimes—say when I'm in the middle of a sermon, or I'm attempting to shore up the faith of a parishioner—I feel like I'm one of those World War II Japanese soldiers who were holed up for years in a cave on a Pacific island because they never got the news that the war is over. Is that me? Continuing to fight, putting up stiff resistance to godlessness when, in reality, long ago God admitted defeat and left?"

Sybil listened, raised her eyebrows thoughtfully but wordlessly.

"We may be on our own," Simon told her. "A thought forced upon me, not by college or seminary, but by life."

"Oh?"

Loosened by the gin, Simon described his most detrimental college memory—the six months of his mother's cancer, the slow wasting of her body, which shook his sophomoric idealism. During her sickness, he watched not only her body dissipate, but her Christian faith as well. She prayed fervently, asked the congregation to besiege heaven with prayer so that she could live until her son was grown and married, but prayer failed to halt the disease. Within a scant six and a half months, she was gone, let down by her touchingly simple faith. She died hurt, embittered, and bereft.

Simon's candor did not extend deep enough for him to tell Sybil that his most painful postmortem regret was his absence from his mother at the end. His father had called him on the dorm telephone to warn him and, in his monotone, informed him matter-of-factly that the end was near. But Simon's youthful inexperience, combined with anticipation of fraternity rush, convinced him that he had time eventually to borrow a car and drive home on Sunday. It was a misstep, the source of much self-chastisement. She died—gasping, calling for him, his father later told him—just before Sunday dawn.

Unmentioned, though equally painful, was that he had only one college friend to ask for a loan of a car and, even though he was at the party, he had failed to get a bid to join the fraternity.

Simon also excised from his narrative the horrible, final burden his mother had laid upon him. His father told him that his mother had gasped, only moments before her end, "Tell Simon . . . he must pray every day . . . asking God to have mercy upon my soul. Please."

"The day my mother died, I became an adult—the hard way. My father, who was never big on religion, just silently turned away, stealing money from his company in order to get caught and fired, offering grief as his excuse. Suicide without the bravery. He died two years later, alone. Their deaths are my most important God moments, spiritually speaking."

"Important?" asked Sybil.

Simon told her that he was infused with determination to help struggling souls who, having gotten little from the church but a mélange of childish, naïve religious banalities, are forced to confront the tragic challenges of life—and death—with inadequate faith. The "God issue" was relatively unimportant; church was a human institution, a sociological phenomenon, subject to the same dynamics of any other human gathering, or as Saint Paul says, treasure in an earthen vessel. Most clergy were clueless about organizational management. Out of love for his people, he would exchange theological platitudes for solid facts. Community was central, the people gathered in the name of God more important than the God who gathered them. We have in our hands all we need.

"And what about . . . Christ?" Sybil asked.

Simon asserted that Jesus was a wonderful moral example, an inspiring teacher, a genius who was open to the divine. Christ never judged. He was a God-intoxicated pilgrim. Love your neighbor as yourself. Christ has no hands but our hands. The journey itself, not the destination, makes the journey worthwhile.

"Hmmm," murmured Sybil. "And how did you and Mary meet?"

Her question seemed to Simon an intrusion into a story that could be fully told without reference to the Blessed Virgin.

"Not much to tell. Not sure what brought us together. May I speak frankly?"

"Oh, please do," responded Sybil.

"Maybe if we'd had kids, that would have given our marriage a certain rationale. Frankly, it's been a very long time since we have truly been husband and wife," he said, watching for a response from Sybil. "If you know what I mean."

"I like Mary's unsullied goodness," offered Sybil cheerfully. "I am sure that she has many admirers."

"Can you imagine what it's like to live with 'unsullied goodness'?"

Sybil giggled and cradled her Martini in both hands. Simon took a last, emboldening gulp.

"Oh, you poor baby!" purred Sybil, reaching over and, with the tenderness of a mother, brushing a lock of his hair. "Neglected puppy." *The past is an elusive animal,* Sybil thought to herself. *Illusive, too.*

"I—I have just been so damned lonely of late."

"Mia Padre! What an alluring lapse into self-revelation," said Sybil.

"It's funny," he resumed, "I've always been independent, not needing the affection and attention that some men need. Mary's a person without need because she is consumed with everyone else's. Me? I'm a thinker, a learner, but with a softer side. At some point Mary just froze, became a relic of the early seventies, a mastodon trapped in the ice of her own altruistic presumption."

"Let's not talk anymore about Mary. I want to hear more you," she said.

Delighted, he edged closer. "Sybil, you amaze me. For a long time I have admired, from a distance, your vitality, the way you so confidently move in the world."

"Admired me? That's a compliment I seldom hear—never, actually. Simon, you are a man in middle life, horny and self-pitying, and I just happen to be standing here, or rather lounging here, first woman in view," said Sybil, retrieving a cigarette from a silver case (engraved, antique) on the table, lighting it and inhaling (elegantly). Simon thought her—sitting there in the late spring afternoon, ensconced in her chic lair, shrouded in mysterious, upwardly drifting smoke, dismissing while secretly encouraging his advances—just about the most alluring creature he had ever beheld.

Though he was most comfortable with words, without a word he rested his hand invitingly upon her knee, open to her. He thrilled to her warm, firm clasp.

Sybil sat in silence, for a long moment holding his hand, and then she rose upward, leaned toward him, and kissed him on his forehead. Simon closed his eyes and received the gift of her kiss with a delight that he fought hard to suppress. If she had kissed him passionately, sloppily on the lips rather than upon his forehead, he could not have been more aroused. He abruptly stood up and looked down at her.

"Sybil, I've got to go. If I don't, I'll be late for our program meeting." He was lying. He had counted on Sybil offering resistance, and after encountering none, he thought that he ought to slow his downward slide. If he didn't leave now, he would never depart this pleasure dome. He calculated that overeagerness on his part would be unseemly, a transgression upon Sybil's classy demeanor.

"Must you?" Sybil asked. "I'm full of questions."

"I could linger forever," said Simon, "just being here with you in this beautiful room, this safe space. This afternoon has been . . . my salvation." That was the gin talking. "But I can't stay. I long to, in the depths of my soul, but I can't. Duty calls."

Duty, in this case, was an alcoholic cook. Earlier that afternoon, Chef had been found unconscious, toque askew, face down on the floor of the kitchen near a slimy heap of turkey tetrazzini, which suggested, even to an untrained evaluator, that his recovery was not going well. Turkey tetrazzini for the board! Still, Simon thought it would look bad if he didn't check on Chef's off-the-wagon condition. For all of Chef's faults, he would be the devil to replace.

"How sweet," cooed Sybil. "I hope this is not the end, but a beginning."

"This is a glorious first chapter," said Simon, "in a new story, a movie about . . . us."

Sybil saw him to the door as she expertly flicked a bit of ash from her cigarette into a Dresden dish in the hall. All of her movements, even the most mundane, delighted his senses. She gave him a peck on the cheek before he passed over the marble threshold—not too much, but more than he hoped. As he departed, he trembled with excitement, so much so that he had difficulty managing his car down the winding, darkened, pea gravel drive. The drinks, mixed with the conversation and Sybil's kiss, had induced in him a vertiginous lightness that he had not known since he was nineteen. So comfortable with herself, serene and sure, an angel of mercy offering release from his chains, she had opened the door of his dim cell and light, glorious light had come flooding in.

ა

"Let's get going, good people," declared Simon, "time to begin."

"Will we have weekly staff meetings all summer?" asked Grimball, a tiredness in his voice.

"I'll let you know, once I evaluate," said Simon cheerfully. "Serious summer is yet a month away. Besides, this is an 'administrative team' meeting. 'Staff' is passé. I like to think of you as more than a team, as family, really. I no longer call you staff but family, to paraphrase our Lord during one of his staff meetings."

No one laughed, though a faint smile played on Herb's wrinkled face.

"Johnson, the Swanson wedding was a debacle."

"Weddings are one of the few things not in my portfolio," Quail responded.

"It was awful. By the time I arrived, the wedding director was hysterical, screaming, bawling. Clive Swanson was cursing, chain-smoking, pacing in front of the church, plaintively shouting details of his church giving record to the arriving guests. Elizabeth Swanson, never noted for emotional stability, poor thing, was rendered a complete basket case, whooping at the top of her voice about 'we'll never set foot in this GD church again.' Makeup streaming in rivulets down her face. The flower girl, or maybe it was the ring bearer—some kid threw up a large puddle in the narthex."

"And what, pray tell, hath this curious tale of the trials of the petty bourgeoisie to do with me?" asked Quail.

"All were shouting about the stench, like the odor of open sewer, a truly god-awful smell! Well, when I entered the sanctuary, I discerned the source. The Koreans! Rotten cabbage, soy, kimchi. In insolent disregard of our sacred covenant, the Koreans had been cooking. Cooking! Were they not told that they were free to worship God, to sing their praise songs, to clap, engage in fundamentalist interpretation of Scripture, run naked down the aisles if they wished, but they were *never*, under any circumstances, ever to cook? Were they not told?"

"Of course they were," sniffed Quail. "I remind you that you were warned by the Presbyterians that if you let those Koreans in our building, you would regret it. They multiply like rabbits, present themselves as poor, oppressed immigrants when in truth they are a bunch of savvy, cutthroat business types and high-priced software engineers. Just try to limit their prerogatives in the building, much less suggest that they come up with more cash, and it's 'me no understand your language.'"

"You know very well that my first choice for ethnic was Nigerians. Anyway, damage is done. You're in charge of the building." Simon assumed a calmer tone. "Tell them that we've had enough. If you must, learn Korean to make Kim understand. Thank God I had the presence of mind to turn the air conditioning fans on high, so within a few minutes the stench in the sanctuary was reduced to that of a poorly kept barnyard, bad but bearable, though the little flower girl, or whatever it was, missed the wedding. They pushed a handful of pills down poor, hysterical Elizabeth so we could proceed. She managed to get down the aisle and back, but I'm sure that by the time those barbiturates got to her she had no inkling that she was at a wedding."

Glumweltner assumed the unaccustomed role of peacemaker and inserted his ample self between them, saying, "His daughter always was a spoiled brat. Word in the church is that they needed a quickie wedding. The odor had to be tough on a two-months-pregnant deb." He grinned a cheeky, pink smile.

"Speaking of olfactory and culinary matters, how is dear, besotted Chef?" asked Grimball, attempting to assist Glumweltner in his pacification efforts.

"He'll make it, though his doctor has told him his liver is well on its way to complete ossification. What a sad waste of talent. He must lay off the hooch," said Simon.

"Well, thank God!" sneered Glumweltner. "The thought that we might have to continue on as the Body of Christ without the sustenance of his astounding turkey tetrazzini had me on the verge of despair. You know what they say: a church travels on its stomach." He felt his ample stomach rumble, reminding him that it had been a good three hours since breakfast.

Sam reported on the new switch box for the east wing.

Eleanor obsequiously reported on the Children's Sabbath complete with a focus on the work of UNICEF and the ecological danger posed by Styrofoam cups.

"Thank you, Eleanor, thank you," said Simon, cutting her off. "Stephen, speaking of kiddies, did you ever find time to meet with young Jack Hodges?"

"Sure did, we've met twice, or at least one and a half times, counting the conversation we had in the shower at the health club," replied Stephen.

"Convocations are being held in the shower? Where, pray tell, do I sign up?" Grimball sang forth.

Disregarding Grimball, Simon declaimed, "You know that I am basically an idea person. Hope Township, Children's Sabbath, the annual garden party were exciting—yesterday. Today, old hat. Any church that fails to be culturally sensitive, to surf the next wave, will find itself standing on the street corner trying to hitch a ride."

Let's all settle in for the sermonette, thought Glumweltner. *God, I hope it's shorter than last week's.*

Mousy Eleanor thought only, *I hate you.*

"Wait a minute," said Simon. "The most important Sunday of the church year looms: *Mother's Day!* And have we seized the opportunity

God has offered? If we can't leverage affection for dear old Mum into an attendance bump, we ought to surrender our clergy credentials."

"And how, may I be so bold as to ask, are we to make money off dead mothers *this* year?" asked Glumweltner.

"That's where you talented people come in. Let's brainstorm on ways that we can make a boon of Mother's Day. Here's an idea: Why don't we have a contest to see who will contribute the most to our church's, uh, 'Mother Fund'? People vote for their mothers through their contributions. The man—surely most of the contributions will come from men—who donates the largest amount in honor—or memory—of his mother wins. The contributor's mother will be featured that Sunday with, well, with her picture in the bulletin and a tribute! A full-color picture."

"Are you serious, Simon?" asked Quail with a look of terror mixed with queasiness.

"Color is three times as expensive as black-and-white," commented Andrea.

"What a marvelous idea. In this congregation, there's got to be enough wounded male psyches from manipulative moms to send all the staff to Cannes," declared Grimball, clapping his hands with mock glee, ridiculing both Simon and his enemy, Quail.

"A gift to Hope is cheaper than long-term therapy," added Glumweltner. "Mine, in her maternal ineptitude, pumped me with so much chocolate cake, consigning me to a lifetime of enslavement to the strictures of Jenny Craig, Inc."

Stephen was loving it. He glanced across and down the table toward old Herb, who stared upwards. He was sure that Herb knew more than he let on.

Before Eleanor could testify to her hellish life under her stepmother's regime, she was muzzled by Simon's frown.

Was Simon too indulgent with his staff? His charitable disposition toward their jabbing and poking arose out of his humble recognition that, unlike them, in his sermons he was given license to take occasional swipes at the world's folly. One of the joys of preaching is the joy of verbally assaulting those people and events that one resents. The poor musicians had no one to attack but themselves.

"They braved stretch marks to bear us. Let's have a special push for Mother's Day, details to be hammered out later," pronounced Simon. "Here's a challenge. Come to our next meeting prepared to share with our Hope family one thing, just one, that you will do differently in the next three months—one thing that could have a positive impact on attendance. God doesn't take a vacation!"

Plug the product, mused Grimball.

ဢ

Quail slunk back to his office to lick the gashes he had received at the staff smackdown, slamming the door and instructing his assistant that he was not to be interrupted due to pressing deadlines. He locked the door as a precaution, opened the bottom drawer of his desk, and poured himself a stiff drink in a plastic cup, unaware that every time his secretary heard the lock click she knew full well what he was up to. The doctor had forbidden him to consume alcohol in the hope that abstinence might quell his turbulent stomach. Slumped down in his chair, Quail was like a wad of crumpled paper that had been tossed toward the wastebasket. He was losing ground, and the cause of the slippage was clear: a shift in his relationship with Simon.

Though Simon thought differently, they had never been friends. And yet Quail had rested secure in the assumption that Simon needed him as both brains and brawn behind Simon's ephemeral achievements at Hope. Someone had to pull the strings behind the scenes. But with each staff meeting, and each increasingly lousy interaction with Simon, Quail sensed that Simon's gratitude for what he had wrought at Hope was dissipating.

To give the devil his due, Simon was an innovator. He was a self-confessed neophile, losing interest in things quickly after they were begun. Simon's main pastoral achievement, Quail had always thought, was his realization that most people go to church for purposes of self-medication. And Simon was a master at responding to their need for spiritual anesthesia, which he administered in large doses during his Sunday performance. True, Sunday worship was Hope's piggybank. But in recent days, Quail discovered the shadow side of Simon's upbeat, positive-thinking theology. The incurably positive leader needs—indeed requires—things to go well, and when things don't, he shows his fangs.

The alcohol emboldened Quail to think the heretofore unthinkable—could it be that good old Simon had overstayed his welcome at Hope?

ဢ

Midmorning the next day, Stephen was noisily banging a box of art supplies down the hall past the Walter Rauschenbusch Lounge—felt markers, glue, rubber bands, and tape—essential tools for his planned Sunday evening student Bible studies. A prayer group huddled in the lounge banged the door shut as Stephen thudded by.

"Hello, young Princetonian scholar!" a high voice hailed from behind.

He turned and saw Jane, alias Miss Marple, bearing a bucket full of mostly wilted flowers. Wearing green galoshes and a faded blue nylon jacket, she could have passed as a bag lady.

"The gospel continues to leap over all boundaries into every corner of the world. The truth marches on. Crucified Jesus is spectacularly raised from the dead, and I respond by heaving buckets of spent foliage, you by toting a big box of arts and crafts kitsch. How well did seminary prepare you for such sacred labor?"

Stephen was grateful for the interruption.

"Altar Guild flunkee at work here. I'm only allowed by Madame Mussolini and her jackbooted liturgical minions to do the scud work, relegated by her royal highness to cleaning up the trash and leftovers after divine service. The skillful arranging and the artistic floral production are reserved for the inner circle of gifted *artistes*, lavender-coated thugs as they are. I'm consigned to the more prosaic task of hauling buckets of dead flowers."

"I'm sure your contributions are valuable," said Stephen lamely.

"You're showing real promise for future ministry, young man," said Jane. "Here you are, only on the job for a few weeks, still fumbling your way along in ecclesiastical *terra incognita*, and already patronizing old women hanging about the *ecclesia*."

Stephen raised his eyebrows in feigned surprise.

Jane stopped in the hall before a painting in a large gilded frame, retrieved by a bygone tourist from a shop in Florence that sells copies, hauled back to Hope, and probably written off for more than it was worth. It was a Madonna and Child, done in the now out-of-favor Mannerist style by a poor emulator of Pontormo.

"Why, I ask you, would anyone place on the wall of a so rigorously liberal Protestant church such an unabashed representative of the most vulgar of Catholic counterreformation spirituality?"

"Beats me," said Stephen, looking over Jane's shoulder, making little sense of the painting.

"Most Protestants are incurable Docetists in my book," said Jane.

"Docetists?"

"Your church history exam? *Doceo,* to seem, to appear. The heresy that asserted that Christ, the Son of God, was not truly, fully human, but only appeared to be so, only seemed so, his bodily humanity a mere veil draped over his exalted, unsullied divinity."

"I nailed the history of doctrine exam," said Stephen with a smile, "and I know Docetism, but why think of that now?"

"All this Catholic mother-and-baby business helps anchor Roman spirituality in the flesh, which of course accounts for the exposed, very Jewish penis of the babe."

"What?"

"That tiny male organ," she said, moving her face closer to the painting, narrowing her eyes, "is a rebuke to those who would detach our Lord from the stuff of this earth, those faint of heart who would deny his bodily reality. Whatever you make of him, he had a body," said Jane, gesturing ominously with one of her buckets toward the naked babe who, in the Mannerist tradition, was almost falling out of Mary's arms. "His penis proves it."

Stephen stood just behind her, taking in the picture at her direction. "The skin looks like it's dead," he commented, "so waxy and gray looking."

"Typical of the Mannerists, my boy. The baby born to die, the nativity followed by crucifixion, Bethlehem united with Golgotha, God with an anatomically correct body, soon to be crucified," mused Jane. "Name me another religion reckless enough to stake itself on such a carnal claim. I love Christianity for its daring assertion of incarnation. Most yokels want their religion to be more spiritual, less corporeal. Oh well. Let's have a smoke. The powers that be won't permit enjoyment of the vile weed within the *sancto sanctorum,*" she said as she set her bucket to the side.

"Er, remember, I don't smoke," said Stephen with awkwardness.

"Oh, excuse me for forgetting what a righteous, unspotted young thing you are! Of course your body is so much a temple of the Holy Spirit that you would never tarnish its bright façade with vulgar habits, would you?"

"Are you making fun of me?" asked Stephen, grinning.

Jane grabbed him by the arm, hugging him slightly, then laughingly led him toward the door at the end of the hall.

"Ravings of a sad, lonely old woman, dear Saint Sebastian. If you try to deal gently with my weaknesses, in the unlikely event that I should discover any of your vulnerabilities, I promise to do the same for you," she said, heading toward a marble bench on the north side of the Jones Prayer

Garden. "Come, let us perch here, on the bench that covers the remains of Dame Judith MacIlvine Jones, a disagreeable old girl if ever there were one, I can assure you. Unlike you, having few virtues, my weaknesses are self-evident. The Stoics like Boethius said much the same. You, man of many virtues, are fated to be surprised when your virtues are revealed to be your weaknesses. Well, this is your five-minute opportunity to humor and to assuage a poor, struggling old sinner." She lit a cigarette, took an experienced drag, and exhaled a cloud of smoke.

"I thought I would be your Saint Stephen, first martyr of the church. What's with the 'Saint Sebastian'?" he asked.

"You were exclusively Saint Stephen until I caught sight of you Sunday in the service, April light bringing out your nice, bronze features, alb formfitting you so well—it was then I thought of the Saint Sebastian conceit. You know dear Sebastian, don't you? Oh, that's right, you are low-church Protestant, blissfully ignorant of Catholic spirituality. Sebastian? Utilized by Roman legionnaires for target practice? His naked, contorted, tight torso became a favorite for altar triptychs in countless convents, giving repressed sisters a brief respite from church-enforced celibacy. Everybody painted him—Botticelli, Perugino, Titian, Guido Reni, and of course, Pollaiuolo. Surely you have seen him, arrows piercing his pure, innocent young flesh. Very Freudian. I hear that sweet, erotic Sebastian is making a comeback among the homosexual community."

"Sorry I asked," said Stephen, shaking his head. "Why do I always get the feeling that you're poking fun at me? Hey, I'm in over my head enough without your making life even tougher," he said with a boyish beam.

"I'm making a feeble attempt at camaraderie," she said. "You misread my humor if you think you are its target. Those of us standing knee-deep in the mud of the trenches of the kingdom must stick together in the battle against the principalities and powers. I felt an immediate kinship with you when I met you with that lithe young woman with whom you are so infatuated."

"A kinship with me?"

"A society of savvy sojourners," she said. "Fraternity of the mismatched and the interlopers, trapped amid a company of enthusiastic ecclesiastical pimps and whores. Like me, you clearly don't fit here."

"How do you figure that?"

"Come now, Sebastian. Has anything that you have seen at Hope suggested to you that you have landed among fellow pilgrims, kindred spirits?"

"Are you—are you referring to the fact that I'm an African American?" he asked.

"Oh, Saint Sebastian, you disappoint me! Of course I'm not referring to any quality so crassly obvious and quite irrelevant as your race. Your race is as uninteresting and as unrevealing as your gender. Such a lot of silliness to make too much of crude biological facts."

She inhaled and exhaled again before resuming. "No, my young friend. You are queer in that you are obviously here in response to a divine summons, on a mission, serving us as subversive secret agent, sent to snoop and then to expose our sham operation. You are God's mole, directing God's undercover investigation into our pompous pretense of being a church. All of this"—she gestured toward the looming building and the bell tower above them—"is an elaborate shelter from the divine, a shield against a God who is determined to incarnate. I'm sure your sincerity threatens many. We have quite a little charade in progress here, interrupted when God intrudes as someone like you who actually takes all of this seriously."

"I don't have the foggiest idea of what you are getting at," said Stephen. His standing by his grandfather's bedside and being prayed into the ministry leapt to his mind as Jane rambled. He loved the way that she insisted on dragging him back toward the inexplicable.

"Oh, you know quite well of what I speak. No credible explanation for someone like you"—another draw on her cigarette—"other than you are unfortunate enough to have had the hand of God bop you on the head and haul you into this sham. It's the call, my dear," she said, lowering her voice in imitation of Boris Karloff, "the dreaded, much resisted call. Oh, God have mercy upon you for the call. The call!"

"So you think my call to the ministry was 'unfortunate'?" Recalling his grandfather's deathbed prayer, he long considered the possibility of that vocational moment being dumb, ludicrous maybe, but not quite "unfortunate."

"Oh, my young Sebastian, your arrival here is our supreme good fortune, though you may come to think that it is not yours, once our arrows make their mark on your smooth, brown flesh. I suspect—and these are the poor ravings of a mere layperson—that your summons, your vocation, your call, your grim assignment of God, your being commandeered or whatever you call it will not be easy. You are here under coercion, victim of divine compulsion. Otherwise, I can't imagine why you, an intelligent, young, gifted, and black man with the world at your feet, would have undertaken such an endeavor. If God has not compelled you to be here, I know of no good reason for your presence." She flicked ashes from the butt of what was left of her cigarette. Then, holding the spent cigarette up before Stephen, she pronounced, "This vile thing serves for me as a sweet *memento mori*. I, in my modest discipleship, shall perish, not at the hands of a rock-wielding mob, as did Saint Stephen, nor due to cruel imperial arrows, as Saint Sebastian, but rather at the hands of a tobacco company, paying them good money to do me in. You, young Sebastian, shall have the privilege, due to your high vocation, of dying more nobly—shot through with a dozen arrows sent into your soul by the sweet, smiling faithful, your body exposed and manacled to the church. How wrong the Docetists were—a God who refuses to alloy himself with our decadent flesh is no good at all. Incarnation!"

Stephen simply stared.

"And as long as we're on the subject of death . . ."

"I believe that you were on the subject of death, not me," rebutted Stephen.

"That's right. I must bring up the really important spiritual subjects when you are too squeamish to do so. (You clergy are such overprotective nannies.) I believe that our great fear of death is not that we fear that the dead shall leave us, but that they shan't. The horror we fear in their dying is not that they may abandon us for some 'better place,' but rather that they will haunt us, making our world miserable with their carping presence. Note the overlarge stones we place on graves. Lord, I hope that this big bench will keep dead Mrs. Jones wherever she is! That's just one of the reasons (and this is solely my modest theory) why people avoid church— church risks bringing them into too close contact with the deceased. This vale of tears is trying enough without being haunted by the undead, those who ought to leave us be rather than loitering here to bother us at the least opportune times."

"I still suspect that you are making fun of me," said Stephen.

"This isn't about you, dear boy. I'm doing a poor job of expressing my deep gratitude."

"Gratitude?"

"Like many mere laity, I feel much indebted to you clergy for assuming the weight of divine summons. We hope that the Lord will be so preoccupied with commandeering the lives of you clergy that he will leave the rest of us damn well alone!"

"Wild."

"*Sursum corda!* In your charmingly adolescent piety, you are a young man set apart, summoned, God's hand upon you taking you God knows where. Quite wondrous, and also a bit intimidating to us lowly laity."

"Sometimes you seem—and I hope you won't take this the wrong way—so cynical about the church, this church," ventured Stephen. "Why are you here every time the doors open, like this morning, doing this kind of work?"

Jane feigned indignation. "That I am attempting to avail myself of God's appointed means of salvation does not mean that I must approve of the inconvenient, necrotic, tasteless means that the Almighty has appointed, does it? Alas, *extra ecclesiam nulla salus.* Shelley, or was it Voltaire—sounds like Voltaire, but it probably was that little fake Shelley—said, 'I could believe in Christ if he did not drag behind him that leprous bride of his, the church.'" As she spoke, she pointed out each word in the air with yet another lit cigarette.

"Besides, if I sound cynical to you, it is simply because of the wisdom of my years. The great A. J. Liebling, my favorite *New Yorker* literatus, said that 'cynicism is often the shamefaced product of experience.' Or as Confucius says, 'The man'—and here I presume the philosopher would include the bothersome old maid—'who understands the Tao in the morning is content in the evening.'"

"Geeze. I better get back inside," said Stephen, embarrassed. "Latin, Shelley, Confucius. Once again, you're pulling me into water over my head." How much was Jane's philosophical/theological brash and bluster due to her being unmarried and alone?

"Not meaning in any way to cast aspersions upon your boss, but I remind you that the Scripture sayeth, 'I am God; I kill and make alive.' That's the one to whom, in ordination, you have sworn lifelong fealty. And as Moses knew, few come close to God without being badly burned by the encounter. Take care, young Sebastian. Keep ever before you how your progenitor, Saint Stephen, ended, and sweet Saint Sebastian too," said Miss Marple as she stood up, straightened her skirt, seized Stephen, and marched him back inside, plodding forth in her green goulashes. "We'll be throwing rocks at you eventually, goaded by our insatiable need. Oh well, I was glad when they said unto me, let us go into the house of the Lord and do the Lord's grubby work. *Labor et Orans.* Surely this will sufficiently atone for all my lies to generations of pubescent dolts, encouraging them to go to college when I knew full well they were just barely trade school material."

"Shush!" hissed someone from the door of the Walter Rauschenbusch Lounge.

"Shush *yourself*. You need not silence me in order to chat with God," Stephen heard Jane retort as he lugged his box down the hall.

∾

"Mr. Kim, well, the thing is that we have been pleased to have you in our church for the past year or so."

"We pleased too," said Kim. "We love our church."

"Well, actually, *our* church, though it is good that you have felt welcome here at Hope, so in a way it is your church too."

"Yes, yes. We all one church. We all brothers in Chwist."

"In a manner of speaking. And you have provided a much needed ethnic, that is, *multicultural* flavor to our congregation," said Quail, "for which Dr. Lupino is appreciative. Diversity is one of our goals, though as you may know we had hoped for Nigerians."

"We like it here. I never thought I serve such nice church as our church," Kim said, grinning from ear to ear.

From there Quail took Kim through a torturous exposition on how Dr. Lupino had directed an "evaluation of our relationship with our Korean friends." When Kim asked, "What you mean by 'evaluation'?" Quail finally mentioned the rancid smell of the cooking, adding that Kim "ignored Hope's competent, consecrated chef" who makes superfluous "amateurs loose in the church kitchen."

Kim, still grinning, narrowed his eyes as if he were trying to crack some incomprehensible puzzle.

"So I fear that we have come to the end of the road, so to speak," said Quail.

"What road you speak of?" asked Kim.

"Why, the road that has enabled you to use the Hope facility at minimal cost, the road that has given you license for full building usage (except the kitchen), although you contribute virtually nothing for upkeep. This road."

"We pay rent every month," countered Kim.

"That's not rent! A pittance. My God, what you pay doesn't begin to meet the cost even for the cleaning of our gutters. Do you think you could go out on the open market and find so grand a place for what you are paying us?" Quail immediately realized that was the wrong thing to say since he was about to insist that Kim go out on the open market and find another place.

Quail noted that Kim's congregation, unlike Hope's, was growing, and growth caused problems for Hope, "unaccustomed as we are to the way that you Koreans multiply. Our antiquated plumbing is sensitive to overuse." He advised Kim to "try the Baptists," who were "more comfortable with the concept of church growth."

"We happy right here in our church," said Kim, the slightest smile playing over his face. "Me Arminian; most Baptists five-pointer crypto-Calvinists."

"Your theology is inconsequential. Dr. Lupino feels strongly that you should seek another road, a more suitable . . ." He cut himself off, not wanting to sink deeper into metaphorical mire.

"Is this about money?" asked Kim. "Go ahead. Name price. Kim try beg people for love offering, though many my people have tough time right now. Dip in technology stocks crucify us. So why this church rich but still want to squeeze Koreans?"

"Now that's just unfair," said Quail, his voice rising. "After all that we have given—in sincere Christian hospitality—for you to imply, no, to outright assert that we don't want you here, is terribly unfair. If you only knew how expensive this building is to maintain, you would understand why we must be vigilant in our stewardship of this architectural treasure. The cooking is but the tip of the iceberg."

"What iceberg?"

"My God, man, it's a figure of speech! A, a . . . *metaphor!*"

Kim seemed not to be getting his drift, so Quail plowed on. "We no kick you out. Rather, we are offering to help you find a more suitable location for your bourgeoning congregation. Perhaps something evangelical."

"We like this place. Though sometimes my people ask why no peoples from your congregation ever worship with us. Now Kim know," he said with quiet, disarming determination. "You no like Korean peoples."

"One of your annoying tendencies is to move into this sort of pig Latin whenever the conversation is not going your way, Kim. My God, you have a degree from one of our finest seminaries. This me-no-understand-your-language is disingenuous of you, if not downright deceitful."

"It my seminary, not 'our' seminary," said Kim, his eyes now steely and focused upon Quail. "You no go to Princeton."

Kim rose. "Kim understand. Can we pray before I leave?"

Sensing a devious attempt to maneuver him into a difficult bargaining position with this prayer ploy, Quail said, "That's unnecessary."

"There always need for prayer," said Kim as he turned and left, muttering something in Korean—maybe a prayer, maybe a curse.

"I've never known a Korean who wasn't a fundamentalist," Quail observed. He sought consolation from the bottle in his bottom desk drawer. Once again he had been asked to do the dirty work of the church, and once again—in an institution full of lily-livered business virgins and commercial incompetents—he had demonstrated his sacred worth.

ᖇ

Simon was dispirited by his initial look at the lections appointed for the Sunday creeping toward him. Dutifully obeying the liturgical directives of his seminary professors, he had fallen into the practice of preaching from one of the assigned lessons of the Common Lectionary. Why? Scripture kept lurching toward some wild assertion, or lapsing into some improbable attribution of divine prowess, utterly unpalatable to modern, thoughtful people, remote and insensitive to human need.

The challenge he faced this morning was not so much with the arcane intricacies of biblical interpretation but rather how to mine the Acts of the Apostles when his brain (or some other organ) preferred to focus only upon Sybil. Ah, she was special! While he had dared to hope for a relationship with Sybil, he was unprepared for her receptivity, her unabashed encouragement, her eagerness, even. In just a few weeks, he and Sybil had moved from a vague, fond wish in his mind to much more. She was teasingly flirtatious without being vulgar. She knew art. Had traveled widely. Although she had never known a life that was not well financed, she was wonderfully unspoiled by her resources. In a word, nonchalant.

She also knew how to move. It was hard to believe that Sybil had not been a dancer. *Lithe.* That's the word for her—*lithe.* She knew how to hold a glass or a cigarette lithely. She was a character in a Noel Coward play, yet even lither.

Admittedly, the invocation of some biblical text, preferably just before he rose to speak his sermon, had the effect of bestowing upon his sermons an air of authority and weight. His use of the lectionary Scriptures was his sole curtsy to the tradition, and what harm in that? Fat chance that any in the congregation would ever take the trouble to ask, "What do these sermonic musings have to do with the Scripture that has just been read?"

Again this week, as in so many others in Eastertide, only a portion of the first lesson, Acts 2:41–47, held promise, if for no other reason than its sheer absurdity: ". . . many wonders and signs were being done by the apostles. All who believed were together and had all things in common; they would sell their possessions and goods and distribute the proceeds to all, as any had need . . ."

He smiled at the incongruity of Acts 2:41–47 in the context of Hope Church. (The only thing that enabled them to say with conviction, "In God we trust," was that the phrase was imprinted on currency and coin.) If Acts is truthful, why do none of the gospels speak of this redistribution of wealth? (Well, there was Jesus and the rich man, but happily, the rich man disobeyed Jesus' "go and sell all that you have and give it to the poor.") The author of Acts has a penchant for exaggeration. Easier for a doublewide tractor trailer to parallel park in a handicapped spot than for a trustee of Hope to squeeze into the kingdom of God clutching his stock portfolio, Lexus, debutante daughter, trophy wife, and widescreen, high-definition TV.

He wondered what Sybil was up to this afternoon. He had been a model of self-restraint, not suggesting to her that they meet this evening. He had a committee meeting, but nothing that could not easily be disposed of. What he most wished was for Sybil to call, to say that she couldn't live without him, that he must drop everything, rush right over and make her day. But there had been no call, and it was close to five.

The last time they were together, he had noted that Sybil was not afflicted by that malady that strikes so many women her age—sagging upper arms. Sybil was not only lithe, she was taut. Her tennis had paid off. *Taut.*

Though the absurdity of the text from Acts aggravated Simon, his fertile imagination uncovered a creative entry point for this Sunday's sermon. Experience had taught him to focus upon the most ludicrous aspect of a given biblical text as a way of hooking listeners. He was blessed, though more traditionalist preachers might call it cursed, with a congregation that appreciated a preacher who helped them—with a minimum of intellectual fuss and bother—to dispose of biblical texts that were impervious to thoughtful interpretation. Thus inspired, he began to tap merrily.

Perhaps there was a time when readers took such claims literally. Our forebears in the faith were distinguished by their fervor, not their intellectual rigor. Now, in the aftermath of whatever happened at Easter, their challenge was to engage life in the light of their inner experience of what had occurred in (they assumed) the resurrection of Jesus. They had a collective emotional experience (that we now call 'resurrection'), leading them to unusual spiritual practices.

Our challenge is different.

(Pause for emphasis, followed by a move toward recommended action by the listeners.)

Our task is to rethink the faith, to engage in the bold, risky work of reframing the faith in a way that is more suitable to the demands of our age. While we honor the achievements of our ancestors in the faith, we recognize that unlike us, they lived in a time of great poverty and imperial oppression, so their too enthusiastic claim that they now had "all things in common," selling their possessions and distributing them to the needy, is understandable, but only as Semitic hyperbole.

We must venture forth spiritually. We must think globally, that is, inclusively, yet always in the spirit of Reinhold Niebuhr—realistically.

It may have been enough for the primitive church to laud the efforts of a few who, in the first flush of religious devotion, sold all their possessions. But the long-term applicability of such behavior? Living in a democracy, having positions of social responsibility—as people in this congregation tend to do—we must be more thoughtful than they.

Here Simon decided to refer to the historical figures in the windows of the sanctuary. They, in their day, refused to swallow whole the Christian faith pushed upon them by the ecclesiastical establishment. They creatively, courageously reworked the faith to suit their needs. At first he thought of Margaret Sanger, but there might be some smart aleck who would bring up Sanger's eugenics—one of the challenges of preaching to an informed congregation like Hope. True, Sanger wanted fewer yellow and brown babies, but if they could overlook Paul's homophobia, why quibble over her eugenics?

He used Jane Addams and her Hull House as his prime illustration, carefully distinguishing her from Jane Adams the actress. The use of a woman, any woman, was sure to appease half the congregation. As he spoke, he would gesture toward the window for effect.

I give thanks that Hope is a place where thoughtful people can engage in honest, forthright reconsideration of the faith. I am sure that most of you have been attracted to the Hope family because you are the sort of person who refuses to take things at face value.

"They held all things in common." Really?

My eye falls, rather, upon the words, "many wonders and signs were being done by the apostles."

He recalled one of Sybil's paintings, a strange blue-and-green night vision of a German brothel, *Nacht Wunder*. She was a wonder, day or night, a sign, to be sure. Oh, that Sybil might call and make his day.

That which marvels me, is not divine wonders sent from heaven, but signs and wonders wrought on earth by a humanity come of age. In our wrestling with the faith, in our creative reworking of the ancient Semitic tradition, we are working "signs and wonders" in our own day. We, who have made such strides to overcome centuries of racial prejudice and traditional economics, are continuing the best of the apostolic tradition. We are Jane Addams. We are living the resurrection faith as we think our way into a new day, all under the benevolent, watchful eye of God, who wants us to be all that we can be.

Looking back over what he had written, Simon was well pleased. He was particularly fond of his closing reference to God—spiritual without being preachy.

Simon's practice was to construct a full manuscript to ensure right wording, then, usually on Saturday mornings, transpose the manuscript into outline. No one could accuse him of slavery to his notes. Early Sunday morning he would do a run-through before a full-length mirror, noting opportunities for gestures, attentive to pacing and tone. Eye contact is essential. The ideas must be right, but even more so the gestures.

In the final moments of his sermon construction, just before he put the thing to bed, he modified the conclusion to read, *as we think our way into a new day, a thoughtful church for thoughtful people, using the gifts that we have been given—particularly intellectual gifts—all under the benevolent, watchful eye of a generous God who wants us to be all that we can be.*

After a moment's pause, he modified the final phrase to *who trusts us to be all that we should be.* He liked the moral tone of the imperative. Simon was a master of cajolement.

Slamming his desk drawer, sighing heavily, he abandoned restraint. Obeying his fulsome heart, he risked a call to Sybil.

∾

She had surprised Stephen earlier. "Could I come by and talk to you some afternoon?" asked Alexis. All Stephen knew about her was that she was the (hot) girlfriend of the (overly pious, exceedingly white) Jack Hodges. He really liked the way her voice sounded over the phone—throaty, raspy, but also sweet and seductive. So Stephen's first real opportunity to offer pastoral care came when he received a call from a (very well-built) young woman who was only slightly younger than he.

On Thursday the two convened in Stephen's little office. To prepare, he had straightened his desk by first tossing some of the books and papers into a bottom drawer. At last he tacked up on the wall his college and seminary diplomas; if this didn't bolster his credibility with Alexis, it would at least strengthen his own self-confidence. After further consideration, he retrieved the books and stacked them on the shelf behind his desk.

After politely inquiring about her summer job—she was a lifeguard, Stephen learned, which explained her deep tan and her raspy voice (probably had to yell at pool brats all day long)—Stephen ventured, "You said that you had a problem to discuss?"

"Well, I'm not sure if it's my problem or Jack's. Maybe this is really just a hang-up with me. I don't know. But I wanted to talk about it with somebody, a pastor like you, who has had more experience in this area than I."

Stephen thought—with consternation—about the few areas in which he might have had more experience than Alexis. He had been told, in his Introduction to Pastoral Care class, that he tended to talk too much, that he needed to engage in calm, empathetic listening, let the client do the talking. He had also been warned about proper pastoral boundaries when counseling the opposite sex. So he just sat there, smiling, intent on looking interested in what she had to say, but silently, calmly.

"Well, you know Jack's big story. Last semester, Jack had his awesome 'religious experience.' And, well, that's just about all he's been able to talk about since. He so badly wanted me to have the same experience, and I really wanted to please him, so I guess I sort of faked it, telling him that I had also had an 'experience'"—here she made air quotes—"that I felt the same thing he had felt, that I had asked 'the Lord into my life'"—more air quotes—"and all that. But I was just trying to be nice."

Faking a religious experience to please her boyfriend? That's new. She really looked good in her shorts and tight T-shirt. Athletic women always got to him. He wondered what Alexis looked like in a two-piece.

"And maybe this is the way you are supposed to act when you are really a Christian. But it's all Jack can talk about. What's the difference between religious fervor and spiritual obsession? Overnight he's changed from a nice guy who was fun to hang out with, who had a good sense of humor—a normal college guy—into this superreligious expert who has taken Christianity to the googol degree and bores everybody, slapping them in the face with Scripture and trying to drag them toward Jesus."

"And this has put a strain on your relationship?"

"I tell myself that I'm concerned more for Jack than for our relationship. He is no longer Jack. We've been together now for over a year. Jack told me that he wanted me to totally give my life to Christ because he didn't want to see us 'unequally yoked,' whatever that's supposed to mean. Is that how Saint Paul put it?"

"I guess," said Stephen, bluffing.

"Jack made a big deal of dropping out of his frat, saying that he, as a Christian, just couldn't sit by and tolerate the behavior of the other guys. I couldn't help thinking that he dropped out, became the big martyr, just to show everybody that he was so damned popular that he could pull a stunt like that," she said, shaking her head.

"Hmm," said Stephen, posing as thoughtful and analytical.

"And we have really tried to be open and honest in our relationship. I got burned bad by my last boyfriend. Jack and I have really tried to share everything. That's why we both decided that we would wait until marriage, or at least until after we're engaged, to really sleep together. So we could share everything. Of course, that doesn't mean that we are not normal; it's just that Jack, that is, both of us, have some boundaries in our intimacy that we don't cross. You know what I mean?"

Stephen, who for the last few minutes was feeling very, very uncomfortable, didn't respond. He fought back the image of Alexis in bed, angry with himself for his dirty, wandering mind.

"But it's like I'm not with the same person anymore," she complained.

"Do you think that Jack looks down on you just because he thinks he's taking his religion more seriously than you do?" asked Stephen.

"To be fair, I think that Jack works real hard not to look down on anybody. He says that he's more aware of his own sin than ever before, though I can't figure out what sin he's aware of since he's one of the best people I've ever been around. Squeaky clean. It's just that he wants us to share everything in common, to in all things be 'one flesh,' like the Bible puts it. So he wants so bad for me to think, to feel, and to experience what he has. Know what I mean?"

"I think it best for you to just try and be as patient as you can with Jack," said Stephen.

"And how do I do that? Got suggestions?" she asked.

Was she offended by his comment?

"To tell the truth, Alexis, I sort of know how you feel. Jack and I have had some conversations, and there are moments when he really annoys me with all his Jesus stuff," confessed Stephen. "So I guess when I say that you ought to be patient with Jack, I'm really talking to myself, trying to increase my patience with him."

"Really? Gosh. That helps. Like I thought that you, as a minister, would think that I was some kind of a real loser for not being as much into religion as he is," she said eagerly.

"Hey, think how old Jack makes me feel. I'm a pastor, for God's sake, or at least somebody trying to grow up and look like a pastor. How do you think it makes me feel for a younger, better looking jock to come in here and sound like he knows more about Jesus than me? He can quote Scripture I've never even heard of. Me, paid to be the Jesus expert! Jack is tight with the God I'm struggling to get to know."

Alexis giggled out loud. "That's great. I can't tell you how much better that makes me feel to hear that from you. That's just how I've felt."

Stephen immediately regretted that he had put things that way. "Look, Alexis. I'm happy for Jack. And I confess that I'm just a bit envious. He appears to have had an experience of God that I can, at this point in my own faith development, only dream about. But let's both remember—that's *his* experience. Not mine, and from what you say, not yours. But it's his and that's great. We just can't let Jack's experience sit in judgment on ours."

"Right. That's helpful too. Thanks. Good advice."

Stephen continued. "When I was a kid, I heard a preacher say that God doesn't call everybody the same way in the Bible. 'When God calls,' he said, 'God calls you by your very own name—Moses, or Saul, or Mary—not by somebody else's name.'"

"That's really, really great. Thanks. You've got a way with religion. I really appreciate that," said Alexis. "You are good at this stuff. Knew you would be. How did you know that you were supposed to be a pastor?"

"That's a long story," said Stephen. "I'm sure you don't want to hear all those gory details."

"I'm sure that I do, but I don't blame you for not wanting to get into all that. I bet it's hard going around with a sign on you saying, 'I've been called by God.'"

"Is that what you think about ministers?" asked Stephen. "That we've got signs on our backs? 'Caution: Don't Follow Too Closely—Called by God.'"

Alexis giggled and then disarmed Stephen by jumping up and hugging him, which he knew was not an appropriate thing for him to do, but what was he to do when a parishioner did it to him? "I'm so glad that I came and talked to you. I've never talked to a preacher who was so good at making things understandable and helpful. Thanks. I'll not take any more of your time. Thanks. You're great."

When Alexis breezed out the door, Stephen sat there for the longest time thinking. What had he said that was worth saying? How could his babbling have made any difference?

Yet she had said that he was helpful. Maybe more was happening in his conversations with people than that for which he was responsible. Was this the much discussed "ministry of presence" that was the focus of his pastoral care course in seminary? Don't worry about what to say; just be there with people, a ministry of presence. How could he be sure that what he said to her was a genuine attempt to be helpful and not his attempt to come on to her?

As he sat for awhile musing on ministry, he looked at the two rows of books that he had put on the shelves—books that he had been required to buy in seminary, many of which he hadn't read. Now that he was actually in ministry, would he ever read them? Could what he really needed to know about being a pastor be found in a book?

He picked up the absurdly large bundle of keys on his desk. Maybe there's not just one key to the kingdom. Why in God's name didn't somebody reduce the number of keys it took to get into this place? Six master keys?

As Stephen walked to his car, he called Thea, checking on the details for their dinner this weekend. He gave thanks to God that they were so much in sync with one another. She said that she could tell, from the sound of his voice, that this had been his best day at Hope.

Still, one of his great challenges in making this church job work was Thea. Last year he had given her some books to read, a little theological assortment. His hope was that if Thea read what he was reading, she would come to share some of his enthusiasm for ministry.

"When you are a cultural anthropologist," Thea attempted to explain, "you look at things more deeply than the average person. I am trained, when looking at the artifacts of culture, to be a skeptic."

Thea's skepticism, if that was what it was, wasn't very well thought through. It wasn't the result of some anguished, failed effort to believe, a dead end reached after a long journey; it was the befuddlement of the person who never takes the first step. But maybe Stephen was being defensive. He loved her whether she ever reached the point of belief or not.

It was a mistake to give her the books. She claimed to have read them, but when Stephen tried to discuss them with her, he doubted that she had. She said that she liked the "progressive stuff, sort of," but even that sounded like "folk discussing the nature of Martians. I just don't get it."

That was Thea. It wasn't that she was opposed to what he was doing with his life. She just didn't get it. Would she ever? When one day they got married—and they surely would—would Thea be supportive of his vocation? How could she if she thought that it was little more than a group of dumb people sitting around talking about the possibility of life on Mars?

∾

Mary entered her kitchen through the garage's side door. The phone was ringing. Mary did not own a cell phone, due to certain moral misgivings about the corporate practices of cellular companies. Burdened with a bag of groceries from the food co-op she frequented, she leaned forward, once in the kitchen, and kicked the door closed with her left foot.

"Hello, Lupino residence," she answered.

There was a short pause before a hesitant, barely audible woman's voice said, "I—I have some news for you. I am telling you this as a sister in the Lord. I . . . I want you to know that your husband is making a fool out of you with another woman, a member of the church."

Mary smiled slightly, raising her eyebrows, and pressed the receiver close to her ear, listening curiously. She was disappointed not to immediately recognize the woman's voice.

"And I—I want you to know that lots of us think it's a terrible shame. Many of us so admire your witness. And of course we believe in forgiveness of sin and all that, but you can still hate the sin and love the sinner. What he's doing is not right. You have many friends who care. We just—I just wanted you to know."

"Thank you," said Mary softly, politely. She heard the phone on the other end click.

Mary replaced the receiver in its cradle, feeling a bit smug in having her suspicions confirmed. Since Easter, Simon had seemed different. She marveled that he found time to engage in extramarital activity. He was a good manager indeed.

She felt . . . gratitude. Simon had apparently moved toward the separation that she had often contemplated but had been too busy to initiate.

She was also learning dimensions of Eastertide that she had not previously known—a resurrection, if true, is bound to release diverse reactions in people, good and bad. "Though I don't believe adultery is anywhere recorded as a reaction to the empty tomb," she said aloud, apparently to the refrigerator.

She quickly unloaded her groceries, pleased that the assorted vegetables made the refrigerator look less bare and neglected. Then she carefully placed the organically grown arugula in a prominent position in the vegetable bin.

Simon hated arugula.

❧

At long last, the zenith of Hope's year—the evening of the much anticipated garden party in the garth of the church, tenth anniversary of the gala soirée. The garden party had been the invention of Glumweltner; it signified that Hope was no ordinary church, that here culture and art mattered, that the winter of discontent was over and summer at hand, that "people like us" really appreciated good food and well-played music, and so forth. Ten years later Simon had conveniently forgotten that Glumweltner was the originator; he claimed credit for the event, even asserting, in a sermon on Mary Magdalene at the empty tomb, that the garden party was a sort of enacted parable of the resurrection.

Guests gathered for an hour of champagne, repartee, and ogling. The women wore evening dress. More than a dozen men wore white dinner jackets, thus taking a moral stand, showing their allegiance to an earlier time when people knew how to behave and events like the garden party were typical. One could blink one's eyes and for a moment believe that the seventies had never happened and that people with values like those of the majority of Hope's members were still in charge.

Tickets went for three hundred bucks a couple, not only because the event was alleged to benefit "the many ministries of Hope," but also because the ticket price excluded those for whom such a gathering would have been uncomfortable.

This year's theme, "An Evening with Sondheim," featured the music of Stephen Sondheim, particularly his popular Broadway musicals. The garth and the passageways were stuffed with scads of spring flowers. A few years ago, Swank Blackstone—the town's most expensive florist, not even a communicant of Hope—got into his florist's head that he had been miraculously saved from death after contracting AIDS. In gratitude, Swank made a public deal with God in which he promised to give free flowers to the Hope garden party—for as long as he got good HIV checkups. When he made his pact with God, Swank assumed that his remission would be brief. His miscalculation had by now cost him a fortune. Bouquets of mostly daffodils and tulips—the price tag for finer flowers would be prohibitive, even as a divine offering—had been placed on every flat surface in the Gothic Hall. Two of the guests were even now taking a phone photo of Swank's hefty arrangement of flowers near a grisaille window depicting Christ's temptation.

Simon arrived unaccustomedly early, having planned unobtrusively to depart just after people moved into the Gothic Hall for the program. Quail—who had been present for thirty minutes under the pretense of watching over Chef, and who had managed to guzzle two glasses of bubbly in defiance of doctor's orders—saw Simon enter and knew, by his early arrival, that he was up to no good.

Though he was loathe to offer Glumweltner any encouragement for his schemes and extravaganzas, Simon found the garden party unobjectionable. Congregants who had moved heaven and earth to position themselves in upscale neighborhoods could, through the garden party, guiltlessly live where their cupidity had carried them and still receive a gracious pat on the head from Mother Church. Periodic acts of contrition were essential for a thriving church like Hope—the annual Christmas appeal for the homeless, an hour a month working at the soup kitchen, a discarded evening gown given to Mary's minions and destined for the Clothes Closet. All these charitable endeavors cumulatively suggested to Hope's membership: Never mind the actual words of Jesus; *Pax vobiscum.*

Simon valued the garden party as an efficient opportunity to rub elbows with movers and shakers of his congregation. He positioned himself near the entrance, in a tux, greeting the men with hearty, masculine handshakes, pastorally pecking the women on their cheeks. He stood, of course, by himself. Mary despised the garden parties, attending only one—ten years ago—which she vowed would be her last, and Mary was a woman of her word.

Simon carefully confined his social intercourse to chitchat—easy since everyone else had the same goal in mind. One jovial couple—Simon had not the foggiest idea who they were—laughingly lifted their glasses, saying, "This is our first church where wine is served, and good wine at that" (in Simon's experience, they would be short-termers at Hope).

Incorporation

The man who asked, "Simon, what would you estimate to be the percentage of our budget that goes for mission and benevolent work?" was easily deflected by a counter-question, tossed out to those nearby, regarding the prospects for the Chicago Bears next fall.

Quail had been instructed to monitor Chef's fluid intake for forty-eight hours prior to the party, and early indications were that the booze patrol was effective. Chef could be heard, officiously presiding in the church kitchen, screaming orders to half a dozen assistants and loudly cursing two dozen, tuxedo-adorned adolescent waiters from the church youth group. When Chef was on the wagon, his version of Beef Wellington could compete with that of any restaurant in town.

At eight, the suburban lords and ladies were herded toward the flowered archway and then into the Gothic Hall, done in an "I Love New York" theme, despite the pots of daffodils on every table. Spying young Jack Hodges, resplendent in a tux, a gorgeously bronzed young woman on his arm, Simon disappeared, camouflaged by a crowd of random seniors whom he judged to be more of the Hope Happy Hearts than evening soirée types. Periodically the door to the kitchen would open on the hall and a bevy of teenaged table servers would emerge with trays and salad plates, sometimes with Chef's curses wafting out of the kitchen.

Simon mingled among the bright company, managing never to get trapped in any conversation beyond polite greetings. Then, as he had planned, he expertly, surreptitiously slipped from the throng and eased his way unnoticed out the side door of the garth (he had earlier checked to insure that the door was unlocked and accessible to him for his getaway). Scurrying to his car in the darkest corner of the lot, he sped across town on the winds of eagerness to his much anticipated meeting with Sybil.

"It's fine with me to go to the garden party. I love those evenings," Sybil had said. Mildly chiding her for her imprudence, Simon had explained why social events at the church, with the two of them in close proximity, would be unwise.

"Any person looking into my eyes when you are nearby is sure to see how things are between us," Simon had said. "We dare not risk it."

"Suit yourself," she had said.

Free of the grip of the party, Simon wheeled into Sybil's drive, the trip from the church taking him a scant seven minutes. When she came to the door, Sybil looked radiant, stunning, and serene. Thus commenced their fourth assignation.

The two quickly sailed beyond the city lights into the darkened countryside for a tryst at Café Vienna, which overlooked the East Fork River.
Sybil suggested taking her car, which was fine by Simon. In the driver's
seat of the Mercedes, her hand draped languidly over the steering wheel,
she was luscious. By the time they arrived at the café, they could enjoy
little of the river's romance, since it was quite dark. But they didn't mind.
For one thing, the East Fork was hardly the Blue Danube, and for another
thing, darkness suited Simon's stratagems. He had thoughtfully made arrangements for a table toward the back, in the shadows, reserved under
the name Charles Lewis.

"I'll put the two of you in our Lafayette section," said the maître d'.
"May I help you with your jacket . . . Ms. Lewis?"

He led them to a small, dim corner, just as he had been previously
instructed (and tipped) to do.

"How is this, Mr. and Ms. Lewis?" asked the waiter. Simon was fairly
sure that the man's repetition of "Mr. and Ms. Lewis" was intentional—and
malicious, even after the fifty-dollar predinner tip.

But it would take more than a cheeky waiter to ruin Simon's evening.
In fact, the waiter's impertinence served to heighten Simon's excitement.
As he helped Sybil with her menu, he felt like a small boy engaging in wonderful mischief, pleased by her exposed shoulders, invigorated by a peek
over her plunging neck line. It was a perfect place, just the right evening
for *liasons dangerous*, indulging in forbidden fruit (and some grown-up
hanky panky).

Simon had lamb, seared rare, with mint sauce, because he recalled
hearing Sybil talk about how good the lamb was at some restaurant in
New York, though he was surprised when Sybil ordered the roast duck.
The meal seemed to Simon the best he had ever eaten, except for the dis-
appointingly predictable zucchini. The post-paschal lamb was rare and
bloody, though Sybil said that her duck was a tad dry.

"I want to make believe," said Simon, "that we are having a romantic
tête-à-tête in a little Left Bank bistro overlooking the Seine."

"I don't think there are any such bistros," dismissed Sybil.

"Set the scene. Tell me about Paris. Tell me what it's like to live free of
drab, bourgeois confines. I want to smell the croissants and taste the wine.
I want to hear the honking taxis. I'm Gene Kelly and you're Ginger Rogers.
Tell me what might have been."

"Simon, please. Nothing could be more blah and bourgeois than my
business-driven family. And I know very little of Paris. As I told you, I was

a messed-up kid incarcerated in Switzerland. My most vivid high-school memories are therefore of boring Swiss prep-school boys' fumblings and various sorts of illicit drugs slipped past the nuns rather than romantic locales in Paris." She ate with her fork in her left hand, he noted.

"But you, my dear, have lived. You have traveled. You have had the life I desired but never achieved," said Simon as he gazed at her, displaying regret intended to awaken her sympathy.

"Really now, Simon, for you to talk like that only shows that you know very little of me," she gently chided. "There's not much of me to envy, and I question the intelligence of those who do."

She seemed to tire of dinner table banter, suggesting that they adjourn to the patio overlooking the river. There they found a corner, leaned against the railing, and gazed into the almost total darkness, the river flowing somewhere below them.

Finding it difficult to elicit a recounting of her intriguing past, Simon reverted to the subject with which he was most familiar—himself. It is commonplace for an infatuated man to assume that the object of his crush has a proportional interest in him. Simon talked at length. As Sybil sipped her wine and listened to his monologue, she periodically raised her eyebrows—signifying a modicum of interest. Simon's first-person narrative described his parents, his hometown, the drugstore where he worked after school, and his inability to go on the senior class trip to Washington because he lacked the funds.

Then he talked about the path of his career, his mother's untimely death, and again he went over his memories of his year in Scotland (which in his imagination had been magnified until they were all out of proportion). Sybil politely did not interrupt him with a reminder that he had narrated much of this to her a couple of weeks ago. They (he more so than she) spoke in low, hushed tones, he occasionally stroking her arm when he wanted to emphasize some point that he was making, she staring into the dark. He suggestively placed a hand upon the small of her back. She did not refuse.

Anyone who might have happened upon them on the restaurant patio would have easily concluded that the two were engaged in a full-fledged tryst, though anyone would have also seen that he appeared to be more heavily invested than she. As for Sybil, she continued to be impressed by Simon's unreliability as a witness to his own life, though she had long since given up trusting any man's estimation of himself.

At that very moment, unseen by the dawdling paramours, a decomposing body floated by.

Simon—who had exercised calculated, heroic self-restraint in the past few weeks—thought it wise to risk a brief reference to his marital situation as a way of testing the waters.

"I'm sure, should things work out as I feel things might, as I pray things will, I shall need formally to end my lamentable marriage. Of course, you and I both know it hasn't been a real marriage in an awfully long time."

Sybil's only response was to smile and lift her eyebrows knowingly as she sipped the last of her dark red wine; she was, Simon presumed, in full sympathy with the path he was taking.

"When that time comes, there is no prospect of it being a bloody sort of divorce, and all can be accomplished without any sacrifice in my career," he continued. "No one will be surprised, I can tell you. Least of all Mary. I don't expect much fallout from the powers that be at church. I chastise myself for waiting so damn long to bring things to a head. Uncharacteristically indecisive of me, I can tell you."

Sybil continued to sip her wine and stare into the dark—smiling, saying little. At one point, she did ask casually, "But why should you want to go through all that rigamarole?"

"So—so that I can focus more exclusively on you, on us," Simon replied. "I want a new life, and I want you to take me with you. I am a bird wanting only to be free. To soar. I want to swing open the door of the cage and fly to freedom with you."

"Well, that's wonderful, but back to your impending split with Mary. All I ask is that you keep me out of it. I've had more experience with marital breakups than I care to tell. It's never as simple as one thinks, no matter how bad the marriage, no matter how well-intentioned the disputants. And I want to make clear that I never, as God is my witness, *never* intend to be a participant in the ritual of Holy Matrimony. Been there, done that."

Sybil's last remark was disconcerting, jarring. However, when he tossed it about for a moment in his mind, as he was to do frequently in the days to come, he thought it unsurprising. He was sure that once things were tidied up between Mary and him, he could easily lure Sybil into deeper waters. Although she had failed in her previous attempts at being married, she had never tried with him. He would need to be patient, but once finished with Mary and luxuriating in Sybil, a willing captive in her gilded cage, his way clear and without impediment, he was sure that his mix of self-sacrifice and self-restraint would pay off.

Though he wished Sybil would respond more actively, he took her body language as confirmation of the course that he was pursuing, despite any reservations she may have voiced. In his mind he filled in her great silences with his own eisegesis of her feelings. Rather than a turnoff, he found her reticence appealing, classy, and enticing, as he found just about everything she said or did, even what she refused to say or do.

Was she intentionally attempting to arouse his desire with her coquettishness, or was this just her way with men to whom she was attracted? When she played hard to get, she was irresistible. The candlelight and darkness, the intrigue, Sybil a woman of mystery and diamonds, the secret rendezvous at the riverside, the blood red lamb, and the wine conspired together to make for a dizzyingly magic evening.

Of course, there was no way for Simon to know that as they talked of romance on the patio, down below, a now mutilated body bobbed by— that of a prominent member of the congregation, one taken by the same river that seemed romantic to Simon.

Later Sybil thrust the sleek, black Mercedes out of the restaurant parking lot, laughing with Simon as they gave some couple a scare, brushing past them on their way out, and sailed back towards town, averaging at least ten to fifteen miles an hour over the speed limit. Sybil at the wheel, Simon snuggled close. On this delightfully warm spring night, with the top down and the wind flowing over them, allowing his hands to be guided by impulse, Simon took flight, reborn—or at least twenty-five again—for the first time in a long time happy, redeemed.

"I am so very content," he whispered into her ear, placing his hand atop hers on the gearshift, giving her a boyish smile. Though she said nothing in response, Simon surmised that she was being silently reflective, thoughtful. Possibly she expected more this evening, if he knew anything about women. He didn't want to appear pushy, adventurous, too eager, and certainly not desperate. He had made a couple of moves, had put a few things on the table for her consideration so that she might grow accustomed to the idea of the two of them together, happy and free. Warmed by the wine, for now that was enough.

When they reached Sybil's house just before midnight, they stood in front of the door like teenagers on a second date; Simon dared to hold Sybil tight and kiss her passionately, unreservedly, lifting her close to himself, moving his hands up and down her soft, naked back. She responded in kind, which indicated to Simon that he had been wise not to expect much more at this point. He had not arrived at his destination, but he was clearly swimming in the right direction. His careful calculation not to rush things, just as he had planned, put everything right on schedule.

"Good night, my love," he said as they parted. She showed him a beguiling, knowing smile as she turned, fumbled the key into the lock, and slipped into her lair.

So there was a good God after all. Between Elm and Jackson streets, Simon recounted the indignities that he had suffered: custodianship of a decrepit spinster of a church building, parsimonious trustees, unruly confirmation classes, clogged plumbing, an unbridled staff, carping evangelicals, disinterested teenagers, condescending laity, unproductive secretaries, ponderous Scripture, pompous musicians, a preoccupied wife. It was as if at last his sufferings were being redeemed. At last a recipient of grace, he was being given a gift. He offered a wordless prayer of thanksgiving.

As he drove home he had the good fortune of finding a station that was playing Sinatra. Sailing along darkened streets, considering the last years of his marriage, comparing their drab, gray lifelessness with his present vitality and soaring euphoria, Simon thought to himself, *C. S. Lewis was right. We are "much too easily pleased." I see it so clearly now. I have contented myself with far too little. But, by the grace of God, there is still time.*

He was blissful, soaring, as Ol' Blue Eyes sang,
I've lived a life that's full
I've traveled each and every highway
And more, much more than this, I did it my way.

5

The Fifth Sunday of Easter

Quail was perspiring heavily even before he stooped and entered the organ chamber. At his age, and in his degraded condition, climbing the fifty narrow stairs from the balcony all the way up to the chamber—without air conditioning, in this early summer heat—was foolhardy.

"God, it must be over a hundred degrees up here," he panted to Grimballs. "And musty too. I supposed at this height, even with the air conditioning blasting below, it was hot as hell up here, but my God."

"From now through the rest of the summer, temperatures stay well over a hundred up here. But you shall sweat even more when I show you what's facing us," said Grimball. "Talk about hell. This old girl may be about to keel over, sad to say. That makes her similar to most every seventy-five-year-old woman I know."

"I thought you told me that we were all fixed up with that restoration work we did a few years ago," said Quail.

"Must I explain this to you yet one more time? That was not restoration, only minor repairs. There's quite a difference between repair and restoration. A long way between renovation and restoration, for that matter. I have attempted to enlighten you on multiple occasions. I even attempted to get that old spinster Niculous interested in the project. I hear he's loaded and got nowhere to dump it."

"Hardly know him," gasped Quail.

"Now I shall show you. I'm surprised that you so quickly forgot. And the repairs were over a decade ago, by the way." Sweat was beginning to mat down his dyed hair.

"Repair, restoration, renovation, who gives a damn? All I know is it cost a fortune," said Quail, wheezing, wiping the sweat from his clean forehead. "If it's not the pipes to the toilets, it's the pipes on the organ. This building will kill me."

"Now see those large pipes over there," Grimball said, pointing to the gigantic lead pipes that filled the rear of the room. "Those are among the most troubling. The *bombarde*, for instance—so important to us when its full thirty-one feet are booming to the congregation. An informed eye would note the crimping, better known as 'smiling,' that is occurring toward the mouth. See it? The weight of the lead pipe gradually pushes down over the years, causing the mouth of the pipe to bend ever so slightly. And on top of that, every one of those pipes has a leather pad at the mouth that allows air into the pipe when I push one of the keys on the console. Do you know what that means? Every one of those pads is dry and deteriorated, in urgent need of replacement. Now!"

"Why?"

"Can you think of any seventy-five-year-old leather that's still in working order? Leather gets brittle, dries out, goes bad. And in this heat. Look at poor old Herb's shoe-leather face and you'll see what I mean."

Quail did not laugh. "This heat is drying me out too. The air is thin. And how much will that stuff cost?" he asked.

"Lots. And it's not 'stuff'—it is the heart and soul of a priceless artistic creation. The guys who do this sort of work—one of the best is in Chicago, *if* we are lucky enough to get him—are true artists in their own right. There's no telling how much it will cost. They probably won't even give us an estimate." Grimball's usually well-kept, reddish-blonde hair now drooped in long, wet strings down all sides of his head.

"They will if they do work for us," pronounced Quail, sweat streaming down his puffy, reddened face.

"If we can get him, and if he agrees to come, I will not tolerate your making crude demands upon him," declared Grimball, wiping the sweat from his brow with a large purple handkerchief. "As I say, he is an artist, and one cannot reduce art to gauche monetary calculation. Now, over there, that's where the wiring comes in from the console. Disaster waiting to happen. All must be digitized. That console down below, at the keyboard, has something like a thousand electrical switches. That thing could blow any Sunday, and if it did, this whole beast would be brain-dead. Silent as a corpse. And then, pray tell, what would we do?"

No response from sweating Quail to Grimball's alarmist rhetoric.

"And how would you look, pray tell, if word got out that you knew we were in trouble but you sat on your miserly little butt and did nothing? Picture the congregation sitting here silently on a Sunday morning underneath a mute organ. Picture Simon's indignation."

"Surely you overdramatize, as you often do," said Quail.

"Are you in possession of any electrical appliance that's more than seventy five years old and still in working order? It's not rocket science, is it?" asked Grimball, words dripping with sarcasm as his face dribbled with sweat.

Thus Grimball's grim prognosis. Rust and corruption here, rot over there, neglect everywhere. The organ, Quail was informed, was probably a "mistake" when it was installed. The company that produced it was mainly a builder of large theater organs—which explained all of the superfluous (and now mostly inoperable) special stops with their tambourines, drums, xylophones, bells, and whistles. Fun playthings in a theater or a ballroom in the twenties, but pointless in a church in any age.

"I'm getting light-headed," pled Quail, "I must be near heatstroke. Or heat exhaustion? I can never remember the difference. My clothes are soaked. I feel like I might pass out. You should have told me to dress for this steam bath. Look at my shirt, it's ruined. There's no air in here."

"Alright, alright. Class over. Five more minutes of this bellyaching and I would kill myself. You are next to hopeless as a student of the organ. Just turn around and head back out that door, but be sure that whatever you do you don't . . ."

It was too late.

". . . *dare shut that door!*" Grimball screamed.

Bang! Quail, in carelessly, hurriedly lurching to open the door and escape, managed to shut it, grabbing the knob out of the leather safety loop that held it open and then thoughtlessly allowing it to slip out of his sweaty hand. It locked instantly, slamming shut, a coffin lid whamming down, entombing them in the hell of the organ loft.

"Idiot!" yelled Grimball. "Now you've trapped us. We can't get out of here. God help us! Moron!"

"You mean to tell me that this door locks from the outside? Only the outside?"

"Of course it locks from the outside. Its purpose is to keep unqualified people out. This instrument is priceless," gasped Grimball. "How was anyone to know that someone so dumb as you would ever be allowed in here? For nearly eight decades that leather loop was sufficient. No one has ever had a problem before—until I allowed you in here."

"Well, this damned 'priceless instrument' will be the death of us both," said Quail, his voice barely a whisper, "and all because of your stupid leather loop. We will die up here, sweating to death like dogs, doomed."

"Shut up, you fool," ordered Grimball. "Help!" he screamed at the top of his lungs. "Hello? Help! Anybody? Help! We don't have much time. We're dying up here, like pigs in hell. Dogs, I mean! Help!"

Both of them then tried screaming together. "Help! Help!" Quail unbuckled his belt and let his pants slip down to his ankles.

"What in God's name are you doing?" asked Grimball, a look of horror on his face.

"I'm attempting to survive. You had better strip down, too, if you want to make it through this heat."

They both ripped off their clothes, all but their underwear—blue speedo briefs for Grimball, printed boxer shorts for Quail. In a grand display of desperation, Quail then lunged backwards and grabbed an old broom handle that he had seen resting in a corner. He drew back and began to beat on a large organ pipe in hopes of raising a rescuer. Grimball heaved his girth at Quail, ripping the stick from his hands. "You fool! That's the *tuba mirabilis!* You are desecrating a priceless instrument! It's from Italy! Besides, who will hear us up here? It's a Thursday afternoon!"

"You stupid, dumb . . . asinine . . . faggot organist!" sneered Quail.

Grimball lunged, throwing Quail to the floor, both of them grunting, yelping, rolling in the dust of the chamber floor, one on top of the other, struggling in their nakedness. In his hysteria, Grimball bit Quail on his left arm. Amid the heat and the desperation of their situation, what shred of sanity they had brought with them into the death chamber was now vanishing. As they wrestled, they did indeed sound something like pigs, madly grunting and snorting. At one point, Grimball had the upper hand, wrapping his knees on either side of Quail's chest, bouncing up and down on Quail's bare, fat stomach, attempting to knock the last breath out of him, lacerating his chest with his gold bracelet. After a few minutes of kicking, biting, foaming, and gasping, they collapsed, lying there together on their backs, both of them spread-eagle on the floor in their underwear, sweaty and dirty, blood oozing from the cat scratches they had inflicted on one another's torsos, half-crazed with the heat.

"Oh God, I can't, I can't make it much longer," said Quail softly. "It's Thursday. We are doomed."

"I hope you burn in hell for shutting that door," countered Grimball. "What in God's name did you think . . . that leather strap . . . on the doorknob . . . was for? And that pipe can't be fixed by anyone outside of Italy

... except maybe the man in Chicago ... if we could get him. But he won't come without me to invite him."

"You, you," Quail gasped, "wretched *organist*."

Then they were both quiet, meditative, each staring at the ceiling of the chamber. Their breathing became less labored as they lay in a pool of dirty sweat, both men awaiting their certain, agonizingly sultry end. Contrary to what one might expect of two men in their situation, neither counted his sins—which for both were numerous, including sins of the flesh and of the spirit—nor did either use the opportunity for a last attempt at contrition. Neither made any gesture of obeisance. And neither dared to pray.

For his part, Quail meditated upon his ex-wife and how gladly she would receive the news that he had sweated to death like a dog, or a hog, or whatever, alone with a man whom he hated. The woman would never get her back alimony now, damn her. Serves her right. Damn her and her attorney. She and she alone had rendered him so destitute that he had been forced to push Niculous out of town (so he assumed) with just the barest threat of extortion for a good cause. While his hatred for her had been moderate and self-centered, now, realizing that he was near the end, he gave full reign to his contempt for her—for her collection of worthless, antique coffee mills that she took with her when she left, and for the way she had expertly squeezed him dry in the divorce settlement.

Grimball, on the other hand, gasped for breath, the heat searing his lungs, and lay there wondering what sort of memorial service would be held for him and whether Glumweltner would pick the right music or insult his memory by using a lot of nineteenth-century trash. Glumweltner would jump at the opportunity to make a final mockery of his artistic achievements at the organ. Everyone knew that Glumweltner had always resented him because he, unlike Glumweltner, had attended a first-rate conservatory. Glumweltner's D. Mus. was based on a short, derivative study of the choral music of Thomas Tallis, which was about as useful in his work at Hope as a study of the songs of Britney Spears. Thomas Tallis! Nasally music came into his consciousness. Morbidly correct English music. He was getting the fate he deserved, he admitted to God, for so thoughtlessly inviting an idiot like Quail into the sacred precincts. How he wished he could have died in combat with a more worthy artistic opponent.

Enslaved on the banks of the river Styx, Grimball cursed himself for not leaving detailed instructions for what was to be done at his funeral. He had often thought about last rites but had never gotten around to it because the church had failed to provide him an administrative assistant.

Who would have thought that he would die at Hope Church; this was only a way station, he had assumed, on his ascent, not the end of the line. And why had he not indulged in even more sinful acts, things he had secretly thought about doing but lacked the courage to do? Why had he not gladly moved from salacious imagination to action? All this—his life snuffed out, his career ended—for want of one small leather strap, a strap that any fool could have seen should not be thoughtlessly removed. A damned strap.

So this was hell: to be trapped with a man you detested, locked in sweaty embrace, the death throes of the doomed, and to die anonymously, all because of a lousy leather strap.

Then, just before Quail slipped completely out of consciousness, the hellish quiet was ruffled by a voice, barely audible, down below. "Hello? Dr. Grimball? Hello? You up there? You OK?" It was the sound technician, who, in checking the soundboard for next Sunday, happened to hear muffled banging as well as what sounded like guttural animal sounds emanating from the area above the chancel.

"Oh God. Help us. A key. Get the key! We don't have much . . . longer" gasped Grimball as he crawled on his stomach across the dirty floor toward the grill.

"You stupid, stupid fool," was all Quail could manage to whisper, being immobile on his back and nearing the seventh circle of hell.

The downstairs janitor, who had now joined the technician, shouted up, "You know that you don't let us have no key, Mr. Grimball. Remember? You said that only a qualified professional could get in the organ chamber. Remember? You said that nobody is allowed in there without your permission. We don't have no key."

"You idiot. You . . . organist," said Quail. "You didn't allow them to put this on the master key system? I had sent out a directive that clearly . . ."

Quail dragged himself across the floor, shoved Grimball aside, and, grabbing the grill of the organ screen, pulled himself up with his last ounce of strength. Through his tears and sweat, he yelled back, "Idiots! I order you as your chief supervisor. Get up here . . . *now* . . . and if you must, break down the damn door!" Issuing this command sapped all of his strength, and he fell back upon the floor, weeping.

Grimball simply lay on his back and, through tears, chuckled hysterically to himself.

The door, though metal, was surprisingly easy for the two saviors to kick in. When they did, they were treated to the sight of two middle-aged men—one naked down to his briefs, the other in boxers—drenched in sweat, smeared with dirt, crawling on their knees toward the open door. Grimball was engulfed in tears, weeping profusely, mumbling incoherently, "Never again will I allow a nonmusician . . . It's from Italy . . ." He struggled to his knees and then fell into the arms of the janitor, to the janitor's dismay, whimpering something about "the strap."

"This damn building will kill me," Quail said. It was his benediction to them all as he slid on his pants and staggered down the stairwell, shirtless, sockless, shoeless, beltless, damning Grimball, cursing organists, indeed, cursing all church musicians everywhere.

꙳

Stephen was bitterly disappointed. The Hope Floats trip—his first undertaking, planned, guided, and led by him from the ground up—was a bust. How could something so well conceived have been such a flop? Designed to be a great way for high school–age youth to blow off steam the first week after school let out for the summer—presented to them as a high adventure, group-building event—was a fiasco. How was he to know that this week was hallowed by local high schoolers as a time for unrestrained carousing at the beach? That was their idea of celebrating the end of the school year—losing themselves in mindless, alcohol-induced bliss, not some dumb float down the local river. Only five of the more than sixty prospective older youth signed up. Luckily, this afforded Stephen time to cancel most of the raft rentals without a great loss. But when the big day arrived, only one youth actually showed—one. James Thomas. One lousy kid.

"Well, James, looks like you and me is all there is," said Stephen, surveying an empty parking lot. "Beats me. I just don't understand."

"I figured as much," James said quietly. "All the kids go to the beach the week after school is out. It's like a tradition. Go get wasted for the week."

"I wish somebody had been nice enough to tell me," said Stephen. "This was to be when I got to meet everybody, the kickoff for the summer and all. And why didn't you go to the beach with the rest of 'em?"

Immediately Stephen wished he hadn't asked.

"It's OK with me if you don't want to do this," said James. "It's stupid for you to give three days just for one kid, just for me. You got better things to do than to waste your time with a nobody when you wanted to meet everybody."

"No, it's not!" reassured Stephen. "I've been planning this for the last four weeks, and I'm going to do it. You and I will have a ball. To heck with the others."

Without comment, James simply shrugged, walked around to the front of the rented van, opened the door, slammed it shut, and mutely slouched into the front seat. Stephen sighed. Stuck for three whole days on a camping trip with a kid nobody in school wanted to get wasted with at the beach—a lousy beginning for his first summer of youth ministry. He was, step by disappointing step, coming to the realization that the "youth ministry" of Hope was a fiction. "Building an excellent ministry to youth," Dr. Lupino's charge to him, in truth meant "raise the dead."

They drove to the river in almost complete silence. James had his iPod blasting in both ears even before they left the church parking lot. So Stephen listened to the radio, fumbling with the channels every few minutes as they drove through the countryside. After about a half hour on the road, James suddenly blurted, "None of the kids attend Hope because they want to, me included. We're all forced to be there, the few who are there. Hating church is about the only thing I've got in common with any of them. I have to come because Dad's on the board and Mom likes her Bible study group—stupid reasons for me to be there."

"Did they force you to come on this trip?" Stephen asked hopefully.

"What do you think?"

This kid had an attitude, for sure. Stephen wished to God that he had some backup plan, some legitimate excuse to spend only one overnight on the river. But he had already planned for a van to be at the pickup point the day after tomorrow. So he was doomed to three long, boring days of sailing downriver with the King of Sulk and couldn't figure how to get out of it now.

Over the next day and a half, James communicated with Stephen only sporadically, a cryptic comment here, a wordless shrug there. How could anybody, even a disgruntled teenager, have so little to say? Stephen patiently waited for James to open up, to respond to something, anything. But no, James just sat there, half-heartedly paddling in silence for hours, making no response to the egrets along the riverbank, seeing nothing curious about the fish that jumped up out of the water in front of them on the second morning, having no reaction whatsoever even to the used condom they saw on the second afternoon, and ignoring the mysterious half-full jug of milk that floated next to them. This guy was determined to be impressed by nothing in the world.

Incorporation

The river didn't help. The water level had subsided in the weeks after the most recent rains. A trip that was supposed to be something of an adventure now consisted of a slow, leisurely float downstream through water that resembled congealed gelatin more than wild rapids. When, every hour or so, they came upon some rare stretch of white water, Stephen looked eagerly over the prow in the hope of excitement. *Please let this be challenging*, he thought. *Please let our lives be threatened. Please let our raft be ripped apart by a rock. God send Leviathan to eat us. Anything.* The raft would pick up speed, but only briefly, bumping along through the bogus rapids, then settling back into a boring, dead drift.

When asked to look for firewood, James did so, but without comment or any trace of enthusiasm. Stephen chattered away to himself, hoping by chance to hit on something—sports, current events, the weather, girls, the Dow Jones Industrial Average, the movement to legalize marijuana, anything—that might pique James's interest. Nothing. Occasionally James would actually stare up at Stephen, but then would give him a look that said, "You are an idiot. If you don't want to be stuck here with me, think how I feel about you?"

As they sat in silence on the second night, watching their small campfire dwindle and sputter out (*nice symbol for the whole venture*, Stephen thought), a desperate Stephen finally broke.

"Look, man," he hissed through gritted teeth, "I can't take any more of this! You're driving me nuts. I think to myself, 'Maybe I was like you when I was sixteen.' I think that maybe you are just mad as hell at your parents for making you come on this trip. I think maybe that I was as screwed up as you when I was your age. But I can't take any more. I should be in the arms of my honey and I'm stuck out here with Holden Cauldfield! You probably don't even know who that is, do you? Say something! Talk to me!"

James looked across at Stephen and mumbled sullenly, "You were never like me. I am mad as hell at my parents, but that doesn't have a damn thing to do with you. This trip sucks."

Stephen said, "OK! Good for you. Now we are getting somewhere. Nice comeback." He couldn't help thinking how very plain and awkward James appeared, even in the dark.

"Shut up," said James. "I'm going to bed." He turned to straighten his sleeping bag on the big rock where they were perched for the night.

"Not on your life," said Stephen, grabbing James's shoulder. "Look. You are going to talk. You are going to tell me something I don't know.

Secrets. I'm a pastor, and I went into the ministry, broke up with the girl who I thought I'd spend the rest of my life with, made my father really angry by not going to law school, and alienated most of my college friends because I need to hear other's secrets. I'm a sick voyeur. So, you are going to talk to me and tell me every damn thing you know, every dark, dirty, demented thought you've ever had in your whole miserable little sixteen years, all of it, or I'll take this hatchet and make you an Ethiopian eunuch!" He lunged at James, seizing him by the collar of his jacket, pinning him to the ground, holding the hatchet menacingly over him.

James's eyes were wide with terror as he struggled with Stephen. "Man, you are nuts! Get off of me! Let go of me!" he screamed.

Stephen relaxed his grip and fell back in loud laughter, pulling his knees up to his chest and rolling on the rock.

James screamed into the darkness, "God help me! I'm trapped out here in the middle of the jungle with a nut case. Help me! Somebody! Anybody! I'm only sixteen! I'm still a virgin!"

Stephen shook with even more uncontrollable laughter. James laughed, too, bending double as he lay on the ground.

Stephen picked up the hatchet by the blade end and, pointing the handle at James, said, "I mean it. You start talking, and do it now or I'll use this thing. Facts! Lies! Secrets! Bullshit! Your favorite band, anything! Talk, damn you!"

James continued to laugh so hard he could barely speak. Only gradually he got words out. The first were, "Do you have a joint?"

"What? No! I want you cold sober when you are talking to me!" said Stephen. "This is *The Real World*, *Reality on the River*, *Church Trip Survivor*, *Big Brother*, and I want to know everything. Our own little reality show, right here and now."

"Well, I'm the kid no parent ever wanted," began James, in a soft monotone. "My parents are embarrassed to have such a below average son in such an above average neighborhood."

"Don't exaggerate or embellish," said Stephen. "Everybody disappoints their parents. You aren't that special."

"Shut up. When I want your psychoanalysis, I'll ask," grinned James. "Mom pays a guy two hundred dollars an hour to analyze me, and he has got an advanced degree in it so don't even try, you pop psychologist hack."

"Continue," said Stephen as he smiled and poked the fire in futility.

"So they sent me to a school they can hardly afford. I was the one person in the world who actually wanted to go off to school, but they wouldn't trust me out of town, so I'm here at this school that I hate and where everybody hates me. My dad doesn't make near enough money to put on the show they think our neighborhood demands. The only useful thing that I learned at their precious prep school was how to smoke dope! Ain't that rich?"

"So you hate the school?" asked Stephen. "You aren't that special."

"Thanks for your pastoral comfort. I'm at a school where the kids who aren't stoned are going to a bunch of Ivy Leagues that I don't have a prayer of getting into. And the kids who are stoned think I'm pitiful, a fake, a poser. Our school is divided into all kinds of cliques and gangs that fight with each other but unite over one thing: I'm the uncoolest loser they've ever met. Actually, everybody—teachers, students, janitors, and maids—got together and voted me the Most Pitiful of the Junior Class."

"Cynicism in one so young!" mocked Stephen, trying to sound like W. C. Fields. "I've been accused of that myself."

"It would all be funny if it weren't hell," said James pensively.

"It can't be as bad as all that," said Stephen half-heartedly.

"You sound like my dad. You mean you went to seminary for how many years so you could make some stupid comment that even my dad could make with no training?"

Looking at James, Stephen laughed, "You're right. It was a stupid thing to say. I don't know why I said it. I guess I said it because, well, like you, I feel so out of place. I feel so over my head. I felt a lot like you feel when I was sixteen, but about some different things. Talk about pitiful. What's pitiful is that I'm nearly ten years older than you, have been to Princeton Seminary even, and I feel a lot like a screwed up, dorky, loser of a teenager!"

"Shut up you nerdy little preacher, you nerd, you dork," James said with affection. "It's really nice to hear that my pastor thinks I'm a screwed-up loser."

Thus began hours of conversation—the two of them sitting on a high, flat rock overlooking the East Fork River under a canopy of blinking stars, talking well into the night. They lay back, each stretched out on his sleeping bag, and looked up into the sky. James talked about his two years of seeing a shrink, about the ways in which he was an embarrassment to his parents, about his older sister at Michigan who could do no wrong in the eyes of the parents, about his misery at school.

Stephen told James that while his was an uneducated opinion, whatever James was, he wasn't stupid. They talked girls. James admitted that he had yet to go out with a girl on anything resembling a date, and Stephen told him to relax. That would come with time. Eventually women came around. They learned to appreciate men who weren't jocks, but it would take time. Being in a regular relationship could be a pain in the butt at times, Stephen informed him—lots of phone time, full weekends, sharing, and talking about feelings.

James boldly asked, "Tell me about Thea. How did you know you were in love?" Then, "Have you ever cheated on her?" And finally, "Did you have sex in college or wait until afterwards?"

To the first question, Stephen answered, "Still not all that sure." To the second, "No, absolutely not." And to the third, "None of your damn business, kid."

Stephen did tell James that he and Thea, though very much in love, were still "in process." He told James something that he had never told anyone else, that Thea really didn't understand "the ministry thing" but that he was hoping once she saw him in action, in ministry, she would know how this is what God wanted him to do.

"I can't tell you how much more I enjoy bunking on this hard rock by the river with you than being up at the university lying in her arms," Stephen said to James with a grin.

"I guess I'm with Thea. I don't understand this ministry thing about you either. Does this mean that you, like, really think that there may be a God up there, somewhere beyond all that darkness?" asked James, staring up into the star-studded midnight sky.

"No," answered Stephen.

"No? Did you say no? Then what the heck are you a preacher for? No? You mean to tell me that you're working for a boss who doesn't exist?"

"No, I don't think there's a God up there, out there, hiding in the dark," Stephen explained. "I think there's a God down here, in here, in the dark. God with us."

"Hmm. I hope you are wrong about that," said James. "Wouldn't life be easier, things less complicated, if we could really prove, beyond a reasonable doubt, that God wasn't there, nothing beyond the blank sky and nobody down here next to us who cares, nobody to judge us, nobody looking down on us, nobody telling us what to do, nobody and nothing ever bothering about us?"

"Intriguing thought," said Stephen. "Not one I have ever had. God's existence always seemed self-evident to me. In fact, I've always felt sort of intellectually inadequate because I never really had any doubts about the existence of God. I sort of envy your doubt."

"I didn't say I doubted God existed. I just said that I doubted that it was a good thing for us if God existed," countered James. "Is the God who is, good or not? I just don't know."

"I need to talk to you about going to seminary," said Stephen, though James couldn't see him smile in the darkness. "They would give you an A+ at Princeton for that atheistic thought you just had." They laughed together.

At some point during the night, when the conversation lulled, James, looking down on the torpid, dark river below them, admitted, "You know, I've always been sort of terrified of water."

"Really? You don't show it," said Stephen.

"Acting!" shouted James. They laughed. "I must have had some kind of trauma as a kid, with my old man throwing me into the pool to sink or swim or something. It's just like something he would do. I still am, like, the worst swimmer in the world. But sometimes, when you look at that river below us, it seems almost like it wants us, like you could dive in, choke for a minute or two, let the water sting your lungs, and then settle back and sink, go with the flow, and you would be no more trouble for anybody."

"Paul said that when you go under the waters of baptism, you die," Stephen noted.

"Sure, like a baby could die with the two drops of water we put on their heads at Hope," James said.

Stephen made no comment. Whatever issues James had, Stephen knew that he was not equal to the task of finding a solution. Stephen felt he was in over his head when the talk turned from sports, girls, theological abstractions, music, and TV toward adolescent angst, maybe because he had too much of it himself. He was relieved when James again asked, "What kind of music do you like best?"

They slept until midmorning, covering their eyes against the rising sun. After a breakfast of a couple of energy bars and soft drinks, they paddled on down the river. James talked constantly, sometimes asking questions like, "Tell me one more time why you think you might be in love with Thea?" This was followed by, "When did you know what you wanted to do with your life?" And then, "So you really believe there's a God who gives a shit about us after all? I just don't get it."

Late in the morning, as they paddled themselves through a particularly slow stretch of water, large trees leaning inward, shading most of the river, James said, "I know that you would rather be anywhere than stuck out in the middle of nowhere with a nobody like me."

"My friend, you are wrong—once again. This is becoming my best day of the past month. Until we got out here, I didn't realize how confined I've been, how shut up, hemmed in, claustrophobic. Out here, away from church, it's like I can breathe. I've been in a room with no windows. These are the best talks I've had in my whole, mediocre two months as a pastor. You're the first person who's treated me like the person I thought I was called to be."

"Whatever," James said, and smiled.

Later, when they had finished their lunch, they pushed the float into the water for the last afternoon's run down the final stretch of the sluggish river before the car park and the waiting van pick up.

"Oh my God!" screamed James, pointing at something on the right bank of the river ahead of them. There, caught in the branches of a dead tree overhanging the river, was a body, or what was left of it, bobbing with the current. The carcass was morbidly white, naked except for some undershorts pulled down toward the knees, and missing one arm. It appeared to be a man, an older, bald-headed man.

∿

The next morning, Stephen, washed and recovered (though with the disgusting image of the rotting corpse forever etched into his brain), heard an always cynical and sarcastic Grimball picking out some sacred piece on the piano in his office. He decided to take the opportunity to unburden himself. He went down the hall and risked sticking his head into the music office. Grimballs, looking up from his Steinway, greeted him with, "Now what can I do for the newest, brightest star in our little galaxy?"

"Thanks for letting me barge in like this," said Stephen. "You have been really the only person on staff to reach out to me," said Stephen.

Grimball held up his finger in mock rebuke, "It's 'family,' Stephen, 'family,' not the cold, impersonal (and therefore truthful) 'staff.' Church requires you to keep our euphemisms in working order. And you are so adorable, why would anybody not want to receive a reach from you?"

"Right. Well, this is something serious that is really bothering me. I just don't have anybody else to talk with. And maybe I'm making too much out of this. I just don't know. And I really want you to tell me if I'm off base with this, but I've had something happen to me that I just don't know what to do with," said Stephen.

"You seem disturbed," said Grimball in an unaccustomedly serious tone. Swinging his knees over the piano bench in order to face Stephen, he said, "I'm flattered that you came to me, glad to know that you have a confidant other than that sad, big-bosomed old lady with smoker's breath with whom you are rumored to fritter so much time away. I knew that God had a special reason for preserving me from Quail's attempt to sauté me in that damned death chamber. Do continue."

Stephen knew enough not to comment on the story of Grimball and Quail's brush with death that was romping round the congregation. "Well, aside from seeing my first dead body, which has shaken me badly . . ."

"I can match you shake for shake. Quail almost made me a dead body!"

Stephen did not respond.

"Well, uh, Thea and I celebrated our first anniversary this past week . . ."

"Congratulations," said Grimball. "Young love is such an encouragement to us lonely old folks. One full year together; that's longer than most marriages around Hope."

"And we wanted to go someplace real nice to celebrate, since I'm now getting a paycheck. I wanted to have something to look forward to after the failure of the float trip. Well, anyway, we went to that Café Vienna south of town, the place that overlooks the river."

"Excellent call. I've been there a number of times," said Grimball. "I'm sure that you found that the damn river looks better when seen from above in a fine restaurant than it looks while eating beans out of a can on its muddy bank. Glad to know that you young folks appreciate quality. Best lamb in the Midwest. Wonderful desserts. I suppose you didn't have the extra dry martinis, did you? With a lemon twist, they're positively scrumptious. Sledgehammer to the brain."

"We had a great meal. Just perfect," Stephen continued. "But as we were leaving, as we stood at the entrance to the parking lot, trying to remember where we had parked, this big, black Mercedes just shot out of the parking lot. You could hear the tires squeal. I had to pull Thea back to the curb or the monster would have creamed her. I got a good look at the driver and passenger—and I cursed them when they raced by. It was a convertible, and because the top was down, even in the faint light of the parking lot I clearly saw Dr. Lupino in the passenger seat. Laughing. And the driver wasn't Mrs. Lupino."

"Hmm. Interesting. Let's see. If I had to guess, I would expect it had to be Sybil Vestal," said Grimball. "She has a black Mercedes ragtop. She has been a wonderful supporter of our music program. Quite a looker— smartest dresser in the congregation, save for Eleanor White, who, though she buys her stuff off the rack, manages to look classy in anything. So? Well, well, our pastor is stepping out, is he? Well, well, well, well, well," Grimball said, smiling, seeming to relish the thought.

"So she is a member at Hope?" asked Stephen.

"A lifetime communicant. Strikingly attractive woman of the world, probably our most sophisticated. I'm rather surprised that she would fall for Simon, and just a tad surprised that Simon would set his sights as high as her. Sybil could have any man she wanted. In fact, she has wanted and had dozens in our fair city—all colors, all ages, all persuasions, I hear."

"And maybe none of this is my business. Maybe this is the way that things are done here. But I got to thinking that, well, if I saw the two of them, surely I'm not the only person in town who could have seen them together."

"Possibly, although few in the congregation are likely to be clientele of Café Vienna. I know I've never sighted any of them there. And while I'm always grateful for any salacious rumor to be tossed my way, why did you pick me to share this delicious morsel of gossip with?" asked Grimball.

"Certainly not to gossip," said Stephen defensively. "Like I said, you are my friend, the only person I know whom I can trust with this. I just wonder if I have some sort of responsibility to say something to Dr. Lupino."

"And why in God's name would you do that?" asked the organist. "I can't imagine that conversation would go well."

"Wouldn't this imperil his ministry if it got out?" asked Stephen. "Couldn't this damage everything if word got out that our pastor is cheating on his wife?"

"That's hard to say," said Grimball reflectively. "In some more conservative churches, yes. But things are changing, my boy. Why crucify the pastor for doing what half the congregation does routinely and gleefully? A raunchy little romp is becoming run of the mill in our second-rate Peyton Place. Why should you and your beloved be the only ones so to enjoy one another, just because of the privilege of your youth?"

"But Dr. Lupino is married!"

"Yes, but have you no heart for Simon's marital confinement? Surely he must be miserable living out a life sentence with a virtual Mother Teresa!

I suppose your goal, in any airing of this with Simon, would be for Simon to take hold of the situation. I doubt that anybody who knows him, or the lousy state of his alleged marriage (little more than pious window dressing at this point), would be utterly shocked by this affair. I have enough faith in Hope that Simon wouldn't suffer much congregational censure. Still, when it comes to judgments about clergy and their exploits, people can be opprobrious. The laity are sometimes guilty of double standards. It might be helpful for him to be given the opportunity to manage things; he so loves a managerial challenge."

"So maybe let's just leave things as they are?" asked Stephen hopefully.

"No action could be the best plan of action for the moment. Simon could easily resent your interference and, in his resentment, make things tough for you. Count on me in the meantime to keep this in confidence. I can simply keep alert, and we can both pray that this was a happenstance revelation that God has reserved just for you and your beloved. For now, I would advise you to tell no one else about this. Have you?"

"Nobody! Not even Thea. That night I just stood there with my mouth open and didn't say a word. It really messed up the rest of the evening for me. I wouldn't dare spread this kind of rumor around," said Stephen.

"Good idea. A less principled and more conniving young man might attempt to leverage information like this somehow to improve his subordinate status, but I'm sure that wouldn't occur to a nice young man like you."

"What? Like blackmail, extortion? Nobody would do a thing like that," exclaimed Stephen, "particularly to the guy I owe my big break in ministry to."

"Of course you wouldn't. I'm just thinking how fortunate Simon is to have a young man of your character who can be trusted with such potentially damaging information. It's downright providential. So let us just keep this between the two of us, man to man, so to speak. I'll keep my eyes open, my ears cocked, and should I think it's good to say something to Simon, so that he can be proactive, I will do so, but not unless I check with you. And of course, I'll not mention by whom I came into the possession of knowledge of his little escapades. Promise. Lips sealed."

"Thanks," said Stephen. "And should you think you ought to say something to him, I hope you'll make it clear that I came to you out of genuine brotherly concern for his ministry. This is all so new to me."

"As you noted at the first, we are friends," said Grimball, reaching his hand toward Stephen's.

Not three minutes after Stephen was safely out of sight, Grimball carefully closed the cover to the Steinway, put away his music, and made a phone call. "Simon, can you see me sometime soon? It's a matter of some urgency. This afternoon? Excellent. I believe you'll be interested. I'll scoot down the hall and be in your office in a jiffy."

ᘒ

"You may celebrate that I've eliminated your Korean problem," Quail announced to Simon at that week's staff meeting. "Tony Soprano couldn't have been more effective, though it will cost us a couple of grand to do it—conniving Kim could talk you into paying him a thousand bucks while thrusting a dagger through your heart. He's a tough cookie, Kim. Tried to play hardball. But it's done."

"We didn't have a Korean problem, I remind you, before you muffed things, Johnson. Besides, I simply asked you to rectify our dilemma with the Koreans. Did I ask for their banishment? I always thought they contributed to our diversity."

"How did you expect me to solve the problem without exiting them?" asked Quail.

"Will you be taking Kim's payoff money out of your salary?" asked Simon absently, intending the question as a nasty jest. As he said it, he stole a glimpse toward Quail's left arm and thought he could still see Grimball's teeth marks from the organ chamber debacle. He smiled.

Quail was almost grateful for Simon's wisecrack. It was a public demonstration of what Quail had been silently putting up with in recent weeks. While Quail and Grimball had not spoken since their showdown, even Grimball grimaced at Simon's abrasiveness. If Quail was imperiled, who was safe?

Undeterred, Quail continued, "I have also tidied up after Chef served that rotten chicken salad to the Women Aflame Bible Study Fellowship last Thursday."

"How positively Christian of you," chimed in Glumweltner, sounding exactly like Orson Welles in *Citizen Kane*. "From what I understand, with masticated, poisoned food being ejected from both ends of half the old girls in attendance, there was quite a mess for you to clean up."

"We had three of them at the doctor's office, pumping their stomachs. A half dozen more vomiting their guts up for the next six hours. How drunk does Chef need to be not to know that the electricity is off and the refrigerator has become an incubator for salmonella?" asked Quail.

"Johnson, how incompetent need our building staff be to take thirty hours to flip a couple of breaker switches?" asked Simon with chilliness.

"You would have to be either crazy or dead drunk not to know that the chicken salad was gone," countered Quail. "That chicken had to be as green as the lettuce. Don't blame this on me or Sam. The outage was complicated."

Sam sat in seething silence, refusing to be drawn into the clergy squabble, knowing from experience that when clergy show their claws, somebody gets bloodied.

"Is there anything we can do to help Chef with his problem?" asked Stephen, sounding like the naïve kid he was. "Don't you think it's sad that we're in the business of redemption and recovery and have one of our own in that condition?"

"We're in the business to redeem and to recover?" asked Quail. "We're in the business of hospitality and the providing of services. Our food isn't up to the standards of a second-rate Holiday Inn."

"Holiday Inn would be facing a multimillion dollar lawsuit if they had poisoned as many old ladies as Chef," said Glumweltner.

Stephen boldly attempted to change course by saying, "I would like to get staff feedback on the idea of a youth mission trip."

"Feedback?" asked Simon with eyebrows elevated and eyes wide. "I was under the impression that you had already received feedback—no."

"But it just seems to me that we spend so much money on ourselves and so little on anybody else, that it's just bad Christian education to let our youth think this is the way the church is supposed to be."

Simon, if you let the kid in the pulpit more often, maybe he wouldn't use staff meetings for his sermonettes, Glumweltner thought to himself.

Out of compassion, Simon did not respond to Stephen's Thought for the Day. Quail, raising his eyebrows, an unaccustomed smile on his face, looked at his cell phone, thinking, *Well, Simon, you've got a problem with your show kid, don't you?*

Grimball, in chorus with Glumweltner, smirked. Although the organ-chamber episode—the news of which, Grimball had learned, had been telegraphed with glee far and wide throughout the congregation by Glumweltner—had forced a serious breach in their relationship (such as it was), the prospect of Simon in discomfort (brought on by a pious young associate) united them in mutual delight. It was a joy to see Stephen so innocently and unintentionally bring out the worst in Simon. Only old pastor Cohellen seemed to be listening with interest to Stephen.

"But if I'm going to try this, I need to get moving as soon as possible with the planning and fundraising and all."

Simon spoke in an unaccustomedly slow, exaggeratedly distinct voice. "Stephen, Hope *is* church as it's supposed to be. I thought we had fully discussed this. After your 'Hope Floats' flop, and after the legitimate reservations that were raised around this table about your proposed missions adventure, as I recall, your persistence surprises me. This is a matter of insurance coverage, not Christian mission. Let's discuss these matters together, you and I, in a forum other than this meeting?"

Stephen felt young and stupid. "Fine. Sure. You and I can discuss it later. Sorry."

"So, is this the place to discuss our growin' problem with the plumbin'?" asked Sam. "Or is it too public?"

"Plumbing?" asked Simon, looking down the long table at Sam.

"Yep, this old girl,"—Sam had the annoying tendency to refer to the building in the feminine—"is on her last legs. God help us if the authorities ever discover the asbestos. Short circuits in the wirin', leaks in the roof, but the plumbin's going to do us in first. Old girl's got clogged arteries. Just can't have a seventy-plus-year-old system without issues. They used lots of cast-iron pipe back then, and with the settlin' of the building, normal deterioration and all, actually we have been fairly lucky that things have flowed as well as they have over the years, but now . . ."

"Sam, get with Johnson, present this to the trustees, not to the staff," said Simon. "This is building and grounds business. And for the love of God, please do something that can help us avoid the calamity that occurred in the kitchen last Thursday."

"Well, you'll all be concerned when we get backed up toilets some Sunday. That's sure to suck the Holy Spirit out of us," Sam retorted.

"Oh, my Lord in heaven, perish the thought! Sewage in the sanctuary!" cried Grimball in feigned horror. Briefly the noxious sight of Chef's turkey tetrazzini was recalled to Glumweltner's mind.

Simon brightened, deliberately changed the tenor of his voice, and said, "Let me thank all of you for the great job you did to make the garden party a delightful evening. Good show, well done. First-rate."

Glumweltner startled. "I'm surprised to hear you say that, Simon. I understand that you were unable to be there for the whole evening, that you missed much of the dinner and the entirety of the musical program," said Glumweltner. "I hope that you were not ill." He let his voice rise ever so slightly on the word *ill*.

Stephen tensed and stared down at this lap.

"No, a pastoral emergency, actually," said Simon, scrutinizing the faces of those about the table for any telling expression. He saw no cause for concern, though he did not note Stephen's averted gaze.

"Poor Chef was quite exhausted from the rigors of producing the Beef Wellington and the broccoli with béarnaise. Poor thing has been confined to bed for three days now," said Grimball. "His embarrassment over the Thursday Women In Heat, or whatever they call themselves, took its toll. His cross to bear."

Widespread giggling around the table.

"By the way," inserted Quail, "I'll be out for much of next week."

"May we ask for what reason?" asked Simon, not looking up from the opened folder before him. "This is a busy time for us, as you know."

"It's personal," replied Quail.

"Let's do send Chef a get-well card, shall we?" chirped Grimball. "'Wishing you a speedy twelve-step recovery.'"

"Yes, and let's keep Chef in our prayers," said Simon, adopting an unctuous pastoral tone.

"Earthquake in Afghanistan and famine in sub-Saharan Africa! Our Blessed Lord has more important matters to attend to than Chef's liver," whooped Glumweltner with a hearty laugh. "Let's limit our Chef-care to the card."

Fat Glumweltner's reference to earthquakes and famine induced in Stephen the momentary recognition that he had lost all contact with, or even much interest in, anything going on in the real world. If there were killer earthquakes or invasion by Martians, he wouldn't know about it. He would still be plugging away here at church. He hadn't even purchased a TV, not because he couldn't afford one but because this room, this build- ing, these petty people had become his cosmos. *Very sad*, he admitted to himself as he stared across the table at the obese, self-satisfied, and rather repulsive choir director.

The meeting, so exhausting for the staff in its internecine jabbing, was at last over. As the spent participants finally exited the scene of their contest, Simon looked over at Quail gathering his papers and said, "John- son, a moment please."

Quail sighed with annoyance. "Yes? What is it?"

Simon paused just a moment to allow the room to clear, then said, "Johnson, old man, I know this has been a difficult time for you."

He is not going to rub my nose in the organ chamber fiasco, is he? Quail thought in horror.

"I just wanted to say that I hope that recent events, the Hope Township challenge and all, don't spoil our relationship. I really appreciate the work that you do for us. We mustn't allow the pressures of the job to consume us."

"Yes," responded Quail flatly.

"I know that you've got what it takes to get us through these, uh, challenges. Please forgive me if in any way I've been overbearing or insensitive."

"Yes," was all Quail said, clutching his little stack of files to his chest, turning, and exiting into the outer office.

To have offered forgiveness, only to have it flung back in your face, Simon thought, now alone at the table, *is the most stinging of rebukes.*

∞

Later that afternoon, Glumweltner waddled into the administrative suite and, as he chomped a cinnamon roll and swigged a coffee, asked Simon's assistant, "Simon yet heard about old Niculous?"

"Has Mr. Niculous at last turned up?" asked Cloe. "I need to get last month's trustee report from him. I've been waiting since before Easter. Not like him to be so late."

"He has turned up. My source at the police department told those of us at the coffee shop that they found him yesterday afternoon."

"Police? Where the heck has old Niculous been hiding? Some secret love nest?" asked Simon, joining their conversation as he emerged from his office with a cup of coffee. "Police?"

"In the river," said Glumweltner.

"Did you say 'at the river'?"

"*In* the river. *In* it. That's right, Simon. Cops found old Niculous, naked except for his skivvies, hanging in the branches of a tree that had fallen halfway across the river with the rain and all. Their theory is that Niculous must have bounded off the 201 bridge over the East Fork, sometime just before Easter."

"Oh my God!" exclaimed Cloe. "No!" She began to cry as she fumbled for a tissue.

"Why on earth would Niculous do a crazy thing like that?" asked Sam. He had been working in a side office filing invoices. "Was he depressed? Never seemed depressed to me. He had plenty of money, so that couldn't be it."

"That sweet man!" sniffed Cloe. "That's just the worst thing I ever heard. Simply awful."

Eleanor, hearing the fuss, now entered the office, speechless.

Glumweltner continued his report to the gathering flock, his speech partially distorted by the remains of a sweet roll: "When the river finally went down a few feet, after all the rains during Holy Week, well, a couple of fishermen or somebody discovered Niculous hanging in those tree branches, arms outstretched, just hanging there. Legs rotting off. Naked as a jaybird, like I said, except for his undershorts."

"Spare us the gory details," said Quail, who had now joined them, having overheard the exclamations as he passed by in the hall. "No way to talk about a trustee who was a friend of mine. Simon, tomorrow you'll have the full report of last quarter's financials."

"He was always the sweetest person to work with," said Cloe. "This church never had a more loyal, devoted member. How awful. Just one of the finest Christians I've ever known."

"'Friend of mine?'" scoffed Simon. "Since when were you and Niculous buddies? Man, that couldn't have been a pretty sight, body exposed out there, decomposing," said Simon. "And this is the first I've heard. So much for my being the Senior Managing Pastor and on top of everything. Of course, Niculous didn't have any family to speak of, at least none around here. I just figured he had gone off for a fling or something, though I don't know why I suspected Niculous of anything so adventuresome. Throw himself off a bridge? Overly dramatic. Out of character, I'd say. A couple of weeks ago, I heard that they had found his car at the strip mall near the 201, but I didn't know what to make of it. Sad."

"Wait a minute," sniffed Cloe. "Wait just a minute. Stephen said that he and the youth saw a body floating in the river. I'm sure he said it. That had to be that dear sweet man . . . What on earth did he do to deserve this? How could this possibly be part of God's plan?"

"Speaking of plan, should we plan on a funeral soon for what's left of Niculous? I vote for next Tuesday. With no family, couldn't make much difference when we do it," said Glumweltner. "I assume we won't need a choir."

"Niculous was a trustee. He was a faithful something or other of just about everything in this church at one time or another," said Simon. "Surely we can mount an ensemble, perhaps a quartet? At minimum a solo? Snappy rendition of 'The Trumpet Shall Sound'? Couldn't you get Mack to get off work and sing for fifty dollars? Niculous was fond of Handel, or at least he bankrolled 'Messiah' one year, as I recall. Or maybe a spiritual? I'm glad to hear that Stephen's float trip was good for something."

"Fine. We only live to serve. The main question is, without a family, who will pay for the service?" asked Glumweltner, barely looking up from his calendar as he licked the sugar off his fingers.

"Simon, I don't mean to sound insensitive, but I see no reason for a showy outlay for a man with no family and, I suspect, about as many friends. What real need is there for mounting a full-blown service? Apparently Niculous, for all his Christian faithfulness and holiness, quite willingly chose a most impious exit. Surely graveside remarks are adequate," said Quail, attempting to convey detachment.

"That's got my vote," Glumweltner chimed in. "Graveside without benefit of musicians is quite enough. After all, dear old Niculous was eager enough to get himself deceased and interred. Why deter him any longer from his goal?"

"Johnson, you frequently worked with old Niculous. Do you know what would possess him to do such a thing as this?" asked Simon. "He wasn't a fisherman, was he?"

"He was on and off the finance committee. I wouldn't say that I frequently worked with him, though I found him quite inoffensive. Pleasant but reticent. I really saw very little of him in recent years. Odd character, I thought. When we talked, it was all business," said Quail, fighting back the temptation to say, "Which would be good for some of you to take as an example."

"Ah, the mysterious, secret lives of church people," said Glumweltner. "None of us knows what anybody is capable of at the right time. Niculous was a lifelong bachelor. Maybe he was struggling with his identity, his orientation or . . ."

"Preposterous," said Simon. "Never saw dear, sweet, unoriginal Niculous struggle with anything. Never was there a man more gullible and credulous. None of us has to give a reason for entering this life; why should we have to come up with a reason for leaving? OK, it's Tuesday at two. Graveside. Music minimal."

"I give thanks for having known such a sweet man," said Cloe, dabbing her nose. "It's all such a mystery. We just have to accept these things as God's will."

"I give thanks for a Managing Pastor who at last seems to be getting the point about our financial condition," muttered Quail. "I wonder if he left a suicide note?" he said to the group, relieved when no one responded.

"I shall miss him," said Simon as he moved back toward his study. "Violent end for such a sweet-spirited man."

Eleanor, even though she could not have known Niculous with any degree of intimacy, was overcome with tears and would require the rest of the day to recover.

"Oh, Dr. Lupino," sniffed Cloe, "Yet more sad news. Sarah just called with word that young James Thomas has OD'd. Doesn't sound good. He is on life support at the hospital, East Side, intensive care. Critical."

"James Thomas? Oh my. Niculous was unfortunate; Thomas is a tragedy. Well, see if somebody, maybe Stephen, can go over there," said Simon. "Poor kid. I'm booked this afternoon. That kid has always been a problem, hasn't he? This'll kill his parents. His father has been on the board. Wonder if they'll be alright with a service at the funeral home. More fitting than at church. You know, don't you, that these things tend to come in threes? Please get ahold of Stephen and ask him to handle things. The experience will do him good."

"Seems like we've had more deaths than at any time since I've been at Hope," whined Cloe. "Lots of trouble all around."

"Which is one reason why I've been concerned about the rising median age of our congregation," lectured Quail. "When most of 'em are over sixty, funerals become our main ministry." As he spoke, he made a heroic effort to demonstrate to all present that the discovery of Niculous' noteless, enigmatic end was of not the slightest concern.

As he had during many past performances, Quail was lying. While attempting to feign indifference, his mind flashed back frightfully to Palm Sunday afternoon when he had cornered Niculous. Alone together, Quail had shown the pitiful, trapped little man how he had (unintentionally but irrefutably) unearthed a surprising, dirty secret: Niculous had been pilfering the trust fund of a senile dowager of the congregation, taking advantage of his position to empty the fund of a million or more. Though Quail had tried to make it clear to the little crook that he did not care about the immorality of Niculous' actions, he knew that Niculous did care, and cared deeply, and therefore would be a fit subject for a bit of blackmail. That was all Quail had intended. He had only wanted harmlessly to leverage his serendipitous discovery into some assistance with his personal fiscal plight, asking Niculous for a couple of hundred thousand, just enough to get his head above the rising waters of his delinquent alimony.

Now Quail was stunned by Niculous' cowardice, his moral rigidity that had led him to nosedive into the East River rather than do business with an accuser. Why didn't Niculous man up and simply pay him to keep quiet? Quite sad that Niculous was so tightfisted that he would rather end it all than pay this modest business expense in order to bury his guilt forever. Probably the self-righteous prig didn't trust him. Who could have known that pious Niculous would become unglued by a reasonable demand and dive off a bridge in hysteria? Well, it couldn't be helped. Niculous' insufferable sanctimoniousness had led him to a stupid end. *Let that be a lesson to us all*, Quail thought to himself as he hastened toward the administrative suite with a calculated guise of cold unconcern.

∾

Early the next morning, Stephen stepped out of the shower, dripping across the badly dated and stained green shag carpet of his apartment. He stood before his mirror, toweling dry.

"In the words of the great Saint Paul, 'Glorify God in your body,'" intoned Stephen, in perfect parody of a preacher. "Any of you ladies out there who want to be taken to glory tonight by this great bod?"

He presented his nakedness before the mirror for critical, corporeal self-examination. His initial assessment was that, unfortunately, his friends were right: he was skinny. Though he had worked out at the gym religiously—not as much as when he was in seminary, but better than weekly—he still looked boney. He had tried, for all of a week, one of those protein drinks and had focused on core exercises. Far from seeing the advent of six-pack abs, he saw exposed ribs. What did Thea see when she looked at him? Was she as attracted to his body as he was to hers? She didn't seem very much into the physical part of a relationship, but maybe that was the way with all women. Was he a turn-on or a turnoff?

Here he was, twenty-five years old, and still he looked to all the world like a gawky teenager. It was humiliating. "Yep. I really do have a body fit for my role—a wimpish, flat-chested, scrawny kid unsuited either for real work or getting down and dirty. Only thing I'm fit for is being some nice old white lady's sweet little tea-sipping parson."

Glancing at himself one more time as he donned his undershirt, Stephen said ruefully, "As the grea-a-a-at Saint Paul, defender of slavery and women's silence, put it, 'who will rescue me from this body of death?'" The sight of his body and the thought of death brought to his mind the picture of the rotting, naked body in the river. It was disgusting to contemplate the fate of all bodies, God's ultimate intent for all bodies, whether well kept or not.

When he was fully dressed, wearing a light blue collared shirt and khakis (being a youth pastor has its privileges), he glanced one more time at his cell phone, sorely disappointed that Thea hadn't texted since the day before yesterday.

Suddenly his phone vibrated in his hand. Before looking at the caller I.D., he excitedly answered, "Hey, babe! Girl, I was just thinking of you."

"Stephen? Is this the Reverend Stephen Smith?"

Stephen froze upon hearing Cloe's nasally voice. "I'm sorry, I thought . . ."

"Yes, dear, I know what you thought. Dr. Lupino asked me to call you and ask you to go by the East Side Hospital. That's East Side, not over at Mercy. He told me to call you yesterday afternoon and, what with all the tragedy about Mr. Niculous and all, I simply forgot. And by the way, that body you saw in the river—Mr. Niculous, longtime member of Hope. One of the sweetest people I've ever worked with. And now little James. I hope we're not too late."

"Not at all. But who is in the hospital? Too late for what?"

"Oh, young James Thomas. Room 503, at least that's where he was yesterday."

"James? What? What's wrong with him?"

"I hear a drug overdose. But that's just hearsay from Sarah at this point. They say he's on life support. Self-inflicted, we presume. Very, very sad for the parents. Doesn't your heart just go out to people at a time like this? Did you know this was what you were getting into when you took your ordination vows? Better get right over there, dear. Don't let me keep you. Mr. Quail was just saying that you ministers will have to get accustomed to dealing with more of this sort of thing."

Stephen mumbled his thanks as he flipped his phone closed. He stood there, immobile, for what may have been a full ten minutes. Then like a robot he turned, took off his shirt, slipped out of his pants, and mechanically put on his only pair of dress pants, his shirt, tie and sports coat. Now properly attired for tragedy, he took a deep breath and said a prayer, one that he had used more than twice in the past couple of weeks: "God, I'm drowning, over my head here." Then he left, feeling empty-handed, without a script, underprepared for his biggest pastoral crisis.

6

The Sixth Sunday of Easter

Simon should not have waited until so deep into the week to work on his sermon, but this had been a busy, distracting week that invited procrastination—overflowing toilets, poisoned old ladies, congregants morbidly gobbling up handfuls of pills, others dead in the water. But then there was Sybil. An early Thursday morning glance at the assigned lessons for the Fourth Sunday of Easter did not provide encouragement.

The Acts of the Apostles in the Sundays after Easter seemed intent upon a reiteration of the huge gap between the church as it was and the church as it actually is. Why belabor the matter?

He read the appointed first lesson from Acts 7:55–60:

They covered their ears, and with a loud shout all rushed together against him. Then they dragged him out of the city and began to stone him . . . While they were stoning Stephen, he prayed, "Lord Jesus, receive my spirit" . . . when he had said this, he died.

Hmm. The stoning of Stephen, first martyr. Headline: "Young Guy Gets Clobbered." Stephen Two, namesake of Stephen One, a nice boy who had never gotten stoned, could be on his way, before the end of the week, to being stoned. Oh, the irony.

Perhaps a sermon on religious fanaticism and where it leads? But that's not the problem around here. He had taken a couple of jabs at fanatics just last Sunday. Wouldn't want people to think this was an obsession. His flock was fanatical about sex, money, their children's upward mobility, and their own smug well-being, but God knows they extol moderation, caution, and balance in all things religious.

What about the second lesson, 1 Peter 2:2–10?

A stone makes them stumble and a rock makes them fall. They stumble because they disobey the word, as they were destined to do. But you are a chosen race, a royal priesthood, a holy nation . . . now you have received mercy.

He sighed and began tapping at his keyboard.

It's humbling, really, to think that God has chosen us, despite any of our flaws, to be God's chosen ones in the world, priests to the world's forsaken. We have been commissioned to show to a hurting world the human face of divine mercy.

Delete that last and change to read, *to put a human face upon obscure and all too elusive divine mercy.*

He continued:

As Saint Teresa, or some other woman saint, has said, "Yours are the hands of Christ"—yours are the only hands God has.

He deleted this last sentence. No need to be excessive in his flattery of the congregation.

I know my many weaknesses, my failings. And God knows, as your pastor, I know yours!

They always appreciated humor, particularly in the form of pastoral self-deprecation.

When our epistle speaks of a "holy priesthood," it's not talking about me or other clergy in this congregation. It's talking about you! This is the Protestant doctrine of the "priesthood of all believers," arising out of the ashes of spent Roman Catholicism. You are a "priest" working in the world in God's name. Like the "priests" who preside here on Sunday, you preside at Christ's more important liturgies on Monday—at the office, in the marketplace, over a cup of coffee, at cocktails at the club, in the classroom.

Was "liturgies" too high church? He modified the phrase to read, *you preside in God's transforming work in the world on Monday.*

From here he enumerated some of the many ways (in truth, nearly all of the ways) that Hope Church evidenced its participation in God's "holy priesthood"—the clothes closet for the poor, abortion counseling, the downtown food pantry, the urban ministry center, generous benevolent funding, Simon's service as advisor to the City Council on open housing, his chairmanship of Rotary's annual turkey giveaway, the men's group's donation of over a thousand dollars' worth of contraceptives to Family Planning, Inc., the church's construction of a waiting room for a clinic in Honduras, Chef's "many contributions to the feeding of the homeless" (actually there was but one in the past twelve months—Chef had dumped some leftover quiche after the Church Women United luncheon had flopped), along with the many people (at least two or three) who marched in the Freedom of Choice rally in Chicago.

Upon further consideration, he excised the clothes closet reference; no need to incite more congregational adulation for dear, dour, devoted Mary.

In a world in which divine mercy is in short supply, you are the only mercy that most hurting people will ever meet. It's up to you to do the work of God in the world, or that work won't get done. Remember: Yours are the only hands that God has. You! You! You!

The sermon ended with a reiteration of a textual snippet for validation.

But you are a chosen race, a royal priesthood, a holy nation . . . now you have received mercy.

"That ought to hold 'em for another week," he muttered aloud as he hit print on his computer. Simon wanted his sermons to be his own little means of helping his congregation receive mercy. There were pastors who lacked the empathy to show grace to outwardly successful people. Simon liked to think that God had given him a charism for seeing through their apparent success and contentment to their suppressed, but real, cries of pain. Here was young James, whose parents had undoubtedly planned and sacrificed (the former more than the latter) in order for him to grow up in the right part of town, only to have it end with James's self-imposed exit. Or Niculous, prim and proper little man, diving off a bridge. Only the coldest of cold-hearted clerics would fail to feel sympathy. Ah, the desperation suffered by those afflicted by the twin curse of indecision and irresolution!

"God we gather weekly thee to bless," Simon hummed as he watched the printer spit out his sermon, "for well-prepared food to eat and a fashionable address."

His telephone buzzed. The whining voice on the other end belonged to one of the women in the congregation. He recognized the complaining, nasal twang but couldn't positively identify it, so he faked it. She was desperately searching for something inconsequential related to the women's midweek Bible study. He got her off with a minimum of effort, amazed that she had obtained his cell number.

ℛ

James? In a coma at the hospital, "not expected to make it"? It was surreal. "Hope you are not too late"? Just last week they were floating down the

East Fork. Maybe James was a screwed-up kid, but no more so than half the youth at the church. With fear and trembling Stephen drove toward the East Side Hospital to fulfill his assignment as the sole ministerial representative from Hope Church. A more senior, more experienced member of the staff should be doing this. He was only the youth pastor. Only twice had he been thrust into a family crisis, in both cases while working at an inner-city mission during seminary. He didn't really know the people.

This was different. He had spent hours alone with James. In fact, in his weeks at Hope, James was the only kid in the youth group whom he had really come to know, certainly the only one who had responded to him. His sole disciple. Maybe Cloe was being overly dramatic. Lots of kids tried the suicide thing, just to get attention. Surely that was the case here. How could he spend three whole days with a young man and not know that he was contemplating swallowing a bunch of pills? He went back over their long, nighttime conversation, trying to recall anything James said that might have been a clue or a subtle cry for help. The kid seemed down, but when had he crossed the line from being sixteen and depressed to being disastrously self-destructive?

Oh God, don't let him die, he prayed. The words wouldn't stop ringing in his ears: "think it's a drug overdose," "we presume it is self-inflicted," "very, very sad," "not long." So there he was, in his midtwenties, fresh out of seminary, speeding at ten miles an hour over the limit toward the center of a storm he would give anything to avoid, a complete incompetent, praying, nothing to equip him for such a task but a lousy Pastoral Care in the Suburban Parish course taught by a clueless dingbat. He tried to banish the image of James laughing at his jokes, there at the riverside.

Stephen rushed from the section of the parking lot designated for clergy (somehow, it reassured him to park in a spot marked Clergy Only), walked briskly into the hospital, past the desk—stopping briefly to show his heretofore unused ministerial ID—and took the steps up to the fifth floor, thinking that the climb would settle his nerves. He took a deep breath, straightened his tie, and stood before the door of room 503. He knew enough to double check the nameplate on the door; he was surprised to find no name. He peeked inside the room. The bed was neatly made and empty. No sign of James or his family. He stood there staring at the forlorn, vacant room; having gotten himself psyched for an encounter with somebody in a coma or just coming out of a coma, with worried parents hovering nearby, he was strangely relieved to be met by nothing but an empty bed. Perhaps James had been moved to intensive care. Or maybe there had been a miracle.

"Are you looking for 503?" asked a nurse wheeling a cart behind him. Stephen made a numb sort of nod.

"The boy expired about six this morning. Joseph's came and got him about seven," she said without looking up as she moved toward the next room. "Sad."

The bottom dropped out of Stephen's stomach. He gave no response to the nurse but thought, *Expired? You mean dead? Too late for what? And what is "Joseph's"?*

He staggered down the side stairs, steadying himself on the railing, and stumbled out of the impersonal, antiseptic building. All he could see was the hospital bed, its emptiness, the sight of which was worse even than the sight of the decayed body suspended in the tree. Now, "Joseph's has him." Where once there had been a life, a future (however uncertain), a soul in need of grace, there now was nothing, not even a name. A great kid, vaporized. He could see James grinning in the middle of the night, holding up his knees and laughing on his back on the rock. James in the parking lot the last day when he said, "Thanks."

He so wished that he could have gotten here in time.

Or did he? He could picture James's parents, wailing and crying, maybe even enraged. What would he have said? What kind of pastor wants people in grief to disappear? Maybe every pastor, for all he knew.

Is one supposed to say to them that James committed, that is, "took his own life"? Stupid phrase. James didn't "take his life." It was never James's life to take.

If Stephen had not been so dazed, he might have noticed Johnson Quail being rolled down the very same hall on a gurney by an orderly. Quail lay there, clad in a hospital gown, groggy from having been through a complete upper and lower GI exam, including a degrading colonoscopy. He recognized Stephen passing through the hall but said nothing, still weak and dizzy from the anesthesia and from having his colon so thoroughly explored.

Stephen felt like a coward as he sat there in his car, immobile in the hospital parking lot, staring at nothing, lacking the resolve even to put the key in the ignition. Should he have had prayer before he left the empty hospital room? No. He would have looked even dumber in front of that nurse, standing there, praying to an empty bed.

Just then Stephen was startled by a sudden, hard rap on his car window. A fat policeman, already sweating at this early hour of the morning, stood there scowling, holding a piece of paper up before him. Stephen rolled down his window.

"So? It isn't enough that you've got your own section, but you also have got to park in a handicapped space?" growled the little man. "Here. Hope you enjoyed your free parking place. You preachers are somethin'."

The cop shoved the ticket at Stephen through the open window. Stephen wiped his face with his sleeve and dumbly reached for the ticket.

"What's your handicap, preacher—you can't read?" asked the cop, grinning. Stephen could see that he wasn't even a real cop. He was a hospital security cop.

Wordlessly, Stephen nodded, turned his head, looked out his front window and saw the words *Handicapped Only* staring him in the face. He sighed and rolled up the widow, and the cop, underarms drenched with sweat, waddled away, stuffing, with difficulty, his ticket book into his hip pocket.

"Damn," Stephen said as he stared at the ticket—one hundred dollars!—shoving it into his glove compartment. After slamming his fist into the steering wheel in despair, he checked his GPS and, sure enough, Joseph's was the name of a funeral home at 507 Oak Avenue. He wanted to call Dr. Lupino for backup, but he didn't dare. Stephen pulled out of the lot and headed for the house of the dead, driven by nothing but a dogged sense of duty.

Probably the family will be there. Say to them, "I'm so, so, sorry." Don't mention how James died. Look sad. Don't ask questions. Tell them what a great guy James was. Then he thought of James, looking across at him in the van, smirking and silent, and then his final word to him, "Thanks"—and Stephen, relinquishing all pretense of professional calculation, lost it.

❧

Though early morning is an unconventional time for a romantic rendezvous, Simon and Sybil sped southward, her convertible's top down in the warm breeze, sailing the countryside, thus certifying that theirs was no conventional affair. That they were now meeting in the morning Simon took as confirmation that their relationship had progressed beyond a passing fling. As usual, she was at the wheel and he close beside her, his body conforming to hers; he wore a disguise of sunglasses and a brown cap, she wore a smart, mauve, ultrasuede jacket and black slacks that fit her just right. They talked, but not much. Though more of an activist than a contemplative, Simon was enthralled just gazing at Sybil—wind in her hair, driving with command and confidence, the shape of her face ideal for a sharp pair of designer sunglasses, she resembled an advertisement in *Vanity Fair*. Her Mercedes sped them toward Nirvana, some Shangri-la reserved just for them (otherwise known as the river overlook car park about twenty minutes south of town).

While Sybil drove, Simon fiddled with the dial on the radio until he had found a station playing oldies (very oldies):

When you walk through a storm
Hold your head up high
And don't be afraid of the dark . . .

"Ah, 'Carousel,'" said a wistful Simon. "Played the lead role of Billy Bigelow my junior year of high school." He sung along robustly,

And the bright, silver song of a lark . . .

"Kitsch," pronounced Sybil.

Walk on, walk on, with hope in your heart and you'll ne-ver walk alone!
You'll ne-ver walk alone . . .

"Did I tell you that you were enchanting?" asked Simon as he leaned toward her.

"What's that about my ranting?" shouted Sybil over the roar of the wind and the road.

"Yes, yes, yes to everything. I'm in ecstasy! Ranting, raving ecstasy!"

"You say you need to pee?" she shouted.

You'll never walk alone.

He leaned over and planted a passionate kiss. Without slowing, she pulled out her lipstick, pursed her lips, and, looking in the rearview mirror, refreshed her trademark bright red. Simon's resurrected libido surged in response to those rubicund lips.

∾

"Tumor in the colon, it seems. Wish I could break it to you in a more gentle way," said the oncologist. "Of course, you said that you wanted the honest, unvarnished truth. There 'tis."

Quail sullenly thought, *If I asked for truth, I lied.* He had always found truth, particularly medical truth, overrated.

"We have got some stuff we can do, chemo and all. I guess you know that's not a pretty picture, but I think we could slow this baby down, at least—that is, if that's the way you want to go," continued the doctor, who seemed intent on being unsettlingly casual, almost lighthearted, as if Quail had a rash. "Get some rest and we can talk about our plan of attack before you are dismissed tomorrow?"

Quail did not respond as the doctor zipped out of his room. For the first time in his adult life, he was terrified. Doctor-talk of "plan" and "attack" was malarkey served up to dummies. He wanted to cry but had no experience in weeping. He thought that he ought to pray, but praying, this late in the game, seemed hypocritical. His overriding concern was what Simon might do if he got this news. There was probably no reliable way to keep it quiet. Possibly that young, minority associate had indeed espied him this morning, helpless on the gurney, and might even now be blabbing to everyone. Experience had taught him that a show of weakness before an enemy like Simon, or in front of the laity, led to trouble. Never let them see your mortality.

Just when he was taking his career to the next level, on the threshold of his big break, a lousy malignant devil threatened to haul him to hell. Why him? After all he had done to keep a roof over God's head. Of all the luck, all the lousy, friggin' luck. What sort of God would blame the suicide of a hypocritical, parsimonious little thief on him?

∾

True to its name, Oak Avenue was lined with large oaks—and also, to Stephen's dismay, with no less than three funeral parlors.

"Zip code of the dead," Stephen muttered as he scanned the street for Joseph's. "A city this size can support three funeral homes, and all on the same street? How many dead have we got?"

Joseph's gave Stephen the creeps—white columns, calligraphied sign out front, decorative wrought-iron furniture in the front yard, another sign reading Chapel of Rest pointing the way, all saying, as innocuously as possible, "Dead Bodies Right Over Here."

He opened the door carefully. A chime sounded. Inside, everything was muted, hushed, clean, and old. Boxes of tissues. Soft, syrupy organ music being piped in. The place was frozen in the fifties, like a set from some black-and-white horror movie, a faintly churchy smell, and everything creepy.

No one greeted him, even though he heard the chime as he entered. He was glad not to be welcomed. He saw an open book on a gray metal stand: Register of Guests. The book said it was for Ida Sara Ketchum. Sure enough, in Viewing Number Two, just behind the register, he could see an open casket from which the powdered nose of an old woman poked up like a white rosebud.

"Gooood morning," said a soft, mellow voice from down the hall. "May I be of heeelp?"

Stephen saw an older man in a gray suit sliding toward him. A funeral director dressed for the part. You could have picked him out of a lineup. Stereotypical all the way down to his muted gray, expertly knotted tie and oily voice.

"Is there any family here for James—James Thomas?"

"We have James here," said the unctuous mortician, "but we just got him about an hour ago, so he's not ready quite yet. And of course, none of the family is yet here. Are you a friend?" The man said "frieeend" so that his voice went up an octave, probably to convey sympathy. He sounded creepy.

"No, not exactly. I'm—actually, I'm his—his pastor," Stephen stammered.

"Really? That's wonderful," said the man. "His pastor. Just wonderful."

"Actually, just his youth pastor," Stephen corrected.

"Youth pastor? At Hope Church? That's wonderful. I am Fletcher Joseph," said the man, presenting Stephen with a limp, white hand, which Stephen shook lightly, hesitantly, feeling faint disgust. "That makes two from Hope Church, what with nice Henry Niculous, though there's more of young James for us to work with."

Stephen saw the body dangling over the river, naked and awful. It was particularly horrible to know that he and the rotting corpse shared the same church.

"Uh, wonderful to meet you, Mr. Joseph," said Stephen. A week ago he had no had occasion to deal with the dead, now he saw bodies everywhere. In his nervousness, he had echoed Joseph's overused "wonderful"—a stupidly inappropriate designation of this whole, horrible moment.

"You must be new in town. Wonderful," said Joseph, as if infected by an outbreak of banality. Stephen assumed that this was code for "I didn't know they hired them a nice Negro at Hope Church, how very . . . *wonderful.*"

"I hope that you and I will see each other often, that you will look upon Joseph's as family," said the slimy man. "We're all just family here."

Stephen suppressed a laugh at the absurdity and improbability of the man's statement. This guy would be his last choice for a cousin, even a distant one who was white. Maybe the only way you can get through a sorry job like his without hitting yourself in the head with a hammer is by abusing common sense and degrading language, giving free rein to illogic and cliché.

"Sorry not to have James ready for viewing, but as I said, we just got the body. Just call me Joseph of Aramathea."

Getting no response from Stephen, he added, "Patron saint of us undertakers."

Still no change in Stephen's expression.

"Gospel of John? Jesus' undertaker? We're the last act in every crucifixion."

"That's alright," muttered Stephen. For some reason he shook the mortician's hand and said awkwardly, "See you later, Mr. Aramathea, I mean Joseph." He turned and rushed past two floral arrangements and the boxes of tissue. He struggled for air, thinking about the rotting body by the river, thinking about James's body waiting to be made up by the mortician. Staggering out the front door of the mortuary, heaving, steadying himself on one of the white columns, he was fearful that he might faint or, worse, puke.

But no sooner had he made it to the bottom step than he looked up to see a man holding onto a woman, both with red, swollen faces, making their way toward him up the walk. The man's hair was the same shade of brown as James's hair.

"Er, good morning," said Stephen, immediately realizing the ridiculousness of such a salutation on the worst morning of their lives. "Are you the—are you James's parents?"

They stopped and stared at Stephen. The man seemed to bite his lip and nod assent.

"I'm so, so sorry. James was a great guy. I really got to know him on the float trip. The only one who came. He . . ."

The couple just stood there.

"James shared a lot with me on the trip. We got close," Stephen chattered on, thinking that it might be some comfort to the parents to know that their deceased son had been close to a pastor.

Mr. Thomas nodded. Stephen thought he heard Mr. Thomas mumble a thank you. Then Mr. Thomas was led away by James's mother, past Stephen and up the steps toward the front door of the funeral home.

Stephen left them to their dead, walked out to his car and, once inside, melted into tears like a blubbering child, head against his fists on the steering wheel. "James was a great guy?"

Four years of college, three years of seminary, turning his back on law school, all dressed up in a coat and tie for the delivery of a cliché empty of consolation to a couple of parents in hell.

Maybe it was because of the mortuary, and his exposure to death and to Mr. Joseph, or having his nose rubbed into his own ministerial incompetence, but as Stephen sat there, he remembered the Shinto shrine that he saw outside Kyoto, Japan, the fall semester he was in Asia. Hundreds, maybe thousands, of cheap, grinning, plaster dolls surrounded the red Japanese building, each doll holding a small windmill. He would never forget the eerie sight of so many cherubic, pink-cheeked Kewpie dolls holding up plastic windmills, each one whirring in the breeze.

He was told that the dolls were put there by women who had had abortions, one doll for each aborted fetus.

Over the course of human history, billions of people had died. They died in different ways, but all fell into the limp hands of someone like Joseph. Death was so very natural and normal—ruthlessly democratic—yet it took only one death to undo Stephen.

I would have given anything to talk to Thea, he thought as he slid into sleep late that night. Then he had to confess to himself, *No I wouldn't.*

"Now I know why so many funerals are held in mortuaries or at the graveside," he said aloud in the darkness. "It's a full-time job keeping the dead away from the church and the living."

Assisted by six beers, lying on his back with arms extended as if nailed to a cross, he slept, fending off visitation by the intruding dead or by the God who, in the words of Meister Eckhart, "becomes and unbecomes."

∾

Late that same afternoon, Sybil and Simon sat on a large white brocade sofa in the expansive, light-filled living room of her tastefully accessorized home, sipping wonderfully cold, dry martinis, even though it was still early. It had been quite a day.

"You know, I'm developing somewhat of a crush for your young associate, the Reverend Mr. Smith," said Sybil, totally out of the blue.

"Sybil!" exclaimed Simon. "You couldn't, you wouldn't."

"I could, but I don't know that I would," said Sybil. "I'm not sure the young man is blessed with enough imagination for me to enlist him in a remake of *The Graduate*. Since he is clergy, he is probably risk averse. I expect that he believes in going by the book, sticking with the program. I might bring to mind his mother more than a potential playmate. No doubt he is cursed with an overbearing moral sensitivity, God help him."

"Sybil!"

"On the other hand, perhaps a woman of the world would do him a world of good by caressing him gently into the duties of manhood. Someday you worldly, so well-adjusted middle-aged men will learn how deeply attractive awkward innocence and naïveté are to women of a certain age. Something about that dark young man all done up in a virginal white frock, speaking of mysterious matters, cincture tight about his narrow waist . . ."

"A well-kept physique doesn't hurt either, I'd suppose," said Simon.

"That too, but one can find as good or better on any weekday afternoon at the gym. Indeed, I have."

"Sybil!"

"It's the innocence, the holy artlessness, the youthful gullibility that's irresistible," said Sybil, a naughty, conspiratorial tone in her voice.

Simon didn't want to show his full shock lest he himself appear innocent or awkward. God help him if Sybil ever thought him provincial. Still, her comments, though playful, were alarming. "I doubt that Smith is all that innocent. After all, he's black and it's America. I expect he knows a lot more about us than he lets on," said Simon.

"I'm not sure how much Stephen actually knows about matters of injustice—Daddy and Mummy are doctors in Elmhurst, I hear—doubt he suffered much prejudice in his neighborhood," Sybil declared. "Not exactly a *Raisin in the Sun* situation."

"Why do you know so much about young Stephen?" queried Simon. "Sybil, you haven't made naughty with our innocent young, have you?"

"Don't be ridiculous. I've always envied juveniles for their spiritual effervescence. Seems to me that God gives us his best stuff while in adolescence; then the Almighty loses interest in us as we age. Ever heard of anyone having a religious experience of note after fifty? I expect the church would suffocate if it did not seek out those of Stephen's age, those who are still spiritually capable. But don't worry—as I said, young Stephen's awfully earnest, which means that he may also be rather dull. All I said was that around here innocence is such a rare quality that I find it appealing, an evanescent, rare flower that just begs to be laid hold of by the stem and plucked, root and all."

"Well, I'm sad to thwart your pedophiliac designs, but young Mister Right Reverend Stephen has become somewhat of a nuisance," said Simon. "I am about to rid us of the self-righteous little prig. Enjoy him while you can."

"What do you mean? I thought that everyone had received him quite well," said Sybil. "I thought that he was hired to validate our inclusive, open-hearted spirit at Hope, and that he was fulfilling his function quite nicely."

"Nothing personal. Just efficient management. If you don't manage a church staff, they'll manage you. True, I could find myself short of help in the future, what with Johnson's sad circumstances."

"Mr. Quail?" asked Sybil in surprise.

"He seems gravely concerned. Of course, Johnson is always deeply concerned whenever the news, good or bad, is about him. Hard to tell if it's serious, but he's in for some sort of diagnostic test. Sounds ominous. I doubt it will be good."

Simon grinned as he casually put his arm upon her shoulder, reaching to place his drink on a nearby mahogany table behind the sofa. "But enough of my subordinates. Since you aren't impressed with *my* innocence, what *do* you like about me, dear one? Let's not talk about anyone but us. Neither my immature associate nor my terminal old assistant is of great consequence. Stephen's wings are about to be clipped. Can't quite chin the bar. Now, how dost thou love *me*, dearest one? Let me hear thee count the ways."

"Oh, let's see. I'll have to think about that," Sybil kidded as she kicked off her shoes and slid her naked feet up on the sofa and underneath her buttocks. "I know this sounds terribly paradoxical, but I like the way you conduct yourself at business, around town, especially church. The way you make church itself business. It's as if you know the score, as if you know that it's all a game, but still you play the pretense—mostly without anger or insincerity. You go your way confidently, without arrogance, guile, or bitterness. That's important to me."

"I guess," said Simon. They sat in silence for a minute or two, staring past their drinks out into the back garden. He took her compliments as an encouragement to unburden himself.

"I sometimes, lately, have this dream, really terrifying," confessed Simon.

"I almost never have dreams," responded Sybil. "I find them all frightening. I am bothered by anything beyond the safe confines of the here and now. I usually take a pill in the hope that it will stifle nighttime intrusions by the irrational. But go ahead, if you must. Tell me your fearful dreams."

"In my dream it's like I'm drowning, going under for the third time. I'm just treading water, just trying to hold on, gasping, grasping. I keep trying to make headway in the water, but I can't. I just paddle in place. And I shout but nobody answers. I wonder when my strength will end and I will sink. Then I wake up in the proverbial cold sweat, gasping, thrashing about."

"And what do you make of your dream?" she asked, suspecting that he was lying.

"I think it means that I'm miserable, Sybil. And only you can save me. I'm going down and I'm terrified by the thought that you will not reach out to me, my nymph, sweet little savior."

"Really now, Simon. Must you be melodramatic? Your dream is probably occasioned by your having to bury that sweet Mr. Niculous after his demise in the river. That's my guess," said Sybil, brushing aside Simon's moment of self-revelation. "Your dream doubtless has more to do with the unpleasant duties of your job than with your infatuation with me."

"Though I've done it a hundred times for others, putting Niculous in the ground somehow did give me a new sense of urgency. For us all, there'll be a day when there's no tomorrow. What a pointless little life he lived."

Sybil perked up. "See? I like the way you move about the world free of the moral baggage that weighs down lesser men. Everything just seems so refreshingly straightforward, as if you have learned some dark truth, yet proceed without complaint or regret. You've ventured a forbidden peek behind the curtain, and now you know that there's nothing there, no one to censure us. All things are possible."

There were many moments with Sybil when one couldn't tell if she was being bitchily sarcastic or alluringly affectionate. She was a great mystery—deep, irresistible, unfathomable—and Simon loved her inscrutability.

"Humm, is that all you love about me?" Simon asked playfully.

"Simon, whatever do you mean?" Sybil arose, put down her empty glass, and moved toward her bedroom, unhooking the back of her blouse as she went.

He trailed behind, saying, "You know, just this week a member of our staff said to me that I seemed like a new being."

"What ever did he mean?" asked Sybil casually as she stepped out of her slacks.

"Well, I think he was referring to my new life, to us."

"Us?"

"Yes. At first, when he said it, I was embarrassed, concerned even. Was my happiness so apparent? Was my joy putting me in jeopardy?" Simon sat down on the edge of the bed. "But as I considered the comment, I thought it confirmation of what I was indeed feeling in my soul. I'm in a whole new world."

"Such a sentimentalist," scoffed Sybil. "Turn off that light. I find it distracting."

"Ah, 'men love darkness rather than light,'" said Simon as he leaned across the bed and reached for the switch, relishing the midnight dark in the middle of the afternoon. "Glad to hear that women do too."

∾

"Well, you must be the new one! I've been looking for you," hailed an older gentleman cheerfully.

Stephen was returning to his office from a late afternoon meeting of the student ministry council where he had been sitting for over an hour with a grand total of three people—one slouching, resentful teen and two anxious mothers—getting nowhere. Fitting ending for a disaster of a day.

"Yep, I guess that's me," replied Stephen. The old man was smartly dressed in a blue blazer and red necktie, light gray trousers and shiny loafers, red handkerchief peeking out of his blazer pocket. *Quite a dresser for his age*, Stephen thought.

"So? Are we going to hear from the man upstairs this week?" the man asked with a leer. "The front office?" he grinned.

"Uh, well, good question," responded Stephen.

"He comes, he goes, but when, nobody knows! What are you doing for the advancement of the company today?" he continued.

"Uh, another good question," said Stephen. "I fear, not much. But I like being reminded by you that's what it's all about."

"Yes, yes, that's what it's all about. Look busy. Remember, if the householder had known when the thief was breaking in, would he have been asleep?" He raised one finger, pointing it aloft, closing his eyes as he spoke.

Stephen stood there in the hallway, fascinated by the man, enjoying his playful biblical allusions, grateful for his exhortation. "You know—and maybe this is just because I'm new and inexperienced at this sort of work—but one thing that's bothered me is that it just seems like there's a lot of busyness, meetings, appointments and all, organizational machinery clanking away, but not much real Jesus in any of it. Not much of the kingdom in this 'company.' No 'man upstairs,' as you say. So I'm glad that you have called me back to the real point of my being here."

"Well, I don't know who you are or what you plan to do with us, but I'm watching you, sneaking about. I'm not fooled!" said the man, a look of anger on his face, his eyes ablaze, staring intently at Stephen. "Jesus my ass. I wonder if you are attempting to rip us off? Are you some kind of con man!"

"Excuse me?"

"You, you fake! Have you ever been in the business? Why aren't you in your office? Damn it, how dare you?" With that the old man rushed out the side door, walking hurriedly toward the east parking lot and muttering aloud, "Jesus Christ!"

Stephen stood there, frozen, flabbergasted. A moment later a woman came hurrying down the hall, calling in a loud, shrill old lady's voice, "Simeon dear? Simeon?"

"Has he gone?" she asked Stephen as she looked out the window, scanning the sidewalk. Before Stephen, still disoriented, could respond, she answered herself, "Yes, there he is, I thought I had lost him."

"Is—is he your husband?" Stephen asked.

"Yes, of course. Were you attempting to engage Simeon in conversation?"

"Yes, I did. We had an interesting chat," said Stephen. "I was fascinated by what he had to say."

"Fascinated?" she asked in amazement. "Ha! I would love to have heard your 'interesting conversation.' Poor, dear Simeon lost his mind more than four years ago this fall!"

"Really? I—I couldn't tell," Stephen said.

"You couldn't tell? I wonder about *your* mind! Simeon thinks we're living in Connecticut! Do you mean to tell me that you just had a conversation with Simeon and couldn't tell that he was out of his mind? He hasn't known what he was doing for years! Most of the time he thinks he's running a supermarket. Complete dementia. Complete."

"No, well, I guess, come to think about it . . ."

Mrs. Mason pushed the door open, laughing to herself as she hurried after her husband, shaking her head in amusement, "Couldn't tell that Simeon is out of it! My, my. Siiiimeon! Now you just wait right there, Mama's coming!"

⁓

Late that night in the parsonage, as Simon lay in bed, feigning sleep while Mary slept heavily, for consolation he turned toward the other side of the mattress and from memory conducted a topographic survey of Sybil's body. Once Simon thought that he had reached an age at which professional achievement excited him more than women. He had secretly feared that he might be cast as a contemporary version of the medieval castrati. Back then the church neutered selected boys in order to preserve their clear, high, prepubescent voices for the singing of the church's most difficult music at Mass. The castrati, so it was said, grew to be large, handsome young men, but in their forties, their bodies became grotesque, and though deformed in service to the church, they were cast aside with revulsion.

Having given the first decades of his life to the church, Simon feared that he awaited a similar midlife fate—a discarded, deformed eunuch in the house of the Lord.

His feelings for Sybil indicated that ecclesiastical castration can be miraculously reversed. Sybil had resurrected in him a reinvigorated sense of his self-worth. His gerontic tumidity confirmed it. In Sybil, God was offering him the gift of a tomorrow.

Ascension of the Lord

O n Wednesday evening, while Simon had surreptitiously worked the night shift at Sybil's, Stephen engaged in other nocturnal endeavors. He shared one thing with his ministerial supervisor: unwelcome, unsought dreams. In the last couple of nights, his dreams had taken an ugly, ominous turn, outdoing any of Simon's. He would be walking down a road in the dead of night, led by a clawing, paw-like white hand that had to be Joseph's, pulling him forward as Stephen stumbled. Stephen woke in a sweat, shivering with fear, exhausted, the rest of his night ruined for sleep, disgusted by the obviousness of the dream.

In another, Stephen would be alone in a room, like a doctor's waiting room, sterile and empty. Not even any old magazines to distract him. He wondered for whom he was waiting. Finally, a door would open, and standing in the open door was his grandfather, smiling, but in a sinister kind of way, with an oxygen tube attached to his nose, saying, "He can see you now." And Stephen would look through the door, past his grandfather—into an empty room.

At least he didn't have to participate in James's funeral. Of course, he would never have expected to assist with the Niculous funeral, but he had offered to help with James's service, assuming that since he was the only person on staff at Hope who knew James, he would be expected to do the funeral, or at least to assist.

"No, for these sticky situations, people want the Senior Pastor," was the rationale Dr. Lupino gave Stephen. He was disappointed in himself to feel relief for not having to say the last words over James's body, considering that he hadn't been very good with words for the grieving parents.

Were his nightmares the result of seeing Niculous in the river, or were they due to his visit to the morgue? His grandfather's parting words, perhaps, or the result of church? Church and death go together. Some churches even bury their dead under the flooring. He had seen as much in London. Jesus said that "God is a God of the living and not the dead."

But Jesus' pastors are lords of the dead, dutifully touching that which nobody else dares to touch. Something about church had peeled back the protective veneer between Stephen and whatever it was that was out there (or maybe in here?) that lay buried during waking hours. In sleep, the dead arose and haunted him. The past weeks had been the longest time of separation from Thea—testimony to how this church had confined him and consumed his life.

Groggy, gulping a Red Bull for breakfast, Stephen considered the day that lay before him—Thursday, Ascension. Easter, the Great Fifty Days of Joy, was ending; Pentecost and the promised (or threatened) plunge of the Holy Spirit loomed. But first Jesus must leave. Stephen leafed through his devotional booklet, *Greeting the Day*, and found the assigned meditation. The lesson for Ascension was of course from Acts 1:11, "This Jesus, who has been taken up from you into heaven . . ."

Stephen ignored the devotional, written by some retired pastor from Minnesota, who urged readers to "look up" and "to ascend from the ordinariness of everyday life." Instead he simply meditated on the biblical passage. "This Jesus, who has been taken up from you into heaven . . ."

Got that right, Stephen thought. *Jesus has left the building. We're mired down here; Jesus has ecaped somewhere vaguely up there.* Jesus gone, incarnation reversed, and the church in response throws a party on Thursday (even though Hope, he was fairly sure, had never observed or even mentioned Ascension). God up and out.

Funny. When Stephen was a mere layperson, before hands were laid on his head and the Holy Spirit invoked upon him, Christ seemed readily at hand, so close that he could command Stephen to break up with one girl and go after another, deter him from law school and prod him toward seminary, annoy him when he was in the middle of something really pleasurable and make him stooped with guilt over stuff that everybody else thought was OK. Christ too close for comfort.

But now that Stephen was clergy, working full time for God, he couldn't get a visitation by Jesus for love or money. Jesus was always talking to his followers back in the Bible but seemed nowadays to be maddeningly coy. Jesus chatted it up with untrained laity but went sullen and silent around the clergy, his field assistants attempting to keep things together for absent Jesus. Would it kill Jesus occasionally to say something encouraging to those who were doing the heavy lifting in the kingdom of God?

Jesus, I'm out here working by myself, Stephen thought. *Even the most mediocre of pastors would have come up with something wise and wonderful to say to an attractive young woman seeking help with her religious fanatic of a boyfriend, or to a screwed-up teenager contemplating suicide. How about a little help with the lifting, Jesus?*

From these Ascension meditations on mute Jesus, Stephen turned toward a brief consideration of the epistle for the day, Ephesians 1:15–23, a hymn to the greatness of Christ: "And he has put all things under his feet and has made him the head over all things for the church, which is his body, the fullness of him who fills all in all."

There's the church, God bless her, under the heel of Jesus, dirt under his feet.

The church, the Body of Christ? *This* church? Christ's Body is in bad need of a workout.

He would have a ton of stuff to discuss with Thea tonight on the phone, if she had time to listen. On this Ascension, Christ sails up to heaven and one of his young assistants in the hinterland stumbles, trips, and falls face down, mute in the muck and mire.

Reveal thy glory! Do something!

∾

That Thursday Simon did not arrive at church until midmorning, having indulged in an extra long workout at the gym. He was more motivated these days, more intent on keeping in shape. Anybody could see the beneficial results on display when he showered, though only Simon knew the reason.

As he sprinted up the walk from the car park and into the administrative suite, he felt light and cheerful, young and alive, grateful that he had not neglected his middle-aged physique, energized by interests other than the church.

Simon was surprised that Cloe uncharacteristically failed to reply to his hearty, theatrical, "Gooood morning!" Startled, she looked up from her computer screen.

"Dr. Lupino, you will want to see this." Her printer began to buzz, ejecting paper, a hard copy of the email she had been reading. (Simon widely boasted at having very little technological proficiency, dismissing email interaction as "quasi-communication" that was inappropriate for Christian conversation. "Nothing beats face-to-face in an incarnational faith," he had lectured. He therefore assigned Cloe to receive, sort through, and respond to all of his email.)

Cloe handed Simon the paper, saying, "It's anonymous. I know you have a rule not to read anonymous letters, but I figured that you'd want to see this one."

Simon looked down at the piece of paper. While there was no change in his facial expression, Cloe was sure that she saw him blanch. He said nothing as he turned, entered his study, and slammed the door behind him. She turned, raised her eyebrows, shook her head slightly, and resumed her work, hearing only the muffled sound of Simon talking to someone on the telephone.

∾

Shortly after putting away his devotional booklet and checking himself in the mirror, Stephen heard his cell phone vibrate. He took the call. Just his luck—Jack Hodges. "Stephen. Just heard about James. Man, that's terrible. He was a lot younger than me. But I knew him. I coached his soccer team when he was in the seventh grade and I was in high school. Man, that's really a downer. Did you get to talk to him before he died?"

"No, I think he never came out of his coma."

"Was there any warning? I mean, do you think he actually committed suicide?" asked Jack earnestly. "Somebody told me that that's the 'unforgivable sin,' but I don't know. Of course, like you, my big question is, do you think James was saved? That's what I always ask when something like this happens. Don't you? Most kids his age probably think they will never die. I know I did when I was that age; I was immortal. Didn't give the first thought to heaven. And I really haven't seen James in a couple of years. Have never seen him at church. Did you get to talk to him about his walk with Jesus?"

"Jack, I'm sure you mean well. But I just don't want to talk about this now. This thing with James has really thrown me. I'm not in a mood to analyze it right now. OK?" Then, his voice rising, Stephen said, "And look, Jack, let me tell you something, you've got a hell of a lot to learn about, well, everything." With that, Stephen smacked the phone shut.

As he drove toward the church, he chastised himself for his show of annoyance at Jack's sophomoric religiousness. Normally, he was not so blunt. Why had he gone off on poor, stupid Jack? Stephen was forced to admit to himself that one reason he found Jack so aggravating was that Jack reminded him of other overly eager evangelicals Stephen had known in college. That is, Jack reminded him of who he himself had once been. There was a time when Stephen knew more about God than he knew now.

Incorporation

Once, Jesus was available. But today, with Jesus ascended and absconded, Stephen wanted to put his fist through Jack's ivory-white, perfectly polished teeth.

❧

"I would advise you not to be overly confident about what you have been indoctrinated to regard as reality," Jane said casually, as if she were counseling Stephen on how to change a tire. They sat together in the pleasant air on a bench in front of the coffee shop in the early afternoon. Stephen had learned to be grateful that most of their friendly discussions quickly inflated into airy metaphysics. He was eager to get his mind out of the mortuary, out of the river, too. Jane was Stephen's sole theological interlocutor, so Stephen had therefore dared to confess some of his Ascension morning thoughts on the absconding God. Jane brightened, took the bait, and was off to the races, philosophizing.

"Frankly, I'm little convinced of your *deus absconditus*. God has always been closer at hand than I desired. To my mind, we know much more of God than we've been able to process."

Sip of coffee, puff on her cigarette, then she continued, to Stephen's delight, "Of course, I'm a Platonist at heart. I do not refer to Platonic notions of the onerous body; I'm too Jewish to fall for Plato's degradation of the somatic. His typically Greek dichotomization of body and spirit holds little allure. As you know, we honorary Jews look upon the body as good, not fallen. As Paul says somewhere, and I'm sure he said it at the nadir of his pastorate, in some quarrelsome congregation—he had many, I remind you—that he would prefer to be out of the body but, God be praised, he's stuck in the body, at least for the time being. That's us, as I see it. Stuck in the body. Stuck as a body for the time being."

Jane's body-talk prompted Stephen to envision James on a mortician's steel table, naked and bloated, a dead dog on the highway, Mr. Niculous hanging from a tree.

"No, dear Saint Stephen, my Platonism is mainly epistemological. I believe that Plato was onto something: this world, for all of its apparent stability and tangibility, may be a mirage, shadows thrown upon the wall of the cave in which we are chained, a poor substitute for the ideal, that is, the real. I understand that Neoplatonism was the rage in the early days of Christian philosophy. The work of dear Boethius comes to mind. He warned us not to be fooled by surface appearance. Amen! How I despise this modern arrogance that looks upon all this"—she waved her hand, holding her precious cigarette, in a wide sweep encompassing the sur-rounding street scene—"and says, 'Well, this is it. We've fully explained everything to our smug self-satisfaction.' My motto is 'put not all thy trust in things visible and temporal.' Doubt what I say? Remember, my dear boy, that we have spent years indoctrinating you into the supreme, modern article of faith:'What you see is all you get.' Period. What closed-minded conceit! What deceit!"

She inhaled, then expelled the smoke in a small cloud above her head, took another sip from her paper cup, raised her eyebrows as Stephen let go a little cough, and continued. "Who knows? That may be one way of explaining how you got hijacked. You are intelligent, sensitive, a keen observer. Therefore, young Saint Sebastian, you are bright enough to know that this world is not as substantial as your teachers have tried to convince you. You, in your considerable intelligence, hanker to view the world *sub specie aeternitatis.* Have you not found the church—yes, even this pale, latitudinarian substitute, even this contemptible *ekklesia* called Hope—to be occasionally porous, permeated by the divine?"

Stephen relished her philosophical ramblings, his sole exercise of three years of seminary theology courses, one of the few moments in the day when he suspected there just might be a theological rationale for his being here in the first place.

"And what of your theology, young Sebastian? How would you char-acterize your views of God?" Jane asked at last.

"Well, I guess at seminary I learned a theology of humility, a theology based on obedience to the first commandment—'thou shalt not make for thyself any graven images.'"

"And how, pray tell, do you propose to pull that off? This was pre-sented to you by your Princeton professors as humility?" asked Jane.

"Sure. Most of our theologizing, I learned, is little more than a series of attempts to imagine the unimaginable, to construct gods in our own image, that is, idolatry. God is distant, unavailable to our meager human mind."

"It sounds to me as if you learned theology that is in truth anti-theol-ogy," said Jane bluntly. "It's a *non sequitur.* Part of me would like to believe that God is beyond our imagining! In my little life, I have found God to be quite otherwise. Anything but apophatic, I can tell you," she said, shaking her head, laughing to herself. "How I wish for unavailability and incom-prehensibility! I could then live my life as I damn well pleased! My images of God could hardly have been self-constructed. If I were devising gods for myself, I would have devised a more congenial little god than the one for whom you are working!"

Just then an old man in a wrinkled, dirty suit shuffled up to where they were sitting. The two sidewalk theologians looked up at him and braced themselves for a request for a handout. They were surprised when he asked, "Can you tell me where we're all headed? Kids blowin' themselves up in schools, oil spills, the end of Goldman Sachs, and what else? In God's name, what else?"

"Sir, though your questions are titillating, you are clearly inebriated," said Jane, standing up and cheerfully patting the old man on the shoulder. He reeked of alcohol, and worse. Jane picked up her things to leave, snuffing out her cigarette in her cup.

"Good day and God's blessings upon both you teleologists," said Jane as she tossed her cup in the trash and departed. "Sir, I know too well where we're all headed, no time left for speculation. Try your questions upon this dear young man of God."

Bustling her way down the street, Jane espied a sign in the widow of a dress shop that read, "Help Wanted. Inquire Within," and shook her head, frowning at "the spread of silly California New Age spirituality, even here."

Annoyed by Jane's callous dodging of a brother in need, Stephen asked solicitously, "Can I help?" He stood up and offered his hand to the disheveled old man.

"You can if you got some answers without the bullshit," replied the drunk, burping and swaying as he spoke.

"Let me see if I can help," said Stephen. "Do you want help?"

"What kind of smartass question is that?"

Stephen flipped open his cell phone, did a quick Web search, and was relieved to discover an address for the Helping Hands Alcohol Information Center, located no more than a couple of blocks down the next street. Thank you, Lord.

"Let's walk together. I've got some people who can help you," said Stephen to the drunk.

The man narrowed his gaze, peered into Stephen's face with a touch of apprehension, but docile as a newborn, he allowed Stephen to lead him through the café's cluster of tables and toward the corner. When they reached the intersection, the man startled. "Wait a minute. What the . . . Do I know you? Where are you tryin' to take me?"

"A place where there are people who know how to help people with your sort of problems," Stephen said in his most reassuring, pastoral voice.

"What problems? *You're* the one who needs help!" the man said, wrenching his arm away from Stephen's grasp. "Who are you anyway?" His voice rose. "What the hell do you want with me? Help me my ass!"

Terror spread over the man's face. As the streetlight changed and Stephen attempted to guide him across the street, the old man began pulling away. He dug in his heels as he shouted at the passersby, "Help! I don't even know this guy! He's trying to take me somewhere I don't want to go. Help! I'm being used!"

Stephen pulled him toward the street and into the crosswalk, restraining the man while smiling at all who paused and stared. Because it was a nice, warm day, Providence had provided for the maximum number of persons strolling down the street with all the time in the world to gawk. Stephen mumbled to the onlookers, "I'm trying to help this man. I'm a minister." He showed his best sanctimonious smile. "I work at Hope Church."

"Why should I give a damn where you work? Does that make right what you're doing to me?" shouted the old man, "Let go!" By the time Stephen had pulled him to the other side, the light had changed, traffic was moving into the crosswalk, and the man was whooping at the top of his voice, "Help! I don't even know this kid. He's taking advantage of me just because I ast a queshun. Sweet Jesus!"

Stephen was mortified, hoping that no one would attempt a rescue of the noisy old drunk. Stephen smiled apologetically at perfect strangers, some of whom laughed as he coaxed and dragged the old man toward the help center.

"I'm doing an intervention," he explained to a particularly curious woman. "I'm a pastor. I'm trained."

Midway down the next block, the struggling old man, gritting his teeth and resisting Stephen's urging, socked Stephen hard in his right side.

"Hey! Stop that," ordered Stephen. "That hurt."

"You damn right, and I meant it, you jerk," hissed the old man.

For a man in your sad shape, you sure are a strong old buzzard, thought Stephen as he urged him another fifty feet. By the next corner, the man had ceased shouting and struggling, thank goodness, and was plodding along next to Stephen as if he had finally realized that he was doomed to being helped. Stephen was relieved when at last they reached the building at 3487 and he saw the small sign reading HELPING HANDS CENTER. Unfortunately, the sign also said Third Floor, Suite 2.

With one arm Stephen pushed through the revolving door. With his other arm he pulled the staggering, wheezing man into the moving door with him. Being stuck, even for a moment, in the door chamber with the old drunk made Stephen reel; the man's odor was as pungent as an alleyway in August. In the lobby, when a neatly dressed older woman exited the elevator, the man called out to her plaintively, "Madam, can you help a poor man? This black guy is trying to take me to a place I don't know where. For the love of God, get the police or somethin'. Help!"

When the lady paused and looked at the two of them, Stephen muttered, "I'm a minister." The lady moved quickly out of the lobby.

"That's ther trouble with this country," mumbled the man, "nobody wants to take responserbility."

Stephen then pulled the man into the elevator, with one hand pushed the button for the third floor, with the other gripped the old man's arm, and prayed that he could endure the stench while they ascended.

The Helping Hands Center, it turned out, was a lone secretary seated behind a desk. When Stephen swung open the door, he inadvertently shoved the old man near her, and she leaned way back in her chair. From the look of horror on her face, Stephen guessed that despite the assortment of pamphlets on her desk—"When Someone You Love Is Addicted," "The First Step in Recovery Is Asking for Help"—this was the first face-to-face encounter the woman had ever had with a drunk.

As he held tightly to the man's collar with one hand and gestured with the other, Stephen explained, "This man would like some help with his problem. I met him on the street, just a couple of blocks away, and have brought him here for you to help. I'm a minister. I'm Stephen."

"How did you get up here?" the woman responded. "We give out information, pamphlets, things of that nature. We're information, not treatment. Who told you to come here?"

"But I—what can *I* do with him?"

"Hey lady, I'll take some information," the old man said, giving the woman a toothless smile. "I'd like one of them pamphlets. I got into this mess with this black kid just tryin' to get information."

She thrust "Resources for Recovery" into one of his gnarled hands and quickly retreated to her place of safety behind the desk.

"Well, what can we do?" Stephen asked. "It was all I could do to get him in here. We've got to help."

"I'm here by myself," said the woman in a shaky voice. "We're informational, not therapeutic. I'll have to go downstairs and ask Mr. Gunderson what we can do. You cannot leave that man here. We've never . . ." She grabbed her purse and keys, slipped sideways from behind the desk, and, carefully keeping her distance from Stephen and his ward, disappeared when the elevator door opened.

"I'm worn out," said the old man. "I got to sit down. You have next to killed me with your Godawful tryin' to help me. My mistake was to ask you anything, damn you."

Stephen guided the old man into a metal chair next to the desk and took a seat beside him, saying, "These people are professionals."

"You, you goddamn do-gooder! Did I ever ask you to take me to this place? Did I? This is America! I've got rights," slurred the man. "We've got a Constatushun, and the last time I checked it still meant somethin'. Fool."

Moments after this philosophical/constitutional outburst, the old man passed out, mouth gaping wide, sort of snoring as he slumped over in his chair, saliva dripping down the left side of his chin.

Stephen sat next to him, keeping him from falling out of his chair, and (because he was working for Jesus) allowed the stench to waft over him; he felt nauseous and also righteous. He was discovering that it was all well and good to speak of ministry as reaching out to those in need, but to touch (and smell) the wretched of the earth—that was something else. Sitting there, sick from the odor and the wheezing, Stephen admitted to himself that if he couldn't actually do some good for someone in pain, he couldn't stand to be around them. That this old man was beyond help, and had no desire to be helped, exposed the limits of Stephen's expertise in Christian ministry.

Ever so carefully rising, Stephen regained his professional composure, sobered up by a drunk. He stood up quietly and tiptoed out the door, softly closing it behind him. Then he sprinted down the hall, hit the steel door to the stairwell with a bang, bounded down the three flights of stairs like an Olympic steeplechaser, flew into the street and ran off without once looking back, distancing himself from the drunk's reproachful, unassuageable need.

∾

On his way to the administrative suite that Ascension afternoon, passing the portraits of the eight dead pastors, Simon experienced a fleeting, wistful sense of envy for these who had come before him. Oh, to have been a cleric in the fifties when American, liberal Protestantism was ascendant! These bygone pastors built and aspired, initiated and augmented. It was

Simon's lot to officiate over the Body of Christ's retreat and descent. A refurbished wing would be the sole tangible result of his leadership. If Simon had his wishes, he would have spent this afternoon securing new talent, expanding Hope's staff, launching creative initiatives. Instead, he was saddled with the onerous task of ridding himself of an inconvenient young assistant.

Thus, less than an hour after Stephen had returned to his office, sweaty and disgusted after his failed intervention, he was surprised by a call from Dr. Lupino. "Stephen, is it still convenient to meet with me now?" asked Simon, annoyed that Stephen was already ten minutes tardy for their appointed meeting. Simon rarely appeared at the office on Thursday afternoons, and he wouldn't be kept waiting until dark by a bothersome subordinate.

"Sure," said Stephen, horrified that he had completely forgotten their appointment, anticipating another "kid, let me show you the ropes" chat with the Senior Pastor.

Once in Simon's office and settled into his chair, there were no "how are you?" pleasantries. Simon drove right to his subject—the abortive Hope Floats trip.

"Stephen, I would like to hear your version of your recent trip down the East Fork with the youth," said Simon somberly. "More accurately, your trip with *a* youth, *one* youth."

Stephen grimaced. He had not seen this side of the Senior Managing Pastor. "Oh. I'm so sorry that you heard about that. It's one of the biggest disappointments I've had in my whole ministry."

"Did you plan to conceal this from me?"

"No, not at all. It's just that it was a horrible disappointment. Embarrassing. I thought I did everything right with the publicity. Even made personal calls to lots of the kids. More than a dozen signed up but didn't show up. It was supposed to be the kickoff. But I've learned. I now know some things that I would do differently. I'm sort of feeling my way around Hope, getting to know the context, seeing what works and what doesn't . . ."

"Of course, your 'whole ministry' consists of the last few weeks here at Hope. But I'm unconcerned about that. My concern is with the sole young person who accompanied you on the trip—young James Thomas."

"Oh. I just about lost it when I heard that James had OD'd. I've been torn up about it ever since I got the call from Cloe. I rushed right over to the hospital when I heard, but he was already gone. I'll never forget the sight of that empty bed. Then I rushed over to the mortuary. James' parents were sure torn up, and I don't know that I was much help to anybody. I tried, but maybe I let my own grief get in the way of my pastoral care. But I guess everybody has to learn that . . ."

"And you rushed over to the hospital when you heard, Stephen?" asked Simon.

"Cloe told me that you wanted me to be the one to visit James. I figured you wanted me to do it because James and I really bonded on that float trip. Being the only kid who showed up, he had my undivided attention. But I mean, it was more than that. I really got James to open up. Which was one reason why I was so blown away when I heard the news. I want you and everybody to know that I had no warning, no indication. I just can't believe that he was on the verge of something like this. We really talked out some deep stuff on those nights on the river. Are they sure that it was an overdose and not just a mistake? Odd, but with James, for the first time I really felt like a true pastor. And look how it ended."

"So James was dead before you got to see him in the hospital?" Simon asked.

"Right. His body had already been taken by the funeral home."

"That's fortunate."

Stephen wondered why it was "fortunate."

"You say you were in 'great grief.' And what do you mean 'bonded'?" asked Simon.

"Well, you know. Like I say, we got to really know one another. James told me about some of his problems, his issues. I just figured he was a kid who was confused and searching—like lots of kids his age. But I had no idea, no idea at all that any of that would lead to this. He did tell me he had smoked pot, but . . ."

"Stephen, I'll be frank. I'm deeply concerned about your actions on this trip," said Simon. "Deeply concerned."

"Look, I feel terrible about all this too. If you have any advice, anything that could help me be more effective in the future. I have gone over this thing with James a thousand times, asking myself if he said anything that I should have picked up on, anything that might have saved him from this OD thing, and . . ."

"Stephen, take the utmost care in your responses. I remind you that I am duty-bound to report even a rumor that there has been a violation of ministerial integrity rules."

"What?"

"It has been alleged that you and James engaged in some inappropriate behavior while on this trip," said Simon. "That proper boundaries were violated."

"What? Who said that? What boundaries? Look, James talked about drugs, even asked me if I had a joint. I told him in no uncertain terms that I didn't and that I . . ."

"I'm not talking about drugs. I'm talking about whatever happened when you two camped together on those nights by the river. I'm talking about a complete violation of our Safe Sanctuaries policies."

"What?" said Stephen, horrified. "You can't be serious! Who would say such a thing? Unbelievable! Do you think that James and I . . ."

Simon waited, making room for a long, awkward pause that simply got longer; Stephen had no words, but like a dazed defendant just sat there with his mouth agape. Then Simon said in measured tones, "Stephen, young James was a deeply disturbed young man. It has been alleged— someone has said that it appears that you may have taken advantage of his . . . confusion, that you may have violated his trust. We have all counted on you to understand the boundaries, the professional demeanor required of you, the difference between a young man moving toward adulthood and a mature member of the clergy, one entrusted with the lives of sometimes fragile, vulnerable young people."

"Why would anybody dare suggest such a thing?" asked Stephen, staring dumbly at the carpet. "It's unthinkable. Do you mean . . ."

"I am not here to put you in a position of confirming or denying these charges. As I said, the less you say, the better. It appears that there are those who, trying to make sense out of James' tragic end, have wondered just what happened on this float trip. It's understandable for people to wonder what could have driven this bright though disturbed young man over the brink."

"James' parents have said this?" asked Stephen. "Well, I can set them straight right now. Nothing happened on that trip. Nothing! This is crazy!"

"I am not at liberty to say more, Stephen," said Simon. "James' parents have suffered enough. You must have no contact with them. Did you not know that no adult staff member is ever permitted to be alone with a child or teenager, sleeping next to one another, camping, and secluded in darkness? Your great mistake was to leave the parking lot in a van with one child, only to compound the error by camping with him alone. We have never, in all my time here, *never* had a single violation of proper boundaries or a situation of abuse . . ."

"Abuse? Violation? God, this whole thing's unbelievable! Whoever has said this, even if it was James, is telling a lie, a stupid, ugly lie! I'll fight this. I'll . . ."

"No, I don't think you will," said Simon firmly. "His parents have pulled the plug, and we are well on our way to James' funeral. James is quite beyond confirming or denying anything."

"No!" cried Stephen. "So that's why I wasn't asked to help in the service. Thought it was odd. And I don't think James tried to end his life. And his parents didn't pull the plug. I ought to know. I was there. The one person there. And there's no way that anything about the float trip, anything, could have driven him to take his life."

"Son, I am uninterested in your opinion of what is odd. You were the one person who was there, alone. You put yourself in an inappropriate situation with a minor—and that is indefensible. All of this now renders you quite vulnerable, which is why we have our policies in place. For your sake I am trying to redeem an ugly situation. You have also, by your actions, made the church itself vulnerable, so far as litigation is concerned. There are people who would be delighted to corner a rich church like ours."

"But this isn't true!" cried Stephen. "It's all just . . . just a lie!"

"Son, in the church, what is true is never as important as what is perceived to be true. In our profession, appearance is everything. Public opinion is reality. And as for what you do or don't think, it hardly matters; you have, by your own careless, immature—if not downright perverse—behavior, placed yourself in jeopardy. Even if we could say that drugs or alcohol were involved, that's no defense. That you would presume to fight these charges confirms how little you understand of the demands of ministry. Who would believe you? And even if nothing untoward actually happened out there (aside from your allowing an already troubled young man to stare at what was left of Niculous), who would say that you have not cavalierly disregarded and violated our Safe Sanctuaries policies? I'm disappointed that you can't immediately see what a sad, painful situation this is for me."

Stephen tried to speak, shaking his head back and forth, but he could say nothing—he had been reduced to a wordless, powerless, defenseless little boy. It was Joseph's all over again; he was Niculous's corpse rotting in a tree, worms crawling in and out.

"Stephen, I hope you know how painful this is for me," said Simon in an even, pastoral tone of voice that made hearing his words immeasurably worse for Stephen. "I placed great faith in you, went out on a limb, bestowed trust. I am confronting you, not because I want to, but because it's my sacred duty and because, though you may not be able to recognize it, I am your friend. I want the best for you, even in this sad circumstance. Let's handle this here and now, in the confines of my office, rather than running the risk of this getting out. It wouldn't be pretty. Even if I am successful in managing all this, keeping it from the congregation and prowling lawyers, it is bound to be an embarrassment to have gone through all the effort to make a good hire and to have offered an opportunity to a talented young man like you, only to have it terminated in two months."

Stephen stared dumbly into the void.

"There will be those who, of course, attempt to play the race card, saying that your departure is due in some way to discrimination. Actually, my extraordinary leniency toward you may be due to my tendency to be more than fair whenever race is a factor. I hope that I am not exposing Hope to the risk of litigation through my softhearted compassion. We will have some explaining to do. Still, it can be managed."

"This is so wrong," said Stephen. "Wrong."

"Well, what can you do to make it right? That should be your chief concern," said Simon, affecting a more cheerful tone. "You must quickly regroup. Your time at Hope is, of course, done. But not necessarily your ministry. With my help, this can be redeemed. One can recover from lapses of judgment. *Elsewhere*. Say nothing. Would only make matters worse. I will simply announce that you have resigned and that you are looking for a situation that 'feels like a better fit.' Yes, that's the thing. We can both pray to God that no one will make a connection between the float trip, James' untimely death, and your departure.

"We could tell people that you quickly discerned that Hope was just not the right fit. They can then jump to their own sordid conclusions or show you compassion. Be sure that you don't criticize Hope, much less me. That would make you look bad. Whatever you do, you don't want to push me into a position where I would have to say more than needs be said. It could damage you professionally. Forever.

"Actually," Simon said, snapping his fingers, "that your only real project was such a flop could be just the ticket. Yes, that's it: you took personally the failure of the float trip to materialize. You were despondent. I tried to build you up, but you thought it best that you should just leave. Yes, that will win sympathy in the congregation and achieve the desired effect: the switch-off of their brains. The multitudes want to believe the best about clergy. You quietly exit amid widespread murmuring, 'Such a nice young man, and with so much promise too.' I'll write you a glowing letter of recommendation. You could easily land on your feet. My good word will open doors. Yes, that's the thing. See? No cause for despair. Here's a tissue."

Simon's words were body blows. Moments ago, Stephen had been unable to speak; now he was almost unable to breathe. He mustered a half nod toward Simon, as if to assent to his execution, then rose and, at Simon's direction, without making a scene, made his way toward the side door, the one Simon always offered to people in distress who, after a chat, needed a discreet exit.

"I'll shoot that recommendation letter to you. Why don't you clear your stuff from your office this evening, but after the staff has departed? A minimum of fuss. Yes, I'll manage this crisis for you. No problem. You'll see."

As Stephen stood in the doorway, the last words he heard were, "And Stephen, please be sure to turn in all your keys to Cloe."

Angry and helpless, he thought how bitterly ironic it was—though he had little stomach for irony right now—that he had been mightily struggling to do just right as a pastor, only to be booted for something he never would have done.

He thought of James, silenced by death. Grief overtook him, and shame. He was ashamed of himself for wishing that James wasn't dead so that he could testify in his defense. He saw Mr. Niculous hanging there, naked, half-eaten by worms after having jumped (or else dumped) into the river. And now it was his turn. *Homo homini lupus.*

No sooner had he staggered out of the shadow of Lupino's inquisition than Stephen felt another odd sensation—a vague sense of relief. He felt like a character in a gospel miracle story, like a blind man whose sight has been incomprehensibly restored him. Amid the gathering dusk, he made his way into the garth and headed toward the side door to the hall that led to his office. As he walked through the garth, he looked back toward Hope's tower, rising above him, red and golden in the dying sun, a monstrosity horrible to behold.

"I didn't even want to be here," he muttered as he fumbled for his keys and trudged down the darkening hall to his office. There he collapsed into his chair and slammed the door, paralyzed.

ॐ

Unknown to Simon, at the precise moment he was solving the problem of an upstart associate, a potentially deadlier dilemma was brewing in Johnson Quail's office.

"To tell you the honest-to-God truth, I'm unsurprised," Quail said to the two trustees, Hank Judd and Tommy Goodwell. Quail leaned back in his chair to convey a sense of authority, thrilled to have such men of the world—a certified business type and a liberal lawyer—in his office, seeking counsel.

"You have relieved me of a great burden. I have felt professional concern, fearing that I was derelict in my duties as CFO in not finding a way to bypass Simon and alert our lay leadership to the precariousness of our financial situation. Revelation of this mess would have killed poor Niculous," said Quail, overlooking that he had played the key-though-unintended role in Niculous's demise some time ago.

"I should have known that astute businesspersons such as you would be fully cognizant of the impending Hope Township disaster. I want you to know that I have tried, desperately tried to redeem this situation. At last I feel that I need not bear this burden alone. Are you planning on asking for Simon's resignation?"

Both men seemed startled by Quail's question.

"We haven't gotten that far in our thinking," said Hank. "I guess I was hoping that Simon might help us dig out. From what you say, he doesn't seem in much of a mood for that. We can always hope. It's hard to imagine Hope without Dr. Lupino."

"True. You know, of course, that I am Simon's dear friend of long standing," Quail was quick to add. "I would hate to see anything hurt him. I am always on Simon's side—usually. But this is an unusual situation. Sometimes my dear friend is his own worst enemy, I must say. I admire the way the two of you are able to put aside your own genuine, heartfelt affection for Simon and do what is best for the future of our beloved church. I fear that I've been guilty of letting my friendship cloud my judgment. I can tell you, from years of experience, that in any charitable organization, appearances are everything. We must handle this in such a way so as not to upset our major donors, put feelings aside, keep focused on the future of Hope. That's the main thing."

Thus Quail calculated that he, not Simon, was to have the last word. Allow the elders to heap on Simon all of the sins of their managerial ineptitude and then drive the scapegoat into the wilderness—a pleasing scenario.

"And Reverend Quail, how are you doing?" one of them asked, solicitously, "with your treatments and all."

"Fine, just fine," he lied. "Everything is just fine. You are kind to ask, though my personal trials mustn't influence your actions. I leave these matters in your capable hands. Again, let me say, as a financial professional, how much I admire your initiative. And your professional demeanor. Too often the church is guided by mere emotion. Now's the time for clear, sober financial thinking, attentiveness to facts rather than feelings, realities rather than relationships.

"We are doing dear Simon no favor by pulling punches. The sooner all this is resolved, the better for everyone, including him. I can't tell you how relieved I am to know that I do not have to bear this cross alone."

Then, out of his excitement at sitting in the driver's seat, Quail had the temerity to compare himself to Saint Francis, who had been told, allegedly by a talking crucifix, to rebuild the tottering church of God. Together, they could overcome Simon's miscalculations and, like Saint Francis, rebuild. Judd and Goodwell, though they were intelligent business people, were still laity, and they sucked up Quail's blather with eagerness, falling enthusiastically into his embrace.

"Oh God, please let me live," Quail prayed aloud as he watched them exit, shaking their heads and casting down their eyes in grave concern. Studying their departure from the vantage of his office window, aware of a pronounced growling sensation in his stomach, he made his solemn petition to heaven: "Don't let me die before I crush that sonofabitch."

∾

Stephen sat in his cell for the rest of that slowly dying day, immobile, stunned, defeated, until darkness fell. There was no light except for a shaft of white that cut through his office's slit of a window from the floodlights outside. Thank God he had stopped his infantile sniveling. Now, in the emptiness, rage became his sole consolation. Damn all of them! He so wished for Thea. Seemed like ages. Oh, to lie with her, held close in her arms, safe, loved and caressed like a child.

It had crossed his mind to call his mentor, Jane, his only surviving friend at Hope. Surely she could shed some theological wisdom upon this ungodly injustice. But that would be unfair to the sweet old lady. Maybe Simon was right: nothing could be said in his defense. So now it was night and the end of the story, his clergy career abruptly terminated before it began.

In his office, now a locked black box, Stephen's rage boiled. He beat his fists on the desk. He kicked the trash can. These actions he took as positive signs that he was turning his inner hurt outward, seeking its proper object—Hope Church. He tended to take too much responsibility upon himself, turning his hurt inward. He had been told his tendency toward the passive-aggressive was typical of clergy.

This time was different. He had done nothing wrong, never laid a hand on James. The thought made him nauseous. How he wanted to teach them a lesson. Burn the place down? Kill somebody? Maybe he was the only one to learn from this—the stupidity of the life he was attempting to lead, the futility of throwing himself away for nothing.

He noticed a lone envelope on his desk. He rose, split it open in the darkness, pulled out the letter, and held it up to the faint light at the window. It informed him that his fine for parking in the handicapped space at the hospital, due to an error by the officer, was actually two hundred dollars, not a hundred. Dropping the paper to the floor, he collapsed again into the chair, cursing like Job the day of his birth.

During one of their infamous coffee shop conversations, Jane had said the memorable words, "God is a great teacher; unfortunately, he kills all of his pupils."

Now, school was over. After some time—perhaps it had been hours—his fury infused him with the strength to struggle out of his chair, get up, and stomp out of his office, carrying with him nothing but a box with a few books. His nicely framed seminary diploma he had dumped in the trash can. He fussed and fumed across town to his apartment. Entering, he dumped the books, which had been of only marginal use to him as a pastor and were now worthless. Sitting on the edge of his unmade bed, he called Thea and, when she didn't answer, again left a plea to join him on his last night at Hope before tossing his phone across the room in frustration.

He cleared his whole apartment in less than an hour, cramming what he could into his car and dumping the nonessentials in the alleyway out back. His material possessions were few, and his list of essentials had diminished considerably in the last few hours. Less than two months ago he had unpacked, ready to begin a new life at Hope. Now, each item tossed into the trash felt like a funeral. There wasn't much to retrieve after picking over the carcass of what was left—shortest run on record in the whole history of Christian ministry.

His only experience of loss as deep as this one had come in the week after his grandfather died. Tossing his grandfather's old photographs, Medicare receipts, military service records, and other ephemera had been one of the saddest moments of his life. He now relived that sadness. Everything consigned by death to the trash pile.

When he came to the two big boxes of files and papers, his complete store of wisdom from his years of theological education, he took a deep sigh and determinedly heaved it into the alleyway. If it was sad to dispose of his grandfather's treasures, this was worse—a ritual of relinquishment, an indecent burial of his theological career.

Upon seeing the cover of a binder that read "Calvin 101," he felt not only sad but stupid. Not a single book from his seminary days had been opened since he had been at Hope. Church History. Theology. Pastoral Care. Homiletics. As each volume hit the trash pile, he pondered the huge gap between seminary and church. Only the course he had endured in Abnormal Psychology and Spiritual Development came close to being relevant, and that was because everybody at Hope was nuts. The actual church, as opposed to the church hypothetical, had nothing to do with books.

The best years of his life (and a small fortune) squandered in the study of arcane drivel in preparation for the dumbest job at the most pointless place on earth. He was a chump.

His last act of burial was to grandly toss on the pile his master's hood, clerical collar, and clergy shirt, graduation gifts from his mother. He had worn the collar only once—on the day of his ordination. His mother didn't even approve of his becoming a pastor, regarding his vocation as a passing phase, like when, at five, he wanted to be a fireman.

His hope was that some random homeless drunk, going through the pile of rubbish, would find the shirt, collar, and hood and wander the streets asking for a handout of free booze, backed up by his Princeton credentials.

He made another pleading call to Thea. This would be one church service she would enjoy. Again he checked his voice mail. Nothing. Stephen stood in the middle of his little kitchen, surveying what was left of his first apartment. As he stood there, he cradled an absurdly large plastic bottle of cheap, peach-flavored vodka, at least three years old, which someone had brought to a birthday party during his seminary years; Stephen had reserved it for just the right occasion. He then left his empty apartment (he didn't lock the door, or even shut it—he was a month ahead in his rent anyway), bearing the libation to his car, vodka consecrated for such a night as this.

Stephen bolstered himself with chicken chow mein from the Chinese restaurant on Second Avenue. Holding the box in his lap, he ate the stringy mess as he drove, making his way through dark streets back toward Hope Church for a farewell Compline, slobbering the chow mein down the front of his shirt. It was midnight. He let himself in a side door for last rites, then flung the whole ring of keys out into the yard behind him once the door had been opened.

"Keys to the kingdom, you thieves! Help yourselves to all the leftover mints and used Sunday school pins you want!" he shouted into the darkness as the keys clanged against the wall of the west wing and fell into the shrubbery.

Abandon hope, all who enter, Stephen thought. He groped through dark hallways until he reached the lightless sanctuary, swigging the vodka. If Thea had called, he fantasized about begging her to join with him in some dirty, sacrilegious act before the Hope high altar. That would fix them. But there he was, alone, with no illicitness to fling in their face but cheap vodka. Because the only windows in the cavernous sanctuary were stained glass, it was as dark as the cold side of the moon. Stephen felt and stumbled his way down the aisle past a few rows, then slid down a pew toward the back of the sanctuary. Thus begins the Liturgy of Self-Consolation in the manner of our Lord in the Gospel of John, Wedding at Cana—with the consumption of a large amount of alcohol, inducement of the Spirit by spirits, this time not in blood-red wine but rather in peach-flavored vodka.

His eyes were dry. And now wide open. When wronged, his usual response was hurt, turn inward, lick his wounds, and curse himself. This time he was angry, defiant toward the true perpetrators of injustice against him. Though it was dark, he saw everything twenty-twenty. He cursed Pope Simon for not standing up to the rumors and defending him. "Damn you!" he shouted, his voice echoing back at him in the cold, empty church.

He swilled the burning, sweet stuff. *How much would it take to kill me?* he wondered. It would serve them right to find his body putrefying under a pew when they showed up to praise God on Sunday. "We killed our pastor! That is, just a youth pastor. We've been bad! We lost our Neeeegro! God have mercy!"

Liquid dribbled down his chin. Images flooded through his defenseless mind as he recalled every accursed thing that had happened to him in the last two months. He saw faces, heard bits of conversation. While the room began to swirl and swing around him, a phantasmagoria of grinning, slobbering, hideous spirits sneered at him. Then Jane's knowing but beneficent smile. The plaintive face of James, too. He lay down on his back on the pew and stared into the nothingness, dying to be blissfully blind, smashed, praying to be as crazy as the old drunk on the street.

Sometime before dawn he was startled awake. Bright light streamed through the large lancet windows, all twelve of them. Everything blindingly blue and eerily ethereal. He pulled himself up by clutching the pew in front of him. The sanctuary had melted into streams of light flooding through each window, blinding in its sinister brilliance. He strained and stared dumbly at the General William Booth window, one of his favorites, but Booth had become bizarre. Oh, God! It was Simon dressed in a dark blue Salvation Army uniform. Simon had this silly, pious, self-satisfied look on his face as he reached out to a small, grinning black child, offering bread. Next to him was Mrs. Lupino, in a Salvation Army bonnet, tambourine in hand, but with her shriveled breasts exposed. Squinting, he made out the figure of Grimball, also kneeling, hands folded sweetly in prayer. In the next window John Brown had been supplanted by Johnson Quail with a glowing halo around his glistening bald head, a large, bloody pike in his hand, a small black child kneeling before him with hands lifted up in supplication. And Alexis in a tight T-shirt that left nothing to his imagination. He lurched about in horror to see Abraham Lincoln's Union Army uniform stuffed with Glumweltner's fleshy corpulence, looking like Porky Pig.

And when he turned his head to the left and strained to see the figure in the Margaret Sanger window, he was almost unsurprised. Jane veiled by a cloud of cigarette smoke, mysterious, alluring, and sick. Was he drunk or dreaming? And high above the altar, with hands outstretched—what was left of his hands—was a pallid gray figure, arms spread as if nailed to a cross. Or were they outstretched in blessing? It wasn't Jesus. It was the dead man caught in the tree in the river, Mr. Niculous, grinning at Stephen as if they now had something in common.

Stephen was relieved to find his own face nowhere among them. He wanted to be the audience, looking up at the show, but penetrated by the eyes of the freaks in the windows, he felt as if they were the audience, looking down at him.

Stephen fell back on the pew, repulsed, defying a strange magnetic pull. All of them, the good and the bad, all being wrenched away from whatever security they clung to in futility, all caught in some irresistible, fearsome dragnet, pulled through the narrow needle's eye of judgment, the veil pulled back, the door swung open, the whole lot dragged toward the river, the deadly, cleansing, dark baptismal river.

He clutched the sides of the pew, dug his heels into the floor lest he be pulled down by the undertow. Everything floating, swept toward the naked crucifix that loomed over the mélange of queer saints without virtue, reprobates reluctantly redeemed, doomed to gather at the river, struggling to be free of the deadly, tightening grasp of a God too gracious to make proper distinctions.

∾

Later that morning, probably about nine, the Downstairs Maintenance Manager, listlessly pushing a dust mop down the left aisle, found the lifeless body of a young man in jeans and a T-shirt sprawled halfway on and halfway off one of the pews toward the back of the sanctuary. He smelled him before he saw him. At first he thought it was the body of a vagrant, some street person needing a bed for the night. It had happened before. Then he recognized the disordered heap as the youngest member of the church's professional staff.

"Boy! What are you doing here?" he asked, shaking Stephen's shoulder. "Did you sleep here last night? What you think you doin'? You awake?"

Groggy, rubbing his forehead, Stephen replied, "No, here's where I died."

The janitor watched as Stephen sat up, rested his head on the back of the pew in front of him, then attempted to gather himself and his belongings. Brushing aside the janitor's offer of aid, cradling the empty vodka bottle, Stephen, vertiginous and queasy, slid out of the pew into the aisle. To his surprise, he stood upright, and summoning a shred of dignity, he wobbled toward the nearest exit.

"You better not do that again. I can tell you. That stuff will poison you, make you sick, make you go blind," preached the janitor.

"It cured me—opened my eyes, actually," mumbled Stephen. No sooner was Stephen out the door than he lost it, hurling the previous night's chicken chow mein into a clump of shrubbery, splattering small chunks of unidentifiable stuff on a memorial plaque that read, "This portico given in loving memory of Arthur Rogers, beloved husband and church trustee. Daddy, we miss you. AD 1931."

As he wretched he recalled a story he had heard in a seminary lecture. As a youth, Kierkegaard's pious father, in despair at his debts and life's misery, stood on a windy hill in Jutland, shook his fist, and cursed God. Thereafter, the elder Kierkegaard's life became prosperous and happy.

Wiping vomit from his chin, Stephen pushed himself into his car, making a solemn vow never again to enter a church. William James declared that he had to inhale a strong dose of nitrous oxide, laughing gas, before he understood Hegel. A quart of vodka enabled Stephen to comprehend the whole of Christ's sorry Body. Now, for the first time in a very long while, he was free. He could see. Things were at an end between him and God. He was happily alone. Jesus had risen, ascended, and left. Never would he tell anyone about this Ascension night and its vision. Never would he entrust his life to wishful inventions.

And never again would he ingest either chicken chow mein or peach-flavored vodka—if he lived past this morning.

∾

Midway through the service that Sunday, as the first lesson for the Sixth Sunday after Easter was being intoned (Acts 17:22–31), when the pimple-faced teenaged lector (cursed be Student Sunday, thought Simon) got to the phrase, "so that they would search for God and perhaps grope for him and find him," Simon, unburdened and in a highly impish mood, looked out into the congregation, peering toward Sybil's section, and thought how wonderfully rich was the word *grope* in this assemblage. He smiled incautiously. Sybil looked wonderful, even from this distance, displaying a mauve pashmina with a just-right gold broach on her left shoulder. Even in church she was a skilled practitioner of flair and accessorizing. Happy the man who gets to grope, he mused.

Simon had considered preaching on this text, Paul's speech at the Areopagus, as a rare biblical example of a reasoned defense of the faith. But he had reconsidered, uncertain if Paul's speech to the Athenians was rational.

The second lesson was 1 Peter 3:13–22, something about Noah and baptism having "saved through water." Unbridgeable.

Simon's target was the appointed gospel, John 14:15–21:

Today's gospel is excerpted from a redundant section of the Gospel of John: "If you love me, you will keep my commandments."

What does that mean?

"Love" is an abused and ill-defined word. A distinguished writer has said, "Love has been reduced to a feeling, a vacuous, free-floating sort of emotion without content or substance."

The "distinguished writer" was Simon himself.

And how odd of our Lord to link "love" with "commandments." Can love be commanded? Can someone be ordered, coerced, to love someone else? That can't be real love. Besides, Jesus' "if" makes love conditional, commodified; I give you this in exchange for your giving me that.

Many of you know how maddening it is to have someone say, "If you really, really love me, then you will—fill in the blank for yourself—for me." That's not real love! Love, true love, is unconditional, inclusive, accepting, affirming, and utterly gratuitous. Love is more than mere groveling obedience. Love that is based on freely given response and affection—ah, that is true love.

Real love is precious, the holiest, purest gift one can give another. In the gift of love is the highest exercise of our humanity. That sad, cold person who is unable to give or to receive love is hardly human.

His anger at Mary had birthed this thought in his sermon, though surely none of his listeners would make the connection.

Religion, any religion, is about love. Sadly, all religions tend to turn what should be a freely offered experience of the divine into hard rules and regulations, moral prescriptions and ethical injunctions, as if love could be commanded!

Glumweltner, staring passively across the chancel to the soprano section, thought, *If Jesus had any standards, he would descend, rip Simon out of that pulpit, and cram his fist down his throat for preaching such blasphemous drivel.* A smile broke on the choirmaster's fat, red face at the thought: Jesus standing before the astounded congregation, saying, "That man's an idiot! What claptrap and twaddle. I'm taking him out."

Therefore, for each of you my prayer is that you will know the mystery, the wonder of receiving love from another and the privilege of offering love to someone else. I think this is why God put us on this old earth. God is love. Love really is all we need.

If anyone were listening closely, comparing Simon's tone and presentation with past sermons, that listener would have detected a striking earnestness in Simon's voice. Simon's unaccustomed sincerity was unnerving for some in the congregation.

Grimball, perched on his organ bench, thought only, *OK Simon, you've hit your allotted twenty minutes, let's begin to shut down the rhetoric. Conclusion, if you please.*

Glumweltner, having now dismissed the sermon as an object of his attention, gazed more intently across the chancel at the sopranos who sat opposite him and thought, *I wonder if that new girl has a boyfriend? She's quite hot.*

Not listening, though his head was turned toward the preacher, was Johnson Quail, eyes open but not seeing, feeling a vague but unmistakable pain in his belly. He presumed the throb to be the tumor, growing steadily, greedily doing its dirty work within him, metastasizing from his gut through his whole body, seeking out each crevice and pore, augmenting itself, malignantly, slowly possessing, quietly summoning him—and not one single soul either to notice or to mourn God's wrath at work. The tumor that had taken over his every waking thought now took over his body, cell by cell. Terrified, powerless, he heard nothing but the gnawing, omnivorous tumor. Quail sat near the Margaret Sanger window, next to a trustee and her husband. How long did he have? How painful would it be at the end, he wondered, as the tumor silently slithered through him, steadily wrapping itself around him, taking him to a place he could not resist.

Although Stephen had secured the services of the youth ushering and reading this morning, Stephen was not in the congregation, nor would he ever be again, and few inquired into his quiet departure.

When, after the sermon, Simon descended the pulpit, during the first notes of the wonderfully fortuitous last hymn ("Love Divine, All Loves Excelling"), with a sort of silly smile upon his face, he surveyed the congregation, his eyes again searching for Sybil.

All loves excelling, joy of heaven to earth come down . . .

Sighting Sybil, he was sure that today she sang with unusual authenticity. The source of her zeal must be him, must be them. He thought perhaps he saw in her eye just the hint of a tear.

∽

"Hold your voice down, fool!" Quail shouted at the wild woman. Two rather hefty ushers wrestled with her in the narthex as the last hymn rang out. Quail had been summoned, during the opening notes of the hymn, from his accustomed position toward the rear of the church, awakened from his meditations upon mortality by a frantic usher.

Quail was aghast to find a wildly dressed older woman, in some sort of Eastern-looking get up, pulling and pushing against two ushers, strangling one of them by the long end of his tie, shrieking, "I'm the prophet sent to warn this church. God is not mocked!"

Though Quail ordered, "Hush!" she kept shouting, "Judgment is coming! The flood!" and other incoherences.

"Call the cops!" Quail commanded, annoyed that the usher had delayed coming to this action on his own. As the usher unclasped her so he could fumble for his phone, Quail positioned himself upon her flailing left arm. She was surprisingly strong, in the way insane people tend to be. Twice she kicked Quail, once in the groin.

Changed from glory into glory, 'till in heaven we take our stand . . .

"You're hurting me, you silly bald fool," she hissed.

"Good," he sneered.

"Let's take her out," Quail said to the beefy man who struggled with her right arm. "The recessional will be here any minute."

"Take her out?" he asked.

"I mean," Quail responded, "get her outside."

Before they could tame her, she broke free and, in an instant, grabbed a hymnal off a nearby side table, drew back, and threatened to heave it. "Back off, you ministers of the devil!" she spat.

One of the ushers, an insurance actuary, ten years ago a college football player, dove for her. As he did, she slung the hymnal, which narrowly missed him and sailed into a small stained glass window in the narthex, shattering the glass.

"You witch!" yelled Quail. "You just destroyed the Virgin Mary! That window is irreplaceable!" Quail joined the group who had now wrestled her to the floor and were dragging her toward the doorway. "I swear to God, you will pay!" He gave her a swift kick in the side for good measure.

With difficulty they hauled her, just as the crucifer, acolytes, and choir burst into the narthex from the sanctuary.

'Till we cast our crowns before thee, lost in wonder, love and praise.

"You'll be sorry!" she screamed. "House of the Devil!" By that time an exhausted and sweaty Quail was relieved by a couple of younger, fitter men who pinned her on a memorial bench in the prayer garden, having been reassured, "Cops on the way."

"Don't step on that broken glass!" ordered Quail. "We'll need every piece for the repair."

"You're all Satan's bitches!" the woman screamed.

Awaiting deliverance by the police, watching a gang of grown men made to look like fools, Quail thought, *Lady, you're not as crazy as you look.*

7

The Seventh Sunday of Easter

Monday morning, Eastwood Cemetery. Seven fresh graves had been opened since Easter, only two for members of Hope. Black tin markers displayed each new resident's name, neatly enshrined in plastic envelopes. James Matthew Thomas. Plot 1286. Occupied after a short reading by Simon, selections from the works of Maya Angelou, followed by a prayer by Herb Cohellen. A soloist sang "Danny Boy" before dirt was dropped on the coffin.

The other grave, plot 1342, was that of Henry Wiltonson Niculous, beneficiary of a longer service before fewer mourners.

Though James and Niculous had never met at Hope, they were now brothers, as it were, united (as is all of humanity) by the fact that their divergent paths had led to the same end.

Rigor mortis occurred within about four hours of James's death. He lay in a gray casket, his body displaying (to the casual observer) few signs of decomposition. With time, it would disintegrate. Every body—high and low, those who die violently and those who slip quietly into death while in their beds—is subject to identical factors of putrefaction. Death is relentlessly democratic.

Both James's aunt from Chicago and his grandmother from Toledo asked for the casket to be opened so they could view the body. Seeing is believing.

And so these bodies, nothing but dust, lay there, dependent upon the possibility that the same God who made the world out of nothing might make something out of them in their now degraded state. They lay facing east, awaiting Saint Paul's promised "redemption of your bodies," unless the Sadducees were right, in which case they would rest without hope.

∾

"Yes. I did want to speak with you, directly with you. May I ask who was responsible for the Negro spiritual that the quartet sang at Niculous' graveside service?"

Simon listened to Glumweltner's response. He knew, of course, that Glumweltner had chosen all the music.

"I am not offended that they were off-key," said Simon, his voice rising in anger. "No, my concern is more fundamental. My objection is the selection of the hymn . . . for a man who met his demise like Niculous."

He listened.

"No, this has nothing to do with suspicions of incipient racism. I could care less about the ethnic derivation of the song. And it makes no difference if the song's theme was eternal life. The song was tasteless and even offensive to many, an embarrassment."

After a moment, Simon was compelled to add, "No, I'm not accusing you of bad taste."

Pause again.

"Gerald, have you lost your mind? At the burial of a man who perished by drowning? 'Shall We Gather at the River'?"

∾

Stephen crashed back at his barren apartment, overcame his horrible hangover, and vegetated, ashamed that he had turned to the bottle to help him make it through the night. Getting drunk and getting wasted—the conventional, young American male way of muddling through—was nothing to brag about. In his mind, his unoriginal behavior validated that a person like him was unsuited to an unconventional vocation.

He had lost his cell phone in the recent apocalypse, suspecting it to be hiding under one of the back pews. Thus he had heard nothing from Thea, nor had anyone heard from him. On Wednesday afternoon, deep into his enforced exile, he had shaved, fished out of the trunk of his car his sole coat, tie, white shirt, and gray pants and went reluctantly toward the Thomases' house on Eastover Lane.

Before a white-trimmed brick home, with yard so severely manicured that it resembled that of a bank, he took a breath, steadied himself, said a prayer, and stepped out of the car—right into a large lump of dog feces, deposited by nothing less than a Great Dane, sliding five or six inches through the fresh mess. Damn. He expended the dozen feet from his car to the Thomas's front walk attempting to scrape his shoe.

With trepidation, he rang. If nobody answered, at least he had tried, pressing the bell for three measured rings, "In the name of the Father, and the Son, and the Holy Spirit." He was sure he reeked of dog poop.

To his disappointment, the door was opened by a woman with red, puffy eyes. She was dressed in a housecoat at two in the afternoon.

"Mrs. Thomas? Uh, remember me? I'm Stephen. The minister from the church? That is, youth minister. Former youth minister, that is."

"I know," she said softly and, without expression, stood aside in the open doorway.

As he entered the darkened living room, Stephen weighed the meaning of the words, "I know."

She offered a soft chair next to a table with a vase of flowers beginning to wilt. The flowers had to be from Joseph's. The room was dark, musty, confining and close. The chair devoured Stephen; he struggled to sit upright.

"How are you doing, Mrs. Thomas?"

"How do you think I am doing, Stephen?"

"Er, lousy?" *Damn*, thought Stephen.

"Yes, that's what James might have said, 'lousy.'" She smiled faintly and closed her housecoat around her knees.

"Uh, Mrs. Thomas, I thought so much of James. In my whole time here, uh, James was my closest friend. The loss of James is about the worst thing that's ever happened to me."

"You are nice to say that."

He was faintly aware of the odor of the dog poop mingling with that of the wilted flowers. He looked down at the carpet and saw none, though he saw traces on the sole of his shoe.

"No, I really mean it. How is your grief process?" It was a question that he thought he recalled from his Introduction to Pastoral Care course. Nervously looking aside, he saw, dimly, a framed photograph of a boy, clueless, peering out from under a baseball cap that was pulled down to his ears. James wasn't smiling, even for a picture, even back then.

At the sight of James, a deep sadness overcame Stephen. He had gone to the hospital fearing that James might be brain dead, but nothing is as dead as body dead. Nobody wants a spirit; without a body—a confused kid peeking out from a baseball cap—nothing's there.

"Jim doesn't believe in God, not because he has actually thought the matter through, but simply because he hasn't bothered. I, on the other hand, am convinced that God is punishing us," Mrs. Thomas said matter-of-factly, abruptly moving the conversation from grief to God.

Stephen exclaimed without thinking, "Uh, I can't believe in a God who would hurt and punish people like this."

"Humm. In what sort of a God are you willing to believe?" she asked, with more than a hint of reproach in her voice. "Much of the Bible is on my side." Her sarcasm was palpable. "It's consoling to have uncovered a reason. When we rushed James to the hospital, Jim looked at me across James' lifeless body, and I knew. The sins of the fathers—and mothers—visited upon the children. I'm not James' mother. She was a young whore whom Jim stumbled upon when he was at the Bar Association Convention seventeen years ago last fall. She supported her habit through sex. Jim says she stalked him back to his room, fell into his arms. It was a dry time in our marriage. James' sister was only three. We contemplated separation. Her name was Sherry. She told Jimmy that she would scream, call the police, claim that he raped her if he didn't give her money. He thought six hundred dollars was the end of it."

Stephen, attempting to breathe under the burden of so much unsought revelation, risked asking, "Is Mr. Thomas here?" He was ashamed of himself for feeling almost grateful to hear that James's mother, this cold woman in such agony, was not James's natural mother.

"Upstairs, in bed, gazing at the ceiling, looking for a better answer," said Mrs. Thomas rather coldly. "I find that strange. If you don't believe there is a God, why ask for answers? Jim fell into severe depression at the demise of Anderson Consulting; how could he possibly summon the resources to deal with the loss of his only son? Jimmy was always weak."

Stephen couldn't form words.

"So, two or three months later, here was Sherry, in town, pregnant, threatening this, demanding that," she continued. "After Jim's tearful, pleading explanation, I was devastated, livid, and I"—here her stern countenance begin to break and her eyes moistened—"I demanded an abortion. Jim begged me, won me back. So, not being able to toss this embarrassing baby away, we lived a lie, telling everybody that we had tried to get pregnant, that we so wanted another child, so we adopted through a law firm that specialized in this sort of thing. So there we are with a baby boy to be baptized at Hope."

"So you think that God is punishing you for your husband's . . . indiscretion?"

"Jim's one-night stand is nothing. No, ours is the failure to see God's offer of a second chance. The sin is our ingratitude. God offered a gift, redemption, a vocation. And we were too cowardly to receive it."

"But, but you adopted James, and you were wonderful . . ."

"I'm sure there were rumors at church. I had my little life all planned out—successful attorney's wife, nice family, afternoons beside the pool at the club. James' misery was God's judgment upon our empty dreams.

"He was smart. When he had trouble in school—no friends, feelings of inferiority—I knew. Our sin was finding us out. Sitting through all the sermons, regular attendance at church, and we can't face the fact that life is messy, we are sinners, and we all need forgiveness?"

"I—I just don't see why you are punishing yourself," Stephen pled.

"Odd. You preachers tend to focus on God as the 'giver of life,' when the thing that gets me is not God's giving but God's taking," she said reflectively. "Oh, my. I have frightened you. I was only trying to explain. How difficult it must be for a young man like yourself to be forced to consider the sort of God with whom you are working.

"Of course, I'm only a layperson, but in my experience our sins are usually due to incompetence, or stupidity, rarely to deliberate malice. And God help you if you ever refuse God's gift."

With that, Stephen made an awkward exit, although it felt more like an escape.

"Kind of you to come by," Mrs. Thomas said, closing the door behind him. "I doubt that we shall be back at church. Nothing more painful to endure, for people like us, than a happy church."

He heard the key turn in the lock.

It was a revelation. What James's mother thought that he—a klutzy youth pastor—had or hadn't done on the river had nothing to do with anything. Nobody cared if he was James's friend; they were determined to make him the best friend of God.

He rushed down the well-trimmed walkway, gasping for breath, desperate to breathe air free of dog poop and death, glad to escape that dark living room, seeking a place where nobody talks about punishment and sin.

Getting back into his car he noted on the floorboard an antique, brass key. At once he recognized the key as belonging to a door at Hope, the lone survivor of his late-night key toss. He would keep it for old times' sake. In a heightened theological state, Stephen stared at the key and noted that there was no way to tell what a key was for if you had never seen a key at work. Nothing in a key's appearance explained its purpose. Like so many things in life, a key's meaning is not self-evident; it had to be discovered— or else revealed.

Why must things be so freaking mysterious? he thought.

As he drove away, Stephen had the embarrassing thought that even a slimy mortician like Joseph had an easier life than ministers. Undertakers had something useful to do after a death. Clergy are forced to handle "remains" that can't be embalmed or buried.

Nearing the street where his gutted apartment waited, Stephen remembered Jane's pronouncing with mock solemnity, "A priest! Only you, the unspotted and unblemished, are permitted to enter the sanctuary of Melchizedek, only you peek behind the veil. Ah, what terrors you will see!"

∾

Though the day was beautiful and he was carefree and brimming with delight, Simon risked work on his Sunday sermon. He chastised himself for his failure to be true to his management principles: Get the repugnant out of the way first so that one has unencumbered time for the more congenial.

To be sure, he had had little unpleasantness in recent days, aside from annoying staff and a couple of inconvenient funerals. Such vexations come with the job of leadership. "My, you are cheerful," Dora Grantham had said to him at the club. Though he had never cared for Dora, he took her greeting as an indication that his internal condition was showing. It was good to have others—even Dora, whose hair tint changed with the seasons—see it in him.

He had come by the club, keen for a "Sybil sighting"— she was often at the Club for Thursday tennis. But he had been disappointed. How inconsiderate not to let him know her tennis had been canceled, he had later teased over the phone. That he projected a cheerful countenance, even in his disappointment at not seeing Sybil, was testament to the reality of his love, the depth of his passion.

First Lesson, Acts 1:6–14. The "two men in white robes" asked the disciples, "Why do you stand looking up toward heaven?" Some potential there—our work is on earth, not in heaven. Dumbly staring into the sky, disciples fail to see the truth that is more mundane: we have everything we require right here on dependable *terra firma*. Some Christians get so worked up over the life to come that they fail to live here, now.

Everybody already believes that sermon; no need to reiterate the obvious.

Perhaps a linkage of the assigned gospel, John 17:1–11. Jesus bids farewell to his disciples with a long, redundant prayer. God is in heaven; we are on earth. Give thanks that you discovered Hope, church of responsible, self-directed adults who walk without crutches.

Who among them wouldn't love such a homily? Think for yourselves. Live the questions. Dare to stand upon the moderate, middle ground.

Destination in sight for Sunday's sermon, mind unburdened, he found himself wondering what Sybil might be up to. Surely she was awake and prowling by now. In his mind's eye, he could see her—long fingers cradling a gold-rimmed china cup as she drank her second cup of dark French coffee, perhaps at the antique wrought-iron table in her garden.

The sermon finale could wait. He had accomplished the most arduous task of sermon preparation—devising a snappy idea. As Simon tidied his desk, he again had the uncanny feeling of being scrutinized. The pesky bird had at last given up its incessant tapping at his window. Was his email secure? Surely Mary wouldn't stoop to hire a private snoop. Still, once lawyers descend, smelling the scent of a fresh kill, and the divorce wheels begin grinding, people do funny things. As the Lord warned Cain, take care, for sin is crouching at the door.

ॐ

Even as Simon was concluding his first pass at a sermon for Sunday, Stephen drove through early afternoon rain to Thea's, determined to reach her apartment before she returned from the library. He was now nearly fully recovered from his nocturnal vigil in the sanctuary, his four-day funk, his botched reach to James's parents, and any effort to figure out what had happened to his life. Now, showered and shaved, after a week of dreamless nights (thanks be to God) on a bare mattress, he was on his way back to the land of the living, seeking solace from the only person in the world who could save him from his morass of self-regret.

Since Thea was so wrapped up in her studies, he would come to her, camp at her apartment, revel in her consolation, and consider which step to take next. He would need to exercise restraint in sharing his feelings;

Thea had little tolerance for sniveling. On the other hand, now that he was done with this "church stuff," she would be pleased. He could at last land a "real job," they could move in together, she could finish school, and they could get on with life in the real world.

The prospect of her saying "I told you so" displeased him, though he deserved it. As he drove through the rain, the windshield wipers seemed to move in sync with the White Stripes' "Denial Twist" on his iPod, the edgy screaming complaint of Jack White matching his mood.

> *. . . think holding hands is all in the fingers*
> *Grab hold of the soul where the memory lingers . . .*
> *never do it with a singer . . .*

He might tell Thea about his afternoon visit to Mrs. Thomas, sparing her the gory details. But he would tell no one, not even Thea, of his strange night in the sanctuary, sniveling and smashed. People like him—people groomed to be mainline Protestant, people with good grades at Princeton Seminary, people who don't believe that Elvis is still alive but who do believe that the folk of Roswell, New Mexico, are nuts—didn't have stuff like that happen, even when drunk.

> *. . . people get confused and they bruise*
> *Real easy when it comes to love . . .*
> *Just because she makes a big rumpus*
> *She don't mean to be mean or hurt you on purpose, boy . . .*

The door to his intended future had been shut. Now it was up to him to discover the key to unlock another. Stephen had no plans, other than to get the hell out of Hope. He would chill at Thea's, get a new cell phone, a new address, and first thing Monday, a new vocation, this time without God.

ᘇ

"No, as I've told you, I have no idea where Smith is," Quail told the two worrisome mothers. "Yes, I see on the master calendar that you were to have a parents' meeting this afternoon. Yes, it's odd that he forgot, though of course he is young and is therefore susceptible to having a distracted mind."

Quail, aggravated by the bother, seized a nearby phone and punched in Simon's extension: "Have you any idea where Stephen is? I've got a couple of mamas in a dither because they were to meet this afternoon but there's no Stephen. His office door was wide open. They say things are in disarray, though I told them that is the usual condition of his office."

A pause while he listened. "I know that he is accountable to you, which makes it odd that you know nothing of his whereabouts."

Simon informed Quail of his discovery of Stephen's inadequacies, which had led him in recent days to regard the young man as "somewhat of a disappointment."

"No, I didn't realize that he tends to be high-strung and impulsive. I thought that his greatest fault was immaturity. It's good that you have given him some time to think about his future. Thanks, anyway."

To the two parents standing by, he said, "Dr. Lupino knows nothing of Stephen's whereabouts either. Leave a note." Then, glancing at his watch, "Oh, my. See? I'm late to have my body pricked and poked as if it were a slab of meat."

∾

Stephen got to Thea's at about six-thirty, a little later than he had wanted, due to the evening traffic. He pulled his packed car into the first open spot, a couple of blocks away. Parking was always at a premium in this part of town, near the university. Retrieving his backpack, he walked briskly toward her apartment through the drizzle, thanking God that he had someone who would understand.

About a half-dozen doors from her apartment, on the sidewalk across the street, Stephen stopped. In the late afternoon light he saw Thea, unmistakable in her faded blue denim jacket, standing outside her building—and holding hands with some tall guy. In the wet mist, they were playfully talking, he looking down at her, she preening on tiptoes as she talked.

He was paralyzed. More than a hundred feet from them, even in twilight and drizzle, he could read the guy's face—he looked down at Thea in a way that only a boyfriend is supposed to look. She was on tiptoes, shaking her head in that cute way of hers.

Stephen turned, retreated quickly to his car, at a run. He sat inert for maybe half an hour, raging, switching off the music, the White Stripes' *Get Behind Me Satan*, just as the band bellowed,

> *We all need to do something*
> *Try to keep the truth from showing up*

After a time of sickened slobbering, sneezing and wheezing, he drove slowly by Thea's, looking up at the light in her upstairs apartment. Stupidly, when he asked Jesus for help, only one biblical text came to mind: "Don't fear those who can kill the body." *Would to God that she had murdered me rather than cheated on me,* he prayed.

He headed out of town, not stopping until he returned to his empty apartment just after midnight. No need for his key as the door still stood ajar, just as he had left it. He thought about getting hammered—he didn't have the guts (or the gun) to blow his brains out. Trouble was, after the church episode last week, he was frightened of booze. About three that morning, he collapsed into sleep. He awoke at ten, lying on top of his mattress, after a fitful, incoherent, but dreamless night, blinded by meddling morning light in his denuded apartment, a failure at both love and work, exhausted and alone, angered by the sun.

Lying there, meditating upon the worst week of his life, he composed the three-point speech that he would have given to Thea had he the courage to confront her:

1. She was crazy, cruel on top of that. For her to mindlessly toss away all that they shared for a random guy was insane.

2. He didn't deserve to be treated this way. She who always took delight in being so direct and blunt in what she said, didn't have the decency to look him in the face and tell him it was over.

3. He had always been faithful, except for one night a couple of weeks into their relationship (and they were hardly even dating then), a one-night stand with a Baptist in a dingy room at Union Seminary in New York in which he was actually innocent and which meant nothing to him anyway. And he had never again strayed the whole time he was with Thea. Not once. So there. End of sermon.

Finally, he resolved to get up and go home to his parents' place. He would shamelessly tell them everything.

Less than an hour later, however, the prodigal came to his senses, recognized his ridiculousness, lost his nerve, stopped and headed his car in the opposite direction. He wouldn't give his father the satisfaction of having him crawl back home on his knees, nor would he give his mother the chance to say, "You were too good for them. I've always said, church people are the worst."

The next afternoon, still licking his exit wounds, Stephen's cheap new cell phone buzzed. Thea? Of course not. It was that kid Jack. He let it hum, then kick into voicemail. A bit further down the highway, aimlessly driving away from home, he forced himself to listen to the message. "Hey, man. I just heard that you are no longer at the church. Don't know what that means. They said they didn't know where you were. I'm hoping you get this. You wouldn't believe what I had to go through to track down your number. Just want you to know that you are my spiritual mentor. I hope that you aren't thinking about leaving the ministry. You're what a pastor ought to be. Alexis and I are both torn up. You're our spiritual advisor, man. I know that you think I'm dumb, so maybe you don't care what I think anyway. Hey, maybe you don't know it, but God really worked through you to say some real gospel truth to me. So, maybe this is the Lord talking and not just an annoying, dumb little brother in the Lord. Just kidding. But think about . . ."

Here the voice mail terminated. Stephen hit delete.

It was awfully hard to think when you had these church people pulling at you. He needed to escape, to put miles between himself and the whole, stupid, clawing, bumbling, boozing, screwing bunch. He would get out of here. Crash at a friend's. He had offered himself to the Body of Christ only to be beaten, stripped, and left half dead in a ditch by the side of the road. Now he was tossing baggage—memories of great times and dreams dashed—throwing it out the window as he drove through the Midwestern countryside, the quiet calm of which was interrupted by stretches that looked more like wasteland than heartland—darkened suburbs, strip malls, rusting factories, trucks passing in the night. Better to toss things before they are ripped off.

In his exodus, Stephen thought of all the obvious, exclusively human causes for what he had mistaken as a "call from God." Everything that Jane reverently named "call" could be more easily explained. His vague, distant relationship with his parents, his need to be needed, his insecurity as a black man in a racist society, his longing to be accepted and loved, his overblown sense of responsibility for everything that was wrong with the world. The list was endless.

Perhaps these honest ruminations accounted for Stephen's feeling a sense of freedom, which grew as the darkened countryside sailed past him. In his honest admission of the human causes for what he once thought was "vocation," he felt, even in the midst of his hurt and anger, a gradually growing elation. He had lost much in a brief space. But loss, bitter though it was, also rendered him free of encumbrances. He had complained that the church was too confining. But he was on the verge of admitting that the church hadn't imprisoned him; the church had dragged him where he didn't want to go, forced him to peer into the shadows, ugly places everybody else avoids. At last he was free to refuse. Let the dead bury their own damn dead.

Unharnessed, uncommitted, unfettered, emancipated. Processing while he drove through a blighted landscape near dawn, he had the odd sense of reentering the world that had almost slipped away, a world that he had renounced without knowing it, a world more congenial than the cage in which he had been confined for the past three months.

He now knew the reason for the gory end of his time with Thea. He had indeed cheated on her, but not in the usual sense; he'd had a fling with the church, not another woman. No flaw in their relationship gave rise to Thea's deceit and infidelity. They were perfect together. Everybody agreed. They clicked from their first date at Dan's party. Their two years and three weeks were untroubled. There was one and only one thing on which they disagreed. From the first, she had said of his vocation, "I just don't get it."

She hadn't dumped him; he had dumped her. He had been unfaithful, a naïve kid seduced by a cheap, broken down, painted whore, caught by the clutching, grasping, cold arms of *Mater Ecclesia*.

As the eastern sky gradually lightened, then became golden, he had driven into a new day. He wasn't working through his grief, as some inept pastoral counselor might put it. He was having his first taste of new wine, life among the free, the unattached, and the unpretending.

Arriving at his friend's apartment at midmorning, he was greeted with, "Man, you can crash here anytime you like. My place is your place. I know what you're going through, know what it's like to be cheated on. I've been through this breakup scene more times that I can count. I can sympathize."

No, you can't, thought Stephen. *All of your women have been psychos. And what's happened between Thea and me is the least of my breakups.*

∽

Simon was home by five, bolstered by two drinks for his long delayed declaration to Mary. He sat at the kitchen table (utilized no more than a dozen times in the last year for a meal together), drumming his fingers upon the plastic-coated top, unsurprised that it was nearly six and no Mary. As he sat in silence, he contemptuously surveyed the austere scene—never a home, actually, more like a cheap motel with its barely furnished, store-bought interior, appointed by a woman whose tastes in decorating seemed to have been informed by East Germans. Beige to the point of being oppressive.

They could easily have afforded better on his salary and parsonage allowance, or by using Mary's inheritance. Mary, of course, lacked the graciousness to live in a finer house, even her domestic decorating determined by her rebellion against her upbringing. So everything—from the dated kitchen (avocado green) down to the ready-made print curtains in the living room—was overly sensible, arrogantly understated in order to flaunt parsimoniousness as a high moral virtue. The furnishings looked liked government issue or a set for *The Brady Bunch*, only cheap. Mary's sole gesture toward kitchen beautification was a carved plaque of Bob Marley as Jesus, done in the Caribbean-mission-team-souvenir genre.

He thought of his parents, nestled—no, willingly imprisoned—in their white, utilitarian bungalow. At least they had an excuse for enduring more than forty years together without public complaint. No religious compunction kept them from ending their marriage; they simply couldn't afford a split. The thought that he was venturing where his dear, drab elders dared not induced in Simon a flutter of self-contentment.

He heard Mary's Prius crunch into the gravel driveway at last.

"Mary, we need to talk," Simon blurted out as soon as she had entered the kitchen, attempting all the gravitas he could muster. Mary, model of haggard, pious preoccupation, mumbled that—this being the evening of a particularly important meeting of the finance committee for the Women's Safe Harbor Home—she had no more than fifteen minutes to spare.

Unknowingly, she stiffened his resolve by flashing her I LOVE HAITI T-shirt as she peeled off her jacket and tossed it over the chair. Surely she knew how he detested a woman of her age and figure in a T-shirt of any sort. He took the shirt as a sign confirming the propriety of his designs for the evening's colloquy.

"Surely they can get along just this once without you," said Simon. "I have been waiting for days to speak with you and can wait no longer. You have been home hardly a single night for two weeks," he added strategically, marshaling his forces and softening up her defenses for the bomb he planned to drop.

"Well, what's this that's so important that it absolutely must be discussed this evening?" Mary sighed as she plopped her keys and her oversized, handmade Honduran peasant straw handbag on the kitchen table.

"Please, let's sit down," Simon suggested.

Mary headed out the kitchen and down the hall toward the bathroom, saying, "I said I was in a hurry, Simon." She shut the bathroom door almost in his face as he pursued her.

If she wanted it presented to her while she sat on the toilet, he would oblige. Refusing to be deterred from his mission, Simon began talking loudly to the bathroom door: "Mary, dear, I have three things that I want to say."

"Sounds like a sermon launch," he heard Mary jab from inside the bathroom. "Should I settle in for the homily? Three platitudes and a poem?" Though her voice was muffled by the closed door, he heard amusement in her voice, could see her smiling to herself, rolling her eyes.

Standing in the hall, Simon delivered the short address that had been forming in his head over a couple of weeks: While he loved her—always would, in a way—they both knew that they had grown apart. What sort of marriage is it when two people rarely have physical contact, go separate ways, pursue separate interests, and hardly bump into one another except at church? His reiteration of "separate" was by design.

"Is it a healthy relationship when the two never break bread together?" he asked rhetorically. While marriage is more, but certainly not less, than physical proximity, marriage is a mutual sharing based upon compatibility, communication, caring, and a host of other practices. A two-way street. A more than fifty-fifty proposition. A relationship. A journey.

He heard the toilet flush. Otherwise there was no indication from Mary that she was still alive as Simon continued his exposition on matrimony, lobbing a barrage of pious platitudes her way. As a Christian communicator, he was accustomed to speaking truth to people who didn't want to hear it, and he wouldn't be stopped now.

Emboldened by her unresponsiveness—perhaps she was stunned speechless by the veracity of his discourse—he continued his soliloquy, noting that though their present arrangement may be sufficient for her needs, he was going through a vulnerable time just now, needed companionship more than ever. A fellow sojourner. His work demanded a soul mate to support him in his ministry, and . . .

"Word is that you are paying court to Sybil Vestal," Mary blurted out in the midst of whatever she was taking so long to do. "I presume this is what your self-obsessed rambling is leisurely meandering toward."

"What?" was the best retort Simon could muster. "Who—who told you such a thing?" He leaned close to the door.

At last Mary emerged from the bathroom, wiping her hands and leading Simon back into the kitchen. He thought he detected a faint grin upon her face as she said, "Simon, please don't dissemble. Surely you must have surmised that I knew," said Mary. "I and the entire church."

She pulled out a kitchen chair and sat down casually. Simon stood over her for a moment and declared, "Sybil and I have become dear friends. That's all I will say about that."

He jerked out a chair and sat opposite her at the plastic-topped table. Though they had been married for years, and he thought he knew her well, Simon read nothing of note upon her broad, worn forehead, framed by her plain pageboy cut.

"Are you not sleeping together?" she asked in words so direct and brusque that Simon could hardly believe they were coming out of her pious, thin, unlipsticked lips. "If you can truthfully say that you are not, then your lack of interest in things carnal is astounding. They have pills that are said to be most helpful for men of your age. I get ads for them all the time on my laptop," said Mary with hostility, an emotion that, until this evening, Simon thought her incapable of expressing.

"That's disgusting. That you would descend to such common, low insinuation! Sybil and I are fellow sojourners." Furious, he looked away from her, across to the stove.

"Please, Simon, spare me the sermonic posturing and righteous indignation. When I heard of your trysts with Sybil, oddly, I was encouraged. You never invited me to accompany you to the Café Vienna, and only rarely have I seen you take a drink, even though I thought it might improve you. For some time I have feared that you were losing your ability to feel, your capacity to care, that you were incapable of making love to anyone but yourself."

"Mary! How dare you?"

"To put at ease your troubled mind, you have my consent, if not my blessing, to pursue this tawdry, unrealistic little affair of yours," she said, as if to conclude the conversation. She grabbed her keys, muttering, "Sojourners!"

"Then you won't hinder me from asking for a divorce?" pushed Simon.

"Do you really require a divorce?" asked Mary with a contemptuous sneer. "As you say, we haven't a marriage worth troubling a court to terminate. Divorce seems boringly bourgeois, too severe for your level of veniality. Divorce me in order to remarry? Do you actually believe that a woman like her would be interested in a formal alliance with a man such as yourself?"

"What, pray tell, do you mean by 'a man such as yourself'? And by 'a woman like her'?"

"I had presumed that we had reached an arrangement. You pursue your life and I, unhindered, pursue mine as we both attempt to retrieve some semblance of happiness in our autumnal years. It seemed an appropriate stratagem, considering the circumstances. However, if our unstated pact is now unworkable for you, then you may dissolve what's left of our marriage. Could be expensive. Although you have always enjoyed living beyond your means, aided by my inheritance, I want you to know that I have no need of making any claim upon you," said Mary in a droning, matter-of-fact tone as she twirled her keys.

"Just like you to insinuate that I haven't provided for you, that I have failed in some way, that this whole thing is my problem alone," said Simon, now trembling. "Your feeble pretense at graciousness is galling."

"Simon, Simon, surely we can discuss this like two beyond-middle-aged adults," said Mary, becoming ever more businesslike even as Simon became more enraged. "You have presented this as your problem. It's certainly not mine. I'm willing to provide assistance with your problem. Be grateful that I am showing solicitousness, though we know that gratitude was never one of your virtues."

"You—you act as if our years together mean nothing," said Simon, trying to sound hurt.

"On the contrary, 'our years together,' as you so elegantly describe our mirage of a marriage, obviously meant more to me than to you. I was willing to continue 'our years together,' but you wish to sue for discontinuance. I have just reassured you that I will not resist, that I will go on living, that I will continue my interests, and that you are free from any economic impediments, though I do question your absurd fantasy that you are divorcing me in order to marry Sybil Vestal. It's laughable," she chuckled.

Simon banged his fist on the table and pushed back his chair. "I can't tell you how thrilled I am by your 'assurance' that you will be damned fine without me. I come here in an attempt to let you down easy, to share my heart, and you take this as an opportunity to dump on me your resentment and scorn, to suggest that we've been living off your inheritance, to impugn my, my *masculinity!*"

Mary reached across the table and attempted to take Simon's trembling hand. "Oh Simon, try to use this as an opportunity to tell yourself the truth. It's yourself that you are attempting to 'let down easy.' Well, come down as easily as you like. Yet I must say that I am genuinely concerned that you are setting yourself up for deep disappointment. I can't imagine that Lady Sybil is actually interested in marriage . . . again. While I'm surprised, principally because I thought we had worked out a mutually beneficial pact, of sorts, I am pleased that you have found someone to comfort and support you in your advancing years, to fulfill your needs. I know how important that can be."

"What? Mary, does that mean that *you*—that you have found someone to meet *your* needs?"

"Are you referring to Hank?" Mary asked casually.

"Hank Judd? Well, I'll be damned! Hank Judd! That effeminate, limp-wristed little squirt, Hank Judd. He's got to be, what, twenty years younger than you? It's revolting."

"Don't exaggerate, dear," Mary said with an impish grin. "Hank's comparative youthfulness is but one of his virtues."

"You've slept with him! It's unthinkable!" exclaimed Simon. "You, you . . . How dare you?"

"Really now, Simon, moral indignation doesn't become you. I won't indulge in sordid confirmations or futile denials. Besides, are you in a position to condemn? You need not bother yourself with what I—or Hank and I—have done, or by what we have left undone."

"Hypocrite! What would the church say if they knew their Blessed Virgin Mary was nothing but a crude cougar sleeping around?" sneered Simon, staring away from Mary. "And with a lawyer!" he mumbled toward the refrigerator.

"Now Simon, no need to be unkind. Hank and I enjoy a relationship that I could not begin to explain to you. Equals, comrades-in-arms. You're not the one to preach against the sin of hypocrisy. All of us are just poor, struggling sinners. You know that I've always been more concerned about social sin than personal peccadilloes. Hank and I are just two people who care about the same things, feel the same hurts, share the same passions, and . . ."

"Including a passion for a romp between the sheets," Simon seethed. "Probably cavorting at the homeless shelter, making whoopee while taking a break from Meals on Wheels!"

"If you insist on being unpleasant," said Mary, gathering her things, "I'll leave you to your childish pouting." She stood up and pulled her shabby denim jacket from the chair. "I suppose I should hire myself an attorney, just to keep everything in order. Come to think of it, I already have an attorney, don't I? But Hank wouldn't trouble himself over such a humble separation," she said with a bit of a giggle. "Can't do it before next week as I've got—that is, Hank and I have this big Healthy Homelessness rally this weekend. Help yourself to the spaghetti casserole in the fridge."

Then, pausing before the door that led into the carport, Mary turned, smiled incongruously—making sure, he suspected, to rub his nose into the words on her T-shirt—and said, "And Simon, please have a nice rest of your life. I mostly enjoyed sharing two-thirds of it with you. God bless. And may my fears of your impending disappointment be unfounded."

And then she left, without a hug or even a polite gesture, closing the door behind her, leaving Simon to stare for the longest time at the shoddy Kenyan teak salt and pepper shakers that Mary had lugged back home after one of her missions. He heard the insipid sound of her ecologically sensible car crunching out of the driveway. Then the maddening silence, allowing her words to resound in his brain. Despite Mary's cruel rhetoric, Simon hoped for just a hint of a tear in Mary's steely, unmascaraed eye. For the first time in their marriage, Mary had surprised him. She had hidden her mysteriousness until the end.

Simon turned and mechanically opened the refrigerator door. He grimaced. As he suspected, the so-called spaghetti casserole was nothing but a heap of Mary's whole wheat, vegetarian lasagna, which she knew he loathed. Gazing at the brown, glutinous glob—pieces of rock-hard, raw zucchini stuck out here and there through the goo of the pale, organically grown tomato sauce—he muttered, "When I think of the money we've wasted in the past ten years to feed her vegetarian, locally grown, free-range food fad, she's got her nerve rebuking me for squandering her inheritance."

Tossing and turning in his lonely bed that night, Simon was unable to shake his growing conviction that whereas ordinary folk plop into misery because of a few unfortunate decisions, clergy get screwed by Providence through no fault of their own. Although Simon aspired to more closely resemble his mother—the innocent, God-bereft victim—it appeared that he might live the second half of his life as his father—another God-rebuked, unlamented practitioner of professional suicide.

Worst of it all, the church worships Mary as a living saint, a God Almighty Midwestern Mother Teresa.

8

Pentecost

" R ead it and weep," said Quail as he dropped the morning paper on Simon's desk without so much as a good morning.

The headline instantly assaulted him: "Church Guilty of Sin of Racism?" Simon scanned the story. Kim telling the reporter—"humbly"—that his congregation was one of the fastest growing in the city. Kim expressing gratitude to Hope Church (even though he had been given an hour and a room for worship no one else had wanted and a broom closet for an office), how happy they were at Hope, how God had blessed them while at Hope, how God's hand had supported them during their days at Hope—even though they had never been permitted the use of Hope's beautiful sanctuary. On and on. Nail Kim to a cross and let him star at Oberammergau!

Then Kim telling the reporter how hurt and shocked he was to be told that they were expelled. Now churchless, his people knew not which way to turn—testimony concocted to melt even the coldest, moneygrubbing, guilty Caucasian heart. Kim "reluctantly" reported derogatory remarks that had been made (by unidentified persons, "I rather not say name") about Korean culture that sounded—and how this "pained" Kim to say it—"racist." He had been in much prayer since having his Korean culture evicted. Now, a nomad like Father Abraham before him, Kim testified that his heart had no anger because Jesus had been so very helpful in enabling him to forgive the vicious, racist injustice that had been perpetrated against him and his sweet, loving, harmless, defenseless congregation.

"The conniving little Korean creep!" hissed Quail as Simon threw the paper aside in disgust.

Incorporation

The reporter had taken it upon herself to phone a couple of churches. Unfortunately for Hope's public persona, First Presbyterian Downtown—whose pastor had offered the right hand of Christian fellowship to "our Korean Christian sisters and brothers in their time of need"—said that their congregation was honored and humbled to show hospitality to the Koreans. The Downtown Pres pastor was confident that his congregation, "which has always been committed to racial inclusiveness and multicultural sensitivity, much more so than any other congregation in town," would be pleased as punch to welcome their persecuted sisters and brothers.

"First Pres having nothing left but a few dozen old ladies, God knows they've got the room," Quail muttered in rebuttal. "We do ten times more for this town than that dwindling band of octogenarians. The conniving little Korean now in league with a neo-calvinist clod! I'd hang both of 'em."

The paper explained that attempts were made to contact the Reverend Johnson Quail (erroneously listed as "Senior Pastor of Hope Church"), the clergyman who had summarily put Kim and his fellow Korean Christians on the street. The paper reported that Mr. Quail had refused to comment.

"Liars," insisted Quail. "I received not one phone call. Not one."

"Well, I hope you wouldn't have said anything if they had called," said Simon. "It would have only made your botched mess worse. 'No comment' is always the best comment of the church when pilloried by the press. You know you are not the most gifted of religious communicators."

"*My* botched mess?" spewed Quail.

"Yet another screwup," said Simon in resignation. "I ask you discreetly to handle the Korean thing, the God-awful cooking smell, the kimchi, and suddenly it's a full-blown crisis with screams of 'racism' and—worse—cultural insensitivity, blemishing our reputation as one of the most caring, committed, and progressive congregations in the city. And these slick Koreans miraculously transformed into innocent victims! We've been made a joke by the jerk at First Pres, who got his seminary degree online! Good work, Mr. Johnson!"

"You dumped this mess on me," said Quail slowly, glaring at Simon. "You thought it would be so cool to give those Koreans run of the building—and for no rent to speak of, I might add. You are now . . ."

"While you were fuming and fussing about Hope Township, a real disaster was upon us. Please, no blaming and whining. I expect you to fix this. Fix it! I don't care how bad your stomach feels, get with Kim and find out what he wants. They've all got their price, despite this pious gibberish. Mammon is the only language in which Kim is fluent." Simon once again lowered his estimate of Quail's pastoral gifts, looking upon him as a master carpenter looks upon a roofer.

"It'll cost us," said Quail. "Oh, it just breaks the heart to see him and his poor, oppressed Koreans wandering the streets, asking only for a place to praise the Lord. Ivy League software engineers badly playing sufferers for Jesus in their BMWs, Italian shoes, and designer suits!"

"For God's sake, fix it!" yelled Simon, regretting that Quail, outmaneuvered by the Koreans, had pushed him into uncharacteristic unseemliness.

Quail smiled as he moved down the hall, ignoring Eleanor and a group of mothers in the Walter Rauschenbusch Lounge, yet wondering why she had need of so plush a location for a children's ministry meeting. Simon was spinning gloriously downward, out of control. Second Samuel 22, one of his most beloved texts, rose in Quail's heart, giving him a great sense of satisfaction: "Thou has also given me the necks of mine enemies, that I might destroy them that hate me." Authorized Version.

ळ

The bishop (whom Simon had once or twice publically referred to as "He of the dyed comb-over") waddled into Simon's suite late the next afternoon, grinning from ear to ear as he did on every occasion, whether presiding at a state funeral or bending over for a prostate exam, oblivious to how his crooked, bad-looking teeth rendered a smile a bad idea.

"Simon, you are looking good, as always. Fit as a fiddle, eh?"

Though our Lord said that "the eye is the lamp of the body," as Simon peered into the pig-like eyes of the bishop, he found them to be inscrutable, showing no indication of what he was up to on this forced visit. Simon surveyed his superior: balding pate, remaining hair brushed to the side and tinted a Grimballish hue, gut hanging over belt, bulging blue blazer, neck encased in a too-small clerical collar, absurd looking pectoral cross that served only to call attention to his gut—in sum, a ridiculous figure. He suspected that the bishop—when he was present in Hope's massive sacred precincts—suffered from a fatal case of pulpit envy aggravated by an edifice complex. When in God's name would the man finally cast aside his dated blue blazer, grey pants, and sixties loafers and don a dark suit more appropriate to his episcopal ring?

A businesslike thank you was Simon's terse response. It was their first face-to-face in three years. They had suffered a couple of church conferences, in the same room, but no more. Simon's elevated situation enabled him never to soil himself with denominational politics, and he had zealously disregarded denominational responsibilities; church politics and denominational trivialities were the bishop's obsession.

The only credible reason why the porcine prelate had dared to intrude into Simon's domain was that he wanted something. Simon had heard that the regional judicatory was strapped for cash. If the bishop needed rescuing by Hope, then he and his bevy of sycophants should have been present at the Hope Conference. He was sure that the bishop coveted an invitation to preen at the conference—an episcopal dream to be realized only over Simon's dead body.

There was talk of the "fine spring we're having," inquiries into Hope's financial health during these trying times, and assorted inanities followed by the bishop at long last saying, "Now Simon, I have come to talk about a matter of some importance. Surely I don't have to reiterate how very much I, and indeed the whole church, admire and are energized by your leadership here. Hope's physical plant looks just great."

"Thank you." Simon could almost feel the bishop's hand slithering into his trousers to lift his wallet.

The bishop righted himself in his chair, shifted his big bottom, straightened his crotch, and continued with growing unease, "You have had a remarkable ministry. Some record. Those of us who met you in your first days of ministry knew that you were destined for greatness. I said to myself, first time I saw you, 'Now there's a man on his way up, for sure.'"

Simon marveled that the bishop was under the delusion that he gave a damn what he said to God, or to anybody else, about him.

"And yet, all good things eventually run their course, so to speak. The good Lord grants each of us a season for ministry, and then we move along to greater challenges, new venues, greener pastures."

Simon knitted his brow and said, "I'm not sure where you are headed with this, Henry. I don't follow."

"What I mean to say is that your Parish Personnel Committee has been in consultation with me, and they have noted . . ."

"What? You have been talking with *my* PPC without notifying me? That's outrageous! Henry, what were you thinking? You know that you are bound to notify me before any interaction with my lay leadership," said Simon, his voice rising. "What sort of sneaky, discourteous . . ."

"Now Simon, no need for unpleasantness. The PPC just wanted to chat. And when we talked I realized, by gosh, that I might be helpful to them and that it might be for the best to keep this *in camera, entre nous*, so to speak," said the bishop. "I'm eager to engage these sorts of things with a minimum of fuss and bother, by gosh."

"What fuss and bother?"

"Well, it seems that, in the informed, prayerful judgment of the PPC, who all greatly admire you, your time of leadership here is at a plateau, that it would be best for all concerned if I worked with you to craft a next chapter."

"Next chapter? Plateau? Are you insinuating that I should . . . *move*? Are you talking about my leaving Hope? Is that what you mean by all this euphemistic, 'next chapter' gibberish?"

"Simon, I'm here as a brother in Christ, as someone who might be helpful in avoiding unnecessary fuss and bother," said the bishop, flashing a yellow, crooked-teeth grin.

"Oh, I bet you would! How you would love to invite some loser to waltz right in here and scoop up the goodies of my visionary leadership at Hope! 'Fuss and bother'? Well, if you think I'm going to play dead while you prance about playing Mr. High-and-Mighty M'Lord Bishop, you have another thing coming. I've sacrificed too much, worked too hard to step aside for anybody. I've built a four-million dollar building! I'm a tither! Bishops move on the chessboard only one way—slantwise, deviously. I'll fight you on this, Henry, fight you in public, I'll . . ."

"I—I would not advise that, Simon. A number of, shall we say, *troubling matters* have been alleged. Fortunately, the rumors seem to have been confined to a few *cognoscenti* on the PPC. But we must work with alacrity lest the congregation hear of this. Yessiree. Not that I'm giving credence to any of that, nosiree. In my experience, when there's restlessness within a congregation, where there's the smoke of ugly innuendo, invariably there's the fire of real problems. I am uninterested in hearsay about your personal life or certain staff problems. We do well to treat this as a simple administrative decision."

"Which means?"

"Well, it means that we say that your fruitful ministry here has come to conclusion—no, a culmination—and that you are a man of action, a man who loves a challenge. You'll know just how to say it, I'm sure," said the bishop, smiling.

"What 'troubling matters'?" demanded Simon.

"Simon, the future of Hope is the main thing. As you know, this church accounts for nearly a quarter of all our mission and benevolent funding. Why, if Hope went south, it would be the end of our children's homes, our camps programs, our Fall Festival of Faith Auction. I'm sure that you are aware that, for all your obvious virtues, you can be somewhat

difficult—not for me, of course, but to some of the laity. And I'm not referring to the carping complaints about your borrowed sermons . . ."

"What?"

"Doesn't bother me a whit. Nosiree. After all, what is truth? What
preacher worth his salt has not swiped a phrase or illustration without
proper attribution? While there are those who complain that you are slow
to acknowledge your mistakes and . . ."

"What mistakes? How dare they? You didn't even have a camping
program until I pushed it and Hope financed it back in my early days."

"Simon, surely you agree that it's better for all concerned, certainly
better for you and for Mary, and in a way better for me, well, better for the
church, if we keep this low key. I always hate to see the church become
mired in fruitless moralizing over bedroom behavior. Terribly distracting.
He said–she said squabbles are toxic for a congregation. If the laity pressed,
then by gosh, I would be duty-bound to order some sort of investigation, a
public inquiry, possibly even the press, and none of us want that, do we?"

"You are blackmailing me? 'Bedroom behavior'? You should be supporting me, defending me, not conspiring with lay insurrectionists in a
public lynching. Is this revenge orchestrated by my sacked youth pastor?
Quail! Nail my hands to the wood and hoist me over Golgotha!"

"Simon. Please. I'm a bit taken aback that this has caught you off
guard. Your indignation validates some of your critics' judgments. Surely
you knew that eventually there would be a day of reckoning given some of
your unguarded actions. I waited in order to be sure that what I was hearing from the PPC was not limited to a few malcontents. As it turns out,
the concerns are widespread and, I may say, at least in the case of the PPC,
remarkably well documented. I'm trying to be helpful in moving things
along without a public fuss," said the bishop. "That's my main job: to insure
that nothing negative leaks into the public domain. Yessiree."

"How long has this, this conspiracy been afoot?"

"Actually, the PPC has been working for some time," said the Bishop,
"though I was summoned only about a month ago, perhaps two months."

"That's outrageous!" shouted Simon. "That gang of inept, small-
minded, conservative . . ."

"I was actually impressed by their thoroughness, quite professional,
evenhanded. They were considering broaching this with you before Easter,
but I urged restraint. Only one person on the committee was steadfastly
behind you, that unfortunate Mr. Niculous. After his sad passing, well, it
left a unified committee to ask for your removal."

"My *removal*?"

"Mr. Niculous urged restraint. Now they are eager to move forward."

"This is my reward for twenty years of service! Secret meetings with the bishop! Conniving! And not one word, not a hint to me," Simon raved, clinching his right fist. "I knew Niculous had neither the anguish nor the imagination to kill himself. He was tossed off a bridge by that damn committee! It's a murder, not a suicide!"

"Now, now, Simon. No need for histrionics. You'll require your wits in the next few days. Yessiree," said the bishop.

When the bishop was on the offensive, Simon found him annoying; when solicitous and patronizing, he was contemptible.

"Next few days?" Simon trembled. The silly little man had done his homework, aligned his thugs before he made his move. It was injustice of staggering proportions, betrayal analogous to the Passion of Christ.

"Now Simon, your legacy at Hope is well assured. Yessiree. Reverend Quail tells me that Mr. Niculous left his entire estate, rumored at two million, to the church."

"Quail tells you? Why wouldn't he at least tell *me*? I'm only the Senior Managing Pastor! That money is the answer to our prayers."

"Possibly Mr. Quail was reluctant to inform you because the bequest was designated for 'the securing and the support of the very best pastoral leadership for Hope Church.'"

"This church already has the best pastoral leadership," Simon jeered.

The bishop continued, "Though they have not put it to me in this way, I'm sure that the PPC was prodded by word of the bequest. They thought, what with the rumors and all, the accumulating problems, the Niculous bequest provided a propitious time for a change. The PPC's read on your situation has been confirmed by Herb Cohellen, and you know how Herb has always supported you."

"Senile Judas!" sneered Simon. "He never served a congregation of over two hundred members."

"Simon, please. Take care not to overreact, or to badly react. You would be unwise to personalize this or to become defensive, much less vindictive. Gosh, that could damage your ability to move into a commensurate position elsewhere. Think things over, ponder your next move, take a month or so off for reflection . . . and prayer. We could say that you were due a sabbatical. Yes, that's it, a time to recharge your spiritual batteries. This is like the first day of a whole new life. A breath of the Spirit. Rebirth. You'll see."

This horrid little man—giving directives, prattling about prayer as he colluded with his enemies to shake the foundations of this church, to rip the doors off their hinges—Simon found dispiriting in the extreme.

"I'm sure that you will know just how to handle this. You always do. Why don't we say that you will, in due course, send me a letter stating that you believe that you have now accomplished a body of work, that you feel need of a challenge, that things are going so well that you can turn your attention elsewhere, et cetera, et cetera. You are so good with words. The sort of letter that can be shared with the public, saying something without saying anything of substance, that sort of letter. Pass by me any communication, just to be sure that we're all on the same page. Seize the high ground," said the bishop as he gathered his battered, brown briefcase and rose to leave. "The good Lord aids us, yessiree. Onward. Invictus! Excelsior!"

The bishop may have gushed other claptrap, may have offered Simon his hand, may even have invited Simon to join him in prayer. Simon heard nothing. As the bishop waddled out of his office, Simon stared out the window, gazing vacantly across the lawn. In the twilight, the window became a mirror in which he saw his own face looking back at him, gaunt, aged, anxious.

Then he saw the small brown bird—which had wasted days pointlessly pecking feverishly at the window—perched upon the sill, probably exhausted, roosting on the window ledge. The bird looked up at him from the ledge on which rested a small stack of sticks, the beginning of a nest.

Simon heard a far-off rumble. Though there had been no storm warning, sure enough, above the trees, lightning flashed across a darkening western sky. Large, heavy globules of rain began to drop. Though he grabbed his coat and dashed out of his office, the rain soaked Simon on his escape. Although he had little inclination toward the arcane, he was feeling engulfed by mystery: Why had he sacked a young associate when his real enemy was that Judas Quail? Was a dead man, through his bequest, controlling the future of the church? Who blabbed about him and Sybil? Were the Koreans working retribution?

Or was God, busy behind the scenes, not as gracious as Simon had led his congregation to believe? Was God the giant fist squeezing the breath out him?

∞

Quail had already endured a grueling day, what with Chef's unfortunate accident as he was preparing his rendition of spaghetti di Napoli—dropping three gallons of boiling water, scalding himself painfully up to his torso. His profane howls had echoed from the church kitchen and could be heard down the corridor as far as the Christian Fellowship wing as he was carted to the hospital. Chef was so drunk at the time that he was partially anesthetized and thus was spared the agony that would have afflicted a sober person. "My goodness," Quail had quipped, "if Chef had taken the cure, his burns would have been unbearable."

Presently Chef was confined to a hospital bed, happily sedated—as close as he could hope for heaven.

Having been subjected to the indignity of yet another enema and lower GI exam earlier in the week, Quail had another crisis to manage. Misfortune doesn't spare the unfortunate. That crazy woman, though duly warned, was back at Hope, just before closing time, raving, demanding an audience with "a Revrent."

Quail's secretary had burst into his office, saying, "She's back. She says that Satan has got us."

He had urged tighter security, had determined the cost of a state-of-the-art system with cameras, one that would give secretaries and others the opportunity to screen quacks. (It was awfully difficult to get them out of the church once they were in.) But the security system was on hold, like everything important, due to finances. Right now, he would have gladly paid from his own fortune—had his ex-wife not beaten him to it, and Niculous declined to augment it, preferring instead to squander his fortune on a place for himself in paradise—not to have this insane woman in his outer office.

She was on her knees, mumbling, eyes closed, hands together in supplication, on the floor in the middle of the office. His assistants had fled to the safety of the Walter Rauschenbusch Lounge.

"Now look here. You were warned. I'm calling the police, and we will trespass you, so help me God!"

She began screaming, "Is the world dying or being reborn? Day, or is it night? Is Satan Lord? If you were a *real* preacher, instead of a damn church administrator, you'd know!" Then she was again prayerful, sitting on the floor in the middle of the outer office, immobile as a rock, only her lips moving, her eyes locked shut.

"Simon has simply got to hang around here more and carry his share of the load," Quail muttered as he dialed the police. Over his shoulder he said to the praying woman, "And I never want to see you again in this building unless you are clutching in your wrinkled old hand a check for the nine thousand dollars that you owe for busting the Virgin Mary window."

Incorporation

Looking up from her prayers, she pronounced portentously, "She wasn't a virgin."

∾

Simon required but an hour to reconstruct his dignity after the bishop's wretched inquisition. He rushed out to his parking spot through the downpour, jumped in his car, and retreated to Sybil's for full restoration. At this point, if he felt remorse, it was for his own stupid determination not to cause harm to Hope. Looking in his rearview mirror, the church tower diminishing behind him, he thought, "Thank God I'll have this money-sucking monster off my back. It's some other sap's to feed, somebody else's leaking roof and backed up plumbing. Conscientiousness led me to indecision and look what it got me," he growled as he slid around the corner of Elm and Locust.

Speeding down Elm, he indulged in momentary self-reproach: "And to think I almost sacrificed Sybil, us, because of my fidelity to my vocation! God was trying to give me happiness and love, and all the while these Judases were scheming against me!"

He was strategically repositioning: "To hell with them. I've a life beyond church. I'm not losing my church; I'm on pilgrimage to recover the years the locusts have eaten. I will demand a satisfactory severance in exchange for my not telling the world the truth. If I go, they can damn well pay me from the confounded Niculous bequest!" As he waited at a stoplight, he concluded, "It's never too late to follow your heart."

He zipped into Sybil's drive, and his spirit leapt when he saw her. She was in the process of locking her front door, adjusting her large, dark glasses. She wore a strong lime-green skirt and blouse pressed close against her, matching heels, with a smart, shiny green, short raincoat, open at the knee. She turned and glanced toward Simon's car. After a quick look in his rearview mirror to brush back his hair that had been platted by the rain, he bounded from his car, leaving the door open as he rushed up the steps toward her, then knelt prostrate at her feet.

"Sybil. I've been a fool to wait, to hold back," he said breathlessly. "Now I'm throwing," he gasped, "caution to the wind. Now it's time for"—another gasp—"us. I care not what the congregation thinks. Let's go away, my love. A cruise, perhaps. Not the Caribbean, the Mediterranean." He clutched the hem of her raincoat with one hand, one of her finely turned calves with the other.

"Whatever are you talking about, silly man?" said Sybil, looking down at him with a smile as she pulled herself from his clutch. "So sorry not to be able to stay and entertain you. Come inside, dry off, and help yourself to whatever is in the fridge. I'm meeting Carol and Janie about the Spring Show, and I'm late already. Make yourself at home. See you later."

"But Sybil, everything's changed. 'Lo, the winter is past.' The church no longer stands in our way. I've been a fool to delay. 'Set me as a seal upon thy heart.' The good news is that my marriage is over, completely free, now my life is . . ."

"Simon, got to go. I'm late," said Sybil as she leaned down and pecked him on the cheek. "We must make all the arrangements for the menu. A bit of controversy over the salad. You know how obsessive Janie can be about such matters. Such a little bore, that Janie."

Her impish harshness, which he had previously found delightful, now felt ominous. He grabbed for her arm but she scooted down the steps and flew away, her tires churning pea gravel in the wet driveway. She tooted the horn, casually waving to him as he stood helplessly on the steps.

Simon turned, sighed, and retrieved the hidden key from under the pot of hydrangeas, opened the door, let himself in, poured himself a tall drink, and plopped down on the sofa, listening to the rain in Sybil's garden.

Yellow eyes glared down at him in the gathering dark, the only thing he could make out in the large, dark painting over the mantle. Her Expressionists were guarding Sybil's inner sanctum, Germans gazing accusingly. He turned away from the disagreeable paintings and looked out at the more pleasant vista of Sybil's garden. Through the rain, he scanned the panorama—made to look wild and beautiful, somehow reassuring in the twilight, misty and indistinct. Things are more appealing when blurred. As a preacher he was in the business of offering greater clarity and definition to the world, bringing reality into focus. But gazing at the garden in the rain, he had to admit that few things gain beauty through greater definition.

He had read that the aging Barbara Walters had directed that a thin film of petroleum jelly be applied to the lens of any camera that filmed her doing an interview. The declining Martha Stewart used the same technique; a smeared lens did what even a well-applied makeup job could not. Cursed with large hips, Martha also took care not to get caught by the camera in front of a kitchen counter, or so he had read. Clarity increases understanding but diminishes beauty. Yes, there was a definite aesthetic appeal to reality viewed through fog, the hard facts obscured. Those gigantic ceramic pots must be Italian, maybe even Greek. He was certain that they were old.

As he recounted the events of the day, he could not shake his uncanny premonition that he was being watched. Like a lobster shedding its shell, he lay there vulnerable and exposed. Alone in the dark, he anxiously looked about the living room, but he saw nothing that cared.

∾

As he gunned his black Buick down Hope Boulevard following his fateful conversation with Simon that wet afternoon, the bishop must have been preoccupied. Why else would so cautious and circumspect a man have shot into a major thoroughfare without looking both ways? No sooner had the bishop poked the Buick's nose into Elm than there sounded the shrill, falsetto horn of a green Triumph convertible and a screech of tires. The Buick halted in midturn and the bishop watched as the Triumph skidded around, missing his car by no more than a couple of feet. The bishop gasped, put his hand to his heart, and smiled lamely at the Triumph's driver, seeking forgiveness.

The driver was a teenager who flung the car into reverse; almost as fast as it had swerved to miss the bishop, it now sped backwards until it was even with the bishop's car.

"You stupid old fool!" screamed the teenager. "Damn you!" Thrusting his right forefinger in the sheepish face of the bishop, he spun off down the street.

"I'm very sorry," the bishop whispered to no one in particular. "I'm only human." Then ever so carefully, looking both ways, he eased out and turned right, pointing himself toward his office. He had traveled no farther than a couple of blocks when he again spotted the green Triumph, now slid at an angle into a parked car, a long pair of skid marks telling the tale. The teenager stood by stupidly, bleeding from his nose, lamenting the crushed left front of his car, which was thrust a good six inches into the parked car's badly damaged fender.

The bishop slowed and, when he pulled up next to the befuddled teenager, lowered his right window and flashed him a beatific grin as he tapped his high, tight clerical collar. He then accelerated, laughing heartily and beeping his horn, leaving the boy standing there in the street, looking stupid.

ᴄᴠ

Chef awoke in the middle of the night. The hospital was quiet except for an occasional bell repeatedly sounding somewhere. He suffered nasty blisters and already peeling skin from the tops of his feet all the way up beyond his knees, coated by a layer of therapeutic grease below his crotch. He was a man afire, an Easter ham simmering in his own juice, Saint Polycarp roasted at the stake, Saint Lawrence seared on the grill.

His greatest concern was for a bedpan. He fumbled for the call device that was clipped to his bed. As he pushed the button, he could hear a buzzer sound down the hall at the nurse's station. Still, no one came. Then, with all of his might, he pushed the button yet again, holding it as long as he could. No nurse. His third and fourth efforts gained him nothing except the sound of the unanswered bell.

Sedated, Chef drifted, his unconsciousness captured by bizarre culinary reveries—heaps of quiche, crème fraiche over lemon tarts, and bloody beef sizzling in the pan. His dream ended badly as he watched a mousse he had lovingly prepared being polluted with dollops of fake whipped topping applied by some stupid church kitchen volunteer. Fools. *If I were God, Dream Whip would be a capital offense*, he swore. A sin. Any kind of margarine too. Especially at church.

In his fits of agonized wakefulness, awaiting a nurse to assuage his urinary discomfort, Chef lay there pondering the irony: the one time in his life when he really merited a good stiff drink, he had landed flat on his back, as helpless as a turned-over turtle, bereft of alcoholic consolation.

If he had his wishes, which he rarely had, he would end his life. *Right now, as God is my witness, I would sell my soul to the Devil*, he thought, *for one lousy bedpan. If I had any friends, they would bring me a Texas fifth of Jack Daniels. They would sit at bedside to comfort, hand me a bedpan, and pour me a drink, straight, over ice. I would pee all over myself, if a nurse wouldn't use it as an excuse to towel me down and put me in hell. I wish I were dead.*

But who was he kidding? Time and again he had lacked the courage to walk suicide's lonely path. Dying you did by yourself. After his third (or was it his fourth?) girlfriend had walked out, he had stayed drunk for a week and was disappointed when he awoke with nothing more than a hellish headache to show for it. Alone. Lacking the guts for suicide, he had taken the route of slow, cowardly, one-day-at-a-time self-destruction, assisted by the bottle.

Incorporation

He had no fear of winding up in hell. Having served on the staff at Hope, he no longer had the imagination to believe in either hell or heaven. No, he would never call it quits because he knew full well that if he ever succeeded at self-termination, the good folks at Hope wouldn't miss a beat—they would flag down the first Mexican caterer who drove by in his van and be just as happy with him, if not happier.

Chef comforted himself with memories of his early culinary successes, recalling his first potato exam at school.

"You have a great future, my boy," said the master chef. "It's not chocolate, but it's a great beginning."

Really? The world outside the Culinary Institute of America knew nothing of the art and the agony, the sacrifice required for good food. And didn't care. Making cupcakes for kiddies and whipping up mounds of chicken salad for old ladies—this was his God-ordained fate.

They wouldn't have run out of wine if he had catered the wedding at Cana.

He might as well have stayed in the army and served up shit on a shingle. Here he was—trained in continental cuisine, master in the culinary arts—trapped where all they wanted was cheap food ladled out thick and quick. Martyr to his art.

Jesus culminated his whole ministry with a meal, vittles put forth as his very body and blood, and commanded his disciples to do the same. Jesus' contemporary followers were quite content with instant mashed potatoes swimming in gravy out of a can.

Chef's grand dessert creations in elegant spun sugar, plated and presented with flair, all three hundred prepared in a substandard church kitchen with only two ovens, neither of which was trustworthy, and who cared? The Body of Christ, shoveled up for you. His gastronomic handiwork doomed to suffer the pulling, chewing, gulping, and salivation of the human maw. He had once worked a whole morning on seven-layered napoleons, two types of custard, chocolate three ways, plated in a puddle of silken sauce—for over fifty, mind you—only to see one of the assembled swine gobble it en masse with one lip-smacking gulp.

Please God, send the nurse. I would give my right testicle for a bedpan, he prayed.

From there Chef's napoleanic art slid down the esophagus and pushed into the stomach where the once gorgeous food was bathed in gastric acid, passed from the small intestine into the jejunum and the ileum, then to the large intestine, churned with bile, laced with bacteria, shoved up the colon, and finally to the rectum to exit through the anus as sewage. *Where is the nurse?*

Thus Chef—lying there alone, in a hellish, narcotic stupor, and in a depressingly meditative mood—recounted the story of life inside out. The whole of human culinary art—millennia of human development, the entire history of gastronomic progress culminating at the summit (Le Cirque in Manhattan)—ending as sewage dumped into the East Fork, everything finished as feces.

"Nurse! Nuuuurse!"

∾

When Sybil showed up, well after nine, she was displeased to find Simon's car, door open wide to the continuing evening drizzle. Shutting his door with a slam, she fumbled with her keys, let herself in, chagrined that Simon had locked the front door. She discovered Simon sprawled in her darkened living room, snoring.

"Simon, what on earth? Still here? In the pitch black?" was Sybil's greeting as she began switching on lights. Simon struggled to sit up, hoping that he mistook the tone of aggravation in her voice.

"Don't," said Simon. "Let's sit in the dark. I so want to see you, to talk. Hold me, shield me against the sadness. Oh my love, at last my eyes are open."

Sybil settled among the pillows at the other end of the sofa, "I'm so peeved with Janie. She decided to be difficult, digging in her heels about the confounded salad. As a matter of principle! So? You see better in the dark? How have your eyes been opened this time, dear?"

"Sybil, I have been a fool, stupidly clinging to my responsibilities, so damned worried about Hope that I have been blind to what I really need, what I really want. Thank God, now I see clearly. I want, I *need* you. Before there were hindrances, limitations laid on my back by my . . . position. Now I'm free, ready to live for me, and I can't live for me without living with you."

"Are you drunk?" asked Sybil. "What is this about? You sound unattractively saccharine."

"I'm talking about us, our future," said Simon, lunging, seizing both of her hands and clasping them tightly. "Us."

"Now Simon. You know I'm not fond of your lapses into adolescence. Have you had anything to eat?" she asked.

Simon's resonant, strong voice began to tremble. "Sybil! Listen to me. I am now prepared to quit my marriage, to walk out on Hope, to throw myself at your feet and to toss everything. For us. I'm yours, all yours. Let's away, now! What was the place you mentioned in the islands, the untouristed beach with the secluded, azure lagoon?"

"You're serious? You're talking out of your head, but you are serious."

"I've never been more serious," said Simon.

Sybil stood, straightened herself, and looked down at Simon on the sofa, his body contorted into a penitent position, left knee on the floor. "Simon, you can be one of the thickest-headed people I know. First of all, let's be truthful. You quit your marriage years ago, or Mary quit—I don't know and don't care. If that death has finally sunk in, fine. Don't proclaim it as news. Secondly, I won't help you play the sacrificial lamb. I've heard you were on thin ice at church, which I found surprising. I figured you had the dolts duped."

Simon's surprise turned to horror as he frantically searched Sybil for a glimmer of affection.

She continued, lighting a cigarette that she consumed eagerly. "You have been a disappointment, Simon. I was quite wrong in my early judgments," she said as she exhaled.

"Wrong? What are you saying?"

"I knew that *I* was in league with Satan, prone to wander. I assumed that you were as well, never suspecting that you actually believed your sermons because I rarely detected a shred of sincerity. I therefore presumed that you might serve as an amusing playmate in my lifelong pursuit of perversity."

"Perversity? You're not so great a sinner as all that, Sybil. I've found you enchanting," laughed Simon.

"How the hell would you know the state of my soul?" asked Sybil with a smirk. "Never once have you inquired. That your silly little liberal theology excludes the possibility of sin renders you completely unqualified to judge such matters. I naively thought that you might have peered behind my façade," said Sybil, staring at her feet. "No, your mainline spiritual ineptitude is showing. As for me, sad to say, the reproaches of my ex-husbands are true. I consent to the accuracy of their assessments. My tab with the divine bartender is more than I can pay. A trapped, self-loathing sinner, helpless and hopeless in her hell-bent descent, I sought to join hands with a few other incorrigibles to keep me company as I fell. Perfecting the sin of using others, I flitted here and there, sucking nectar from each pretty flower and, when they wilted, casting them aside. Devoid of regret, I appear before the judgment empty-handed of anything to commend me. How embarrassing for someone so well financed, and with a master's too."

"Sybil! Come now."

"And to think you gave yourself to a vocation that licenses a professional peek behind the veil. Yet you see nothing. There's no hope for us, whether in pulpit or pew, without mercy. No other hope for you either. Oh that you had the audacity to face the truth. Nothing, nothing except the possibility that whoever set all this up, and who shall one day bring it to an end, is not only powerful but also extravagantly merciful."

"Now you're being the drama queen, Sybil," Simon said as he reached for her hand, hoping that she might be attempting humor. "You can't believe all that, really?"

"Even though you've seen me naked, how little you have seen. Unlike you, I *believe* my lines. At first I thought that you, having spent so much time around the doomed degenerate, understood what you were getting into when you got into me. I talked myself into believing that you might be a bold sinner of my tribe, a fellow dabbler in recreational wickedness. I romantically expected that you might have dared to gaze into depths that I, poor layman, could only imagine. Then came your petty preoccupation with our being discovered, what your board might think, and how poor Mary couldn't live without you. The sneaking and the creeping. Now I hear that you have even disposed of an innocent young associate simply because you feared that he would expose your romping with me. You don't have what it takes for a bracing plunge into the icy waters of adultery, do you? You have the carnal desire but not the moral backbone. Your theology, if that is what it is, forces you still to play the good little boy, to keep in place your well-polished persona, even if you must sacrifice everyone around you."

"Sybil! How could you?"

"Petty little pietist," she smirked. "Disbelieving in a God who forgives, you lack the imagination to believe in Satan. You're afraid to descend the stairs into the dark—worse, too cautious to test the possibility of grace. If all I desired was a romp between the sheets, I would have chosen a more adept playmate. I was bored and you visited me, but sad to say, you brought only greater boredom."

"Sybil, you are being horrible!" Tears formed in his eyes for the first time in years. "How can you treat me like this? How can you be so, so—dare I say it—*judgmental?*"

"Ah, the light *is* beginning to shine in the darkness."

Again he sought her hands. She pulled away, reaching for yet another cigarette. "Poor Simon. You actually believe your oppressively hopeful sermons. You are stricken with the most deadly of maladies, the dumbest of illusions—you think you are good. True, without a merciful God, you must delude yourself or be damned. I'm surprised. I had hoped yours was an act; so many in your profession are adept at sham. I erroneously assumed an experienced sinner lurking behind all that power of progressive thinking. No, you are your sentimental sermons, after all. I'm tired."

"You can't mean what I'm hearing."

"Simon, it's been a long time since you have been truthful; you may have forgotten how. Well, show yourself out, can't you?" asked an icy Sybil as she picked up her shoes, made her way through the dark toward her bedroom, alone, leaving Simon silently to slink away, closing the front door behind him, badly wounded, again orphaned.

ᴏᴡ

"Well, Hank, Simon finally summoned the courage to confess his dalliance," said Mary as Hank folded blankets for summer storage at the homeless shelter.

"Really?"

"Oh, he of course couched it all in nonsense about the death of our marriage, his loneliness, his hurt, his pain. Blah, blah, blah. You know Simon—trapped in himself."

"What are you feeling, Mary?"

"Next to nothing. I should be ashamed. But Simon has had me in training for this day for a very long time. He never really needed a wife, certainly not for conventional reasons. Simon required only a smiling member of his supporting cast."

"So, you're OK?" Hank asked, turning from his work, taking her hands, looking into her face.

"Fortunately, I was never blessed with a surfeit of sentiment. I'm actually somewhat relieved that Simon has at last summoned the gumption to make a move. I thought that his upward ascent was all he needed, along with adoring himself in the mirror of his weekly pulpit performance. By the way, you were right. Sybil Vestal."

"Really? Even though everyone said it was Sybil, what does she see in Simon?"

"Simon is engaging in that predictable project undertaken by many men of his age, that reptilian shedding of skin under the illusion that he's becoming a new being when, in reality, it's the same old Simon"—her voice emphasized "old"—"in a different guise. Poor thing. He thinks we are having an affair," said Mary in a matter-of-fact way.

"Really?" Hank paused, smiled, and squeezed Mary's hand, moving her closer to him. "Are we?"

"That remains to be seen," said Mary with a laugh. "Certainly not in an orthodox sense. Americans' sexual escapades are all that they have left after the death of their gods, gives them a respite from the fatigue of dollar worship, a momentary release from service to their shallow idols. When they tire of breathlessly consuming cars, TVs, and pills, advertising prompts them to consume one another. So very boring."

Hank stepped back and released his tight clasp of Mary's hand. "Real passion arises from sharing commitment to the well-being of others, discontent with the status quo. Concern for somebody else is the real turn-on," said Hank softly. "You taught me that."

Mary giggled a girlish laugh as she reached for another stack of blankets. "Keep talking. You are convincing me that I'm in the middle of an affair after all—torrid lovers amid mountains of smelly bedding, none of which belongs to us. I love you when you talk leftist revolutionary rhetoric. As a passionate crypto-Christian-Marxist, you are adorable. Whisper liberation theology to me; my powers of resistance are crumbling."

∾

Although Simon was crushed, still shivering from Sybil's coldness (and sitting in a puddle after leaving his car door ajar in the rain), he wasn't whipped. He had seen an odd side of Sybil. She was less impulsive than he had first thought. Now, he must set aside all that and resume his professional demeanor, giving attention to the more pressing project of convincing the world that his departure from Hope had been solely at his initiative. No more honorable way to exit than burn out, his bright flame extinguished by their suffocating pettiness. He was overly invested, excessively committed to his congregation, and therefore had neglected self-care. Was that a sin?

Or should he say that he had become impatient with the lack of imagination among the lay leadership, so he had decided to launch in a new direction? Yes. He was too strong to take the burnout defense. He was a man of action beating his head against the brick wall of conservative indifference and ecclesiastical mediocrity. Despite his inherently upbeat and positive nature, he was fatigued after decades of rustic, reactionary resistance. Yes.

The traditional goal of preaching would characterize his departure: hit them with maximum guilt before the benediction.

As he drove through darkened streets, the water on the wet seat gradually penetrating his underwear, thinking these recuperative thoughts lifted his spirits. Refocusing, rethinking, repositioning, retrieving. The spirit had been quenched in him, but only for a time. His incaution was costly but not deadly.

One thing was sure: Never again would he put his trust in small-minded, trivial church pygmies who had made him get down on his knees for a full car allowance! Never again would he be vulnerable to a scheming, lying Judas like Quail.

And never again would he betray his God-given gifts for the upkeep of a useless architectural antique.

He fleetingly thought about praying; many people do at such a time. But the sort of God that he had preached seemed not too concerned with whining weaklings.

He would keep his thoughts to himself.

Simon smiled in self-satisfaction. Already he was pulling himself up, putting things in perspective, validating his sermons. As he drove he composed a brief outline of his virtues, as if he were in the dock defending himself before the court of the Almighty. He had communicative gifts. He was an entrepreneur. Imagination, creativity, excellence were his tri-une talents. Intellectually he was unconfined by the Christian tradition. Psychologically he had resisted suffocation by and dependency upon the church. Sexually, he was unbound by matrimonial constraints. He knew how to connect. Gifts demand respect. Utilizing his connections, he would venture forth, make a fresh beginning. (Perhaps in commercial real estate?) True, a door had closed, but thanks to God, in every ending is a fresh beginning. He began to hum a hymn: *In the bud, there is a flower. In the seed, an apple tree. Butterflies will soon be free!*

Simon thus skillfully refurbished his self-confidence in the scant six blocks between the florist's shop near Sybil's house and Cut-Rate Custom Caskets a block from his own, a once dispirited victim miraculously self-infused with fresh spirit.

∾

Simon's Sunday sermon was produced by mindlessly going through the motions. Countless clergy had done the same. Despite his disaster of a week, Simon managed a Saturday morning glance at the assigned lessons for the Sunday rising up before him like a hangman's noose: Pentecost, 1 Corinthians 12:3b–13.

> For just as the body is one and has many members, and all the members of the body, though many, are one body, so it is with Christ. For in the one Spirit we were all baptized into one body— Jews or Greeks, slaves or free—and we were all made to drink of one Spirit.

Clearly Paul's metaphorical inclinations had gotten the best of him. The church a *body?* He thought of Sybil's body, lying next to his, her sleek, well-defined features a joy to behold, even at her age. He smiled, receiving this vision as a gift on an otherwise morbid morning. Sybil lying on her bed, propped up by lush pillows. He tenderly contemplated that little role of cellulite just above her waist that showed itself when she leaned to one side. Her hips, when exposed, were more ample than he had anticipated, though still more trim than most women her age. She had taken exquisite care of herself, had done what she could, and he admired that in her.

He fondly remembered his first sight of a woman's body. Actually, she was seventeen, not yet a woman, still a girl, yet that primal vision of naked flesh had never left him, and even now filled him with elation, his spirit rising. He thoughtfully assessed his own body, which, though displaying signs of age—an unsightly sag here and an unwelcome, asymmetrical bulge there, an impervious paunch—had been, as a whole, responsibly maintained.

Simon's unbridled homiletical imagination, outdoing even that of Saint Paul, gave somatic consideration to Hope's rambling, crumbling, Gothic (that is, *Neo*gothic) edifice, a bodily nuisance, but inspiring and uplifting for many who didn't know better. For twenty years he served this mildewed Moloch without complaint only to end on this Saturday, grubbing for a sermon, probably his last, delivered to a congregation well trained in complacency. That which others saw as an inspiration, the clergy—who had to raise the money for the urinals, the gutters, and the drains—knew to be an insatiable dinosaur, an occupational hazard. And that's just the building.

Incorporation

We were all baptized into one body. Jesus struggled his whole ministry, was brutally crucified, improbably rose from the dead, and ascended regally into heaven to take his place at the right hand of God the Father Almighty. Then the Holy Spirit descended on Pentecost, shaking the foundations, and what did God get for the trouble?

The church?

If he couldn't talk himself into tackling Saint Paul's allegorical exaggeration in 1 Corinthians 12, Simon knew he hadn't a snowball's chance in hell of thawing his frozen congregation for it. Thus Simon, in his much distracted and still troubled state (though he had expected a penitent phone call from Sybil, he had heard zilch since her tirade two nights ago), moved toward tomorrow's sermon. He had sought consolation in his emptiness and Sybil had turned him away with a stone rather than bread. He was willing to atone for coming on a bit eagerly; all she had to do was ask. What he did, he did for love.

As he pondered his departure from Hope, he remembered the loan that had been given to him during initial salary negotiations. Surely nobody would expect him to repay the two-decades-old, interest-free bridge loan. It was part of his salary, not really a loan. Thanks be to God most who were on the board when he got the loan were now quite dead.

How much alimony would Mary expect? Her wisecrack about their resources originating with her family was surprising. And troubling. Her sweet demeanor (deceptive as always) might shift as soon as she fell into the reptilian hands of some venal attorney. A brief shudder ran down Simon's spine at the thought of the Virgin Mary under the expert management of a savvy lawyer. Perhaps he ought to talk to Quail about formally excusing his loan. But why give Quail an opportunity to alpha-male him? Better to lie low. He could count on finances being so haphazardly conducted at Hope that no one could retrieve the papers; they had not a prayer of collecting once he was out of their employ.

Just then was heard a light but persistent tapping. He glanced over his shoulder. That bird was back, pecking, beating its wings in futility against the glass. Simon rose and rapped his knuckle loudly against the window, hoping to deter the bird. At Simon's tapping the bird flew a few feet away but, once his back was turned, returned and resumed pecking and flapping.

"Stupid bird," Simon said, annoyed by the distraction. "I, seminary-trained scholar, want out, that pea-brained creature wants in. The crazy things we do in the name of love." Smiling, he returned to the sermon.

He resolved to toss the assigned lessons and stand and deliver a slightly updated version of an earlier offering, "I Believe in the Human Spirit," an inspirational address that had arisen in him years ago after reading William Faulkner's Nobel Prize acceptance speech (actually, an article about the speech in *Reader's Digest*).

He would speak of the indomitable human spirit, extolling the way that a benevolent God had given each of us the capacity to rise (here he added Maya Angelou's "And Still I Rise" with a few improvements), to reach, and to strive. He would tell the story of the man who was tragically cut down, in the prime of life, by a debilitating nerve disorder but who, by sheer force of will, had taught himself to drive a car just like Franklin Roosevelt (they loved Eleanor or Franklin stories) and to type with his tongue, even to compete in a regional Formula One rally in Ohio.

He would praise what God does for us, in God's providential care, but he would more highly praise what God chose *not* to do for us, graciously leaving us room to rise, to reach, and to strive. Or perhaps rise, reach, *recover*? Yes, the alliteration worked nicely. *Recover* gave a certain regenerative spin. The unreflective among us regard aches and pains, tragedies and setbacks as bad news. But in the hands of the determined, the spiritually creative, and the inspired, such impediments are gospel, an opportunity for self-care. "Rise, reach, and recover" would form the sermon's rhythmic backbone, a mantra to be repeated throughout, after each illustration. "Rise, reach, and recover." Yes. He was sounding like Jesse Jackson, only white. In all circumstances of life, he would tell them, we can rise, reach, and recover. He had become his sermon. Rise. Reach. Recover.

On Monday he would make his tactical retreat before the bishop could take credit for pushing him out. Looking back, his time at Hope had been, all in all, a good ride. He would say his benediction, not with exalted words of wisdom (their tender ears couldn't take what he would really like to tell them), but rather with a rehash of a sermon from a decade earlier, reprise of a speech that Faulkner gave, surely while drunk, served up with skill to a congregation that was too dull to realize that they were ingesting leftovers.

Rise, reach, and recover—a sermonic perfect fit for Hope. They had risen on the backs of their conniving, upwardly middle-class parents and their legacies. He had witnessed those who had not been so blessed kick, bite, and grab, thus mounting to the summit of the social heap—two cars (and another for the kids), membership at the club, a place at the lake, a poinsettia on the Hope altar at Christmastime and lilies on Easter.

Incorporation

All of them enjoyed thinking that their ascension was the result of their own talent and effort. They were wrong. Luck and good inheritance, along with an unbridled ability to step upon the necks of those who were cursed with less overreaching cupidity and more moral compunction, had more to do with their social location than aptitude.

"My parish, how well I have known them," mused Simon as he exited his office, smiling with self-satisfaction.

9

Trinity Sunday

Grimball's aging, coughing Volvo—which he self-consciously drove to make some sort of point—having choked its way from his townhouse by fits and starts, finally got him to the Hope parking lot, almost the first car that Sunday, arriving well before the start of the pealing bells. As he exited his car, clutching his organ shoes in one hand, locking up with the other, he was accosted by an older woman whose stringy gray hair strayed from under a University of Alabama baseball cap. She reached out and clutched his left arm as she whispered, "God isn't done with us! He's going to kill all of us!"

Having suffered a lifetime of tribulations inflicted by unbalanced amateur musicians who thought too much of themselves, Grimball was startlingly unstartled by this crazy old lady's God-babblings. Another day at the office for a professional church musician. A rotten, horrible odor hung on the woman, no doubt due to her having rifled through the church's garbage, and as she talked she gestured with her right hand, in which she held what looked to be a soiled, red velvet master's hood belonging to a graduate of Princeton Theological Seminary.

"You're telling me, sister. The end is quite upon us. You know not the half," sighed Grimball, grinning knowledgably. His matter-of-fact agreement caught her off guard. She gaped at him in stupefied curiosity.

"Honey, in these last days I know just the person who can help you, a man of God who, though he can do nothing to contribute to your salvation, is in desperate need of your revelation. You can find him burrowed in the administrative suite, busying himself for his nonparticipation in the service today," he said, gesturing toward the side entrance. "Please allow me to guide you to the good Reverend Mr. Quail. Matters eschatological are quite beyond my level of competence or remuneration, I fear. And don't let him take that hood from you; he'd give his right arm (or some other part of his anatomy) to have one of those babies."

"Nobody calls me honey!" the woman retorted, pulling her arm away from Grimball.

"Each of us has a cross to bear, don't we?"

"Are you trying to come on to me?" She shot Grimball an angry, fierce look.

"Just attempting to be your little brother in Christ," Grimball reassured, gagging at her uremic stench, coaxing her up the walk and toward the entrance. Then with his organist shoes in his left hand, he pointed her down the hall toward Quail's office.

"That'll fix him," said Grimball as he skipped gleefully towards the music suite. He had at last evened the score after the organ chamber hell.

"Wait a minute," she said, halting in the middle of the hallway. "Did you say 'Quail'?"

"Yes, sweetie," giggled Grimball over his shoulder. "Quail: a small, dumb, flightless bird that played a bit part in the Exodus."

∾

That day at eleven, worshippers at the main service were surprised to find kindly, retired-but-still-hanging-on pastor Herb Cohellen, vested in white for the Trinity, plodding along as coda to the procession rather than their pastor, whose name had been listed in the bulletin. The *Corpus Christi* was clueless about the disruption that had unfolded at Hope Church. Staff consensus was that they must always protect the congregation from the facts.

In deference to the Sunday, the first hymn was in homage to the Trinity, sung with an elegant brass interlude between the third and fourth verses:

Holy, Holy, Holy, Lord God Almighty! Early in the morning our songs shall rise to thee . . .

"Is Simon ill?" a gaggle of choristers had asked Glumweltner, who, being late, waddled at twice his normal pace into the chancel to ready the rented brass, straightening his ample surplice as he brushed passed.

"I am at liberty to say nothing," he had replied with a knowing look. "Nuthin! And no, I know not where young master Stephen is either, so don't ask. Both are missing in action. Rats leaving a sinking ship, I'd think."

God in three persons, blessed Trinity.

While clergy frequently utilize the Prayer for Others to slip controversial announcements to the congregation, no word of explanation or reassurance related to Simon's absence was forthcoming, even in the prayers. But when a choir member, fumbling with her sheet music, allowed her hymnal to slip between her knees and bang on the marble floor of the chancel, everyone in the congregation startled, an indication that the usually placid congregation was on edge.

Though the eye of sinful man thy glory may not see.

At the appointed place for the sermon, Herb, stooped and frail, moved slowly toward the pulpit, looking ancient as he mounted the steps—Abraham ascending Mount Moriah, Noah taking the helm of the Ark—glare from a bright spotlight falling upon his white hair. Or perhaps he looked Methuselaic merely by comparison with the strained vitality of the pulpit's regular occupant. Fortunately for the congregation, when the occasion demanded antique wisdom, Herb knew how to play the patriarch. And when Herb spoke, his voice seemed to arise from elsewhere:

Even perched here, I can feel your corporate disappointment that you have me rather than our eloquent pastor. As you know, eloquence is not a gift that God has seen fit to bestow upon me, certainly not to the degree that God has given this gift to Simon.

Polite, scattered, deferential smiles throughout the church. They had always craved, but had rarely seen, a show of humility in their clergy. Though advanced in years, Herb still could work a congregation to his oratorical advantage.

My goal this morning is not eloquence but faithfulness. I hope to say something to you before we come to the Lord's Table, something that, while lacking brilliance, at least, by the grace of God, might be helpful.

It was the congregation's first celebration of the Eucharist since Maundy Thursday. Simon was opposed to frequent communion; he based his objection on a notable decline both in attendance and offering on Sundays of word and table.

My friends, it's Trinity Sunday, bane of preachers. The Trinity lies beyond my gifts of explanation. And though I don't recall ever having heard a sermon at Hope on the Trinity, this is the Sunday when all of the lessons remind us that our hope rests in the three-personed God—a challenging assignment for people like us, since we are more accustomed to hope in ourselves.

Herb cleared his throat.

Incorporation

When it comes to thinking about God, Christians have a challenge. We share with many the belief that God is One. But we are no mere monotheists. We hold the astounding conviction that God is God in three ways: Father, Son, and Holy Spirit.

Oh dear, I see from the expression on your faces that I've already coaxed you into perilously deep waters.

Scattered muffled laughter.

Our first lesson from Genesis depicts a God who speaks, who preaches to the dark void, saying, "Light," and there is light. And the light is good. The first sermon preached on the first day was preached by God, not to a sunlit, handsome congregation like Hope, but rather to the dark chaos. Without a God who speaks, summons, and creates, all would be . . . nothing. That there is something—light in the darkness, order amid chaos—is testament to the loquaciousness of a God who refuses to leave nothingness to its own devices.

The preacher paused to draw breath. He bent close to the microphone, knowing the weakness of his aged, high-pitched voice. Thus the listeners heard him breathing, as if he were whispering a deep secret, as if his breath were hovering, simulating the Spirit at creation. Hope was unaccustomedly hushed and attentive as the raspy breath of a preacher who seemed to predate the Flood was breathed upon them.

Viewed from Herb's pulpit perspective, the urbane congregation looked for all the world like lines of birds perched on rows of wires—Mary Lupino, two rows in front of Sybil, gawking upward and intently towards the preacher, smiling with delight at how much more thoughtful was this elderly elocutionist than her soon-to-be ex-husband, and then Jane and her sister, mouths wide open, Jane with eyes closed in delight at the fluency and depth of what she was hearing. Jack Hodges, who had vowed to Alexis that this would be his last Sunday at Hope ("that church is a bunch of hypocrites"), held her hand tightly, all confused by the presence of something unaccustomed, palpably moving among them. Grimball, transfixed on his organ bench, Glumweltner (Buddha surrounded by a choir), and a young woman whom nobody knew, fumbling for her tissue. Two usually disinterested teenagers with atypical, quizzical faces focusing, joining hundreds of others—heads upturned, hungry mouths agape as if dying to be fed by the words of an ancient preacher who preached without artifice or cant, whose voice was high-pitched, breathy, and trustworthy.

It's a childlike story, Genesis, arising out of the world's infancy, when the Spirit of God hovered like a dove over dark waters. I have found in my own ministry—whenever people's lives are thrown into chaos, and circumstances force them to revert, and life renders them once again infantile—that this childlike story of our origins is a comfort: when you turn and become as a little child, and watery, death-dealing chaos threatens, how reassuring to know by heart: "In the beginning, when God began creating the heavens and the earth . . . 'Light,' and there was light."

If this word is true at the beginning, we are justified in assuming it will be true at the end.

Here Herb paused and again cleared his throat.

Now I want to tell you that our pastor, our beloved leader, Doctor Lupino, has decided that his ministry has come to a close here at Hope.

An audible gasp from the congregation.

The years in which Simon Lupino led this flock were among the grandest in the history of this great church. Simon led us down paths we would never have had the courage to walk without his leading. Most of us, including me, are at Hope because of him. You can imagine the demanding burden of a congregation like us. Simon is now taking a well-deserved sabbatical, but our bishop says that Simon will not return. God will not leave Simon's gifts long unused; he will be called to some new work.

Of course, the church is more than its pastor. Hope is a creation of Jesus Christ, his Body on earth. The same good God who gave us light, who breathed into our dust the breath of life, also gives us Christ's Body, the church, and breathes into this congregation life-giving Spirit. It's all gift. The church is convened not by a pleasing pastor but by Jesus Christ. Only God can birth, or kill, a church.

Which brings me at last to this morning's gospel. In the Wednesday morning Bible study we have been working our way through Matthew's Gospel. In chapter 28 the risen Christ prepares his disciples for his departure. And he commissions them to "go into all the world," "making disciples," "baptizing," and "teaching," constitutive activities of any church.

Baptizing, going, teaching—demanding work. How does Jesus expect ordinary, weak, and inadequate people like us to do it?

But then Jesus says, "I am with you always, even to the end of the age." We're not expected to do anything for him, without him. The same Savior who calls us to be faithful to him promises to be faithful to us. "I am with you always."

Another pause with heavy breathing.

Through the passage of time, crises, the rising flood, the change of pastors, life and death, and every threat of the return of primordial, watery chaos, this is the promise that cheers: "I am with you always." For reasons known only to Jesus, we are the form that the risen Christ has chosen to take in the world, his Body.

I can't figure it out.

Yet another long gap as Herb cleared his throat and shifted his notes uneasily.

Paul says to one of his churches: "You are the Body of Christ." We're not a well-built Body—crucified, bearing wounds, weak, bleeding. But we are the only Body he's got, evidence of his reign, we, his sole witnesses. If you are intimidated by such prodigal claims, I am as well.

Time and again, in our ineptitude, we tear his Body asunder, but time and again he breathes new life into our valley of dry bones.

In a moment you will eat the body of Christ; you will have your deepest hunger assuaged, Christ's body and blood will flow through your veins.

Our future as a congregation is in the hands of our bishop; our fate as church, our future as the Body, is in the hands of Christ.

Here he made a somewhat awkward pause, as if a thought had come to him mid-sermon. Looking away from his notes, he gazed into the space above the heads of the congregation.

A ridiculous statement, when I think about it, ludicrous even when applied to a church as good as this one. We, Christ's Body, his grand argument put to a wayward humanity. A strange analogy, a thought that doesn't fit my own experience, I must confess. We, Christ's Body?

Herb recollected himself, looking down at his notes again. No one wanted him to stop; his words were lifting them out of a deep well of banality, enabling them to ascend.

Hope for Hope is not in us. Church, any church, is utterly dependent upon a God who enjoys raising the dead. Hope is in the one who said, "Let there be Hope, and there was." And it was good. The only hope we've got is found in Saint Paul's wildly unguarded "you are the Body of Christ," followed by Christ's even more extravagant promise, "I am with you always."

Amen.

The congregation sat in silence, stunned, overwhelmed, grateful, as Herb turned and made his way down the steps, feeling, fumbling down the railing, awkwardly plopping into his seat behind the pulpit, having let God have his say, now blending into the woodwork of the chancel, unburdened. Some of the flock wanted to applaud, but that didn't seem right. Others had a strange urge to weep but did not know why. Almost all knew that they had been led, in spite of themselves, close to the heart of the matter, the true point of it all.

At Herb's mention of "dead," Quail momentarily thought of Niculous—poor little pious dead man hanging from the limbs of a dead tree—sad to be floating toward him on the same dark river.

The choir required a moment to regroup for the offertory anthem, a choral arrangement of "The Church's One Foundation," accompanied by trumpets and tympani.

The Church's one foundation is Jesus Christ her Lord,
She is his new creation by water and the word,
From heaven he came and sought her to be his holy bride . . .
And for her life he died.

Herb struggled to remove the corporal from the Lord's Table, then faced the congregation with arms outstretched in welcome. The offering was received, plates of money borne by officious ushers, a flask of wine and loaf of bread offered by the Kline family, the littlest Klines bearing oblation for the sins of all.

Bread was broken. "This is my body." Blood-red wine poured in homage to a Savior recklessly willing to sup with those who would otherwise be damned. Processing to the Lord's Table, they were little children moving hesitantly, as if they knew inchoately they had neither reason nor right to be here, other than the graciousness of God. The boldest sinners came eagerly, reaching for the body and the blood, famished, brash to bear *corpus Christi* in their soiled, empty hands.

In their corporate move upon the Lord's Table, considering who they were (and who they had no hope ever of becoming), in their unashamed reception of grace, mouths open like fragile baby birds, in their sweet collective conviction that the body of Christ would be given even to such as them, wounded by grace, they embodied Paul's words: "We carry in this body the death of Jesus."

Midway through communion Herb realized that he had forgotten to give direction to the alternate communion stations. He set down his tray of bread and shouted over the organ, "Excuse me! I forgot. The lactose intolerant among you. Station on my left. Oops. I meant *gluten* intolerant. It's your right, my left." He looked anxiously toward the two teenagers at the station to his left and the clueless looks they returned shook Herb's conviction that they were actually offering gluten-free body of Christ.

"And for our alcoholic friends, the station with the grape juice is . . ." His helpless look at the communion servers failed to elicit any definitive gesture from them that this was indeed where the non-alcoholic blood was being served.

"Oh well, do the best you can. None of us is worthy to be here anyway. Come as you are, wherever you please." Those who heard him laughed. Grimball continued the background organ music undeterred, and communion resumed.

Such a sight—the comforted, the summoned, the soiled, the pursued, the fallen, the foolish, the blessed, the misunderstood, and the misunderstanding—all engrafted, fused, as if clinging to one another, moving as one body, incorporated into some incomprehensible grandeur, rescued, the oddest work of a determinedly incarnate God.

Nearly everyone in the room would be dead thirty years from now, but in that moment, mortality held no terror. Few had come that Sunday expecting to worship. Most, having been taught that faith was a system of thought, were surprised to experience church as miracle. The religion that had been presented to them as wish projection or as personal need fulfillment became, in that moment, gift, corporate revelation made more wonderful because it was unanticipated.

As he played a series of hymns—background accompaniment for the throng streaming forward to communion—cupric-coiffured Grimball, hands moving across the keyboard, stared at the music, but not consciously, lost, a crying, Tang-haired baby, mucus running down his nose in droplets upon the keys, appalled by himself, humiliated.

Extra ecclesiam nulla salus.

"Oh, I neglected to say earlier," Herb clumsily interjected after he had tidied the Lord's Table and just before the beginning of the last hymn, "that our bishop will be our preacher for the next few Sundays, taking the helm. He shall be such a help. Oh yes, I also forgot that the Hope Happy Hearts are planning a cookbook, 'Best of Chef.' They're doing a referendum on your favorite recipes from our Manager of Hospitality, in the hope of Chef's soon recovery."

∽

That night, unseen by anyone, Simon's Porsche slowly processed its lonely way up Hope Boulevard to allow for Simon's morose valedictory on his years at Hope. This was always his favorite vista—flawless, resplendent in floodlights, a glorious apparition—all once his. Twenty years ago he sat here, parked in this very spot, holding hands with Mary, on the eve of his inaugural sermon, disbelieving their good fortune. Tonight Simon sat in kenotic solitude, defeated, despondent, busted and bruised on fine-brushed leather seats.

Unable, despite his swaggering and haughty declarations, to culti-
vate sufficient anger to overcome his hurt, as he looked at Hope, sadness
overcame him. In the last couple of days, he had been forced to admit that
without a congregation, bereft of people whose screwed-up lives required
his pulpit wisdom, he was nothing. A skilled worker of words thrives
upon, requires, the adulation of the inarticulate and the uncomprehend-
ing. Simon knew enough about himself to know that he could not live
without an audience.

More humiliating was his desperate need for this building. For twenty years he had deceived himself, telling himself and the world that Hope
was nothing but a hulking dead millstone shackled to his neck. Tonight he
knew it to be the other way around. Tonight he adored every neogothic,
incongruous inch of this imposing temple—sunlight streaming through
blue windows, the amplitude of the Great Hall, the substantial oak pulpit, the warm, domestic intimacy of the Walter Rauschenbusch Lounge.
Hope's plumbing and circuitry, once derided as crumbling and decayed,
now seemed immortal. Tonight nothing was eternal except that tower rising before him in the darkness. For ever and ever, amen.

Though Simon had redundantly, publicly lamented that the building
was falling apart, was undeniably dependent upon his vigilant stewardship, and was sapping his spirit and the congregation's resources, tonight
the building spoke in a voice as resonant as its biggest bell: "While your
body breaks down and is despised, I'm more dearly loved for my age. I am
still here, and you are not."

Simon mused: If Warren G. Harding came back from the dead, the
only thing he would recognize is Hope. Somewhere there's a sermon in
that.

∽

It was an eventful week for the Trinity. God the Father, God the Son, and
God the Holy Spirit—emboldened by the attentiveness shown in millions
of churches the previous Sunday, perhaps taking advantage of the disruption offered by a brief cessation of clergy control—responded by producing a highly charged week. The Crazy Woman was deadened by Sabbath
afternoon with a shot of potent sedative in her bottom. She now lay co-
matose in the psychiatric section of Mercy Hospital, though she was to
be evicted for lack of funds before the end of the week and dumped at the
County Home. In the prospect that she might one day win her freedom,

Hope Church, in the person of Quail, took out a restraining order, prohibiting her from setting foot within a hundred yards of Hope property.

The small brown bird returned and, when it wasn't working on a nest on the ledge, spent hours each day tapping at the Senior Managing Pastor's window out of territorial possessiveness, stupidity, spirit, or sex, pecking away at the dark window of a forlorn and vacant office that once held the belongings of the Senior Managing Pastor.

Thursday after Trinity is Corpus Christi, but Hope—progressively Protestant—knew nothing of the feast. However, the people of God at Hope, robbed of Simon's ministry, were now powerless to defend themselves against pneumatic, bodily incursions, even on a Thursday. That day, when the bishop issued a statement of "gratitude for Dr. Lupino's dynamic ministry," and blathered that Simon was now free to "follow God's lead even unto ever more promising contexts," even the most obtuse of the laity easily deciphered the ecclesiastical code as "our preacher is history."

When word shot through the congregation of Simon's demise, of his sudden, still-shrouded-in-mystery exit from Hope and the dissolution of his marriage, some walked with a lighter step, receiving renewed faith in a just God. (Corpus Christi is a moveable feast.) Though there was debate over whether the cause for Simon's exit was spiritual, sexual, or psychiatric, glee outweighed gloom. Herb confessed that he had overestimated the laity's capacity for lamentation; something in laity rises at reports of clerical ruin. That a church fails formally to celebrate Corpus Christi does not invalidate its truth.

Nonetheless, Quail moved about Hope's corridors unsteadily. He now labored under a dark secret, traumatized by an ominous event having nothing to do with the demise of Niculous, from which he was by now quite well recovered. Monday after Trinity, Quail received a jolt. Back at his doctor's office to prepare for his regular chemotherapy torture session, his doctor had startled him with, "Well, Reverend, I think we've got an honest-to-God miracle on our hands. Never seen nothin' like it."

Before an incredulous, utterly unnerved patient, the doctor slapped an X-ray of Quail's gut on the viewing screen and proceeded to show how the tumor had "just up and disappeared. A first in all my days of oncology. See for yourself. Gone." Such an occurrence, the doctor assured, had nothing to do with a positive attitude, handfuls of daily vitamins (some secured illegally from Mexico), two searing shots of radiation, or twelve packs of gut-wrenching chemo. "No," said the doctor, "it's an honest-to-God miracle, like Lourdes or Waco. Roman Catholic, even."

After receiving this unexpected and inconceivable news, Quail staggered dumbfoundedly out of his doctor's office, wordlessly clutching a copy of the X-ray, scientific proof of a decidedly unscientific phenomenon. On his escape through the waiting room, a receptionist, or maybe she was a nurse, accosted him and hugged him tightly to her ample, heaving breasts, tearfully babbling, "You must have been living right," and, "God wouldn't do this for just anybody. I've never known anybody to have a prayer answered! A miracle! I guess it's because you are a man of God . . ."

Her smooching clutch was tacky, terrifying. Quail pried the woman loose, pushed past the gathering supplicants in the waiting room who reached out to touch the hem of his golf shirt, and wordlessly hightailed it to the parking lot, embarrassed to the depths of his being. Later that day, drinking himself back toward stability, he had a fleeting urge to be thankful, to say something to God in gratitude, but—having made neither intercession, oblation, confession, nor thanksgiving in years—he had no idea what to say, so he said nothing. Without experience of the miraculous, without even any expectation that there was such, he was flabbergasted. His miracle as absurd as a vision of Christ on a taco, Quail was annoyed with medical science for having no plausible empirical explanation to bolster his disbelief. And as for God, why thank someone for a gift when the gift has not been petitioned?

He resolved never to tell anyone, least of all his ex-wife, especially her—though he delighted in thinking how crushed she would be by his positive prognosis. While Johnson Quail had a theology that charitably excused God for causing tumors in good people, he lacked any theological rationale for God's curing cancers in bad people. He was too old graciously to receive an epiphany and too prideful to be born again. If the church got word of this it would be his ruination.

The Lourdes-like healing served to scour off Quail's last residue of faith. "What sort of God would burden a person like me with a gratuitous cure like this?" he asked his empty living room as he downed another anesthetizing drink. Battered by his realization of reality's unpredictability, he would now be forced, by his miraculous recovery, to confront the idiots at the Department of Motor Vehicles and renew his long-expired driver's license. (A month later, when his doctor called and asked him to testify before the weekly Gastro-oncologists for Jesus prayer group, Quail—horrified by the request—refused, sternly reminding his doctor of the restrictions placed upon him by medical privacy laws.)

Incorporation

For Chef, there was no miracle. The gangrenous infection from his burns raged throughout his already weakened body, processing triumphantly from one organ to the next and, before the end of the week, working an agonizing denouement. On the afternoon before his end, Chef became delirious and confessed various sins to Quail, who had meant only to stop by and check on the financial implications of his condition. Chef wept, clutching Quail's sleeve, and tearfully, incoherently owned up to the violation of a former girlfriend. Nietzsche said that the deathbed is a prime location for showing off; Chef was theatrical to the end.

The next morning Quail returned, claimed the body, and, since there was no one else to assist Chef's leave-taking, signed the papers that sent what was left of Chef to Joseph's. The bill would be paid—delinquently— by Hope Church, and Chef was given—reluctantly—more a curt, dignified disposal than a Christian funeral. Severe kidney failure was listed as the cause of death. A rock-hard liver didn't help.

"Chef's spaghetti di Napoli really was 'to die for,'" was the postmortem pun that Grimball circulated around Hope. Hope Happy Hearts would never publish *The Best of Chef.*

10

Sundays in Ordinary Time

Widely rumored to be having a platonic affair, Hank and Mary threw caution to the wind and attended the Habitat for Humanity Midwestern Assembly in Chicago, a first step toward conjugal union, opening act of cohabitation staged in an altruistic setting, rebuke to those who insisted on giving Mary the benefit of doubt. Less than a year later they would be married one evening at the community center, the wedding party comprised mostly of homeless men and women, the connubial ritual composed by the bride and groom, the sole musical accompaniment provided by a lesbian guitarist who sang two Joan Baez songs, one of which was rewritten to commemorate "babies incinerated by napalm."

Hope regrouped after its brush with the Holy Spirit and moved into the post-Pentecost Sundays of Ordinary Time. Jack gathered a dozen of his college friends who were home for the summer and had a wholesome, two-hour-long, hand-holding-prayer-and-Bible-study fellowship in his parents' living room in which Jack led them in prayer for "a fresh anointing at Hope Church and for the return of the most awesome youth pastor that ever was." Alexis continued not to have the full infusion of the power of the Holy Spirit, and, as Providence decreed, the two broke up shortly after the beginning of fall semester. Jack would never again set foot in Hope—in fact, he stopped going to church altogether until his late forties when, after his wife discovered his marital infidelity and sued for divorce, thrusting Jack into a custody battle for the children, his lawyer advised that church membership would strengthen his case.

"After twenty years yoked to Hope," Simon complained to Cloe in a tearful, late-night phone call to his former assistant, "sacrificing myself in service to others, I have no more to show for it than a cold letter of appreciation by the board, three phone calls from various demented older women, and a severance package that will sustain me no more than six months."

Cloe sympathetically agreed that it was an injustice of major proportion though she failed to report to Simon that, upon his departure, the board had elevated her to Executive Office Manager.

"Everybody knows you have been running the church for years anyway," the Chair told her when he notified Cloe of her promotion.

For a week or so, before leaving town, the prophet without a parish kept vigil at a prominent bar, hoping someone from Hope might appear so he could pour out his heart's grieving and wring them for information. Miraculously, in a week of waiting, no one appeared, even though everyone knew the place as Hope's tavern of choice. That was the laity for you—neither a shred of gratitude nor need of highball to assuage their guilt. The church is the only army that shoots its own wounded, Simon had often prophesied, not knowing that he would validate his words with his life.

Simon's episcopally imposed ecclesiastical exile was brief. Not six weeks after his departure from Hope, he was scooped up by a well-known, doctrinally unconstrained, community-centered, non-denominational, progressive congregation in Pennsylvania at almost twice the salary he had earned at Hope. (The church hired him solely on the basis of two video sermons, bolstered by the bishop's glowingly enthusiastic letter of recommendation, in which he praised Simon for his "personally costly, but inspiring prophetic ministry.")

Now an ecclesiastical free agent, liberated from the encumbrance of denominational meddling, Simon was given (at his request) the title of Community Enabler rather than pastor. In his new situation, Simon felt as if he had been born again, or at least repackaged.

It was his strategic retreat to Pennsylvania, nondescript land of his nativity, martyr for the cause of peace with justice, fairness, and civil discourse. There Simon realized a lifetime dream—TV talk-show host. "Way Out" featured Simon interviewing prominent persons from a faith perspective and also those with a recently relinquished faith. True, the show aired from six to seven on Sunday mornings, which was the best slot they could afford at the moment, but it was undeniably mainstream TV, infinitely more respectable than cable. "Way Out" focused primarily on faith and addiction, devoting a couple of shows each to a selected crav-ing—drugs, alcohol, food, sex, TV, high-church liturgy, surfing the Web, hoarding, autoeroticism, and supermarket coupons. Simon haughtily as-serted that at one time or another he had been a victim of most of these obsessions himself.

Determined to get the jump on this congregation, Simon's first ser-mon opened with this warning shot across the bow:

I have always thought that Jesus Christ's chief virtue was that he was so secure in who he was that he need not claim to be God. Just to be himself—a person serenely confident and comfortable in his humanity—was enough.

His text? "Only a true Messiah would deny his divinity," beloved snippet from *The Life of Brian*. Having thus forewarned the congregation of his intention never again to dissemble in order to ingratiate himself with theologically limited laity, he began a six-week series on "The Glory of God is a Fully Opened Mind."

Simon also began assembling a dream-team staff to compliment his ministry. Thrilling to the freedom of a church shorn of traditional church musicians, Simon put together an electronically (rather than percussively) enabled Sunday service with sound and lighting that would be the envy of any disco. Film clips off the Web too.

For a few months, Simon futilely attempted to pursue Sybil, giving her ample opportunity to join him in his new Pennsylvania parish. Even though he was willing to forgive, Sybil was unresponsive. Eventually he ac-quired other interests, enjoying a fresh church facility—white and gleam-ing and techno, with everything in good order, a minimalist building that imitated the early romantic work of Philip Johnson.

"Never again will I serve a church with primeval plumbing," he de-clared in his first sermon. And Simon now aspired to be a man of his word.

Simon's recovery was wondrous until, about a year later, when he was in Toledo, featured guest at the Entrepreneurial Christ Conference, out for a late afternoon stroll between sessions, he happened to look in a shop window that displayed an engraved, antique silver cigarette case exactly like Sybil's. He was undone. Transfixed, he stood gazing at the case, wanting to turn it in his hand and fondle it, through tears calling out to the empty street, "Sybil, Sybil my elegant muse, my sojourner, soul mate, nymph," pitifully desiring to break the window and hold the box up to his nose and sniff it, shower it with sloppy kisses, overcome with regret at what might have been.

Incorporation

∾

On Friday after Trinity, Sam was ordered by Grimball to dispose of a pest in the sanctuary. Somehow a small brown bird had managed to squeeze its way into the church and had chirped, flitted, and hopped about in the upper reaches of the chancel all week.

"Our service will be destroyed if that damn bird is still fluttering around next Sunday," Quail had said in that week's post-Simon staff meeting.

"We've got bird droppings on the organ console," added Grimball. "Not that anybody cares."

Quail refused to take notice of the organist's remark.

Sam and the downstairs janitor erected—in the left side of the chancel—the tallest ladder they could rent. As the janitor steadied the base of the ladder, Sam ascended heavenward with a broom, planning to wallop the bird as it perched in the left organ chamber grill like it owned the place. While the bird chirped blissfully away, Sam climbed nearly to the top rung.

"You watch yourself now," the janitor instructed from below. Sam took aim, drew back, and then swung the broom in a wide arc, missing the unconcerned bird and losing his balance on the ladder. Accompanied by the janitor's shriek echoing through the sanctuary, Sam wordlessly plummeted, banging his head on one of the choir pews, landing with a mortal crack and a thud.

"My Lord!" was all the janitor could get out as he watched blood trickle from the side of Sam's mouth onto the chancel carpet.

Though a hysterical Cloe got EMS to Hope in ten minutes, Sam never regained consciousness. He died in hospital two days later without anyone eliciting from him the church's electrical circuitry plan.

Quail's calloused comment on the tragedy astounded even his most vicious detractors among the staff: "If Sam had been more careful in his care of the building, that bird would have never gotten in here in the first place."

More than one in the congregation thought: *The bird took out the wrong staff member.*

Herb celebrated Sam on Saturday afternoon in a grand service at Hope that was attended by dozens of sincerely grieving Hope congregants. "I would rather be a doorkeeper in the house of the Lord," was the text for Herb's brief remarks before Sam's pall-covered casket. Sam was lowered into the earth next to his wife, with a graveside committal in which Herb extolled Sam's virtues in building maintenance, making a rather complicated figurative reference to Sam's care of various doors at Hope, asserting that "he laid down his life for Hope." Herb also made a quick linkage to Christ's giving Peter the keys to the kingdom, noting that with Sam's untimely departure, no one at Hope ("our little piece of the kingdom") had a clue which key fit which lock. Herb also mentioned that Sam's wife had been a Catholic.

A week later the hospital returned to the church Sam's sole legacy—a huge ring with a heap of useless, unidentifiable keys.

James's parents filed for divorce in late August. James's father began a postmortem process of following the lonely path taken by his son, drinking himself to death, a procedure that would take three years to complete.

With Simon out of the picture, Glumweltner realized the toll that Hope was taking upon his emotional health. He relaxed, let down his guard, and had a complete nervous breakdown, precipitated by his abortive attempt at the Scarsdale Diet and the departure of all of his tenors for the praise choir of the new independent church on the edge of town. Free to go crazy without Simon's "I told you so," the musician's breakdown was melodramatic in intensity, even exhibitionist. One Tuesday afternoon he was carried out of the music office, with four EMS personnel straining to bear his stretcher, Glumweltner flailing, screaming to high heaven in his best Orson Welles' timbre his loathing for contemporary Christian music.

Glumweltner was diagnosed as suffering from Chronic Carbohydrate Deficiency. After his recovery, in late October, he was enthusiastically stolen by the Reverend Kim (at a maliciously higher salary than he pulled down at Hope) to be the director of his three choirs in what had become the city's fastest growing congregation.

"We rebwanding our church," Kim told Glumweltner (whose name Kim pronounced "Gumwetter") when he was hired. "Switch markets. Upsizing. We bigger than Hope Church in three years or my name not Kim."

"I give thanks to my Lord and Savior Jesus Christ," Kim told Glumweltner on his first Sunday. "When Quaier kick us out, it first day of the best year of my ministry. Now, sky the wimit. You see. Sky the wimit."

With Glumweltner gone, everyone assumed that the organist Grimball had a bright future at Hope. They overlooked Grimball's immortal loathing for Quail, deeper and more sinister even than the near-death experience in the loft. When informed of Quail's miraculous healing, it was the last straw. Grimball ceased his agitation for a fully renovated organ and abandoned church work altogether, absconding with the Steinway in tow—unconcerned that the piano was the church's property.

His departure was a matter of principle. Scandalized by the mounting evidence of the Divinity's appalling lack of standards, Grimball resolved never again to get mixed up in any business associated with one so capricious as God. He began performing nightly, under a lighter-toned, blow-dried coiffure that may be a rag, in a suburban Chicago strip club, The Bouncing Ball.

In his valedictory remarks to the last luncheon of senior female admirers, Grimball asserted, "Sadly, church is all about money these days, thanks to our clergy. There's no integrity anymore. Ladies, I had always agreed with that medieval monk who, comparing the church with Noah's Ark, said, 'If it were not for the raging storm on the outside, we couldn't stand the stench on the inside.' Well, sometimes, gals"—and here he raised his Merlot in a toast—"the stench becomes overwhelming. Farewell and to hell with thee all."

Hope Township went into receivership and was offered to alleged Seventh Day Adventists who scooped it up for a song. The church was left holding three million dollars in debt. (More than one knowledgable source rumored that the so-called Seventh Day Adventists were a front for Kim Ministries, Inc.)

Herb was unexpectedly pressed into a hectic schedule of visiting and baptizing an influx of new member recruits from late summer into the fall—for each one who had recently joined Hope in order to sit at the feet of Simon, many more were awaiting his exit.

"Even at this late hour," Herb chuckled to his Wednesday Bible study group, "I'm still able to learn and to grow in my faith. Church growth consultant wisdom notwithstanding, not everyone joins a church because of its pastor."

Other than Quail and Herb, only one member of the church's professional staff remained at Hope by the mid-fall—Eleanor. She gloated, "I alone am left to carry on the Lord's work." Squeaking about the church's corridors in her tennis shoes, buoyed by an unaccustomed self-confidence, Eleanor was often heard humming Gloria Gaynor's "I Will Survive."

Hope Church continued to be afflicted with electrical and plumbing tribulation throughout the summer and fall. During the middle of his end-of-summer miniseries on "The Blessings and Responsibilities of God's Good Creation," sermons that were contrived to complement the denominational environmental stewardship emphasis, the bishop was informed by the lay leadership that the next senior pastor would be forced into a menacing capital campaign to shore up the building. Ten million would be devoured by the insatiable structure. The looming campaign shortened considerably the bishop's list of eager prospective candidates, though the Niculous bequest emboldened the bishop to assure the lay leadership at Hope that they would have the pick of the clergy litter. It was the bishop's usual line to nervous search committees.

As if to confirm the trustees' assessment, most of Hope was without electrical power (a situation made worse without Sam's healing touch), the people forced to sit in darkness between the Twenty-sixth and the Twenty-seventh Sundays in Ordinary Time, hymns banged out on a rented piano.

∾

For a few weeks after his departure, Stephen, feeling miserable and sluggish, crashed at the apartment of a college buddy; it was an inglorious conclusion to his short run as a preacher. Although Tony was far from being Stephen's best friend, or even one of his favorite acquaintances, he had kept in touch since graduation. Though Tony was not the brightest firework in the show, he could be good company, and Stephen's options for free accommodations were few. When Stephen called and asked if he could hang at his apartment, good-natured Tony's immediate response was, "Sure, you're free to stay right here. Got the room. We'll go out and get wasted as soon as you get here. Then we'll get laid. You'll forget about your women problems in no time."

This exchange reminded Stephen why he never really liked "Tony Baloney," as they had called him in college. Three years of post-college life had failed to contribute a day to Tony's maturity.

"Man, I know what it's liked to get the shaft from a girl; it's happened to me more times than I can count," Tony said the first night, attempting to establish camaraderie.

"My ex is the least of my problems," said Stephen sullenly. "In three months I got booted from a job I didn't ask for, and for which I've spent three whole years preparing. Now, I've got to get a life."

"Man, don't talk like that. Your only mistake was sleeping with an anthropologist. I'll have you fixed up and back to preaching in no time," said Tony, swigging a beer and grinning.

"No, you won't," declared Stephen. "All that's over."

"Over? No, you're just down. You know how it is with you preachers. Once you get the God Almighty call, you have to do it, no matter what.

You can run, but you can't hide. It's the call. And God knows you've got it. You may be an asshole, but you got the call. To tell you the honest truth, back at school, some people resented you because, unlike us—the clueless—you had a call. Relax, get over your funk, and make the best of it. You got the call, man."

"Everybody's an idiot," said Stephen.

"Preach on," grinned Tony. "See? That proves you're just another preacher calling everybody else an idiot. Preach, preach. I may not believe most of that stuff you preach, may not know as much about God as you, but I sure know when somebody's got the call."

"Shut up."

Tony gave Stephen a fraternal nudge. "Well, you may be a preacher but you still ain't good enough to make a saint out of me. Look, buddy, you're down in the ditch, beaten and bloody. Just call me Mr. Samaritan. I'll pull you out, get you bandaged up, and put you back on your ass. You're a preacher and that's all you'll ever be. Of course, with the way you screwed up at that highbrow church, you'll spend your preacherhood at one of them vinyl-sided, low-rent churches with a volunteer band."

"Shut up," Stephen reiterated, unimpressed by Tony's argument that since he was a part-time bartender in a tavern on the edge of town, "we're both in the people-helping business. It's easy to get burned out listening to their problems. You'll get over it."

Two days deeper into his purgatory, Stephen sat with Tony at the breakfast table, gulping down coffee (which he now drank straight black), watching Tony slurp bits of rainbow cereal. Between slurps, Tony asked solicitously, "How you doin', man?"

"I had a rough night," replied Stephen.

"Really? Sorry to hear it."

"Yep. A nightmare. Dreamed I was a pastor at a large church in the suburbs."

On most nights, Stephen was able to sleep—crawling into bed, his knees brought up to his chest in the fetal position, his sleep mostly devoid of dreams, as if a burden had been lifted off his back. His worst night occurred in his first weekend at the apartment. That evening Tony brought home some random girl and Stephen was forced to endure the clamor of their passion until two in the morning. He had wrapped his head in a pillow, but it hadn't helped.

Fortunately, since that night Tony pursued his prospects at her place. Stephen had thus heard no more of their theatrical moans—which he suspected to be a deliberate, malicious attempt on their part to hurt him as he lay in his cell, unburdened, at last free of the penal colony called church, but miserable and alone.

Twice in one week, when Stephen vainly sought solace from Tony Baloney, Tony had stunned him by saying, "You are more like Lupino than you want to admit."

It was one of the few things that Tony had said that made sense.

∾

After those first weeks he had seen little of Tony, which suited Stephen's purposes. He longed to be lonely, to think himself back into whatever game he was supposed to play, not to have anybody tell him what he ought next to do. He hadn't heard from Thea after their one nasty, quarrelsome, brief (and final) phone conversation. She detested Tony, which made Tony's apartment more appealing, though it was humiliating for her to know that Tony was the sole friend Stephen could turn to.

All that Stephen knew of Hope Church was that Sam had busted his head open and died after losing a bout with a bird. Clergy freak show, that place. He had not received the promised letter of recommendation from Lupino. Having heard nothing from anyone at Hope, he wondered if anybody there ever had cause to ask, "Whatever happened to that, er, uh, black kid who was on staff?"

He had evaporated; it was as if he had never existed, as if he had died and his body had been cremated, leaving only a wisp of ash.

What did he care? Having seen more of the church than he had the capacity to comprehend, and much more than he would ever be able to love, Stephen was exhausted but content with solitude and the first fruits of his freedom, just beginning to enjoy the happiness of those fortunate souls who are free of communal muck and mire—the joy of the unaddressed.

Day by day Stephen warmed to the idea of recovering his life. Law school? Master's of social work? Maybe a year or six months working in Japan? Skiing in Switzerland would be cool. Swiss women loved guys like him, so he had heard. It had been the longest time since he had looked at his life and seen such a broad, unconstrained panorama. He was ashamed by how he had succumbed to mindless servitude, bowing and scraping before the baptized, the pretense and the posturing before the suffocating ecclesia. He was a bird who, having just been released from a cage, hopped about nearby the open door, unsure of which way to fly, unacquainted with life outside.

At night, when he had trouble sleeping, he would sometimes have Thea thoughts, seeing her lying there, with morning sunlight showing off her features. But his reverie would always be blunted by the jarring remembrance of Thea's smart-aleck wonderment at how anybody could believe such stuff, her put-downs of the little she had taken the trouble to read of N. T. Wright, her reaching up to kiss another guy. And at that, memory of her became blurred by the acids of hate. He was free.

∽

It didn't last. One late June morning, while still in exile, Stephen received a package, forwarded to Tony's by his parents. Ripping it open, he noted that it was from Hope Church, by way of Cloe. Something he had left in his office, a severance gift that he well deserved, or hush money that he should have demanded?

No. The package contained only an envelope and a book. He opened the envelope first, thinking it might contain a check. It was nothing but a couple of notes, the first a handwritten letter from old, kindly Herb:

Stephen!

Mementos from your admirers at Hope, which number in the dozens, including me, the most devoted. I regret that I was not given the opportunity to give you a proper farewell, but you have probably received far too much pontification from this spent old pastor.

Later I learned that your departure was not at your initiative.

Well done, young Stephen! For a witness so young, even without preaching a single sermon, to be so threatening to the ancient régime that we had to dispose of you—what a prophetic achievement!

Congratulations.

I've always been a bit ashamed that in all my years of ministry I neither preached clearly enough nor enacted the gospel faithfully enough to demonstrate the appalling difference between Christ's church and Christ and thus to earn a dismissal. Look what God hath wrought with you in your first three months of ministry!

I pray that your succeeding years of service will be as adventuresome as your first. We work for an exceedingly fascinating God, don't we? How dare we reduce ministry to something tame?

And the most interesting work of God I've witnessed in recent days is you!

In Christ's Service,

Herb

Attached to Herb's letter was a small note on expensive stationery:

My Dear Reverend Mr. Smith:

Though we never met, I share the grief of many at your unceremonious leave-taking. While I'm sure that you are better off in some ministerial position more worthy of your considerable talent, Hope is the poorer for your departure.

Much of my grief is for my shameful lack of courage. I could have spoken up in your defense when I had a hint of the sinister designs on you. Though I will never forgive myself, I am bold to hope even for greater absolution.

You're so virtuous. Have you a surfeit of the virtue of forgiveness? Will you ask God to grant me yet one more act of forbearance? I'm sure that your prayers count for more than mine.

True, cowardice is only one of my sins to confess—and far from the most heinous—but one must start somewhere.

In such a short time your ministry brought out the best and the worst in us. What more could a young preacher want?

With all sincerity,

Sybil Vestal

Then, as the coup de grâce, Stephen cautiously unwrapped the smaller package. It was nothing but an old book, in Latin no less, Boethius' *Consolatio Philosophiae*—antique, bound in reddish leather with worn gold-stamped binding. Just inside the book he found a note written with a fountain pen, in a frail, trembling hand, on light blue paper.

Dear Stephen:

Last week, without premonition, I lost dear, sweet, difficult Jane. How I regretted that you were not present to give me pastoral assuagement! Jane was my guardian, my spokesperson, my most severe critic. Her beloved "vile weed," which imprisoned her in life, has taken her to her grave.

Surely you know that my dear sister adored you, having high admiration for your gifts. She felt that she really understood you, and, even more surprisingly, she was convinced that you understood her. Perhaps, in the sweet by and by, you shall be good enough to explain her to me!

"Alas, I shall not live to see how God may use that bright young man," she said to me. Little did I know her prescience.

I am certain that she would want you to have her Boethius. That you may be unable to read Boethius' Latin would have been inconsequential to Jane. Cast by God into a world where you must daily deal with incomprehensible ancient texts in long dead tongues, you may value this book simply because it was loved by Jane. Its mysteries are beyond translation. Sometimes we need not understand the words to know their meaning; the dead speak that which we dare not speak to ourselves.

Boethius, imprisoned, awaiting sure and certain death, discovered the truth about this world even while kept in a prison cell of others' cruelty, and therefore (as Jane would surely have me say to you) he was free, having found the truth about God.

Who knows where God will take us from here? None of us can predict the machinations of providential pursuit. Nor can we fully resist. Because Jane loved you, I know she prayed that the story that God is writing with you will be kind. But sometimes God's stories are not. I promise to pray for you, a young man under orders, whose story is not fully his own. Will you pray for me?

Your fellow, reluctant servant of Christ,
Maryanne Whetsell

Stephen cautiously set down the book. It seemed to shine, to glow with mystery. He shuddered. Though he did not know Latin, as he stared at the book, he who had been often so confused now thought he knew. The two letters were a prelude to receiving the ancient book as sacrament, tangible revelation no less than transubstantiated bread placed upon his tongue.

So, this was how it was? His "call" back in college was only preliminary. An hour ago, he wanted solitude. Now, from out of nowhere, without premonition, he had been handed a key. For the first time in a long time he desired to talk, to tell someone the fearful, funny secret entrusted to him.

So, the stories and odd sayings, the demons and the dusty people, preposterous miracles and Jesus the fanatic, wandering Jew back from the dead—all true. He was stunned. His grand renunciation was fake. Glad that no one was looking, embarrassed, he laughed at the strange humor. God had tossed him from the clutches of his grandfather's dying prayer, into the hands of Herb, then Sybil Vestal, even Jack, finally into Jane's relentless reach with Boethius beyond the grave. He saw James, on that last day of the trip, standing there in the parking lot, determined to call him pastor.

More than half the New Testament consisted of epistles; why should he be surprised to receive revelation in a similar way? A book had spoken, the key had turned in the lock, and a door had opened.

James's mother's words haunted him: "God offered us a gift, redemption, a vocation. And we were too cowardly to receive it."

What kind of God stooped to performing such stunts? Stalked, cornered, Stephen felt ridiculous, shoved through the needle's eye of aggrieved resentfulness toward more congenial resignation. The hovering dove descended. A whipped, crucified God he may be, but he could still pack a wallop. Strangely, though Stephen was no better equipped to be anybody's minister, he felt competent, authorized, summoned.

The body-snatcher God who sallied forth from the tomb on Easter wouldn't allow him to stay dead. Despite his earlier adolescent determination to lose himself in lament, to hit somebody, to be quiet and alone, he relented to his inexplicable but undeniable, absurd vocation.

Stephen opened the door, stepped over the threshold, poor in rational justification, yet rich in hope. Beckoned, looking skyward to bright sun pushing through the green, glad for the end of summer, willing to be summoned, commandeered, relinquishing his body to the Body, caught, contra desire, in service to the One who kills to make alive.

Striding down the sidewalk, willing to be led, hands in pockets, gazing up at clear heaven, Stephen answered softly, and with a grin, "I give up."